Rob Walden-Woods spent a great deal of his youth in and around the East End of London. He would, many times, feel the heat generated by the plethora of criminal gangs. In 1965 a much younger Rob, teamed up with three guys from Stratford E15 and together they would frequent gambling casinos and clubs where some of the most violent of criminals would gather. Rob and his mates were witness to many dreadful fights, fights for supremacy, respect and wealth, often with the aim being to take control of the club or casino they were fighting in – with much blood being spilt – on both sides of many a fracas. No quarter was given or taken.

Although fictional *'Violent Horizons'* contains a strong element of the roughness and ferocity of undisguised violence meted out by mobs, crews and gangs, on behalf of their gangland bosses, whose aim was to climb the greasy pole of notoriety.

Older and wiser, you now find Rob more the country gent than the 'pitch and toss' cockney.

Also by Rob Walden-Woods.

Give Yourself Permission to Win.
Give Yourself a Head Start.
Give Yourself an Edge,

Thanks goes to my wife, Jan, for the many teas, coffees and bickies while writing this book. To our good friend, Elizabeth, for words of encouragement. A big thanks to Carron for the *'Butchers Block'* and the many other creative notions.

Rob Walden-Woods

VIOLENT HORIZONS

AUSTIN MACAULEY PUBLISHERS™

LONDON * CAMBRIDGE * NEW YORK * SHARJAH

A CIP catalogue record for this title is available from the British Library.

ISBN 9781528917506 (Paperback)
ISBN 9781528950510 (Hardback)
ISBN 9781528950527 (ePub e-book)

www.austinmacauley.com

First Published 2022
Austin Macauley Publishers Ltd®
1 Canada Square
Canary Wharf
London
E14 5AA

Characters

Eddie Coleman; Main Character

Ma Val Coleman.

Wossname (real name Vince Gander).

Billy Maggs and Melvin Cooper; both hardened criminals.

Plus, a scattering of others… for example, Johnny the Turk. Peter Painter. Boxer Boy. Bomber Brown. Rosie Higgs. Lenny the Scrote. D.I. Mike Bright, Dave Conti and Esme Wren.

Synopsis

The story is based in London's East End. Date line 1960s. The Brothers are in charge; however, Eddie Coleman from the Isle of Dogs is on the up. A young man nursing a tortured soul, because he is different. Different from the run of the mill. Okay, so what's wrong with being a short-arsed, curly haired ginger, pale faced, weak, thin looking young man with freckles? Plenty in the case of Eddie Coleman. Taunted by his father, then regularly and mercilessly at school by the older boys. Enough suddenly becomes enough. A major fist fight close to his home on the Isle of Dogs with a bully boy, emerges as his turning point. Something in his brain snapped. At the age of eighteen, he crash-lands on the deck of London's East End tough playground. From that point on, Eddie is going to be someone to be reckoned with. He was going to be no one's mug. Respect me, was the name of the game. His old man gone, school days well over, Eddie Coleman has aspirations to take on all-comers. Desperately needing to climb the greasy pole to notoriety based on violence and criminality. He recruits like-minded individuals to his crew which expands rapidly. His deeds and wrong doings leave a trail of blood, beatings, robberies and murders in his wake. Violence speaks volumes. It also attracts ;'violence. As Eddie's empire grows, jealous eyes are looking on. Some just look the other way and let him get on with it. Some want what he has got and will stop short of nothing to get it. Gaining control of a section of the East End was not going to be easy. Eddie found though, he had a knack for getting what he wanted, as long as he applied an abundance of terror and mayhem. For his short-lived reign, he seemed to have the Midas touch. Even the law could not touch him, or so he arrogantly thought.

119 Plevna Street; Isle of Dogs

"Eddie...Please. No more violence!" Val yelled at the top of her voice through the open living room window. It was useless of course. Eddie couldn't hear anyway. He was miles too busy kicking the shit out of someone in the road right bang outside the house. He was way too far into revenge mode to hear his mother bawling at him from indoors. Sometime soon he'd wage a hate campaign locally. Then the name of Eddie Coleman will be feared in and around the Isle-of-Dogs in London's East End. But just for the moment, a very unfortunate lad almost twice Eddie's size and stamp had stupidly agreed with his mates up the road a bit, to go and pick a fight. Now, Eddie Coleman was definitely not the world's tallest teenager, at most measuring up to 5ft 8 in his Cuban heeled boots.

Eddie lacked a fair bit in the grim, snarling, sneering face department when required, as in right at this moment. He was more leaning towards the classic angelic look. Being a bit on the slim side but agile, he looked quite the athletic type. Deep blue eyes together with a shock of curly ginger hair.

Pretty boy, he was sometimes known as at school, which of course, was a description he hated with a vengeance. During his early teen years Eddie was picked on throughout his school days when he bothered to attend, picked on beaten about a bit almost weekly. This was carried out mainly by older lads who thought, *Eye, eye here's an easy target, I can take him.* Some would taunt him with a short singing ditty that went something like 'who's got ginger hairs up inside his pants.' The taunting ditty, spread like wildfire unfortunately throughout the school. For young Eddie it had an appalling effect on his general wellbeing, it was something you could not forget that easily. Hatred began to burn inside his curly ginger topped head. Eddie knew the bigger boys were singing the hateful ditty as loud as they could 'cos they were showing out to the girls. The many young ladies that would constantly hang around them, giggling at every word that dripped out of their hero's mouths. *I suppose the guys were definitely going to score with the girls tonight following such a display of bravery,* he mused.

And of course, these young ladies were well out of reach of the young Eddie. Deep down inside, Eddie Coleman's personal worm was beginning to turn and turn bloody vicious. He decided it had to stop, he'd had more than enough of bullying, taunts, kickings and piss taking. Something snapped. He was severely unhappy at always coming off worse. Marching now to a different beat of the drum, and being a ginger top too, can often mean quick to anger, as of this minute. Right now, out in the street, outside his house about to deck an older bigger and much heavier boy who fancied himself as a fighter. At the age of 18 Eddie had had enough, no more beatings. The boot was now firmly on the other foot. Eddie Coleman by means of his anger inside, resembled a live wire. 20,000 volts ready to shock someone, anyone who would dare to cross him, touch him, hurt him or simply take one too many liberties.

Fuses would immediately blow. Eddie had crash landed his plane on the deck and into the world of violence with much relish. He continued to ferociously bang in the punches like pile drivers, one after the other into his enemy's face. The red mist dealing with any counter blows coming back his way that were fast diminishing. For good measure and simple badness, Eddie grabbed the bully round his head with both hands and pushed his thumbs ever deeper into his eye sockets with evil intention. Then resumed punching him in the face again and again.

"Eddie, Eddie, **FUCKING EDDIE,**" screamed his mum again in vain. Val rarely used the 'F' word, but seeing what she was seeing, on her own doorstep, her mouth got much the better of her. In terms of getting Eddie to disengage, Val had about as much chance of calling back a deaf dog from a kiss chase with a disappearing blind moggy. Eddie's attacker was now very much on the defence. He began to cover his face with both hands and lower arms in an attempt to ward off the multiple and heavy blows. He didn't twig. It didn't occur to him that there wasn't going to be the usual and expected end to this horrendous and vicious beating. *You know how it is, shake hands, hug like boxers following ten gruelling rounds, then be bestest mates for life! No way,* thought Eddie, as he danced around the big guy landing well aimed kicks and punches with no retaliation.

The bully boy was on a hiding to nothing and wanted out and soon. As far as Eddie was concerned, he needed to put out a message. A meaningful message. A message that announced he was 18 and now no longer to be fucked with. Take me on at your peril was the message he hoped to transmit. If the big lad didn't scarper soon, serious amounts of blood would flow. Any further damage inflicted might well be a permanent reminder on his now bloodied and swollen face. The fight as far the big guy was concerned was well and truly over.

He ran and he ran fast without daring to look back, just in case a deranged psychotic Eddie Coleman was on his heels ready to haul him down to the ground.

Breathless, bloodied but triumphant, Eddie stood legs astride, head held high, smiling, hands on hips watching his attacker limp and scarper as fast as he could. Eddie turned and beamed in the general direction of his mum, Ma Val. No sign of her. Val had melted back into the living room so as not to be visible to anyone outside the house.

Some of her neighbours had popped out to see what the commotion was all about and she didn't feel like getting the third degree from any of them. One of her neighbours screamed out, "Go on Eddie, fucking do 'im."

The neighbours would make up their own stories between them about the fight outside 119 Plevna Street, then to be passed on to their husbands when they eventually made it home from work or pub, that evening. What the husbands would make of it, was anybody's guess. *Good for my reputation,* he thought.

The stories, however much exaggerated, would be passed on from drinker to drinker in the various pubs frequented by the excited story tellers. Val was dumb-struck. She had gotten used to her boy coming home with the odd black eye or cut lip, but this! This was a new and worrying revelation.

Val Coleman.

Eddie's mum Val, always dressed smart, well, as best she could on their tight budget, somehow always managing to look elegant neat and trim. Rarely seen wearing make-up, Val had a natural beauty, high cheek bones, a tiny turned up nose and a fantastic smile, which gave her the air of a magazine model. Her bleach blond hair was up in bun for once. Usually, it was down to her shoulders. Her slim, almost painfully slim body was now shaking with shock and rage. Shock at watching Eddie half murder someone. Rage for it to be happening on her own doorstep. The doorstep she had donkey stoned for many a year.

The East End way, Isle-of-Dogs or not is always, don't shit on your doorstep. Here was Eddie piling it six foot high. Val's neighbours were all good mates with her. She would be the first in line to help them out, listen to their troubles, put the kettle on, ready to be a shoulder to lean on.

Laugh together when things cheered up, like one of their husbands getting a win on the dogs over at Harringay. She never leant on any of them for anything or tapped them up for a loan or two, it was always the other way around. Val stood staring out into the street, absently pulling at a tiny loose thread of her spotless Aron button thru top, wearing a deeply worried frown. Eddie made his way into the little red brick terraced house through the front door of 119 Plevna Street set in the heart of the Isle-of-Dogs, East London. A two up two down red bricked terrace with bogs out the back. It masqueraded as their home. This is where Eddie lived with his mum, Val Coleman. He slammed the front door hard in defiance, hoping the guy he had just beaten to within an inch would take note and not venture back anytime soon. Eddie's revenge vendetta was only just beginning. War, any war has a certain type of madness attached to it, unless it is borne out of personal reasons; and this was very personal. Therefore legit. This was going to Eddie's war.

Mickey Coleman.

Ed's old man Mickey, was long gone from Plevna Street. So, no male authority in the home to keep Eddie in check. His missing father, when he was around, always addressed Eddie, when he wanted him, by his full Christian name, 'Edward'. When his dad wanted Eddie for any reason, any reason at all, be it for nipping down the Off-licence for some fags, he would scream, "**Edward** get yourself down here pronto." This was the best laxative currently available on the market in the 1960s.

The loudness and venom in dad Coleman's voice would send poor little Eddie straight for the toilet. Thankfully though, because Eddie was apt to roam the streets of the island, he didn't get to know his old man too well.

Mickey Coleman was a drinker's drinker. A dedicated lover of Guinness, especially with a drop of gin in it. There weren't many nights of sobriety at Eddie's house, with weekends being by far the worst. Eddie sadly however, did have a constant reminder of his dad and not the best you might imagine. During one of Mickey Coleman's many nasty drunken rages, breaking up the home's furniture and stuff, set about Eddie in a blind fury and broke his left wrist. A broom handle was whacked a couple of times on to Eddie's wrist, instantly breaking bones.

Eddie was just twelve years old. He had had the gall to stand between his dad and his mum in an effort to save her from even more punches from the old swine.

His wrist was stinging fiercely. Still, he stood up to his dad and landed a well-aimed punch to his dad's guts winding him. Eddie screamed in agony. Coleman senior staggered back in utter surprise. He looked down at his handiwork with the broom handle. Eddie's left hand broken was hanging from his wrist at a weird angle. *Fuck me*, he thought, *he hit me with that!* Hearing the screaming and shouting going on in number 119, the kindly but nosey old meddlesome mare next door, thought it was her duty to call the cops. Mickey of course, as per usual, was dragged away by a burly sergeant whose only feature below his police helmet was a very large and bulbous nose, glowing bright red. He grabbed Mickey by the back of his shirt collar dragging him kicking and screaming off to the local nick.

Two hours including mugs of tea and several fags later and no doubt a couple of hands of rummy, he was back home again with a warning. By now both Eddie and Val were out roaming the streets. Eddie with a makeshift sling for his busted wrist. Despite the cops popping round and questioning all the nearest neighbours, followed by Eddie and then his mum, nobody talked. It was the way in the East End; silence. It was them against us, most would say. Mickey Coleman and his mates at the pub had an entirely different saying: 'Coppers is dirt and dirt is your sworn enemy. Give 'em an inch and they take a sodding mile.'

When Eddie's busted wrist was eventually put in plaster, then broken again due to not aligning with his arm correctly, then reset at Harringford Hospital, most unfortunately for Eddie, it was not the best of hospital jobs. His wrist wasn't set totally in line where it joined his lower arm as perhaps as well as it could have been. As a result, when Eddie held out his left hand, it tilted down and to the left a tad. It played havoc at P.E. time at school. Press ups were difficult to say the least.

Hand stands against the wall, almost impossible. Plus, Eddie needed to overcome a slight problem, when it came to defending himself in a fight. He couldn't make a proper fist with his left hand. So, he had to learn to lead with his right, which didn't come easy. Becoming a southpaw, jabbing with his right seemed to begin with, almost impossible. However, in the end it did lend Eddie a few advantages. To his surprise, as he got into more and more serious scraps, found it would come in very handy. Blokes would not usually be expecting a jab or hook shot coming from their left. To some extent this gave Eddie the element of surprise. Always good in a street fight. Most satisfying when the other bloke is put on his arse more than once. Eddie would stand over his victims, put a boot on the throat and push down hard. There was always the possibility that the boy he'd put on the ground, might jump up and have another go, so, a boot on the windpipe usually did the trick.

The Floozie.

Ma Val often explained to the young Eddie; his dad had gone away one day on a butcher's business trip and failed to come back. The word on the street however, eventually discovered by Eddie, was very different. So that theory was knocked into a cocked hat, soon as you like. The truth was this, Mickey Coleman had fucked off with some large breasted floozie from Westcliff down on the Essex coast. Did a bit of G.B.H. on her old man got hauled up before the beak and charged accordingly, ending up doing a bit of bird at Wandsworth nick. When he was finally released, he and the floozie, settled down to an average life. They rented a three-bed bungalow down on Canvey Island quite close to the King Canute pub. He'd swopped one island for another! Floozie's dad was something to do with the navy, so, Mickey and him had something in common. Gave them something to talk about over a pint or two, given that Mickey, was in the merchant navy, during the war.

Mickey and Floozie went on to have a couple of kids, but never married on account Mickey still being legally hitched to Val. Eddie guessed he'd be the kid's uncle or step-brother or step something or other.

The most haunting news that filtered back was that Mickey had given up the booze, given up hitting women and children and become a bit docile. Lucky miss bloody Floozie! *Hope their offspring don't come looking for handouts from me,* flashed across Eddie's mind.

Some years later, Eddie discovered, Mickey, had purchased and ran, a down-at-the heel D.I.Y shop, in down town Benfleet, four miles or so from Canvey, somewhere near the bottom of Bread and Cheese Hill. Heaven knows where that money came from. Mickey wasn't loaded. Any money that came his way went through his fingers quicker than finely graded sand. Mickey Coleman's last known job before his disappearing act was a meat and poultry buyer up in Leadenhall Market just on the edge of the city's square mile. So, he wasn't into big wages. Occasionally, he would need to visit abattoirs used by the meat suppliers who he worked for. On these out and about occasions, Mickey would train it as a means of transport, then bed and breakfast it for an overnight stay, if the out and about visits called for it. At least that's what he told Val, the lying bugger.

One particular abattoir situated in Hadleigh, not a million miles from Westcliff was a regular out and about location, much visited by Mickey more than any of the others. Val didn't think it was too odd at first, but the visits to Hadleigh became more and more frequent until one day, he visited and never returned home, period. Her reaction was at first fearing for her future, then realised it meant no more aggro in the home. Then it was bloody good riddance to bad rubbish.

Whenever Eddie enquired after his dad with the older generation down at the local, all he would ever get would be a shrug of the shoulders and a throw of a grimace. The body language was all too easily interpreted. It said enough as far as he was concerned. One or two of the old boys who sat around in scruffy pubs all day nursing halves of bitter, explained to Eddie, old Mickey was mad leaving Val 'cos she was a bit of a looker. "I wouldn't have minded given her one myself," one of the old sweats giggled.

"Give it a miss pal, that's my mum you're bloody talking about." Eddie let it pass but noted the comment for the future.

What a Tosser.

Val called out to Eddie, "Come in the kitchen you toe rag and wash your German bands." Eddie might have been 18, and now an accomplished street fighter, but mum indoors at Plevna Street was definitely in charge. Eddie loved this fact. Deep down he totally respected his mum and loved the strictness in the house. It meant he could go ballistic outside when it was necessary and come home to mum's calm rigidity. A few deep breaths then everything would seem right in the world.

"Just like a little Oasis," he would say. Sergio Mendes was on the radio playing something called Bossa Nova music. Apparently, Herb Alpert was up next. Val loved it. The smooth sexy rhythm of the music and the silky voices of the artists singing. She absolutely loved it and would often hum along to the tunes, gracefully swinging her hips to the rhythmic music around the tiny kitchen. Reluctantly turning off the music, she offered up, "Eddie you've got to damn well promise me, that you won't attempt to kill anyone, at least not with your bare hands. Just look at them all bloodied up, and definitely not right outside our house. What the hell do you think the neighbours are gonna do now?

Probably blank us I should think, especially after that display of yours. We have to live here amongst these people. I go shopping for some of them and baby sit for others. There's enough fights and stuff kicking off elsewhere, we don't need it on the island especially so close to home son."

"Ah leave it out Ma. He's a total slag, he had more front than Woolworths. It's about time he and his sodding mates got their comeuppance and for that matter when they're on the deck, their downuppence. A boot stamped firmly two or three times on his windpipe would have sorted him for good. At least I didn't leave him sprawled in the road lying in pools of blood. Anyway Ma, let the neighbours talk. Bloody well let them. Let's hope word gets out, in fact get a load of this."

Ed walked back out on to the street, stood firmly in the middle of the road, forcing the odd car to stop and screamed, "Eddie Coleman is on the fucking war path." The yelled statement echoed around the street with its tight little darkened alley-ways. The message would have been heard way down the road and well beyond. Unlike his boring do-nothing neighbours, he wanted to be somebody and if this was the route to being somebody, then bring it on. "Perhaps, I should chase after that tosser and finish him off good and proper like. How dare he have it away on his toes just when I was just getting on top of him Ma."

When this would-be attacker decided he'd better run or actually risk the chance of dying, Eddie had bawled after the runner at the top of his lungs,

"There's plenty more where that came from pal."

Adrenalin was pumping round his veins, Eddie gulped down some air to slow the rapid heartbeat. He needed control of his body. Deep breathing helped him gain a bit of strength and normality back. It was the way forward. Stay calm, smile sweetly as your sticking it to them. That really spooks people. Stare at them with crazy glazed eyes looking just over their shoulder, as the knife makes its way into flesh and beyond. Eddie was sure the bully boy would get back to his oppo's elsewhere on the island pronto and spill – and he did for at least a fortnight. As a result, Eddies' street rep on the Isle-of-Dogs went up a fair few of notches. Not many would want to cross him now after this turning point.

It flashed through Eddie's mind that a violent money-making career for one Eddie Coleman might be on the cards? A voice in his shell like seemed to be saying that it could be *the* opportunity and it was staring him in the face. The voice in his head went on. *Look around you. Open your eyes to the possibilities. It's been done before and no doubt will be done again. Getting a reputation for being violent speaks volumes. If it can be harnessed, surely hard cash will follow? Someone, will eventually take on the Island*, he thought, *so it might as well be me.*

Eddie ignored the voices in his head for the time being, but, as with all inner voices, they nag and gnaw away. The voice with its messages, drove its way down like an earwig, aiming for the brain, then on into the department labelled up as Eddie's subconscious.

Violence, can be a very strong language and produce results almost instantaneously, especially during London's gangster ridden era of the early to mid-1960s. Parts of London were often seen as the big boys' violent playground. The two brothers in the East of London, Richard's mob over in South London with not a great deal of villainy being employed in-between. So, perhaps thought Eddie, *if the ground in-between was open for business, why not carve it up and give the Isle of Dogs, his own unique brand of violence, mayhem and threatening behaviour.* He even had a moniker for it, 'Eddie's Law.' Money was tight, too tight to talk about. Eddie's little family knew of this more than most. Ideas and thoughts welled up inside his head. Eddie's one and only current income was the dole, or rock and roll as it was called and that didn't amount to much. *Eddie's Law*, he thought, over and over again, until it began to make sense, become real, took shape. To him it made perfect sense, money, status and *respect.* But where to start, the Docks maybe? No, far too ambitious. So where else? How to turn aggression and open violence into those things he craved most, especially respect. To create a small army capable of delivering. What was needed he thought was to take control of the Kingsway Estate just up the road a bit.

Elephants and Rats.

Pimps, pushers, punks and birds on the game. Add on a couple of laddish gangs, all operating their own little quarter of Eddie's potential criminal launching pad, the Kingsway Estate. It was like rats earning a poxy living from all the other Kingsway Estate rats. Situated in the middle of the estate amongst all the back-to-back houses was a little row of shops.

A baker's, a butcher's and candle stick maker's, well actually a hardware shop. Another of the shops in the same row was one that was the hub of the community. An open all hour's style mini market convenience outlet, owned and run by Mr and Mrs Sharif. They stocked anything and everything one could ask for, anything from a pin to an elephant could be found in this essential and wonderful little emporium. Although, there wasn't much call for elephants on the Kingsway Estate. Lovely Mr and Mrs Sharif and their two gentle wholesome little boys were a family much liked by most of the Kingsway community. Always ready and willing to help all their customers, even letting the serious hard ups have stuff on tick. They knew most if not all their customers by name and would welcome them in with welcoming smiles. The Sharif's generally got on with running the business, going about their daily tasks professionally and quietly. Stocking shelves, visits to the wholesalers, sweeping up outside the front of their shop. No task was shirked. They worked in the shop from seven in the morning through eight in the evening at which point they would shut up shop and retire to the flat above. Unbeknownst to Eddie, this busy little outlet was destined to be the central launch pad, the jumping off point for his particular brand of evil doings on the Kingsway Estate.

last Sunday at 4.00 am, the Sharif's shop was broken into by three masked lads who lived in one of the high rises up near Indescon Square. As the Sharif's lived above their shop, they didn't feel the need for any alarm systems. Basing this judgement on the fact, they were living above.

Who would be dumb enough to break in, knowing the owners were just feet above them? Upon hearing a commotion downstairs, Mr Sharif, shot out of bed, guessed what was happening and instructed his wife to call the police whilst he investigated what was going on down in the shop. Mrs Sharif warned him to be careful and vigilant. No amount of damage or stock stolen she said, was worth getting hurt for.

Just observe and let whoever it is down there know that the police are coming and coming very soon. He shushed her and told her to get on the phone immediately. His nightly locking up routine never varied. Empty the till, lock the main entrance door, lock the private door that led up to their living accommodation right above the shop.

He instinctively knew it could only be a break in. Making his way down the hall he grabbed hold of a stout walking stick nestling in the little umbrella stand by the door that led downstairs. Fearing for his life, heart racing, he crept down the back stairs to the shop.

The shop's cash till was in the process of being ripped wholesale from its base located on the shops main counter. Packets of fags were scattered all over the place, boiled sweets and Mars bars underfoot. While all this was going on, Mrs Sharif, acting on instructions from her husband, busied herself upstairs phoning the police before rushing to her young son's bedroom to cuddle and comfort them both. Mr Sharif as quietly as possible entered the shop from his private door at the rear, screwing up his face at the loud click which might alert the intruders. The three masked teenagers immediately stopped what they were doing. They all heard the loud click.

Sensing movement, as one they turned to look in the direction of where Mr Sharif was standing lit only by the faint glow shining in from the lamp post outside, close by the shop. The nearest mask to Mr Sharif was the first to react. He growled menacingly, "Get back upstairs old man or we'll fucking cut you." To demonstrate he meant serious business, he drew an eight-inch blade from inside his jacket. The knife was waved about in a swishing fashion then drawn across the masks throat in mock execution style.

Mr S. was either brave or stupid or perhaps a little of both. Taking no notice of his wife's well-meaning instructions. Taking the initiative and catching the nearest masked hoodlum by complete surprise, Mr Sharif ran the full length of the shop rotating the stout walking stick above his head mimicking the rotor blades of a helicopter, yelling something completely indecipherable. The knife wielding masked raider was definitely caught entirely by surprise, by Mr Sharif's yelling and charging full tilt towards him. Surprised to hell that this horn-rimmed bespectacled little chap in striped pyjamas was at him and closing rapidly. This was not supposed to happen. The stout heavy walking stick connected to the side of the masks face with such force, a fair number of his yellow rotten teeth were uprooted.

He fell to the floor like the stuck little pig he was, spitting out blood and loosened teeth. Mr Sharif thought, *Oh God blimey, one down two to go*. Although Mr Sharif's gander was now well up for the fight, sadly, his heart and lungs were definitely not. He too fell to the floor very nearly on top of the knife wielder who was now nursing his busted and bleeding mouth. Mr S. was becoming dizzy, couldn't breathe properly, was in a cold sweat and clutching at his chest. A massive heart attack had gripped him, overtaking him, forcing him to fall exactly where he stood. He had only recently celebrated his 44th birthday, was in good general health too. Whilst he was writhing and thrashing about on the floor in abject agony, of his beloved shop, hidden to all but mask 1, hidden by the height of the stocked shelves, shelves he had restocked just a few hours earlier. The remaining two masked teenagers could only but stand and stare, unsure of what was unfolding over on the far right of the shop.

19

They glanced at each other then began tentatively to make their way over to where their mate had been dropped. They stood stock still staring in disbelief. One of their gang was decked, spitting blood snot and teeth onto the floor. The shop's owner, they rightly assumed was either dead or dying.

Death or dying or even both, was something these three had not witnessed previously in their young lives. Not been a part of, not even sure it was happening. In a matter of sixty short seconds Mr Sharif finally succumbed to the cardiac arrest. He lay dead, the thrashing and groaning abruptly stopped. Once again, the shop descended into an eerie silence. Eyes staring weirdly and wide open up at them from the floor, tongue sticking out at a bizarre angle. Foamy bubbles emerging from nostrils. This was the masked gang's clue to fuck off and fuck off fast.

The now almost toothless mask got to his feet grabbed his knife from where it had fallen under the coffee and tea gondola, stuck it in the pocket of his army look-alike combat jacket.

The three of them exchanged panicked glances. A silent signal was telegraphed. 'Have it away right now and bloody fast.'

The shop's entrance door although wide open, wasn't wide enough to accommodate all three exiting at the same time. A scuffle ensued, fists, arms, knees, elbows, Doc Martin boots shot out in all directions in an effort to be the first onto the street outside. As they piled out onto the pavement, in the yellow lamplight glow, all three ran blindly in different directions. Had a casual observer been standing nearby they would have likened the scene to rats leaving a sinking ship.

None of the would-be burglars took heed of the distant bells ringing, heralding the imminent appearance of Mr Plod. Scrote and his mates were shit scared. To their tiny and uneducated minds this could be seen as an actual murder and it was down to them that did it, nobody else. Not long after the threesome doing a convincing disappearing act, old Bill arrived in a patrol car. As per usual, too bloody late. Scrote and his two mates had melted away into the rat holes they belonged to.

However, although arriving a little on the late side the old Bill was at least instrumental in calling an ambulance for poor old and very dead Mr Sharif. Following on from the general police enquiries, the only tangible bit of evidence that yielded itself up to the police was a name. Mrs Sharif was able to tell the officers very little, not having seen the masked men. None the less, she heard one of them shouting something to the others as they ran, something she didn't understand. "Oh yes, madam and what was it you heard?" asked officer number one, pencil and notebook at the ready.

"One of them had called to the others don't you bloody well grass us up Lenny, or it might have been Benny or maybe even Henry."

"Thank you, Mrs Sharif, that's very interesting and helpful," the officer said in a mildly sarcastic tone. The police had a name, or did they? One of the two officers who first turned up stayed with Mrs Sharif until a fresh team arrived to look for clues and fingerprints. When they arrived, Mrs Sharif left them to it. Disappearing back upstairs to begin the sad process of contacting her husband's many relatives in India, who would no doubt want very much to be part of the funeral and burial process.

Rosie Higgs.

Val Coleman had always worked and now worked hard, harder and longer hours after Mickey buggered off with the floozie type. Val became the bread winner in their little two up two down. She had worked a longish stint at one of the docks many café's North of the Island, serving fry-ups, bacon sarnies and the likes to the hard-working dockers. Fun, but poorly paid. Val relied on tips from the dockers to top up her earnings, but even they started to dry up. A job for a bus conductor or clippie as it was more commonly known, had been posted up on one of the pin boards at the employment offices in Canning town. Val took a look at it and thought, *I could do that*. The money was almost double what she earned at the docks, even with the tips.

First to apply and be interviewed, the job was hopefully hers. She took up the post when it was eventually offered and became a member of the staff of London Transport.

The pay was far better and instead of free bacon butties she had free access to bus and tube rides. The job meant wearing a uniform of course and this suited Val well. Wolf whistles a plenty on her way to the bus depot and wolf whistles a plenty on her way back home. The uniform supplied was a black jacket and matching trouser set, times two. These was accompanied by a leather money bag for a cash float of a couple of bob in pennies for change. A metal plate to hang a ticket machine on and a licence badge worn on the lapel. The badge consisted of two letters followed by five digits.

It was up to the uniform wearer to supply a crisp white blouse or shirt; flat heels (for ladies) and the outfit was then ready to go. Val, with the help of her old treadle Singer sewing contraption, stitched neat little creases down the front of each trouser leg.

You would have to be very close to see the black stitching. It gave the trousers a 'well pressed' and smart tidy appearance.

What with her long blonde hair and the smart uniform it's no wonder she got loads wolf whistles when passing any building sites on the way to the depot. Plus, the occasional "Can we go for a drink darlin, on me." Then under the caller's breath 'And pretty soon I'll be on you.'

It's a known fact, a number of drivers at the bus depot put in with the depot inspector to have Val as their main and permanent clippie. Some drivers actually fought each other round the back of the depot for the right for her to work on their respective bus. This of course went straight over Val's head. She was far more interested in getting the little brown envelope at the end of each week with a bit of cash in it, so bills could be paid and food put on the table. There was one driver however, she did go a bit sweet on. Elvis, he was known as at the bus depot, being as how he styled himself on the king. His casual manner and rocker style haircut, brylcreemed up with a duck's arse to the back, strangely appealed to Val so, after many requests she went on a date with him. He took her for a meal at a new place called the 'Golden Egg.' A new chain of food outlets springing up like mushrooms. What a disaster. During the meal a shoeless foot found its way under the table they were sitting at into Val's crutch. A bit like a creeping python. At first Val didn't understand what was occurring. The moment she did, her omelette chips and peas, plate and all, found its way into the face of this creepy git. Val wasn't finished. She jumped up, pushed the guy over backwards, chair an all, to the floor and began to grind a stiletto heel into his bollocks. Unable to jump up, he howled and hollered. Val looked him in the eye calmly mouthing. "My turn tosser."

Snatching Val's foot, an attempt was made to pull her to the floor. Anything to stop the excruciating pain to his groin. Rather helpfully the nearest restaurant customer, a strong looking young giant of a lad from Silver Town stood up and said politely to Val, excuse me a moment my love. He placed his own chair over the chest of Val's now ex-date and sat down on it hard, all 16 stone of him. The victim gurgled in more pain, this time to his chest. He quickly gave up the fight and laid still hoping for a truce but Val was not finished.

Grabbing a coffee pot from a nearby table, she poured the hot coffee straight onto his clock-weights, just for good measure. More screaming and howling. Needless to say, the evening was over, finito. Nothing of that night's events at the Golden Egg was mentioned by either of them ever again.

Somewhere at the back of the restaurant was one Rosie Higgs. She knew Val from working with her for a brief spell in a caff job, up at the docks and what's more Rosie had heard a lot on the grapevine about her son Eddie.

He was getting a lot of publicity just lately, what with becoming a wide boy and tear-arse. "Val," Rosie called, "over ere luv, come and have a cuppa and a bite with us." Val looked over in Rosie's direction.

Through the thick layers of foundation and make up on Rosie's face, Val recognised her, only just. She was a little cautious, Rosie was always a bit rough and ready for a bit of a fight. Val had her down as, trollop, so what the bloody hell is it she wants with me?

Walking over, unsure of Rosie's motive, Val stood next to her table and observed a well-dressed young black guy possibly in his twenties in the chair opposite. Rosie introduced him. "Errol, this is Val Coleman, Eddie's mum." Rosie kicked Errol under the table.

"Hello Mrs Coleman," Errol stood up. "Please, won't you sit with us. Let me get you a glass of something perhaps?" *Good looking, well presented and impeccable manners*, thought Val.

"Call me Val Errol and yes thank you, a little glass of apple juice would be nice, thanks."

Errol stood up again and was about to nip off and place the order, but he needn't have worried. The waitress was ahead of him, placing a fresh glass of apple juice in front of Val "On the house Mrs Coleman," she smiled sweetly and explained, "The one you had earlier, was ever so slightly spilled." Val looked up and smiled back at the waitress, with her mouth, but not her eyes. This sort of thing hadn't happened to her before.

Usually it would have been, "That'll be another ten Bob please!" *Was this the beginnings of being an up-coming villain's mum, respect? I'll have some of that*, she thought. *Yes please.*

All the diners in the restaurant heard Mr Creepy scraping chairs, pushing them out of his way, staggering towards the exit, skulking out of the now buzzing restaurant grimacing, clutching his privates.

Mock applause and shouts of "And don't come back pal," from the management. Mr Creepy had the right hump.

"Ok you two, Rosie, Errol, what's on your mind?"

"Nothing serious Mrs C." replied Rosie, "Thing is, Errol's looking for a bit of extra work ain't cha mate?" Rose kicked him again under the table in an effort to get him to join in.

"That's right Mrs Coleman, err sorry Val, I understand that Eddie might need the odd bit of work doing here and there. I can fit in any work to be done with what I do now."

"Oh yes and what is it that you do now?" Errol smiled broadly at the opportunity of explaining exactly what he did, knowing she would not be disappointed.

"My father owns a scrap yard over in Creekmouth. It's mainly for pulling apart old unwanted abandoned cars and lorries and stuff."

"Creekmouth, that's over near Dagenham isn't it? Not called Fords is it?" Val couldn't resist asking.

"No nothing as grand as that Val, (Errol had heard that one a thousand times) but the plant is quite large. We have a melting furnace or smelter on site and employ seven or eight guys all who worked for Fords at one time or another. And, they all hail from the Dagenham area. Cars and lorries are coming in daily now for scrapping even a couple of buses recently, so we might need to expand."

"Forgive me for asking, but why, when you've got all that going for you, do you want to tie up with my Eddie?"

"Contacts Val contacts, I want to meet Eddie and see if we can be of mutual help? We have a good business going and want to keep it that way. Eddie might find that we could be of help to him, as much as he can to us." What was running through Errol's mind was a tidy little earner for both Eddie and his dad's business, namely, Eddie nicking designer cars flogging them to Errol, Errol keeping them under cover in the breakers yard for six months or so, changing the plates, paper work and paint finish. Then flogging them off to anyone daft enough to buy them. This little bit of harmless info, he held back from Val.

Contacts hmmm contacts thought, Val, *no harm in that.*

"So, Val," asked Errol, "what can we get you from the menu?"

Violence Equals Money.

Eddie decided he was definitely on to something. He had handed out a severe hammering outside his house. He felt this could definitely be his way forward in the money for violence stakes. His route to something he now craved more than anything, *everlasting respect*. To become a face to be reckoned with, just by using his fists and wits, and the occasional cut throat razor as opposed to living in fear and at his wits end. The thoughts of a simple but loaded equation, as in violence equals money, should not be the thoughts of an eighteen-year-old East End Lad, or should they? He was getting on a bit with no real job or prospects plus, he couldn't live with his mum forever.

Surely at 18 he should be getting involved in girl chasing, charging around with mates, getting pissed on Saturday nights, nicking cars for joy rides. Trips to Brighton or Clacton. Getting involved in pitched battles on England's Southern seafronts. Who the fuck cares about mods and rockers and their running gang fights on the coast? Let's get stuck against either side, mob handed like and kick loads of sand and dog shit over anyone that gets in the way. Teenage stuff, yes definitely, but 'not violence equals money'. The warm glowy feeling remained as Eddie pictured himself climbing the greasiest of East End poles to notoriety amongst and amid the losers that didn't dare stand up for themselves when all alone out in the scary streets of East London. He sneered as he thought to himself of all those gutless bastards that beat him up after school, jumping out of hedges, grabbing him from behind usually two or three mob handed and never from the front. Always jumped from behind. Gutless bastards.

Thanks guys, you have actually unwittingly presented me with a monumental and not inconsiderable primal urge to improve my fighting skills and improve I will.

Then, I will be back for a catch-up with the lot of you and that's no idle threat. You just bloody well wait and see. You lot are on the fucking kill list.

Eddie's temperament had taken on a new chapter.

His mood, if fronted out, would now rocket from calm to complete and total blind rage, in a matter seconds, no steps in between in. The violence Ma Val had witnessed from her living room window clearly informed her and her Plevna Street neighbours who came out of their houses to watch, now had a potential tear-arse on their hands. There was no doubt of that and, with no man in the house to keep Eddie in check, how was the future going to shape up for all of those that witnessed the heavy and vicious beating.

Most neighbours in the sixties would usually, by-and-large, stick by each other through thick and thin. Some of Val's neighbours however, were having serious second thoughts. Started to look the other way. Crossed the street when they needed to walk past number 119. Ma Val however deep down, found some admiration for her son creeping in. He could now at last stand up for himself big time which pleased her greatly. She had watched him coming home from school many a time holding his arm or leg, whichever had been kicked or punched. Now though, he was fast acquiring a trait much needed for young men making their way hopefully, for a better life and future for themselves and those around them that's not normally afforded in this shitty down trodden neck of London.

Ma Val was, as many others around her, keenly aware of the type of business the brothers had carved out in the East End for themselves, utilising the rule of violence *and* how well off they had become. It was well document in most of the papers, some printing daily accounts. Almost all the locals despised the feeling of oppression metred by the gangs and firms, steering well clear. Leaving well alone if they could. Life was tough enough as it was, without falling foul of any gangland menacing. Val though, dared to dream.

Dared to dream of Eddie on the up in a similar fashion to the top firms, hopefully not killing too many people on the way unless they were wasters or police snouts of course. That was quite acceptable. Eddie had heard of the top firm's code and so had Val. Something like no women or children were to be harmed. If anything, they were to be cherished.

The rest of society, if it became necessary, because they stood in the way would be legitimate targets from their legs upwards. Val had listened wistfully to the lovely stories of how the brother's mum was so well respected and well treated in Bethnal Green. There were stories she heard of how, when she shopped and got to the till the shop owner would politely pack her stuff in a carrier then say smiling, "That's fine Mrs K. Hope the boys are doing okay, have a lovely day now." Much to the annoyance of any others in the shop at the time. For some reason, she always shot to the front of any queue. Was always given the best cuts of meat and so on. *I could do with a bit of that,* thought Val.

Beach Huts and Motorbikes.

Arms folded, still staring out through the living room window, Val began to day dream on a slightly grander level than usual. She dreamed that perhaps her Eddie would be able to grant her a wish once his wallet was bulging and money was pouring in, as she knew it would. A much-cherished wish and in the not-too-distant future please. Up until now it was just a pipe dream, it was beginning perhaps now to become a reality. Val's innermost cherished wish, was a simple one, to her anyway. It was a wish to own a beach hut on the sands of the Costa Del Sol in Espanola, as she like to call it. Much better than plain old Spain.

Val occasionally read magazines at the dentists or doctors. Mostly about a resort called Tossa de Mar. It was right popular in the 60s. Made her giggle a bit, the name, some magazines proudly printed glossy, colourful pictures of the resort. These mags boldly displayed double page spreads in the middle of the magazine. Two big staples spoiling the sea view a bit, she didn't mind though. They went straight into her handbag. Most of the glossy pics were neatly pulled out of various publications and kept safe. Neatly folded up, then placed a little oxo tin box which she kept under her bed. Each and every time she took them out for a look, she would say to herself, "Very nice thank you very much." Val was convinced in her mind, the beaches of Tossa will have loads and loads of beach huts all going for song or at least cheap as chips.

After all, most of the beaches on the south coast like Southend and that, had beach huts. So, why not Tossa? Surely the beach-masters of Tossa were not tosser enough to miss a trick like that even if they were greasy bleeding Spaniards. With a bit of luck, if Eddie was extra kind she could have two, push them together like and knock 'em through as with some of the larger families that do on the council estate up the road from Plevna Street. *Silly cow* she thought, *fuck it, with Eddie on the up and dead set on living it large, what was it he called it, Eddie's Law? I could have a double for me and a dozen more doubles to rent out. I could sit there in my own double in the lovey warm Spanish sunshine, warding off all the greasy gigolos and have a good little earner at the same time.*

Oxo Tin opened, glossy shots of Tossa de Mar spread all over her bed, Val joyfully remembered the happy outings when her mum and dada would take her and her two sisters down the Arterial Road, passed Basildon to Southend-on-Sea. The locals of course aptly re-named it Southend-on-Mud. When the tide went out, apart from a wide strip of stony sand, beyond that, it was sticky smelly mud, as far out as the ray, a mile of mud at least. Walk out there at your peril. The mud could and would bog people down to point of not being able to move. Unsuspecting visitors from the East End out on a beano were often being rescued before the incoming tide sneaked in to claim them, God knows how they didn't drown. But what days Val and her family had on the Essex coast. Dada, Mum, Val and her sisters.

Candy floss, a train ride to the end of the pier, ice creams with a chocolate flake smothered in hundreds and thousands. Mum always bought the girls kiss me quick hats.

A paddle in the briny was a must do thing, dresses tucked into knickers and Dada with his trousers rolled up to his knees. All screaming and laughing when the ice-cold dirty Thames Estuary waters lapped around their ankles. Along the Esplanade was a famous Fish-n-Chip shop overlooking the Estuary and on over to the coastlines of the Isle of Grain and Sheerness.

A large menu board on the front of the building announced in chalk 'Delicious Cod and Chips, Cod caught locally.' If you were to cross over the road, look down over the sea wall at high tide, you would feel it might have been better to state, 'Cod caught at least 100 miles away!'

At high tide, the Estuary waters looked very mucky and murky. Dada on these days out; always insisted he wore a four-corner knotted hankie on his bonce to cover his bald spot. He never went anywhere without a shirt and tie, no matter how hot it got. During the afternoon they would pay the entrance money to go into the Kursaal amusement park which was situated just at the Eastern end of Southends Miracle Mile; so-called as it was a bloody miracle if anybody came off better against the hundreds of rigged one arm bandits in the amusement arcades crammed in together along the mile. Once in the Kursaal, they would have a go at the various amusement opportunities. Dada loved the one called 'Knock the lady out of Bed,' But never quite hit the target with the three balls handed to him by the caller running the side show. The target was situated below the lady laying in her bed for all to see. If he hit the target, her bed would tip sideways. The lady would roll out on to a mattress below, scantily clad of course.

All the young lads nearby would rush over to get a glimpse of her in bra, knickers and stockings, before the bed slowly returned to its base and in she climbed, awaiting the next punter to hit the target. There were bumper cars, Helter Skelter, coconut shies to have a go on. Best of all though was the wall-of-death. The very name struck fear in the hearts of Val and her big sisters. Guys on motor bikes roared round and round the vertical walls at speed, defying gravity.

Tired but happy the family would then head off for home in Dada's old Bedford CA van with its ever-jamming sliding doors. Halfway home up the A127 they often stopped at a café called the Blinking Owl.

This was a haunt for the ton-up boys and their loud, brutish motorbikes. All in the 500cc size engines. Clip on handle bars and shiny exhaust systems. These boys would race each other up and down the main drag between Southend and Romford's Gallows Corner, daring the old Bill to chase them on their puny Noddy bikes.

Val and her sisters would hang around outside where the ton-up boys would be admiring each other's gleaming 500cc bikes, not really noticing the three young ladies hovering and hoping to get a conversation on the go. Norton Dominators, Triumph Bonneville's, BSA Gold Star, they were all there. Sadly, not many of the ton-up lads lived long enough to tell tales of the speeds they reached, usually 100 mph plus. Crash helmets were for whimps in those days. Dada would leave the engine running outside in the car park in case the vans starter motor jammed again.

Nobody in their right mind would want to nick it. The Bedford was well passed its sell by date. When the photos that were snapped during any of the outings got processed and printed a few weeks later, Val would pick out all the ones with a beach hut in the background. These would be special to Val, not because she was present in the photo, often she would stand a little to the left of centre to make sure the beach huts were in full view. Val would then choose the best of them and the best of the best would find their way pinned onto the wall of her tiny bedroom. Ma Val would often lovingly spin tales of these outings to Eddie when he was a lad and growing up, in a sort of reminiscing way. But it cut no ice with Eddie.

His thoughts and ambitions were on a different level to beach huts, candy floss and a quick paddle in the briny. Eddie Coleman was 18 now and anxious to get on with his agenda of violence and mayhem.

Up the Hammers.

Hey Wossname, what's up wanker? Eddie bused it over to his mate's house in Corporation Street, Stratford, E15. Stratford being a parish in the Borough of London and part of the Lower Lea Valley. Stratford localities include Maryland, East Village and Stratford City. Wossname, (real name Vince,) was much like his dad, a big lumbery lad with hands like shovels. He was sometimes known as lubber-lub when he was younger. As he slid into his early twenties, the lub gradually morphed into muscle which gave him a powerful, menacing appearance. Those closest to him though, knew he was but a gentle giant. Always wearing the same worn out blue and green striped pullover from the market in Brick Lane coupled with his fave Levi jeans.

Due to the bulk round his middle, to achieve a comfortable waist size he had to put up with a leg length that was far too long. Thus, he had more turn-ups than was usually acceptable, almost halfway up to his knees it was! Because of his image, six-foot-tall, three-foot-wide in places and super large hands, nobody challenged him on that particular subject. He had a habit of listening with his mouth open almost as if his ears and mouth were linked.

Wossnames dad was a big West Ham supporter. You couldn't miss their house. Stuck well out like sore thumb. It was painted in the Hammer's colours, claret and blue. There was even a pair of crossed hammers painted on the front door. No wonder his misses, Wossnames mum, we think, ran off with a coach driver some years earlier and put down roots south of the river in Lewisham.

Wossname didn't see much of his pretend mum on the basis that she now lived south of the Thames. South of the Thames was basically a foreign country to most who lived north of the river, especially East Enders. It was the East Enders who coined the saying 'All South Londoners are planks.' Eddie had called round to Wossnames to discuss his impending assault on the Isle-of-Dogs, Eddie's back yard. The island as it was more commonly and locally known, was left relatively alone by the more established villains mostly because there was not that much to be gained in terms of villainy. To the north of the island sat the busy wharfs and docks. Gigantic sea going ships being off loaded day and night.

To the East and West, the Thames Loop and the middle bit dominated by Millwall Football Club together with Mr Cubitt's new town, land development areas. Still, Eddie wanted to make a start with his assault and where better than where he lived and was brought up. After all he judged, if old Bill was chasing him following some evil doings or other, he was in the know as to where he could easily duck out of sight. Melt into the Isle-of-Dogs fabric and have it away on his toes pronto like. Same as the black cab drivers of London Eddie had done the knowledge of the Isle-of-Dogs comprehensively from the age of seven.

Yep, the island had it coming. Up West and Park Lane as the saying goes, could wait.

Wossname was a right character. He was some three years older than Eddie. Never worked, never intended to. Not a proper job anyway. But you have to give him his due. He never signed on the 'any-to-come' income. Would not be seen dead in a dole queue, preferring to duck and dive in the moment of each day as and when it presented itself. His money-cash-in-hand, came mostly from selling badges, scarfs, football rosettes and assorted stuff, up at Wembley and a few other footie grounds within a tube ride of Corporation Street. He even did the occasional speedway crowd at Wimbledon's Plough Lane track, home of the Dons, if there was an international being held there. There was always something on somewhere most weekends and it was fair old money too for an afternoons work. He would opt only to do the crowds on their way in. 'Doing the in' as it was known as. Supporters wanted to get their team colours by and large, going into the match.

Some of the other sellers would do the in, the interval, and the out. But Wossname thought that was greedy. Besides which, the interval and the out were never as lucrative as the in, unless there was a really big win and If there was a big win there was always the danger of getting rolled and losing your stuff and hard earned, to some of the unrulier fans, who poured out of the grounds not giving a shit for anyone or anything that stood in their way.

The tale of Wossname being know solely as Wossname, came about because of his inability to finish a sentence without the word wossname. As in, 'Shall we shoot off and have a pint or two down the wossname?' Or. 'Did you know Bert's knocked up that bird Julie and she's three months up the wossname!' So, in the end, wossname it was for evermore!

Eddie knew roughly where to begin his personal assault on the Isle-of-Dogs the Kingfield Estate. He wanted to be accompanied by like-minded mates or mob handed as it were. Blokes who could handle themselves in search of easy money, even if it meant hurting someone. And If anyone did need hurting, Eddie had absolutely no problem with that. However, there were elements other than fists and bovver boots required to attain his aspirations.

His top aim was to financially benefit from his activities, at the same time as getting his name about the island. He bused the four miles or so via the Blackwell Tunnel, over to Wossnames for a bit of a chin wag on his thoughts, ideas and schemes. Why the hell Wossname you might ask? Well, apart from being a big fearsome looking fucker who could well put someone's lights out with a single blow, Wossname had access to a motor. This fact being quite rare in the mid-sixties. The motor or wheels as it were referred to actually belonged to Wossnames dad.

Outside Wossnames house in the neat tree lined road of Corporation Street Stratford, stood, a Ford Anglia 105E Deluxe no less in what looked like Caribbean blue body colour, topped off with a white roof.

Eddie couldn't work out why it was not in claret and blue, up the Hammers and all that, after all most of Wossnames house was painted in the Hammer's home colours and not just the outside. But he let it go. Beggars can't be choosers, Eddie mused to himself. However, the motor was most definitely his dads' pride and joy. Wossname being Wossname seniors only family now, was trusted with the keys to the motor, but only now and then, mainly to pick up Wossname senior after a home game followed by a lock in at a pub, any pub, around midnight.

Lock-ins were very popular in the 60s and Wossname senior was always the best customer to be invited in, frittering his hard-earned cash on far too many black and tans. Plenty of time therefore in the evening for Wossname to drive over to the island, pick Eddie up and go out on the rampage. Especially, on the weekends when the Hammers were playing at home up at the Boleyn ground, Wossname senior was to be found during the morning of a home match, head under the bonnet fiddling with the carburettor complete in the knowledge, that by opening the air inlet just half a screw, and the same to the fuel line, would make the one litre engine a contender for the next British Grand Prix! Not sure if he had Jim Clark and team Lotus-Climax too worried.

Wossname junior knew what was required of him on these home game-lock-in weekends. He needed to stay sober, up to a point, be ready to taxi his dad home in the Anglia, usually at midnight, when the lock-in locked out.

West Hams season of 1964/65 was extremely successful.

They swept aside all before them in the European Cup winner's cup. Hammers scored a notable semi-final victory over Spanish cup winners Real Zaragoza before defeating TSV 1860 Munich, in a fantastic final at Wembley. Wossname senior was of course fiercely and passionately mad about the Hammers and would not hear a word said against them.

Should he over hear anyone bad mouthing his beloved West Ham United during a lock in, he would stroll over to where the guy was standing and engage him in light conversation. Then offer him a cigarette and as soon as the guy opened his mouth to put it in, Wossname senior would make a fist and bang him on the side of his chin and saunter back to his pint. Nine times out of ten the blow given would break or at least dislocate the other guys jaw bone and send him crashing to the ground like sack of spuds. The theory is, you cannot break or dislocate someone's jaw if they have their teeth clenched together, hence the cigarette being offered. Wossname senior had mixed a bit with the periphery of the brother's army and picked up one or two basic operational techniques allied to the gangsters 'terms and conditions' – East End style. Typically involving bribery, mayhem, corruption and the odd bit of jaw breaking.

A Peace Maker.

The Ford Anglia 105E was the first of its kind to have an inwardly sloping rear windscreen. The old Bill had a few of them. These were usually given to stations out in sticks to run around in, a big leg up from old fashion worn out rusty push bikes for coppers riding about with blue flashing lights built in to the pointy bit of their helmets. London cops however had wheels that were a bit more up market. They were chasing robbers and crims and stuff around the smoke in Hillman Minx's and Wolseley's. These were predominately black and more commonly known as area or squad cars.

Equipped with 'in car' to station radios, the occupants usually two uniformed men and one in plain clothes, could scream off to potential crimes in action, arrive hastily with all three jumping out to act as back up for whoever was first on the scene. Wossname senior's Ford Anglia, was not exactly a gangster mobile thought Eddie, but it was wheels.

With wheels one could organise drive bys and stuff. Getaways from old Bill and stuff. Drive who ever to remote spots, like One Tree Island, do them over and drive off stuff. Stuff that Eddie wanted to progress into and fast. He decided he wouldn't get much street cred mooning about on buses even if he did ride around everywhere upstairs. Upstairs deck is where everyone smoked, some so-called hard nuts on the top deck smoked Grand Cigarettes.

The advertising street hoardings just visible from the top deck through the grimy bus windows, carried a life-sized image of a 007 type character dressed in a trench coat complete with a Fedora hat pulled over one of his eyes. The advertising company of brand Grand used the strap line that went 'You're never alone with a Grand'. It was a monumental failure. The brand was quickly dropped in the mid-1960s. However, most of the newsagents around, luckily, had plenty of stocks hidden in their basements so the brand lived on for some time until even these stocks sold out. The slogan did it for some wannabe hoodlums, who used the bus to get here or there smoked a Grand, then went home early to supper with mumsy. Grand flopped. I mean, who wanted to be associated with loneliness? By far and away the top reasoning however, as to why Eddie wanted to befriend Wossname extra specially nicely, Vince bloody Wossname bloody Gander had access to a shooter.

Fuck me, thought Eddie he nearly shat himself at the thought of carrying one about in the clubs and pubs on the island on a Saturday night, getting pissed on his dole money, with the peacemaker as Wossname called it tucked in his belt. A meaningful bulge in his trousers, instantly recognised as trouble. He was tingling all over at the thought and badly needed to get an eyeful of Wossnames gun. The shooter, turned out to be an old American revolver brought home by Wossname senior after the war. Wossname junior called it a peacemaker which wasn't far from the truth. It was clean, tidy but completely knackered. The revolving cylinder didn't revolve. The firing pin had been ground down out of existence, but to quote Buddy Holly, 'Oh Boy' to the uninitiated, did it look sinister and threatening or what.

Especially when held in sinister and threatening hands. Shove it in someone's face and scream, "Get on the fucking floor cunt," would have anyone at the wrong end of the barrel have a pant shitting experience. They wouldn't have the time to work out that it's not loaded or that it wouldn't go bang even if it was. It was jump down on the ground rather quickly and smartish like. This appealed to Eddie big time.

All the bastard cow-son's that hitherto kicked him in the head were quickly recalled. Time for revenge maybe? No bloody maybe about it. He couldn't wait to get started. Eddie asked if he could see the shooter first hand like. He wished to know what it felt like handling serious iron.

Wossname dug a battered shoe box out from the 'Old Mother Hubbard' under the stairs then fished out an oily rag which contained the peacemaker. *Christ*, Eddie thought, *I'm gonna rename it the fucking war-maker*.

"This is definitely pukka matey did your dad ever kill anyone with it?"

"Don't think so," Wossname replied, "Dad wasn't infantry he was in the catering corps. I think the only soldiers he topped was down to his lousy Wossname." This was Eddie's first actual handling of a piece. He lovingly moved it from hand to hand and back again, checking the weight. Mockingly he held it right up close to Wossnames forehead, right between the eyes and pulled the hammer back until, with a machine like click, it sat in the 'about to fire and kill you position.' All Eddie needed to do was to gently squeeze the trigger and Wossnames brain would splatter all over the wall just behind him. Momentarily, Wossname went boss eyed, what with the position of the ugly barrel snout pressed into his forehead right smack above the bridge of his nose. Eddie began to sing very slowly and softly, almost childlike a favourite nursery rhyme that his mum used to sing to him when he couldn't sleep. His eyes were glazed and head titled to one side.

"Half a pound of tuppeny rice half a pound of treacle, that's the way the money goes pop goes the weasel." Ed squeezed the trigger. As the hammer was released, he screamed, "**BANG**."

Anything for the Weekend (Sir)

Wossname fell backward and very nearly fainted in fright. He slowly became aware of a damp patch to the front of his jeans. He'd pissed himself. Inwardly, Eddie felt the massive thrill of someone being shit scared on the business end of a gun whilst in his hand, finger on the trigger.

Top, top power trip came to mind! Wossname knew only too well that the gun was harmless; wouldn't or couldn't shoot bullets, but for few seconds that knowledge went rushing out from his brain, straight out through his backside. The cold calculating almost angelic intense look on Eddies' face it was that really frightened the shit out of poor Wossname and that soft eerie singing. No sneering no snarling and no screwing up of his eyes. Eddie was like an ice man, cool as you like. He was smiling, smiling whilst living the death of Wossname.

"Fuck me Eddie. I've pissed my pants a bit and I think I've followed through round the back. You made me drop my arse, bastard git." Eddie threw him a grimace of a smile.

"Yea, well, you ain't brown bread yet though, are ya pal?" Eddie didn't fully appreciate Wossnames plight and fright, he was well away in some fantasy criminal world of pure and professional violence. This was something he only dared dream of to date. Now he wanted more, much more and fast. It took a fair few minute for Eddie to descend back down to mother Earth. This literally was his first ever come down from a great height. He waited for his rapid breathing to become shallow. Took some serious deep breaths to hasten the come down, to get his mind to stop spinning and heart rate to decrease. Eddie had never in his entire life, ever touched drugs. Never wanted to. Drugs, he had always felt was for hopeless useless losers. Besides which, at best, taking drugs, or popping pills as some people called it, was like throwing money straight down the proverbial.

This gun to the head thing however, was as high as he had ever been. High as a bleeding kite. Eddie had yet to score with a bird. Something to do with being a short arse with curly ginger hair. Freckles on the bridge of his nose didn't sit well with the female of the species either.

Had the odd fumble of course, who hadn't? His mate Timmy Tit Squeeze had given him some ideas and tips on winning birds over. Even purchased a packet of three from his barbers for him. "Anything for the weekend sir?" his barber asked Timmy.

"I'll have a pack of three, but they're not for me." The barber smiled much to himself, having heard that old chestnut about a million and one times before. Doin' a slapper in some god forsaken minging alleyway behind the local Chinky House would be a poor comparison with the high feeling Eddie had just experienced.

This new feeling was going to be his mistress from now on. He was going to love her, look after her and cherish her as best he could. No, Eddie had never got past the fumbling thing with the girls, the odd cloth tit here and there but never a proper stand-up shag or any other position for that matter. Who needs a bunk up when you can get this high without even getting your dick out of your pants he thought? Thing is, this time, it was only role play. No bullets, no firing pin, no real bang. He daren't think of the enormous high he was going to get when it's for real. As in a real working gun, with real bullets making a real bang when he pulled the real trigger, making a real hole in someone's head. *Fuck, let it happen real soon*, Eddie thought.

"Jesus H Christ Eddie," Wossname yelled, "I thought you was a bleeding Wossname, I think I need to go and get changed." While Wossname busied himself upstairs in the toilet Eddie inspected his new but dangerous toy a little closer. He called it his, because now he couldn't bear to be parted from it. No way was he going home without it, no way. In due course he would need to get hold of a proper working shooter together with some proper working ammo. As soon as he got home, he would put the feelers out. But for now, the warmaker would do. He needed to take it home with him and knew there would be a row about it with Wossname. However, if Wossname refused point blank. Then it would be, 'Over his dead body,' he smiled to himself, if necessary.

Fritz.

This particular Peacemaker model, had a seven and half inch-long barrel. It weighed just a tad over a kilo. Quite light for a big looking gun. Jet black, mean and ugly with it, but to Eddie it was a thing of beauty and perhaps a joy forever. He immediately stuck it into his waist band, zipped up his tired old battered brown leather jacket and proceeded to strut around Wossnames back yard drawing it out and aiming at an imaginary enemy. He practised the draw from his waistband a number of times, until he was capable of completing the action in less than five seconds. Wossname non plussed, was watching him out of the open fanlight in the upstairs bog window, trousers round his ankles. Wash, wipe. Wash wipe. "Hey mate, you look like a total dick," he yelled. "No, better still a complete wossname you do."

Oops! He knew he'd fucked up for a moment there, and bit his tongue. Him and his big gob, huge mistake. But being a nutjob and a sizeable one at that, he pressed on regardless of any recriminations from Eddie. "Nobody struts around like that anymore, except in a John Wayne film perhaps." This outburst hit some nerve endings belonging to Eddie, made them tingle for all the wrong reasons. A thought instantly came into his mind to race up the stairs, grab Wossname by the hair pull his head back so that his face would be exposed and pistol whip his so-called mate then and there. After all, Eddie was the one packing the piece. He felt however, this type of action might be a little unfair. To be whipped with your old man's gun barrel in your own bog. Besides which Wossname senior had only just decorated the smallest room in the house, took him the best part of three months. Pistol whipping Wossname would spoil his old man's handy work. Blood snot and tears all over the place. Still, the name calling stung.

Eddie vowed to make Vince bloody Wossname pay for that slagging off sometime soon. For now though, Eddie was going to need access to Wossnames wheels and definitely his shooter for a bit of show. Both items leant a bit of power in the eyes of whom Eddie Coleman planned to threaten, intimidate, rob and maybe even protect, for a fee! He also needed any contacts Wossname might have, that were a bit tasty when it comes to violence and mayhem.

He was sure Wossname had knowledge of names and faces and he was prepared to milk him for all he was worth. From the time those taunts were shouted down from the bog window, a slow but growing coldness between the two of them was spawned. They began to eye each other with a bit of suspicion. Eddie had been the victim of many a name calling and didn't care for anymore, especially from this big lumbering slag. The outburst from his so-called mate especially when it might have been overheard by anyone within earshot was the last thing Eddie needed. What he needed and craved and craved above all else was respect.

The bullying that young Eddie had endured, started when he was at school age, handed out by his dad. What a bastard Eddie thought beating up his own kith and kin. 'Thanks for the confident leg up in life dad.' he said to himself sarcastically. May God spit on your soul when your time comes and if he doesn't I certainly will and piss on your grave. It followed on, taunt after taunt during Eddie's school years if you could call it a school. A school that was run virtually by the older boys with teachers forever being off sick for one reason or another. Old man Evans, the head teacher was tall always immaculately dressed. Suit, waistcoat, shirt and tie, the offing pot. He was known amongst the kids as Fritz, due to his scrubbing brush hair style, bleached white. It always stood up erect and on end. It made him look scary. Everyone saluted him behind his back-Nazi style having already dubbed him with name Fritz. He of course knew it was going on, he tried hard to ignore it. Hitler had done him no harm though as he was a conscientious objector during WW2.

His deputy a certain Mr Roland Quin sported a droopy grey handlebar moustache. Had an enormous beer gut, hence was only able to walk sideways though open doors and, only then if he sucked in his huge gut. He was completely bald an all. So, he didn't have much going for him, apart from his deep trombone style laugh. He too had been tagged with a nick-name like old man Evans. Quin was known as Holy Moly, (here comes) Roly Poly! This on account of his lumbering hulk.

Finally, Fritz had had enough. More than enough of the Nazi saluting and name calling. It finally got to him. He decided to put a stop to the Nazi hand flicks that went on once and for all. So, he made an example of one of us boys in front of the rest of the school. The boy David Dodd was brutally grabbed at random from assembly one morning and dragged to the front by Roly Poly.

His punishment for resisting arrest, trying his best to wriggle out of Roly's grasp was immediately rewarded with a belt or two round the ear from Fritz. Fritz yelled. "Let that be a lesson to you all. From this day on, more Nazi salutes or this will happen again, until it stops." We all jeered and sneered at the cowardly way Fritz had supposedly dealt with the problem.

But of course, we all knew what was to come. We all knew about Dodd's dad and the frequent punch ups he had at the Ferry Inn on Friday nights. The boy Doddy raced crying and screaming blue murder all the way home. It was not long before he arrived back at school riding pillion on the back of his dad's motorbike and open box sidecar combination, complete with decorator's ladders sticking 5 feet out in front. The boy's dad Dodd senior, was an ugly tough looking six-foot bastard. Worked most of his life up on Millwall docks as a stevedore, unloading ships before becoming a jobbing decorator.

He stepped smartly into Fritz's hallowed office, decked Fritz with a crashing left hander, kicked him once or twice to make sure he hadn't died from the blow and walked smartly out again. He didn't say much didn't need to. Neither he or his son Doddy were seen at the school again. But the Dodd legend lived on in the minds of Eddie and others at his school, especially Eddie. Unfortunately, the name calling continued for young Eddie at school, it's not easy when you are four or five inches shorter in your own class year. Eddie dealt with the taunts from the bully boys by memorising names and faces and committing the gathered info to a list inside his head. Right, you mate is on the fucking kill list.

Finchley.

Planning any sort of mayhem by a week in advance let alone a month, was not Eddie's forte. And, of course, where to begin? In fairness Eddie thought he was best suited to handing out creative violence not planning and stuff. His old man being in the Butchering trade for reasons best known to him, would describe to Eddie how to cut and slice fresh meat with the use of boning knives. These boning knives would allow for precision cuts. A quick sawing motion was all that was needed to inflict serious damage to someone's face. Since that epic fight outside Eddie's house, he'd tangled with much tougher opposition, if only to sharpen up his reactions.

Eddie put himself under the wing of an ex-fighter by the name of Johnny the Turk. It seemed like a good idea. Johnny was no more Turkish than Eddie. The nick-name was given to him because of the fleshy lobe of skin hanging from his neck and the way he flew around the boxing ring. Eddie started to frequent a boxing gym for some weight training. He needed to bulk up his frame a bit. The Turk always seemed to be around, mostly sparring with other boxers. Not ultra-successful was the Turk, in his heyday he had been set against many a tough opposition, guys that went on to become semi-professional. Johnny however preferred the amateur circuits. More recently he was pitched in against younger stronger lads who were learning their trade.

Reasonable money was earned from the many side bets for getting knocked about a bit. Thing is, Johnny was a natural southpaw, always leading with his right. Other fighters found this bloody awkward to deal with. It was exactly this skill that Eddie wanted to learn and get to know all about. Eddie approached The Turk, took him out of the gym and across the road for a cuppa. They discussed the subject. Johnny the Turk sighed, "You sure you want this?"

He was peering over the top of his dodgy specs, the left lens scratched to buggery, sipping tea and reading the racing pages at the same time, looking nothing like a fighter. "Definitely," Eddie replied and he opened up on the story about having a dodgy left hand. Johnny winched.

"A broom stick," he spat in disgust.

"Yep," said Eddie.

"Clouted me three times with it. I heard something snap and assumed it was the handle. Well, we know it wasn't now." Johnny chewed this information over in his mind for a full minute, turned to Eddie and told him,

"Yea I will train you. But only on the basis, that when you are giving it large, becoming notorious and feared and you hear I've crossed you somehow, you will remember who trained you and leave me be."

Eddie nodded sagely and left the Greasy Spoon Café on Dalston Lane. When he looked back through the steamed-up glass frontage afforded to the café, he thought Johnny looked a bit pathetic sitting there for all the world to see and think; poor old fucker, making each tea last a couple hours. Talk about don't judge a book by its cover.

Johnny would tear your head off and split down your throat in a second if needs be. Tough as nails him. Under Johnny's expert eye, it wasn't long before Eddie got the hang of leading with his right. In fact, it was going so well that Johnny got him a few bouts organised on the amateur scene.

People would turn up to watch these fights which in turn meant Eddie had an audience. An audience where perhaps he could get his name about as a bit of a fighter. The early three round bouts, one of which Eddie would be fighting in, tended to be warm ups for the heavier weights coming together later in the evening. Johnny acted as Eddie's second. Eddie's first ever three round-bout was about to begin. The ref beckoned both fighters to approach him from their respective corners, said a few words like, "Keep it clean lads, no head butting, biting, spitting, no aiming below the belt and stuff. When you hear the bell come out fighting." Eddie looked squarely at his opponent and mouthed 'you're going down son.' His opponent was completely unfazed. He'd heard it all before. They touched gloves returned to their corners and awaited the bell for the first round. The bell rang, Eddie walked casually to the middle of the ring entirely confident of knocking this guy to the ground. So confident was he, that to begin with forgot to bring his gloves up in front of his face.

His opponent caught Eddie first. This stung him into action, Eddie jabbed at his opponents face with his right fist like a steam hammer. Sadly, it didn't go the way Eddie would have preferred. Eddie's one and only amateur fight in boxing gear soon ended. It ended with him flat on his back halfway through round one. Floored by an unseen uppercut which caught him just above his Adam's apple. Eddie lost his voice for a few days following the short-lived fight, but not his pride. His opponent suffered a severe cut above his left eye from the constant jabbing and needed some stitches. Although Eddie was put on his arse from the uppercut he wasn't counted out, standing up as he did on the count of nine. After much deliberation and due to the blood running from Boxer boy's cut, the fight was counted as a draw. The contest due to blood flowing from his opponents cut above his eye would have been stopped by the ref anyway.

In due course, Eddie was man enough however to want to visit the lad who landed the punch that sent him sprawling. He wanted to tell him well done.

Not many others recently had managed such a feat, albeit in the street and not in the ring. Apart from the congratulations on putting him on his back, Eddie instinctively knew, there was more in the makeup of Boxer Boy, than meets the eye. Something about him Eddie could not put a finger on straight away. He went over to the gym where fighters trained to be aggressive and asked the gym boss if he knew where Boxer Boy hailed from. Eddie explained why he wanted to go see him.

He was given an address on the strict proviso of a peaceful chat only, Eddie readily agreed. Soon, he was on his way over to Boxer boys' home. It turned out, he lived in a tiny bed-sit come flat above Woollies on Ballard's Lane in Finchley. Eddie tubed it to Finchley Central then legged it the rest of the way. He eventually arrived at number 226. The door frame to 226 sported three door bells, none of them with a name tag. Three door bells Christ, more than one flat. He picked the middle one, stuck a finger on it and heard it ring at a distance. He kept the bell push hard in, hoping for a reaction. A window above him was pushed up. A voice yelled "Who is it?" After a bit of fucking around and shouting at each other, Boxer boy pushed open the large front door, nodded sideways indicating Eddie should enter the building and climb the stairs immediately to his left.

"Climb the stairs. Go straight up then first door on the left," he said, "Number 2." Eddie climbed the stairs as requested, noticing one of those push button light switches that when pushed, the hall would be illuminated for just enough time to get to the first landing before it popped out, turning off the light. He swung open the door with a number two roughly painted on it. This led on into a tiny bed sit. A single bed on one side with large bay sash windows overlooking the street below on the other. It seemed to Eddie that Boxer boys' pad was all window and very little pad.

"So, what brings you here then and how did you know where I live?" Eddie looked over Boxer boys' shoulder and blinked in disbelief. The wall behind Boxer boy was covered in rosettes, paper medals and many other boxing diplomas, framed or otherwise plus awards including one or two silver gongs. This guy was definitely tasty and on the up in the boxing world. He could obviously handle himself, Eddie said to the wall,

"I talked to the gym boss in Hackney. He let me have your address providing it would be all peaceful like, you know us having just a chat. He didn't think you would mind, do you?" asked Eddie. No answer.

"Okay, so what do you want and look straight at me when I'm talking to you." The cut above his eye beginning to weep.

"Sorry mate, I was admiring your awards, so fucking many! Look I came out here to say well done you nearly bloody killed me in the ring *and* I was a bit croaky for a while. How long have you been at this boxing lark then?"

Boxer boy growled a reply, "As long as I can remember, since I was about six or seven, still don't know why you are here though."

"I will tell you," Eddie said, "but first ain't you going to offer me a cuppa?" Boxer boy grunted and busied himself behind a curtain in what passed for the tiniest kitchenette in Christendom. Eddie took the opportunity to nip over for a closer look at the wall of awards. All wins! Some knockouts, others full term fights.

Not one loser's medal? And I managed a draw with him, feeling impressed, he thought, *so I didn't make a complete knob of myself after all.*

They had a cup of tea and some Battenberg cake. Fattenberg Boxer boy called it, which was all very nice. Eddie quietly explained his reason for the trek North to Finchley and invited Boxer boy to be his minder on account of being able to throw such a killer uppercut unseen like. "Not immediately but perhaps some way down the road a bit when things took off like in the crime and violence stakes." God knows why Eddie had chosen this guy for this particular job; it just came off the cuff.

He felt drawn to him. He was sure there was more to Boxer boy than meets the eye. There was something to be had from this guy and right now Eddie didn't know what it might be or who it might be.

"I'm not leading you down the garden path pal, it's a genuine offer kosher an all that." Mistakenly Eddie thought Boxer boy would jump at the chance of being a minder, cash in hand no nonsense like.

But, no dice. Straight in, a big no. The big elbow. It was the mention of crime and violence that stopped the job offer in its tracks. Boxer boy harboured thoughts of a professional boxing career. Crime and violence and being a minder was not on his agenda. But as super luck would have it he did know of two possible blokes that might be interested. They were well tasty in the crime and violence department and might well be what Eddie was looking for. According to him, the Stratford two were currently spending a little leisure time on one of the Channel Islands, Jersey in fact.

Keeping their heads down a bit well out of harm's way from Stratford Nick. Apparently according to Boxer Boy, one them was a distant relative of the Brothers but wasn't sure which one, It might even be a complete fabrication. This didn't matter to Eddie. Fabrication or not, he wanted to meet them and soon. '*I knew it*' thought Eddie, this is a good enough reason to be here, I just fucking '*knew it.*' What was it, sixth sense or maybe seventh! Who cares, the two Jersey boys were exactly what he was hunting for. By all accounts these two as yet unknowns to Eddie were on the run. On the run following some house breaking, which took a bit of planning, car nicking, more planning, as it were, to off-load them for cash and a bit of blackmail, even more planning. *Hmm* Eddie thought, *muscle, fearless and planners*.

"Nice CV. Got to meet them!" B.B. said, he would try to get a message to them.

"Try! What the fuck do you mean try?" Eddie was getting impatient wanting to get the ball rolling.

"Jack it in," said B.B. growling again, and narrowing his eyes. "Who the fuck is you, big bad John or something?" Eddie's nerves tingled he felt the blood rushing through his veins, heart beating ten to the dozen, he felt the urge to drop him in his own tiny bed sit, never mind about the fucking awards, this would be a bare-knuckle affair. Eddie's clenched fists began to slowly rise.

"I ain't frighten of you," he said seeing the danger. "Go on then, do your fucking best." Then, in a split-second Eddie relaxed. He took control of his body slowed the heart rate down a peg or two, smiled and relaxed, then smiled again all in a matter of seconds. Killing B.B. could wait. He's just gone to top of the list. Right now, this bloke was his only conduit to the two hard nuts on the run over in Jersey. Besides Eddie remembered, he'd put him on his back once before and rendered him virtually speechless for a couple of days. Not a good idea to start throwing punches, just now. The first job for these Jersey boys, would be to take crowbar to his head and do 'im fucking proper. They eyed each other until one blinked first. Luckily it wasn't Eddie "Wanna nother cupper?" Eddie nodded and smiled a toothy shark like grin.

He sat down on the only chair available, having removed a training bag ready to discuss the where's and whys on getting a meet arranged with the Jersey boys. Later, Eddie found his way back to the island and home, he smiled to himself at having the insight to visit Boxer boy. The news regarding two possible recruits to his tribe was excellent news indeed. The next stage was to wait for a meeting date to be organised. Eddie was more than ready; he figured the Jersey boys fitted the job profile to a T. Have to hope, they want in.

Stratford Police Station London E15.

It was early a.m. on a clear sunny morning when Mike pushed through the unlocked doors of Stratford E15 police Station. There were few people around this early and few cars parked up in the police compound. Conveniently placed from Mikes flat in West Ham Lane, the distance to the station also in West Ham Lane was either a quick jog if Mike was in the mood or a ten-minute walk from where he lived with his wife Sarah and their six-year-old son Leo.

Mike nodded at the duty Sergeant who was manning the front desk ready to deal with the odd member of public dropping into the station to report this and report that. He looked smart with his three stripes and single crown.

Having spotted Mike on his way in Frank straightened his tie and buttoned up his uniform jacket. The sergeant was on his own the reserve constable must have been about somewhere but Mike couldn't see him. "Anything on today yet, Frank?"

"Not too much sir, just the usual, couple of drunks sleeping it off in the cells brought in last night and one missing person."

"Oh, right," said Mike.

"Not another one! Male, female, boy or girl?" asked Mike.

"Young man," Frank said reading from his log. "Early twenties apparently. His lady friend a certain Miss Jenny Web called it in two hours ago. According to the entry in the log it was 04.00 hours. Worried sick she was. Said all the usual stuff, you know, not like him, usually very reliable etc."

"Who's on it?" asked Mike.

"Stan from CID and Sue Harris who's out mobile from uniform."

"Cheers, Frank," Mike replied. "Keep on it and keep me posted. When Sue Harris next reports in, call me."

"Okay sir, will do," came the reply. Mike made his way through several doors and up a flight of stairs then via a myriad of corridors to his office. Here he stopped before going in and smiled at the shiny new brass name plate on his office door. Inscribed were the words 'Mike Bright Detective Inspector'. Mike was rightly proud of his newly won promotion to the level of D.I within K. division. Especially at the relatively young age of 34. He worked extremely hard with all the relevant and required promotion exams, endured many a long night out on undercover jobs, plus tough assignments on his journey to this office and what an office. It could have housed a light aircraft.

Plenty of room he thought, back on his very first day. Today though he opened his office door, walked briskly over to the vast desk and was about to make himself comfortable when the phone rang. Ah he thought, Frank has got hold of Sue Harris. He liked Sue, as a uniformed copper out on the beat she made quite a name for herself with the clear up ratio for petty criminality in the Stratford area. There were many letters being posted in from the general public praising her for having a friendly and professional attitude. It would not be too long before she hit retirement age and would be hard to replace. Mike picked up the receiver, "Mike Bright!" Silence at the other end. "Shit.it must be a dodgy line again." He made a mental note to get maintenance onto it and call B.T. soonest. Again, he announced his name and asked who was calling. This time he thought he heard shallow hoarse breathing almost rasping. What on earth was going on? It was 8.15 a.m. A thought, then a million other thoughts flashed through his mind. Was it his wife Sarah in some sort of distress and couldn't speak? Heart thumping ninety-five to the dozen, he tried rapidly clicking the buttons located in the cradle of the phone were the receiver sits. Nothing….

He slammed the phone down and picked the receiver up again in order to call Frank. Pressing button five would normally get him directly through to the front desk, however, the line was engaged. "Buggeration," he shouted out! There simply was nothing else to do now but nip downstairs to see what the hell was going on for himself.

Coppers instinct had now taken over, Mike half jogged through the corridors then took two steps at a time on the stairs leading down to Franks empire, the front office. Barging though the double doors that led on to the front desk area. No Frank, and still no reserve constable! Where, in the hell are they both? Mike had a quick look round then thought to lean over the chest-high counter. There was Frank, sprawled on the floor with blood spurting from what looked like a vicious stab wound to his neck.

It opened up a nasty gash just below his right ear. The lost blood pooled very quickly, and more was still spraying from the wound. Franks face was contorted with pain and fear, mumbling incoherently. Both of his legs were shaking and juddering announcing the very last throes of life.

"Oh Christ," shouted Mike. In an instant he leapt up smacked the emergency alarm button to his right and the alarm sounded throughout the building.

The piercing noise was meant to summon help in the event of a fray, or disturbance at the front desk and summon it did. Officers and staff suddenly appeared. By now Mike had whipped off his jacket and was trying to tuck it under Franks head as a make shift pillow. His crisp white shirt was becoming splattered with Frank's blood. Mikes knees were soaking up the blood pool as he kneeled by Frank, calling out, "Stay with me Frank, stay with me!" Frank mumbled something over and over again. Mike leant closer; his ear very close to Franks mouth. He was shocked at what Frank was whispering over and over again. Frank knew his attacker! "Call for an ambulance now!" screamed Mike. Mike and the Sergeant were both on the floor behind the high purpose-built reception desk. Frank laying, Mike kneeling, meant they were both hidden from view. Frank was beginning to slip away. "We're losing him," shouted Mike.

The knife or whatever was used to stab Frank, entered the right-hand carotid artery leading directly from Franks heart to his brain. A sure killer blow.

Whoever did this, knew exactly what they were doing. Frank's life was indeed slipping away.

The unanswered telephone receiver was hanging by its cable almost to the floor, swinging gently from side to side like a pendulum slowly ticking away the last moments of Franks life. Mike stood up shocked and stunned, police auto pilot kicked in. "Secure the area," he commanded. A colleague had run for a first aid kit and handed it to Mike.

"Look," someone shouted, two of the station's cars were on fire over in the compound.

"Oh Christ," yelled Mike again above the din of the alarm.

"Ring for the fire brigade but don't touch Frank's phone, use the one down the hall." This particular Police Station, it would seem was under attack.

Jersey.

"Hey mate lost your bottle?" grinned Billy. He knew all too well that Mel was up for this blag. Of course, Billy was only goading, banter between lifelong mates kept each other's spirts up just before a bit of burglary. Billy glanced sideways at baby face Mel who registered no interest in the barbed comment. Billy laughed again saying, "Look mate, no aggro, it's only when the slagging stops and I start being all nice you should start to worry." Again, no reaction. Mel was the naturally handsome type, had no shortage young ladies queuing to be by his side. Especially young ladies who craved a sense of danger. He was the type who treated ladies like princesses. Never letting on what he did or to who. Always looking immaculate, smiling and laughing.

"Give it a miss Billy and keep your eyes open. The villa looks a bloody sight easier to do than the last place we did, up in Kensington. At least this one's empty and we know where to search. Do you remember that old geezer who jumped on your back as we were climbing the stairs at the Kensington drum? He must have jumped straight over the banister to get to you Billy, brave bastard I thought. Good job you were in front though. If he had landed on me and messed up my hair, I might have had to kill the skinny bastard."

"Yea, I remember, the old git nearly broke my back, daft bugger."

Billy was the brawnier of the two. Strong as an ox with a swarthy complexion made all the darker from sitting in the Jersey sun on St Brelades Beach. More courageous than Mel and shrewd with it too. More than happy to lead a villain's life. "We survived it though," sniggered Billy, "you me and the old chap, plus we got a couple of hundred notes for the necklaces." What a laugh the pair had when they were raided by the cops following the Kensington job.

They swarmed in like wasps on heat. The old geezer must have had some high up contacts with the filth. The police steamed in to Billy's house and turned the place upside down, eventually leaving empty handed except for Billy's stash of dirty mags. *Bloody perverts,* smirked Billy.

After they left, Mel said, "Hey mate, do you fancy a couple of slices of toast with loads of butter on top?" They both had a good chuckle. Prior to the uniformed police raid, as a matter of precaution, Mel hid the tom-foolery in the butter, in the fridge, in the kitchen. Not one copper went near the fridge let alone near the tub of butter. All the cops needed to do was open up the Frigidaire, stick a finger in the butter and the game would have been up. The two of them hauled down the nick, up in front of the beak within a fortnight depending on his work load followed by six months inside. The cops had missed the easiest of arrests of the year! The stolen jewellery was right under their noses. Mel smirked "And what about that look on the old boy's face when we tied him up, took off his wee willy winkie night shirt and left him starkers in his back garden. He looked a lot like the old geezer on the tele you know, Steptoe! Not the usual garden ornament seen in and around Kensington." They both grinned, "That would have got us a further six months at least!" Mel pointed out.

Right at this moment in time though, Mel and Billy were in the grounds of a large upmarket very swish looking villa near St Ouen not far from Five Mile Beach, on the West coast of Jersey.

This was a villa they were somewhat acquainted with. Standing some fifty yards or so from the villa they were just under the tree line in the grounds which vaguely passed as the back garden.

This in turn, backed onto open countryside, which was their route into the grounds earlier that same evening. In between them and the target, were two tennis courts and a large outdoor pool, complete with its tailor-made plastic pool cover. Billy and Mel exchanged raised eyebrow glances, very swish they thought. The evening sun, now a golden globe was fast disappearing on the sea's horizon to the West.

It would soon resemble a thumb nail, before disappearing. The villa slowly succumbing to darkness. Inky skies, loomed, dark enough to do the place uninterrupted. They waited patiently.

Jersey in June is especially lovely. Beaches full, Hotels full, all ripe for the pickings as they say. Some of the tourists no doubt would be going home minus the odd purse or wallet. Well, if they would be lackadaisical about the security re their belongings, one could hardly blame these two nice Stratford lads for relieving said tourists of their belongings. It was of course entirely the fault of the tourist wasn't it? Of course, it was. Tonight though, Billy and Mel were after bigger fish as they waited patiently for night to fall completely. This job hopefully would be big enough to get them a first-class flight each with BEA, back home to London airport. Then to cab it round the North Circular and on to Stratford where they could sink a few beers in the Butchers Block on The Broadway. Only when daylight was completely gone would they make their move.

Blood Brothers.

The villa that happened to be on their menu tonight, belonged to a wealthy and successful businessman from Horsham, on the fringe of the Weald, West Sussex. It was his holiday home for when he needed a two or three-month battery recharge. Towards the end of the previous year's summer season, Mr Wealthy had advertised for an Island based interior decorating company. Hopefully one well known for high quality interior decorating workmanship. The brief was to quote for some work in the master bedroom. As a result of the ad Mr Wealthy was approached by an Islander called 'Peter the Painter.' Due to the quality of Peters immaculate workmanship and attention to detail, his reputation was well known on Jersey, Guernsey too for that matter. Peters lavish and expensive quotation for the required work in Mr Wealthy's master bedroom was readily accepted. Mr Wealthy had made some discreet enquiries and was entirely satisfied by what he discovered.

At their first meeting outside the villa, Peter explained, May or June the following year would be the earliest he could make a start. Must be good he thought, with that amount of work in front of him. This impressed Mr Wealthy. When next May eventually came around, Mr Wealthy came over to Jersey. First to drop off some luggage at the villa and second to un-moor his yacht appropriately called 'Nauti-Times' from St Helier's Marina. The plan was, to sail around the Channel Islands for a week or two accompanied by his secretary who he passed off as his wife, to whomever they met on these jaunts. And who would question him? Nobody on Jersey had ever seen his actual wife, poor cow.

Then to call back to the villa in order to inspect the work carried out by Peter. There were no family photos anywhere to be seen in the villa. The only photo of a female which happened to be in the master bedroom where the work for Peter was to be carried out, was a huge black and white print of Marilyn Monroe sexily smiling down at anyone looking up, big enough to hide a wall safe there beyond.

Perhaps the happy couple, while they were over from the mainland might point the bows of the 'Nauti-Times' Eastwards, pop over to St Marlo on the Channel Coast of France, for some sea oysters, washed down with a glass or two of Chablis daaaarling! When the time came for Peter to start the work, his order book, as always, was bulging.

So, he decided, to be able to complete the work in good time, he needed some hired help. Following a job advertisement phoned in to the Jersey Evening Post, a couple of chaps over from the mainland working the season, were the first to apply. Peter was so snowed under he carried out a telephone questionnaire-cum-interview then and there.

He thought he could get away with lower than was the norm on the Island for an hourly rate for these two jobbing decorators, being as they were not Islanders. All painting whites, brushes, paint, dust sheets, ladders and steps, plus lifts to and from the job would be supplied on top of the hourly pay. Billy and Mel jumped at the opportunity. Up until now, they had been working in the potato fields up at Sorrel Point. Despite the warm balmy summer sunnier climes of Jersey, it was continually windy up on the Point, being the one the highest parts of the Island. Besides, it was mostly backbreaking grubby work. "Bloody hell," said Billy, "this painting and decorating lark should be a doddle. I bet we can tap our new boss for bacon sarnies, and a cuppa tea an all!"

Billy and Mel grew up as best mates together in London's East End. Billy was the larger of the two, dark hair, dark skinned like he had a forever tan, had a bit of pikey in him. He was the thinker of the two. Mel was exceptionally good looking blessed with an ever-ready smile and a twinkle in his bright grey eyes.

He was the joker, usually getting away with murder, most of the time. He could joke his way out of the stickiest of problems. Both however were to become in good time, violent thugs. Being inseparable, as very young lads, they would often bunk off of school preferring to muck about in the remaining bomb sites still around in the late 1950s. Days were spent not on maths or history, preferring to shoot down imaginary pretend, German bombers. lob imaginary hand grenades into imaginary nests of imaginary German soldiers. They had been mates since very early school days and regularly looked out for each other. One major incident however, was to bond them together for life, Billy saved Mel's life and Mel never forgot it. Saved him from drowning, he idolised Billy from then on would happily slice anyone into tiny chunks if needs be should they hurt him. One hot summer's day when Mel was eleven, he got into difficulty while attempting to swim in the River Lea up on Hackney Marshes. It had been hot for at least a couple of weeks and Mel needed to cool off. Stripped to his pants he bombed in, as soon as he hit the water despite the warm weather, the cold water hit him. It winded him sucking the air out of him severely. Gasping for breath he was soon out of his depth. Immediately struggling to keep his head above the surface water line. Some older boys on the opposite bank just watched, jeered, smirked and laughed. No attempt was made by them to help Mel. Not Billy though, not a strong swimmer himself leaped in without a second thought.

By now Mel had been swept out in the middle of the river and was taking on water fast. Billy doggie paddled his way over to Mel. With one hand down the back of Mel's underpants grabbing hold of the elasticated top he literally dragged Mel over to a nearby muddy bank to safety then up onto the grassy bank. Billy, still breathing hard sat up and pulled a razor blade out from his trouser pocket slid off the safety device covering the sharp edge and cut into his thumb. Blood seeped from the wound. "Come ere me old China, your turn." Mel turned his head as Billy cut him on the thumb too. "Now," said Billy, "Hold your thumb against mine." After sixty seconds, Billy said, "Right, that's us then, blood brothers now, through thick and thin until we die." The bond between the two of them was sealed for life. As they grew into their teens, then their early twenties, they continually found themselves getting in to more and more trouble with the law. In more recent times they had embarked on a life of petty crime to sustain their lifestyle.

Thing was, for them to be able to avoid capture if at all possible. Nicking a bit here and robbing a bit there. Jump starting cars and flogging them off to anyone with a bit of cash. It gave them enough income to avoid actually working for a living with a few beers on top. "Who the bloody hell wants to work in a bloody factory," Billy stated. Even if it did mean a spell of R and R. The current heads down stint on Jersey was to keep out of old Bill's way for at least six months following the Kensington job, in the hope that when they got back to their old haunts in Stratford, the police would have other things more important to deal with. Little did they know how near they were to the truth.

51

The pair had just left their rented flat in Harve-De-Pas situated a little East of St Helier to begin the first day on the decorating front with Peter, when news was breaking regarding a major incident at Stratford nick. They missed the bulletins that were coming in thick and fast via the BBC news on their transistor radio back in their flat by seconds.

Beggerman Thief.

Peter waited for them at the pre-arranged pick-up point outside the Pomme D'or Hotel on the Esplanade close by the Marina. He was there at 8.00am sharp. The boys actually got there at 7.30, having a cuppa and sharing a bacon sarnie in a nearby cafe. Eventually, they found each other and set off for St Ouen and to the job in hand. Peter was keen to find out what experience the guys had. As they chatted on the way it became obvious to Billy and Mel this bloke their new temporary boss, was a couple of knives short in the cutlery department. Still, who cares they were not finding their way back up to Sorrel Point again if they could help it.

Compared to Sorrel Point, this was going to be a doddle! Soon, the guys found themselves being driven along a tree lined gravel driveway which curved to the right ending up at a most impressive looking villa. The marble steps which led up to the equally impressive gleaming white front door were impressive indeed. The villa was double fronted with beautiful lawns that had been mowed to within an inch. Topiary trimmed and shaped shrubs a plenty adorned the grounds. "Who the hell lives here?" whispered Billy.

"Dunno," answered Mel almost under his breath, "but whoever it is they must be fucking minted." Peter produced a bunch of house keys with a tag attached upon which he had written in red 'customer O'. Peter was very security minded and aware that wherever you look there are thieves about. The 'O' denoted St. Ouen, in case Peter forget his own style of codes.

Should he have unintentionally dropped the keys, whoever picked them up would not have a clue as to whom or where they belonged.

Peter grinned at the two Stratford lads, pointing to the 'O' tapping the side of his nose saying, "Can't be too careful you know lads." He turned to open up the vast gleaming white front entrance door. The moment he turned his back, Billy looked at Mel and mouthed,

"Dipstick, doesn't know were a pair of right fucking tea leaves." Billy pointed a finger at Mel then back to himself and then to Mel again in rapid succession.

"The villa at present is unoccupied." Peter explained the owner and wife were over from the mainland on a short sailing break around the Channel Islands. They would be back in a fortnight or so to inspect Peters' handy work. Billy's thought process was way ahead of Mel's.

All three traipsed down the hall through to where the work was to be carried out, the master bedroom. Then all three traipsed back outside to unload all the necessary stuff in order to get the job underway. "Look now," said Peter. "I really do need to pop over to Gorey. A customer is expecting me to price up yet another job. If you do good here, you might get lucky and be given the Gorey job too. I'll not be gone more than a couple of hours, is that okay with you?" He left instructions on what was to be done and disappeared back up the hallway, out the front door to where his van was standing. In he jumped, fired it up did a quick three-point turn, then drove away down towards the main road. This was much too good an opportunity to be missed. Billy set about inspecting the various contents of various cabinets and various drawers. With a draw pack of say four drawers or more he had learnt to open the bottom drawer first. Stupid people thought.

"I know, I will hide my precious stuff in the bottom drawer. That will fox any would be burglar!" The better reasoning though was this, if you started from the top, you needed to close each draw again to get to the next one down.

This trick of starting from the bottom draw up was quite handy if you were doing a fast in and out job especially with an alarm ringing. Here though in the villa, with Peter on his way to Gorey, time was not an issue. Habits die hard though, the third cabinet of four yielded a trinket box in the bottom drawer.

"Aha," yelled Billy. It was filled to the brim with assorted Jewellery. Lovely looking rings, bracelets, all sorts. "Take a gander at this lot Mel." Mel dropped what he was doing and looked over Bills shoulder.

"Jesus mate, bingo! What do you think its worth?"

"My guess," said Billy, judging by the owners taste for all things expensive, "I'd say a grand or two at the very least my son." A vehicle was heard being driven up to the villa, the giveaway was the tyres crunching on the driveway gravel. A vehicle door was slammed.

"You guys okay?" a voice called out. It was Peter. "Sod it, quick Mel." He'd returned with a couple of cheese rolls for his workers. In the master bedroom, drawers were swiftly closed.

Dust sheets thrown over furniture, by the time Peter had time to make his way down the hall and almost into to the master bedroom, Billy and Mel were whistling and busying themselves stripping Anaglypta paper off the long wall opposite the equally long and very wide bed. Mel purposely positioned his step ladders so the bedroom door would not open fully thus not allowing Peter into the room proper and see how little work had been completed.

Peter said, "When you have a break guys here's some elevenses." He left the rolls on the top of the steps that was barring his way into the bedroom. They heard him mooching off, piss loudly in the toilet up the hall, pull the chain, slam the front door and drive off down to the main road for the second time. "Christ that was close," said Billy. "Good job you parked your steps by the door, good thinking mate."

"Yea well," Mel answered. "I didn't want him to *step inside love.*" He sang the line from Cilla's song, "Ged it? steps against the door to stop him stepping inside." Ever the joker of the two, was Mel.

"Oh well, I thought it was funny," grinned Mel. Billy had to chuckle in the death. "You're always having a tin bath you are mate, it worked though. If Peter had been able to get in, he would have seen zero amount of work carried out and maybe wanted to know why."

Panic over, the search continued but somehow neither of the boys discovered the wall safe behind Marilyn's famous pout. Towards the end of the second week the job neared completion. Peter didn't care for the owner's reaction to him taking on a couple of jobbing decorators. To be fair though, the two Londoners had done an excellent job. Peter did the finishing touches, gloss paint, paper hanging that sort of stuff. He stood back admiring the result and felt his reputation for high quality workmanship would be upheld.

After all the reputation he had gained over the last 20 years or so kept Peter in work, in clover and the bonus of an ever-increasing order book. He might well be lanky streak of piss but in his chosen career, he was a very successful lanky streak of piss. For the two would be villa breakers, it was time to make their move and do a bit of breaking and entering, grab that box of rings and assorted tom foolery in the master bedroom, then have it away back to Harve-des-Pas with their ill-gotten.

Timing.

Eddie Coleman was lying in bed; it was cold o 'clock in the morning. Wide awake his mind was working overtime. What with all the new experiences he had experienced over at Wossnames gaff, gun to the head and shit like that, no way could he get any proper shut eye. He arrived home from Wossnames round about midnight. In total darkness he let himself in. The street lights had long succumbed to stones thrown at them by the kids from the estate up the road.

As he entered, he slung his house key on the tiny hall table, began to make his way upstairs avoiding stairs two and seven. The creaking noise they emitted when trodden on was likely to wake his mum.

She was on an early shift in the morning and would be none too pleased to be woken up in the middle of the night. Some weeks ago, Val had invested a considerable sum of dough, in a chiming mantle clock.

It stood it dead centre on the mantlepiece ticktocking away, parked between two psychedelic lava lamps she got for her last birthday from her now absent old man. Lava lamps were invented by a certain Edward Craven. They had various coloured oozing blobs of wax that would rise and fall in the heated bulb lit glass lamp. Everyone went crazy for them sometimes buying half a dozen at a time. The inventor must have been raking it in. The clock however, was something she bought for herself. It was lovingly polished and cared for. Eddie didn't possess a watch and therefore was only vaguely aware of the time, most of the time! Climbing the stairs, the clock in the tiny front room struck once announcing the time was a quarter past 12. Eddie thought *fuck its later than I imagined*. He'd interpreted the single chime as one o'clock. Gently opening his bedroom door, he quietly closed it behind him. First thing was to stow the Peacemaker. Ma Val would throw a hissing fit at Eddie if she found it, probably chuck it in the Thames and then give him a right fucking bollocking.

He decided, first thing tomorrow, when she was out of the house, to stick it inside the metal wall cistern in the lav. Decision made, he stripped off his clothes until completely naked, slung them on a chair by the window and slung himself onto his single bed. The chiming clock, chimed once again, announcing it was 12.30. Eddie thought that's bloody funny, now it's one o'clock again. This happened again at a quarter to one, one chime, then on the hour of one o'clock-one chime, then a quarter past one, half past one finally at a quarter to two. It was only when the clock chimed twice that Eddy finally knew what the bloody time was. Bugger me I need to get hold of a watch Eddie said to himself. What self-respecting aspiring gangster went around not knowing what the time was.

He made a mental note to pop up West one night engage in a bit of smash and grab, accompanied of course by his Peacemaker. At this point he was falling asleep. As he fell towards sleep, he was saying to himself over and over again, stash the shooter, stash the shooter.

Val was busying herself in the kitchen, then called up the stairs, "Breakfast Eddie, it's on the table, I'm off to work now, don't let it get cold." Eddie was standing on the toilet seat carefully placing the gun in the metal cistern, already in a plastic bag just above the water line. He heard the front door close and trotted to the kitchen, dressed only in underpants.

Breakfast consisted of scrambled egg shoved on to a slice of toast, put on a plate, then covered by a second upside down plate to keep some of the heat in.

A knife and fork ready for the use of placed by the side. He'd better eat it Val thought as she made her way to the Depot. It was eight o'clock and Val needed to clock in at the depot by 8.30am latest. Her bus was due out fifteen minutes later; at 8:45 a.m. besides, she needed to grab her money bag and ticket machine. There had been a couple of sackings at the bus depot recently. One or two sleepy head drivers got their clippies to clock-on for them. Both clockers on and their respective sleepyhead drivers were given their marching orders, on the spot. No aggro, just go.

"Whatever is due to you, money wise, will follow in the post." The Depot Manager informed them. Being the breadwinner at 119 Plevna Street, Val was not about to fall into that particular trap. Her driver could bloody well clock himself on.

Eddie moved over to the kitchen table and woofed down his breakfast. It has been a while since he'd eaten anything. A while since that meeting with Boxer Boy over in Ballard's Lane too. Eddie was itching to meet these Jersey boys. Maybe recruit them into his as yet, small but growing enterprise. His first port of call today therefore, would be the gym in Hackney This being one of Boxer boys' regular training haunts. If he drew a blank at the gym, then it was off to Finchley and Ballard's Lane.

The Team Grows.

Johnny the Turk was hard at it in the ring, sparring with somebody Eddie had yet to meet. The other somebody was at least six-foot-tall with a longish reach.

He looked like he could handle himself in times of trouble. It turns out that Johnny and this guy had never partnered each other for sparring, so it was a bit of the unknown for both fighters. This was 10.00 o'clock in the morning. Grabbing a Coke from the little hole in the wall that did snacks, crisps and stuff, Eddie stood near the ring. Near enough to smell the sweat and hear the swearing and cursing as he stood and watched. The two fighters were circling each other more than punching it out. Johnny caught Eddie's eye and managed a wink. As the minutes wore on the sparring intensified which was not what sparring is all about. Sweat was pouring from both of them now as they danced, weaved and jabbed. It got to crazy levels. This was becoming a full-on punch up. Sparring forgotten it was kill, or be killed. The timekeepers bell on the other side of the boxing ring rang loudly several time, ding, ding, ding' in quick succession. Eddie drank down a few more mouthfuls of his Coke and looked casually over to see who was manning the bell. It was the Boxer boy! This was a stroke of good fortune thought Eddie. No shooting over to Finchley and legging it up Ballard's Lane to that minging bed-sit. And, no stale Battenberg.

Boxer boy by now was up and over the ropes in a single bound before you could say Jack Robinson. He was attempting to separate the now seriously fighting and not sparring partners. The sparring had turned into a no holds East End punch up. Any minute now, the biting, kicking, spitting and head butting would start. Eddie continued watching, watching to see how this was going to develop. Neither Johnny or the other guy wanted to stop. The fight intensified.

Others in the gym doing the weights and general resistance stuff stopped what they were doing, mooched over to ringside, stood alongside Eddie to see what might develop too. No one expected what happened next.

Eddie jumped into the ring accidentally clouting Boxer boy with his half empty Coke bottle as he flew at the fighters. The bottle caught Boxer boy right on the cut he sustained during that bout with Eddie a few weeks ago. After a couple seconds, getting over the shock and with blood streaming down his face from the re-opened cut above the eye, he began laying into Eddie. No gloves mind, bare knuckles. This of course is a big no-no for amateur and professional fighters alike. Boxing gloves protect fingers from getting busted and more importantly faces from getting busted up too, Eddie was having none of this nonsense.

He head-butted Boxer boy immediately, slammed his knee into his midriff causing his opponent to bend forward in an attempt to catch his wind. Eddie finished him off with an uppercut. This was more like it; street fighting was right up Eddie's Strasse. The sparring twosome broke off what they were doing and stood looking at Eddie and Boxer Boy in disbelief. Eddie knew he had stepped over the mark when a door flew open from the Gym's little office and out stepped the manager. "What the bleedin' ell is going on here then?" He was confronted with four guys in the same ring, two dressed for it and two in civvies, one of the civvies, Eddie, standing menacingly over the other one on the canvas. Eddie looked up and began his cool down process.

At the same time Johnny, said to the manager "Look boss," everybody addressed him as boss. "Look boss, it's not what you think!" Eddie cut in and shouted, not worried at all about incriminating himself,

"Yes, it is," he yelled defiantly. "It's exactly what you think it is." He looked around the gym for support.

The weightlifting bystanders slowly nodded in agreement, not wishing to cross Eddie Coleman after what they had just witnessed. Eddie wanted this to look bad on him. Bare knuckle fighting in a boxing ring. Christ, for sure it wouldn't do any harm to his growing reputation for pure unadulterated violence, not at all. Boxer boy groaned as he came around. Above him, staring down, hands on hips, Eddie grinned then grabbed him by his shirt front, lifted him to a standing position and put his mouth to his ear whispering, "Even Steven's pal. Go get yourself cleaned up and I'll buy you an expresso in the Penny Farthing just around the corner." He told Johnny to pop along once he'd tided up. The Turk knew better than to cause a fuss and got on with Eddie's bidding. Instinctively, he knew Eddie would expect him to smooth things over with the manager, clean up the mess and generally calm things down. Call it East End sixth sense.

If you didn't pick up on the unspoken language in this East End hard man's playground, well let's just say it would more advantageous if you did. Johnny smoothed things over and cleared up as requested without questioning why, it just needed doing. Eddie and Boxer boy sat patiently in the Penny as it was better known.

They saw Johnny enter. "Over here," Eddie waved to guide the Turk in their general direction. At the same time, he caught the eye of the young blond behind the counter ignoring the come-on smile and tilt of her head and ordered two more coffees plus a tea for Johnny. While they were nattering, the weightlifting guys and other assorted gym goers were banging the East End drums. Of course, as the story passed from person to person, little bits were added. Eddie Coleman's reputation was nudging further and further up the violence charts. If one was to have believed the end results of all the ensuing Chinese whispering you would be right in thinking, a new nutcase was well on the block. Eddie was unaware of all the marketing going on regarding his particular brand of mayhem as he quietly sipped his espresso coffee. He slipped into quite mode and fell deep into thought.

He couldn't hear the frothing and steaming new Gaggio Espresso machine recently installed in the Penny Farthing as it was spewing out the ordered coffees. His mind was firmly on the future. Progress Eddie thought, this is gold trimmed progress you cannot hold back progress. If you are on to a winner, get stuck in for all you are worth.

Before long, Boxer boy made to leave for his bed-sit in Finchley. As he got up to go, Eddie woke up from his reverie and asked him when they were likely to see the two guys currently on Jersey. Apparently, he'd had word that it was looking like next week, possibly Saturday.

"Were you not going to let me know of this little gem," Eddie said coldly staring intently over Boxer boys' shoulder.

"Well look, what with all the happened in the gym just now, it slipped my mind," Eddie was about to lose it again but thought better of it.

The Penny Farthing was a half decent place, one that didn't deserve to be the centre of a mini riot and get fucked up. So, when Boxer boy left, Eddie sneered at his back muttering much to himself, 'once I've done with you, we are off on a one-way trip to One Tree Island.'

He turned to the Turk. "Johnny, were gonna need a place to hang out. Somewhere we can have meets and stuff. See and be seen. It needs to be well off the old Bill's radar not somewhere well known to them. We need a bolt hole, somewhere we can plan stuff, hide people and gain alibies. Get my drift?" the Turk nodded. "Where?"

"Well, I guess," replied Eddie, "somewhere just about here." He stabbed a finger on a pencil drawn map at Limehouse.

"Limehouse," Johnny said uneasily, "Ain't that a bit near the firm. I mean they stretch out quite a way from Bethnal Green."

"Yea I thought that an all. My thinking is this, if we are only meeting and hanging out in some Limehouse dive, but doing villainy on the island providing we don't give them the hump we might not get a knock on the door see, and if

59

we do there gonna think, just a load of lads showin' out, nothing to write home about.

"Besides word is, they are busy setting up a meet with the mob, which means eyes will be off us, maybe?" Johnny wasn't too sure, but thought he would run with it for now.

"Well, if that's what you want boss, I've got a few boxing mates over in nearby Poplar. I will give them a bell pronto."

"Yea, soon as you can mate, I've got these likely lads coming back home from Jersey soon and I won't want to have a meet in a boozer or something. Walls have ears. See what you can do, by the way did it go alright with gym manager?"

"He was okay about it, I had to scrub the canvas, blood and coke tend to leave their mark," he grinned.

"Johnny, who was that guy you were sparring with not, anything to do with any gangs is he?"

"No Eddie, he's just out of Pentonville and wants to get back into the ring proper. I did the gym manager a favour cause this bloke was about my height and weight so I got in the ring with him for a bit of sparring."

"Well," said Eddie, "when I popped in, the both of you were a level or two above sparring what the fuck was all that about?"

"It's cause I'm a southpaw Eddie, it niggles and rankles some boxers especially if there not used to it. Anyway, my guess is that you are on a hurry up for a safe house, so I'd better get my skates on."

"Yea okay mate," Eddie said, "Just before you go, if that bloke has just done a stretch at the Vill, any idea what he was in for?"

"Attempted murder Eddie. He came home from work early one day and found his old lady in bed with not one but two burly truckers doing what was necessary. Apparently, the bedroom door was lockable so having locked all three of them in he went downstairs and set light to the place. Wanted to smoke them out or something he said. Stupid arse completely forgot he'd locked the bleedin' door. One of the truckers flung a chair through the bedroom window, both then climbed down the drain pipe stark bloody naked grabbing what they could from the washing line to cover their embarrassing bits.

"His misses eventually got rescued by the fire brigade, bit of smoke inhalation and that's about all I know Eddie. He happily told me the story a few minutes before we climbed in to the ring together. Do you want me to arrange a meet for you?"

"Fucking right I do mate, see you here on Friday about the same time."

"Friday? okay will do, by the way what's today?" Eddie smiled to himself and left Johnny to his tea.

Murder and Arson. Stratford Nick.

Shock waves reverberated through the entire building. A murdered sergeant, a missing front desk constable, police cars burnt to a crisp and not yet 08.30hrs Frank Bullymore was officially pronounced life extinct by the ambulance crew and therefore Franks body could not be moved. An on-call police surgeon was summoned to confirm death. Once confirmed, a police pathologist would need to attend the scene. Following a brief examination, Franks body would be transported in a body bag by a police service van or black Moriah to Newham Mortuary close by for a more detailed examination. A post mortem on one of their own was to take place at 14.00hrs sharp.

Mike, wanted to be there with Frank. Everybody in the front desk area, uniformed and civilian staff alike, were either shaking heads in disbelief or simply shocked and stunned into silence. Unable to take it all in. This was the only way to describe the aftermath of the sudden and awful events that had descended upon Stratford nick that early morning.

Two crimes committed at the heart of their Station. Murder and arson. Mike happened to be the highest ranking officer on site.

He needed to shake off what he could of the stunned, shell-shocked feeling. Clear his spinning head and start coppering.

He heard his own voice bark out, "Okay everyone, let's clear the front desk please and turn that bloody alarm off. This whole area is now a crime scene. I want two officers on the front of the building now and two over by the torched cars. Nobody is to enter until a team from the scene of crime boys have gone over every inch.

"I want a team to secure an area around the two torched cars and seal it off. A second team of crime scene officers can move on to that site as soon as they arrive. Close off the front doors. Everybody and I mean everybody will need enter or leave the building by the rear entrance until forensic have finished up and given us the all clear to use the front desk area."

The station was temporarily closed to the public to preserve the murder scene. Very limited access was granted, only to local officers who were attached to K division. A temporary Police Office would need to be set up and manned elsewhere. The town hall was just around the corner so a couple of uniformed officers were sent round to judge if there was anything suitable. Stratford Town Hall is a big old structure.

The blackened stone edifice made it look like a dark and moody place for the towns local democracy to be planned and discussed then re-planned and discussed yet again. Once agreed with the town hall hierarchy, tables chairs and police paraphernalia was hastily set up in the cavernous reception area. This would have to double as a temporary open police desk.

A place where the general public would be able connect with the police and for the police to offer continuity of service to Stratford's residents and businesses alike. Although not perfect, it would have to do. Almost immediately the two uniformed officers manning the temp set up, one sergeant and one constable were besieged by members of the public wanting to know what the heck is going on. Of course, the officers had to be tight lipped. Any hint of a siege would cause panic, probably followed by looting of shops on the Broadway and possibly further murders, carried out on the looters by shop owners.

The two drunks brought in to Stratford nick the previous night to sleep off whatever it was they needed to sleep off, would need to be transferred to another station. Probably Forest Gate or be simply released with a polite bollocking. Mike commanded, "Somebody, please get on the teleprinter and inform up line, so that they can then inform the Assistant Commissioner at the Yard to brief him.

"Then circulate what's happed here to East Ham and Forest Gate Stations. There's a large gym on site at East Ham station, that might make a good spot for an incident room. So, let East Ham know that it might be used for just that. I need to get out of these clothes as they are now classed as evidence." A spare uniform and police shirt were rustled up for Mike to change into so his blood wet clothes could be bagged up as evidence.

An officer was despatched to Mikes home for a change of clothes and to explain to Mrs Bright, that Mike was fine and to brief her on the details of what was happening, down at the station. Next, two crime scene teams were organised by the Assistant Commissioner. ETA at Stratford Nick was gauged at 11.00hrs One team for the front desk area, the other for the burnt-out cars in the police compound. The entire front of the Stratford Police station was sealed off. Signs were hurriedly erected outside close to the main road showing 'No Entry.' 'Police Do Not Cross' tape hurriedly employed in streams around the front of the station.

A hastily erected sign offering instruction for the general public to call into the Town Hall, where officers are available to speak to, was displayed outside the police station. Although Mike held the rank of D.I. all of this effectively was above his paygrade.

Being the first on the murder scene though, Mikes input would be needed as valuable evidence. Initial contact regarding the officer's death had now been passed to the Assistant Commissioner who in turn would appoint a Detective Chief Super or Detective Superintendent whose job it would be to organise a Murder Incident room. In this instance because of its size and location to the murder and scene, they could well take Mikes advice and use the gym at East Ham station.

Marilyn's Secret.

Darkness fell over the villa. The Stratford two, could just see the outline of the building they were about to break into. Billy and Mel were going to make their move for the box of jewellery. "Fuck," Billy hissed, "what the shit is that?" A car was making its way slowly, purposely up the driveway. Main beam set to full headlights almost picking out the two would-be villa breakers. They instinctively hit the deck, diving for cover.

They fell onto the grass; grateful they were a least fifty yards away and still under the cover of the tree line. The car drew level with the villa. Nobody exited. Its noisy chugging diesel engine kept running with full headlights left blazing. Blazing in the direction of the East End pair. Mel slowly inched his head up, very slowly but could see nothing as the powerful lights dazzled him. Vision fucked; he laid his head back down sideways on the damp grass. Head to one side he slowed his breathing. This was scary stuff. Neither had any knowledge of who this might be, the owner perhaps? a neighbour? Peter the Painter? All they could see was headlights. Perhaps it was another team who had come to a break in! Whatever or whoever it was, the biggest job, for them on the Island looked like it was slipping away.

Minutes passed which seemed like hours, suddenly the main beam was set to dipped. The engine remained at idling it was now Billy's turn to inch his head up and he didn't take to well to what he saw. "It's only the bleeding Jersey filth in it," he croaked.

"Well, that's put a damper on our evening," whispered Mel. "Perhaps we should give it the elbow and come back some other time."

"Just give it a few more minutes," snatched Billy not taking his half-closed eyes of the proceedings. "Besides, we can hardly stand up stick our hands in our sky rockets and saunter off all casual like!" A powerful hand torch did a sweep of the villa followed by a cursory sweep of the gardens. The main beam was powered up again and the car together with its occupants slowly disappeared back down the driveway, onto the main road and away.

"Right, let's do the fucking place before they come back. Might be a once-a-week check, once a night or every hour. If it's every hour that give us just thirty minutes tops for the job and to get away," breathed Billy. The pair of them raced the short distance between the tree line and villa, stopping outside the huge window to the master bedroom.

One of the many stone ornaments was hoisted from its plinth and flung at the large picture window. The glass yielded and they were in, Mel stood doggo keeping a flowing drape curtain between him and the outside world. He kept a keen watch on the driveway and the main road beyond. Doc Martins crunching on broken glass, Billy made his way over to where the jewellery box was located and stopped dead in his tracks. The Jersey moon was now in the ascendance its brilliance shining brightly through the open and very broken window. The tooth like jagged remains of glass which had not been cleared around the sides or top of the timber window frame acted like a prism.

Beams of colourful light danced around the master bedroom ably assisted by some of the moon beams bouncing off the beautiful glass chandelier centred above the huge bed. The effect was akin to the glitter ball, reflecting light from a dozen spots trained on it, slowly spinning up at the Tottenham Royal Dance Hall where Billy would sometimes hang out.

It was also a favoured night spot for gangs to have drink or two and of course be seen! One particular beam of moon light, bouncing off the crystal chandelier eerily lit up Marilyn's face on the wall, famous pout and all. "What's all this about Mel?"

There was something not right here. Billy thought he could see a metal outline of something behind the pout, he man-handled Marilyn off the wall and slung her roughly on the bed without a thought to her welfare in a matter of

64

seconds. He almost shouted at what he saw. "Christ, Mel there's a bloody wall safe here, how come we missed it?" Mel turned to look.

"Dunno Billy, leave it mate just grab the Tom I've got a bad feeling about this," Billy hissed then motioned his head towards the wall safe. "let's just have a little peek."

"If we can't get it to open, we we'll grab the tom-foolery and scarper. Be handy if it's got money in there though, be a damn sight easier getting it back home than loads of rings and stuff."

"Yea think of all the butter we would need to pack," laughed Mel.

A quick inspection proved the safe to be locked. Not a combination type thankfully, just a key needed. "Mel, we need a fast search for the key it's got to be close I can almost smell it." Contents from drawer after draw got scattered, on the floor, on the bed, on the furniture, some even made its way onto the chandelier! Eventually the key gave up its hiding place. "Got it," said Mel handing it to Billy.

"Well done mate, where was it?"

"In the bloody jewellery box," Mel grinned. Billy nearly pissed himself laughing.

"Talk about a notable double," he said. In went the key and with a satisfying clunk the front of the safe swung open. Billy whistled, as did Mel who was looking over Billy's shoulder.

"There must be upwards of five big ones there," remarked Mel all fired up.

"Right," said Billy, "let's fill the carrier and have it away in a civilised fashion. The rings and stuff they can keep. Money's far is easier to shift, alright with that Mel?"

"I'm with you pal. The sooner we have it away from here the better."

"The old Bill turning up like that really spooked me." The pair left by the main door rather than the window heading quickly back to the security of the tree line and the shadows.

From here, for the boys it was a case of legging it to the main road by doubling back over the fields. About a mile down the road towards St Helier was a bus stop. Together they sat on the bench provided as if butter wouldn't melt in their mouths waiting to hop on the next bus. It didn't occur to either of them, the money they stole might well have been in Jersey Pounds. Jersey Pounds would be much more difficult to spend unnoticed in Stratford and elsewhere for that matter in London's East End.

They needn't have worried though. When they got back to their flat for a count and divvy up the notes were indeed in English five-pound notes, perfect.

Could well have been Mr Wealthy's secret stash held back from the tax man. Next on the Stratford two's agenda, was to pack a duffle bag each followed by a hasty Jersey exit and back to the smoke, well before the Jersey Police put two and two together and came looking for them. There happened to be an early flight from the airport up at Saint Peter. So, grabbing a taxi, they made their way to the airport well in time for the first Aurigny flight to Eastleigh airport, over on the mainland.

On the short fight which took them across and over part of the English Channel, their pilot flew the Tri Lander at a slightly higher flight plan than the one doing the reverse journey coming back to the Island.

The pilot explained laughingly, "To make sure they actually missed each other during the flight." Tri Landers flew back and forth from Jersey to the mainland offering an air taxi, walk on walk off service for whoever needed it. The boys had originally planned to fly in first class comfort with B.E.A direct to London.

However, plans needed to be hastily rearranged, due to a burning desire to be off the Island rapidly. If the old Bill did visit the villa regularly, they would soon discover the break in. Billy and Mel rightfully thought the police would quickly put a watch on the airport and ferries and stuff. Aurigny flight services, although roughing it a bit by comparison to a first-class job with B.E.A., meant they could at least scarper off the Island that much sooner. Mel looked over at Billy.

"Where the bloody hell is Eastleigh anyway, when it's at home?"

The question only came up because Eastleigh airport was the aircrafts intended destination; and with all that money burning holes in pockets, it was their quickest route to comparative safety, so they took it. "Last time I looked mate; it was down on the South Coast somewhere."

"So, how do we get from the South Coast to home?"

"There'll be a train or coach or something. Anyway, what's the problem, we've got pockets full of readies. We can get a cab back home if necessary." Billy looked around him. The flight was at half capacity. Just them and four others. Their pilot, had one arm over his seat and was half flying, half turned to chat with one of the passengers sitting directly behind him. They obviously knew each other quite well, as the occasional joke made both laugh and smile.

Mel wished the driver would bloody well turn around and get on with his job proper. Mel shouting above the aircraft din, pointing to the floor. "look I can see the sea." He was pointing to the floor of the aircraft's fuselage by his feet. There was a hole about the size of a tanner where a bolt used to be. He could clearly see the water below them. Mel was freaking out. Billy smiled, "man up, you twat," then closed his eyes ready for a doze. Soon, the aircraft circled above Southampton, landed safely, fuselage intact, at Southampton's Eastleigh airport. Billy and Mel being last off, made their way over the tarmac to arrivals. Hunger pangs got the better of them and they decided on some breakfast before working on their next mode of transport. The airports café for a bit of a bite was due a visit.

Billy bought a Daily newspaper and tucked it under his arm. Teas and sarnies trayed up; they made their way to an unoccupied table over in the corner as far away from prying eyes as possible. For the nineteenth time that morning Mel peeked into his duffle bag. At long last, he was rich, rich beyond his boyhood dreams, 2500 sov's was a huge deal. More than enough to keep him in clover for, well, for ages. His first port of call the next day would be Saville Row. Hitherto he'd only been able to wistfully stare through the windows of the professional tailors' outlets in the past. Now he could show em, steam in and go through the fine cloth until he found one that he liked. A top end whistle and flute, made to his measurements. Double breasted with a silk top pocket hankie, that was the ticket!

As they munched into the sarnies, Mel said, "Let's have a butchers hook at your paper Billy." Spreading it out on their table, moving cups and empty sandwich packets to make some room, he let out a gasp. The lead headline hit them both like a lightning bolt straight out of the blue.

Storm of Violence Hits London's Stratford Police Station

D.I. Mike Bright watched the grisly proceedings. Evisceration they called it as the senior pathologist carried out his business at Newham Mortuary. How he can face bangers and mash ever again after doing that two or three times a day thought Mike, I will never know. Post mortems carried out following a criminal act are needed to decide cause of death and indeed decide the state of health of the victim, before death. Medical examiners search for the method of murder, as in Frank Bullymore's case with a view to helping the authorities with their search for the killer. Mike had witnessed a number of post mortems recently. All of the previous cases he viewed were carried out on complete strangers murdered strangers at that.

The body now on the slab was Mikes desk sergeant and known to Mike albeit just for a short while. As the Pathology technician carried out the reconstruction process, basically stuffing Frank's internal organs back inside his body, Mike couldn't get the word disembowel out his head. Such an ugly word but very appropriate to these proceedings he thought. The technician having stuffed the organs back into the cavity of Franks chest and abdomen, began the stitching up programme. Mike whispered to himself, fuck me Franky boy, you've been stitched up good and proper mate. The senior Pathologist already scrubbed up disappeared into an adjoining office to write up his findings.

Due to the speed required by just about everybody involved, he intended to write up the original plus two copies and have the copies sent by despatch riders by 17.00hrs.

One for the Stratford Police Station to be passed on to the murder incident room, and one for the Coroner's office in Mare Street Hackney. Both marked Urgent and Private. Mike signalled his departure to the remaining Pathology staff and wearily made his way back to Stratford nick.

Bomber Brown.

"This look's the business Johnny."

"Thought you'd like it Eddie. you wanted Limehouse and here it is."

"Yea mate, it sure is."

"You might want to give this gaff the once over though, cause there's a private basement area to be had." The outlet they were eyeing up from across Basin Approach looked right and proper as a serious spot for meets, planning raids and general villainy. Sited on the corner of Mill Place and Basin Approach a stone's throw from Limehouse Basin with easy access to the Isle-of-Dogs, geographically speaking it couldn't have been much better. Not too near Bethnal Green thankfully. Licenced for liquor in the evenings, 'The Oasis' had a dual purpose. Coffee house stroke caff by day, drinking den by night.

No live music, but there was a Jukebox hired in well stocked with swinging sixties records, all about three minutes duration. "Looks a bit tasty Johnny. You think we can have access to the basement in the evenings and all?"

"That's about the size of it," replied Johnny. "Exclusive access," he added.

"Right, let's go over and have a butchers hook." The Turks old boxer contacts in Poplar had come up trumps. The Oasis, as it was called turned out to be a bit of a dive. Really, the best that Eddie could have hoped for. Run and owned by an ex-heavyweight boxer by the name of Bomber Brown now in his early fifties and from a long line of family boxers. The Oasis was Bombers retirement pension. Face well scarred up almost in ribbons from at least thirty odd fights, and not all in the ring. What little money he had earned from the boxing game had gone into this coffee bar stroke caff cum drinking house.

However, just lately some unlikely scooter type lads had adopted his place and were becoming a bit of a nuisance. On the odd Friday night, they got lairy and were none too careful with Bombers fixtures, fittings and furnishings. The one-and-only-time bomber complained they turned nasty on him and nearly wrecked the place. Bomber didn't fancy taking them on single handed so, as it happened, he was on the lookout for some way to keep them at a distance. Johnny told him about Eddie Coleman's requirement for a safe place to have meets and stuff so a sort of deal was struck. Eddie was to see to it that no more damage occurred in return for free use of the downstairs area whenever it was required. Both Bomber and Johnny thought pennies from heaven. Johnny could well have over stepped the mark by going above Eddie's head and doing a deal with

Bomber. Now he was here with Eddie, Johnny was beginning to think it might have been a bad idea.

He needn't have worried. As they entered The Oasis, Shirley was bashing out, "I who have Nothing." The few punters who were sitting around barely looked up as Eddie strode in with Johnny the Turk by his side. Johnny nodded to Bomber who was sorting out some stuff for a couple of customers, standing in line at the counter. Eddie had a quick look around. He liked what he saw.

Apart from a few tables out in the open, there were a number of booth type tables offering a little privacy. The service counter ran down the left-hand side almost the entire length of one wall. Sat on top of it were several glass display units, with sticky buns, rolls, cakes and stuff to choose from. The coffee machine, tea urn, till, washing up sink, cooker plus other essential items all on the back wall behind the long counter. The night time diet of booze, mainly bottled brown and pale ale, plus a bottle or two of whiskey were on the shelves of the counter below, not on show.

This was where Bomber worked and slaved. Where he listened to customers conversations about this job and that job.

Also, where he would stand and listen when a customer was apt to tell Bomber his life story. Curtains ran across the widows that looked out on to the street, horizontal style, at half-mast. Anyone walking past on the pavement outside would need to be well above six-foot-tall to see over and into the dimly lit interior. Eddie cracked a tiny one-sided smile glancing around like he was a bloody surveyor! So far so good thought Johnny he took Eddie's half smile as a good sign.

Bomber came over to meet them both. Of course, he knew Johnny the Turk, he'd been in earlier in the week cracking deals but not Eddie. Bomber had only heard stuff about him being a right fucking handful. He towered over Eddie, placed a heavy hand on his shoulder and held out the other to shake his hand. "Alright Mr Coleman, happy to make your acquaintance. I've heard your looking for a meeting house that's off old Bill's radar." Eddie nodded, uneasy at being address as Mr Coleman. "Well, this and the basement, ain't never been raided, the only filth that comes in here is those after a coffee or a cuppa Rosie Lee and sticky bun. I make sure they pay, no bleeding favours for that lot!"

"First off, call me Eddie. Second off, Johnny says no rent to pay. So, what's in it for you?"

Okay, Bomber thought, *okay!*

This guy's straight to the point sharpish like. Johnny jumped in, opened up and outlined the bit about protection for the gaff which would more than suffice. Eddie looked sideways at the Turk inquisitively.

On the one hand he was impressed with Johnny having tracked down and sourced the gaff on great terms and conditions too. No rent to pay, just needed a bit of protection thrown in from his side. On the other hand, he would need to let Johnny know he doesn't want any more deals done in advance. "Okay Bomber Let's have a peek at downstairs," requested Eddie. They followed Bomber down a wide flight of stairs which led directly to the basement. It was pretty sparse to say the least a single bulb hanging down in the middle of the ceiling was the only source of light. Dark corner's abounded and a slight smell of damp accosted the nose. "Where's that door lead to?" Eddie requested, pointing to the middle of the back wall.

"The basements got its own bogs, bit like ensuite, then there's a further door through there, that leads onto the back yard. The yard is well enclosed and private like." Bomber mentioned the word ensuite grinning sheepishly, hoping his limited French was up to the mark.

"Excellent, we can have a Jimmy Riddle without leaving our office. I take it there's somewhere to take a leak upstairs? Don't want anyone wandering down here. They might hear something they shouldn't have, then Johnny here would have to straighten them out in your back yard."

"No worries, Eddie. The upstairs has its own toilets." According to Bomber there is a fair bit of furniture stacked up in a shed out back which could be wheeled in and tidied up a bit.

"Perfect Bomber, just bloody perfect got our own pisser an all. Who lives in the flat above?"

"I do," said Bomber, explaining he owned the lot, the flat, the caff and the basement. "My flat looks out up to Commercial Road and down to the Basin. If you like, I could set up a bell for me to ring, should you need me to give you a warning that old Bill's in the area, good idea?"
Bomber made his way upstairs and left them to it. "Well done, Johnny good stuff. Those mates of yours need a bung to say ta, need to keep em sweet."

"No need Eddie, by my reckoning they would be more than happy to be allowed in, no questions asked."

"Okay mate, tell them it's open doors. I'm gonna grab Bomber and have a little chat about these unwanted scooter types."

"Why don't you nip out to the shed and give the furniture the once over, I'll get Bomber to shift it in here once you picked out the best bits."

"Ok boss, consider it done," came the reply. *Hmmm*, Eddie thought '*boss*'. He rolled it about a bit in his mind. So, Johnny definitely wants in. Won't tell him now, but he could be useful as my partner.

"Tell me about the lads who busted up the place?" asked Eddie as he sat with Bomber in one of the booths. "What do you want me do exactly?"

"Put the bleedin' frighteners on them. I don't want them back in here again, they're bad news they are, roaring about outside on their sodding Vespa and Lambrettas. Sound like bee's in a bleedin' jam jar they do. Some with all mirrors everywhere. They ain't doing my trade any good either."

"Evenings, say seven to nine is when I take the most in cash. Since these turds have become a nuisance, I reckon I've dropped by about 50 percent in me take home." Eddie wanted to know where they came from. Which part of London or was it from outside the smoke. Was there an established pattern of when they turned up and more importantly how many at a time. He wanted to be more than ready. Besides if he did a good job on this load of rowdies, his reputation would be broadcasted all over the place.

The Oasis was a little over two miles as the crow flies from 119 Plevna Street. Eddie reckoned he could jog that in twenty minutes dead easy, Up Marsh Lane up to the docks and then a few back streets to get him outside The Oasis. Armed with information gained from Bomber, he told the Turk, "The best thing would be to deal with this load of scooter louts as soon as poss." The peacemaker was to make its way from its hiding place in the toilet cistern at home along with a couple of baseball bats, a hunting knife and a hammer from Mickey Coleman's old tool box. All squirreled away in the basement bog.

According to Bomber, the Scooter riders usually gathered up in Island Row, roaring around and generally pissing of the neighbourhood, Friday's late afternoon, before descending on The Oasis. The first Friday came. It was now five, Eddie and Johnny sat in a booth furthest from the door. Bombers customers dwindled to a trickle about now before the place getting busier again from seven – until Bomber closed up, around ten. At six o'clock, Eddie was about to get up and leave, when they both heard the unmistakeable whine and exhaust rattle of five or six Lambrettas racing up and down outside.

Johnny the Turk legged it down to the basement and grabbed the hunting knife, hammer and the two baseball bats. The peacemaker was already jammed into the back of Eddie's jeans. The plan was, to make sure all the riders were in. None left outside. Eddie didn't want any stragglers. None left outside able to run. A baseball bat was hidden behind Bombers counter, the other lay across Johnny's lap. Hunting knife and hammer hidden under their booth table, should they be needed. Scooters parked up on the pavement outside, the gang of Mods filed in, jostling, shoving and shouting in an attempt to put the wind up everyone in the gaff. The last dribble of customers hastily left, all that remained was Eddie, Johnny and Bomber. Eddie had instructed Bomber to act normal and stay calm. The scene for Eddie's law was now set.

Mayhem at The Oasis

The Scooter boys collectively called themselves 'mods' this being short for modern on account they dressed modern, talked modern, sported modern hair styles. More importantly they danced to modern music. Usually, the garb worn by mods was suit and tie covered up by a long olive-green Parka type coat, together with a faux fur trim to the hood. Nine times out of ten the Parkas would have badges sewn on, all over. This mob however to a man, had but one insignia on each of their Parkas. It read Totnam Boys, a shortened version of Tottenham. The insignia in white, neatly sewn on in large lettering arched across from shoulder to shoulder on the back of each Parka, couldn't be missed.

Mods sworn enemy in life were rockers, rock and rollers, Elvis types, and yes, a few of the local rocker boys mainly from the docks down at the Basin used Bombers gaff now and then. Bomber believed this was the reason for their Scooter treks across from Tottenham to Limehouse. To seek out rockers and do 'em on their own turf. Eddie and Johnny the Turk completely ignored the team of Mods, sipped their coffees, talked quietly between themselves not even looking up. To the Mods it looked like they might be planning a quite trip to Brighton or somewhere. Bombers baseball bat as he served coffees, was close to hand, as was Johnnies, across his lap, under the table. The commotion and noise went up a notch. Beat music filled the Oasis. One of the Mods had slotted a tanner in the Jukebox and stuck a record on. The Beach Boys were now doing their best to be heard above the racket.

One of the Mods appeared to be conducting the proceedings, shouting and ranting at Bomber to hurry up with the coffees. Bomber kept his nerve and stayed calm. "That's the one I'll front out first," Eddie motioned to Johnny.

"The rest will probably try to scarper so I need you to go over and stand by the door, block the exit whichever way you choose to do it." Eddie stood up as if to stretch his legs. Yawned and stretched his arms up in the air, arching his back in the process.

Totally relaxed and with a casual air about him he walked slowly over to the main mod man. He stood smiling at main mod, waiting for the Beach Boys to stop doing their thing. Mayhem was about to kick off.

As soon as the music finished, Eddie spoke quietly and calmly directly to the main mod. The one who seemed to be the boss, the one slating Bomber.

"Scuse me pal, you're not wanted here anymore, especially after trashing the place recently," Eddie talked almost in a whisper. The main mod walked swiftly over to Eddie and punched him right in the mouth. Eddie swayed a little but was okay with this, he was used to it. It happened to him many times in the past. Eddie ran a hand over his mouth and saw his own blood on his hand. In a whisper of a second he flew instantly into a blind rage. The peacemaker was drawn from his belt, smacked violently into the mouth of his opponent, barrel first as far down his throat as Eddie could force it.

Eddie pulled it out and shoved it straight back in, again and again, main mods front teeth were all but wrecked, leave alone any other mouth parts working or not. "Would you like to hit me again Pal?" Main mod's head shook rapidly from side to side, which didn't do his face any good what with the peacemaker shoved up against his tonsils and beyond. "Would you like for me to shove it up your arse instead." No clear answer.

For good measure, Eddie asked the Turk to toss him the hammer, which he used to smash down on the right shoulder of main mod making a blood curdling crunching sound. A scream emitted from the bloodied mouth.

Agony personified was etched on the remains of his face. Eyes ablaze with total fear, he would not be a pretty sight ever again. Now forced onto his knees by Eddie, again with the barrel halfway down his throat he looked up to see Eddie's eyes glaze over, head tilting to the left a little. At the same time, he thought he heard an eerily hummed nursery rhyme. Transfixed, until now the remainder of the Totnam Chapter suddenly burst into action in a futile almost hopeless attempt to defend their leader. Bomber, despite his bulk was swiftly out from behind the counter, bashing in any mod head that came within bat swirling range. Most of the Parka gang turned to flee. The scene they had in front of them was well scary.

Their boss, was faceless literately, on his knees, claret and piss everywhere with a long gun barrel aiming down his neck roughly in the direction of his arse. The holder of the gun was slowly pulling the hammer back ready to shoot, he seemed glassy eyed, smiling and humming a tune. On top of that, the gaffs owner stripped to the waist was running towards them menacingly wielding what seemed to be the biggest fuck off baseball bat they had ever seen. Johnny nipped past them like a ghost on heat quietly, and unseen. He slid the doors retaining bolts home to be sure there was no escape. At a nod from Eddie Johnny attacked the runners.

The speed of the mod attack was breath-taking. No sooner had it begun; it was finished. No damage to the gaff or any of its content. Only to heads and one particular face. Eddie politely asked main mod to stand as he was now required to give Eddie his undivided attention. Very slowly, he got from his knees to his feet, sure that any moment now the gun still down his throat was going to go bang, tearing his head off in the process. Apart from all the insides of his mouth being reconstructed in a very mixed-up way, his top lip was torn to shreds. "I am Eddie, fucking Coleman, see pal," this he said very slowly, in order to prolong the agony of the guy on the end of his peacemaker.

"The Oasis is now my place, my place to be, my place to relax and to meet my fellow partners in crime. When you can talk proper again and people ask who the fuck did this to you, you can use your fucking messed up boat race as my calling card. Now get your posse of fucking tarts off my property now." Another nod to Johnny prompted him to unlock the door and stand to one side, clutching his baseball bat to his shoulder.

He watched the mods heads down, file out tails between very shaky legs. He was in half a mind to nip out and do some damage to their scooters, but that would mean they would have had no way of leaving the neighbourhood on the hurry up.

Best to let them fuck off. "Well, that's put the tin lid on that lot," smiled Bomber. "Shouldn't be around here again." Eddie nodded, wiping the blood off his gun using serviettes sat in nearest glass.

"I fucking hate flash bastards, got no time for 'em," spat Eddie. The sound of disappearing Lambrettas and Vespas, tails tucked well up their exhaust pipes filled the air for a few moments. As Bomber correctly observed, they would not be back.

Mrs Sharif.

Life as they say, goes on. Mrs Sharif along with close relatives of her late husband over from India ensured correct procedure for her husband's journey into everlasting paradise. The family meticulously carried out the formula required. The bathing and enshrouding of the body according to Sharia Law. The funeral prayer, Salat al-Janazah. Supplication for the deceased and mankind was recited followed by the burial. Mrs. Sharif closed the shop for the mourning period then very slowly began to think about living again after death. The police out of respect stayed their hand. As soon as they spotted the shop had reopened, they were back hoping for more information. Lenny, Benny or Henry had not uncovered anything remotely helpful to the investigation. As per, most if not all enquiries met with the usual wall of silence. Common place for the policing in the East End. Police for most were the enemy. They were forced to resort to old time coppering, long hours and shoe leather reduction. Pulling in and leaning on snitches with menace aforethought. Snitches were considered lowest of the low to all respectful East End villains. Old Bill would bung the snitches a few readies in return for suitable usable information in order to get to the bottom of a particular crime. For some reason, tried and tested snitches living in and around the estate, seemed reluctant to open up. Funny thought the inspector handling the enquiries. During the a.m. and p.m. briefings the name Eddie Coleman kept coming to the surface. Who the hell was he? Not a name he'd come across before. He detailed one of his officers to get some background on this Eddie Coleman. At about the same time Eddie's name was surfacing with the Police, news of the Sharif's break in and subsequent death of Mr Sharif, was reaching Eddie's ears. Val, picked up the news in the bus depot canteen then passed it on to her son. Frankly if you want to know who was shagging who. Who was being done up like a kipper and especially who done over the Sharif's leading to Mr S's death?

It was the bus depots canteen gossip that always yielded the tastiest and most up to date info. Apparently, a clippie was having it away on the side with one of the officers on the case.

The canteen jokers took the piss relentlessly, the nub of which related to not one, but two uniforms on the back of her bedroom door, his and hers!

Result, a true his and hers story. In order to let her lover know it was safe to pop in for ride or two, the clippie placed a box of OMO washing powder in the front window as a signal to her copper lover. For him it read 'Old-man-Out.' He could shoot in for a bit of how's yer father get his end away and get back on to his proper job pronto. A bit like the S.A.S. In and out without knowing.

It was during one of these steamy and sordid little get togethers, lover boy let it slip about the three names. The three names Mrs. Sharif had given the officer on the night of the break in. To date, it was the only lead uncovered by a goodly bunch of uniformed officers who were allocated to the case. The break in happened almost six days ago by now, but still old Bill was no further on than they were on the night of the raid. The majority of the bus canteen fraternity as usual, were streets ahead of the Police. They knew Lenny alright, a proper little scrote he was, rob is own grandmother given half a chance!

Nasty bit of work, and one that in their opinion could well do with yet another spell in Borstal. "Eddie, do you think you can ask around a bit as to where Lenny might be holed up? There are a few blokes down at the depot who would like to get their hands on him.

"Fancy doing the Sharif's stupid git. He should have known better. The Sharif's are well liked round here, very nearly one of us. Here's hoping something really shitty befalls him."

"Yea, okay Ma, I'll ask about a bit." Eddie, knew he would do more than find Lenny. He would find Lenny and give him a fucking good kicking. Batter the fuck out of him and put a complete stop on him. Put him plus his mates out of action permanent like. No more solids for them, Eddie didn't tell his mum that Lenny was one of his worst nightmares when they were at school together. He was a year above Eddie and constantly picked on Eddie, with his mates of course, generally making Eddie's life hell. Eddie juggled his kill list, he demoted Boxer boy to second place, putting Lenny the Scrote up at number one. I'll fucking have 'im, he promised his mum and himself.

Not only get a bit of violent revenge for what Scrote dished out to me at school, I will crack his bloody head open for doing over the Sharif's. All those blokes at the bus depot wanting to get at Scrote,

will be slapping me on the back. I might get one of them to tell old Bill, it's been sorted. They might just turn to dealing with other crimes, like Jack the Stripper, over in Hammersmith. That'll keep them off our case for a bit.

Eddie began to plot his long overdue revenge party, starting with Lenny the Scrote. Another side benefit unseen at the moment, Val Coalman will become someone to be very nice to, once everyone at the bus depot caught on that it was her son Eddie that tracked and closed down Lenny and his mates. First things first though. He would go and see Mrs Sharif. Tell her how sad and hurt he was about Mr Sharif's passing. He would also take the opportunity to offer Mrs Sharif the possibility of some comfort for a small fee, for what took place at her shop, never happening again.

The Oasis Basement

At last, the meet was on. The two blokes from Stratford, back home from Jersey, had listened to Boxer boy's tales. They were dead keen, itching in fact to come face to face with this Eddie Coleman. Prior to the meet at The Oasis Eddie had indeed paid a quiet visit to Mrs Sharif. She was more than willing to have Eddie's brand of law protecting her, her sons and of course her business. A sum of £15.00 was agreed and would be collected by one of Eddie's crew on a weekly basis. With this contract safely in his back pocket, Eddie asked Johnny and Wossname if they wanted to be present at the coming meeting.

They both jumped at the chance, a chance to sit in posing as Eddie's unofficial minders. A quite word with Bomber would be necessary too.

He would have to be alert and wide awake to any filth in the locality, warning Eddie of any impending visits. It was not himself he was concerned about; it was about these two unknowns. According to Boxer boy, they left Stratford for Jersey following a house break-in up West in Kensington then left Jersey rapidly, following a similar break-in.

Odds on old Bill would be on the lookout for them big time. He thought well, there's danger then there's stupidity. He didn't know which was worse.

"Christ almighty Eddie, where'd you get that suit from then, bit snazzy isn't it?" asked Val. "I mean, your only on the bloody dole. What you done robbed a bank or something? that whistle must have set you back a tidy sum."

"Not a penny Ma, mate of mine works down at the dry cleaners. I told him to keep a look out for a two piece that might fit me. Some bloke dropped this one in and was told it would be a week before it was ready.

"So, I've borrowed it, just for tonight like. Take it back in the morning, bish bash bosh, no one's the wiser. It gets cleaned and everyone's a winner."

"Well, I must say you do look smart, pin striped and all, you look like one of them bankers from the city. Are you meeting a young lady, take her out and treating her to a nice meal?"

"Something like that Ma, might be a bit late home like."

"For Christ sake, don't get any makeup on that suit."

"No Ma." Eddie was more worried about getting blood on it.

Eddie raced upstairs, wanting to get a look at himself in the only full-length mirror in the house, in his mums' bedroom. Opening the wardrobe door fully, his reflection smiled back at him. Dead smart he thought, dark blue suit with red shot silk liner. His refection said, "Eddie Coleman, you don't look no cunt in that, talk about clothes maketh the man." Eddie felt fired up enough to take on all comers. To finish off the ensemble he grabbed one of his mum's white cotton hankies and stuffed in to his breast pocket, leaving just a little bit poking out over the top. He didn't possess a tie but his white button-down Ben Sherman shirt in Oxford weave freshly washed and ironed completed the picture. He looked down at his feet. He wished now that at some time or other in his life he'd invested in a pair of black Brogues. Shiny black Doc Martens would have to do. He crashed down the stairs two at a time and was out of the house before Ma Val was able to say good luck, and treat her nice.

Wossname was parked up in the Anglia at the end of the road as planned. Johnny seated in the back. The warm evening was making Eddie sweat a bit with all this clobber on. He was much more at home dressed in jeans, leather bomber jacket and tee shirt. Tonight though, the meet up with Jersey boys dictated that he should look the part, gain the high moral ground as it were.

Eddie, had not an idea of what, if anything, Boxer boy had told the Jerseys about him. As it happens, all he knew about these guys was the house breaking, car nicking and that one of them might be a distant relative to the brothers. Bomber had been briefed about the meet, as had the two waiting in the car. Eddie opened up the passenger door of the and slid inside next to Wossname. "Okay driver, to The Oasis."

Wossname looked at Eddie as if he was mad. "What did you just fucking say?" Eddie grinned then burst out laughing.

"Just trying it out for size mate not taking the piss honestly, just havin a tin bath. Wind your neck back in and see the funny side. It's a sunny Saturday evening and were out to enjoy it so put on a happy fucking face." Eddie turned around to speak to Johnny as they drew away. "You all sorted?" Johnny nodded, opening his jacket to reveal a claw hammer nesting in a shoulder holster.

"Nice one," remarked Eddie. He didn't expect Wossname to be tooled up in any shape or form. He was the driver and needed to travel lightly. He spoke to the windscreen "When we get there, I'll dig the peacemaker out from its hiding place and keep it close by, just as a precaution like." Both Wossname and Johnny the Turk nodded in agreement. Wossname parked up a couple of streets away from the venue. He was pissing himself with worry, not wishing for any damage to befall his dads' pride and joy. The trio entered The Oasis. It was 7.30 pm and a bit lively. Word had got around.

A new team had befriended Bomber and had cleared the way for trouble free evenings for a quite drink or two. A few of the punters eyed up Eddie and his two minders and quickly decided to mind their own business as the trio, made their way to the basement. Bomber had put a rope barrier at the top of the wide staircase to deter any customers wandering below. As Eddie and crew approached the stairs Bomber moved to unhitch the rope barrier and replace it behind them. Eddie whistled as they reached the basement proper. The furniture chosen by Johnny the Turk from Bombers shed had been hauled, cleaned up and spread about the basement.

There were even a few pictures hanging off the walls and a new ceiling light fitted. Smart striped wall paper regency style was hung vertically across the back wall. "Bloody hell," muttered Eddie. "This looks excellent, especially that big desk in the corner with a picture of the Queen above."

The big old kneehole oak desk, complete with leatherette top faced outwards. A table lamp already lit sat on one corner of the desk. "Ah look at that lamp, the top bit has got tassels anging all-round its bottom rim. I could sit behind that desk when we've contracts to sign. Jonny, stick a chair in front of it for geezers we might want to interview. Especially anyone who's crossed us."

Johnny smiled knowingly and nodded to let Eddie know he was on his wavelength. Wossname observed, "Bombers done us proud. Very impressive, all of it and well-lit too."

Wossname and Johnny set about putting several chairs round the big circular table centred in the middle of the basement. Bomber appeared with a wooden crate of beer, some glasses and ashtrays. Boxer boy and the Stratford lads we due in at eight. Suited and booted, well Doc Martened, tooled up, in his very own office, Eddie Coleman was more than ready.

Three Becomes Five

Bomber knew immediately. Two guys in double breasted suits one charcoal grey the other dark blue, well-tanned and looking decidedly dangerous, accompanied by who could only be the Boxer boy, entered The Oasis. Boxer boy was much stockier than the other two, big wide boxers' shoulders and very pale in the face compared to the Jersey tan featured on the unpredictable pair behind him. Boxer boys dress sense quietly pointed out that it mattered not how he looked to the world. Besides he didn't possess the sort of money the other pair were in possession of, having gained a good wedge from their exploits at a villa last week in Saint Ouen, Jersey.

Bomber had been well briefed on who and what to expect. The suited two glanced around the interior of The Oasis with lazy almost unconcerned eyes, sizing up any issues or problems they might need to deal with. One or two of the booths had blokes sitting and drinking. Boxer boy decided to move over to where Bomber was waiting arms folded making his already huge biceps look even bigger and ordered a round of drinks. Beers for his companions, an orange juice for him. Bomber was first to speak to the suits.

"Evening gents, welcome to The Oasis. I believe you're here for a meeting?" The two nodded in unison whilst continuing to scan the interior. Roughly twenty or so drinkers were scattered around the place. Some in groups some alone, a few women were in that evening, standing by the jukebox over by the far wall, singing along to 'Wild Thing' by the Troggs. All seemed as it should be to the Stratford suits. As with most thieves and petty burglars, they had, over time in their young lives developed a nose for trouble and a sixth sense for any old Bill that may be in the vicinity.

Bomber motioned a shovel like hand towards the basement stairs and said politely, "Go straight down gents, I'll bring your drinks in a moment or two." Sensing a trap, all three stood where they were. A few of Bomber's customers were beginning to take an interest in the proceedings. This unnerved Billy and Mel. Boxer boy moved over to the rope hanging between the two top stair posts and peered down the stairs.

"Hi mate," Johnny called out. "Good to see you. Shoot down here and we can get cracking." Boxer boy turned to his companions, nodded and mouthed an okay.

He descended slowly and purposefully to the basement. The others followed cautiously, hands on hidden weapons. "Well, well, well. We meet at last." Eddie sat facing the stairs. He would see all that was going on from this vantage point. He jumped up from his seat walked over to the suits and began the centuries old custom of introductions. First Wossname, second Johnny the Turk and then himself. Billy and Mel looked at all three then at each other and began to relax a little.

Just then, Bomber came down with the drinks, the atmosphere changed from charged to relaxed in a matter of minutes. Billy and Mel could see they were amongst friendly like-minded people. Hands came off of hidden weapons as they began to feel comfortable. Eddie spotted the hand movements and said, "I expect you've come here tooled up! we have too."

"So, in order that we can talk business without worrying about stuff like that, we'll put our bits on the table right here in front of you as a sign of us not wanting any aggro."

Eddie unholstered and slammed his Peacemaker down in the centre of the round meeting table, swiftly followed by the hunting knife which was tossed down rather than stabbed in the table, plus a couple of baseball bats that had been stashed under his chair, well out of sight. Eddie looked at the Turk and nodded. He drew his claw hammer from inside his jacket and threw that in with Eddie's weaponry.

Mel and Billy looked at Wossname who sheepishly pulled a knuckle duster off his hand that he had been concealing behind his back. "Well, that's a fucking fair pile. What were you expecting a bleedin army?" Mel chuckled. Billy too held a hammer, silver tipped with the claw end sharpened to that of a razor blade. It too was thrown into the middle. Mel drew a motor bike metal chain from somewhere inside his jacket, his chosen weapon. He called it his persuader. Carefully placing it well out his reach, he held his hands up in mock surrender. Ever the joker was Mel. Everyone in the basement then looked at Boxer boy. It was now his turn. Holding up his two fists boxer style, one near his face the other extended with malicious intent stated, "These are my weapons but this is not my fight."

"Right, that's got that out of the way, let's get down to business." Eddie motioned everyone to take a seat at the round table, the centre of which was piled high with the tools of their trade. Introductions and information flowed. It was soon becoming obvious that Eddie had something that Billy and Mel wanted a part of. Thing is, do they simply want be part of Eddie's set up, what was it he called it 'The Crew' or did they simply want to hang around for a bit of an adventure. Eddie needed Billy and especially Mel to go out and prove themselves. Apart from the evil looking weaponry laying in front of them, what else could they bring to the table. As the evening wore on, Eddie, Mel and Billy were getting a bit pissed.

They were beginning to sound a bit lairy, swopping tales about fights and general villainy, trying to outdo each other. As the hubbub grew Eddie decided he'd had enough. He stood, scraping his chair back at the same time knocking a few empty beer bottles over from the circular table and began to set out Billy and Mel's first job. "There's a team that needs to know break-ins at Mrs Sharif's shop on the Kingfield Estate will not be tolerated. They've taken one fucking liberty too many. I have information that this team is headed up by a nasty little fucker known to me called Lenny. We call him the Scrote.

"They tried to do over the Sharif's. Sadly, Mr Sharif died trying to tackle them. Scrote got bashed by Mr S and lost a lot of teeth, so that makes it easy to mark him. I want them to know I called you in to sort it. Mrs. Sharif has agreed a good fee for continued protection of her business and her family. You will make it your business to ensure it never happens again. The fee you will collect weekly. My cut will be half you keep the other half. After having a word with Scrote and his mates let me know the outcome.

"If you put a complete stop on them permanent like, there'll be more wedge making jobs for you." It took seconds for the two Stratford suits to make their minds up. They were in!

"Can we hurt them a bit?" Mel smiled in anticipation. Eddie screwed up his eyes. The corners of his mouth dropped, allowing unusually for him, a menacing glare. He stared at Mel for a full 30 seconds.

"That's the whole point of this exercise pal. I want them off solids for a while, if you get my drift." And don't leave them in any doubt who ordered the job either.

"I want them to know who sent you. And, tell the bastards mouths fucking shut to the filth. Any grassing and they'll end up in the Thames hands and feet bound. Dropped off Tower Bridge in a fucking coal sack." Wossname looked at Eddie in awe. Where did all that come from? It wasn't in any of the Dick Tracy books he'd read.

The meeting was interrupted by shouting and banging coming from upstairs. The sound of glass breaking. Bomber appeared at the top of the stairs. "Excuse me Eddie, sorry to interrupt your meeting, I have need of your services, shouldn't hold you up for long."

Unhurriedly, Eddie stood, slid his jacket off, folding it neatly, began to roll his shirt sleeves up having removed the expensive looking cufflinks. All those sitting around the table knew exactly what was about to happen. The fact that

Eddie didn't pick up a single weapon from the centre of the table, was to say the least, impressive.

Turning to Johnny and Wossname, he asked them to entertain his guests as he had a little bit of business to deal with and would be right back. Making his apologies to Mel and Billy, he was up the stairs in three bounds.

Upstairs, a pair of rocker types dockers up from the Basin over by the counter were locked together. One was giving a bear hug to the other and the one being squeezed was nutting the bear hugger for all he was worth. "What started this Bomber?" Eddie asked casually as he walked over.

"Spilt beer, I believe."

"Okay Bomber, stand clear." Eddie grabbed the one doing the nutting by his hair, yanked his head back so far it almost broke his neck. He waited for the scream to follow and it came. At that precise moment Eddie punched him hard on the lower jaw instantly snapping it. He fell to the floor dazed and in serious pain. Eddie then turned his attention to the bear hugger whose face was already a bit of a mess from all the repetitive nutting. With his Doc Martens, he stamped hard on the huggers winkle picker shod feet a number of times, ensuring broken bones to both feet. This of course rendered the bear hugger unable to walk. Eddie moved towards him menacingly, face inches from his. He yelled, "You fucking lot make me sick. You come in here bust the fucking place up over a bit of spilt beer. You're sodding lucky I haven't spilt your blood, now fuck off out of here. And remember any more of this sort of business will be dealt with accordingly." He turned to Bomber and asked in a polite manner, "Any breakages needing paying for Bomber?"

"Nah, just the odd glass or two." Eddie moved to opened the door in order to let them limp out into the night air.

"Eddie Coleman's the name. You've just qualified for 'Eddie's Law'," he whispered as they passed by adding 'be lucky'. The event convinced Billy and Mel, who, from the top of the stairs had watched the goings on convinced them that this was truly a crew they wanted to be part of for definite, never mind the age gap.

Most especially with a psychopath who has a personality disorder as wide as the Thames along with zero remorse in charge. Eddie explained later that his new suit was on appro hence the need for the lack of blood. Laughter all round.

The Clean Up.

A Chief Detective Inspector arrived at Stratford nick in order to organise the Incident room along with a team of detectives ready to investigate the murder of the unfortunate Desk Sergeant. All this in just under four hours from receiving news of Franks murder. Two members of the visiting detective's team were sent to the mortuary to where Frank had been examined, then trolleyed into a holding compartment.

Uniformed officers acted as a barrier outside. Police officers only were allowed to pass into Stratford Station and only then via the rear entrance. The main entrance was still designated a crime scene. The first on the list to be questioned would be Inspector Bright. It was he who encountered the dying sergeant. Mikes office had been turned into a temporary Murder Incident room whilst the large gym area attached to East Ham Station was hastily being re-constructed into the main incident room or hub. Desks, chairs, filing cabinets and notice boards were appearing for the many designated detectives who would 'be on the case' as it were.

Post office telecoms engineers set about installing several phone lines for the inevitable multiple telephone calls in and multiple calls out. The gym at East Ham was comprehensively being morphed into a serious crime incident hub.

A full sweep of the Stratford Station grounds plus all the local streets to search for any evidence, other than that found by the SOCO teams at both scenes needed to be organised and fast. Evidence can get trampled on accidently or on purpose, then lost very quickly.

It was essential to get it underway. The sweep would take place as soon as the necessary number of constables could be rounded up and briefed. A murder investigation was now fully underway. Stratford Nick would be in temporary lock down until further notice. All leave cancelled.

Any officers away on leave were called in to help in any way they were asked. One of their own had been brutally murdered on their door-step. A coming together of minds and individual effort was needed in their collective quest to find and apprehend the killer. What nobody knew at this exact moment was Mike had information on the killer's identity. Frank had whispered a name moments before dying.

So why was Mike not rushing to pass on this highly valuable piece of information that would without doubt, short cut all the usual detectiving? Not to speak of the public monies about to be spent. Was it because his own office had been commandeered? strangers sitting at his own desk, commandeering everything he had worked for over the previous five years, only he would know.

His office was only in temporary use, everything would soon be dealt with at the hub! So why the dark thoughts. Perhaps he thought he might get promoted further up the ladder by apprehending the murderer singlehandedly. Whatever his motive was, on the face of things it could turn in on him. Be a career suicide.

Due to the general commotion and confusion, nobody had yet noticed that the reserve constable was nowhere to be seen. Of course, a quick look at the 'Station In' book would confirm him either in or out if station procedure was followed on such a day. But of course, this was no ordinary day. The Station in book was mistakenly and totally ignored until sometime later on. When it was eventually checked, the reserve officer, one P.C. Halliwell was marked as in. A search for him was conducted. It became obvious within an hour or so of the search beginning, he was indeed missing. One of the uniformed officers who was part of the search raised his thick eyebrows to a fellow officer. "Hmmmm, that looks a bit suss to me."

Somebody leaked the story to the press. It was inevitable. In a matter of minutes, from the original and no doubt well paid for leak, news hungry reporters were gathering outside the Station, gagging for snippets of information. TV cameras appeared. The two burnt out cars had been examined by officers from scenes of crime. Before they left with their gathered evidence, both cars were draped with tarpaulin-like covers that touched the ground. For the time being, the covers kept the press guessing. Before long though, a statement would need to be put together. This was very likely, given the situation as it was to be aired on national T.V., radio and no doubt splashed all over tomorrow's national papers.

Cut and Shut.

"What about it, Eddie," Errol asked. "Your crew lifting decent clean cars from up West and parking them in our scrap yard over in Creekmouth. We'll keep them hidden and under wraps well out of sight of old Bill. Even the original owners won't recognise them when we've done them up." Eddie and Johnnie had met up with Errol at the Butchers Block pub in Stratford. It was midday and although busy, there was none of the usual bandits who haunted the pub of an evening time. Three weeks had passed since Errol floated the idea of a meet between himself and Eddie. He came alone unarmed and smartly dressed. There was absolutely no reason to think that this was nothing more than a business meeting between two consenting parties. "Tell me more about the bit where you do them up." Eddie had nicked his share of old bangers in his time, but only for the badness, then either torched them at High Beech or pushed then into the Thames at Rainham Marshes.

The cars he nicked were easily broken into and easily fired up if you knew which wires to cross. A quick drive round, dump it, or torch it, over and done with. Quality cars, expensive cars would need a bit more sophistication. Eddie challenged Errol on this point. "Look Eddie, it really doesn't matter what damage you do by gaining entry.

"We have a panel beating paint shop plus access to motor parts from a no questions asked supplier in Dulwich. Its sweet Eddie. Okay, not fool proof but with a bit of caution and clever tactics, we can outwit the filth hands down."

More drinks arrived at the table and once again Errol stuck his hand in his suit pocket and dug out yet another fiver, paid and left the change as a tip for the bar lady who delivered the round. Not being wildly savvy business wise Eddie agreed but only on his terms. This was definitely not going to be a partnership, more like an understanding. What was needed Eddie thought with Johnny agreeing was a trial period, see how it fitted in with his other plans. Admittedly, on the surface it all looked fancy and dandy. Eddie needed a regular income for his team plus expenses and here was a money spinner staring him in the face. Once this lot gets going no need to be boracic lint anymore.

A value per car was put forward by Errol on the basis that the higher up the designer ladder they went, the higher the pay-out. Always in hard cash and always on delivery. "There is one other thing, Eddie."

"Yea, I'm listening," Eddie said glancing at Johnny.

"We've been experiencing some problems recently."

"Go on," Eddie requested.

"A couple of break ins, mainly for car parts but more seriously, someone recently gained entry to the office and ransacked the place."

"Nothing was taken, but we have some sensitive printing equipment kept in the office, to do with new paper work for bent cars."

"Bent?"

"Yes, well the street terminology is cut and shut. A car may come in from a road crash as a write off. The back half might be completely smashed up. After the insurance has seen it via an assessor, it's supposed to be crushed. We don't always do the last bit. The back half is cut away, we find a similar model with a smashed in front but with a semi decent back half and weld them together. Clean the weld up, give it a paint job, fresh paper work and its ready to roll."

Eddie whistled. "So where do you off load the bents?"

"We have a small number of car-lots dotted around the East End. Each has a bloke running one, controlled and employed by us. We mix the bents with genuine cars."

"Right, so what do you want from us?"

"Protection basically. Not only the site at Creekmouth but the car-lots too."

"Why the car-lots?" enquired Johnny.

"Well, they are just as important to us so as to be able to move the bents on to the public. Car-lots are seen as easy prey. Cars can be nicked, blokes running them can fiddle. It's all cash for cars.

"And, we have experienced some skimming, you know, punter pays a ton, but just 90 quid is marked down in the sales book. We also have someone going around the car lots on a weekly milk run to collect the sales cash. So, what do you think?" Errol asked.

"I think were in. So, we get paid for designer cars nicked from up West and delivered to Creekmouth. On top of that we get paid protection money for Creekmouth and keeping an eye on the car-lots."

"Exactly," replied Errol. "We also want one of your guys to do the weekly collection. You can take your cut directly from the takings and bring the rest to me."

"How many lots do you have?"

"Half a dozen," was the answer.

"Give us a couple of days. Let's meet again on Friday this time over at the Oasis." Eddie wrote the address down on a paper napkin and got up to leave. "Oh, one more thing Errol, you were with Rosie when you spoke to my mum, what's the story there?"

"Must confess on that one Eddie, I used Rosie to get to you. Hope you don't mind?" Eddie looked straight into Errol's eyes for a moment or two longer than usual. He could see no malice intended and blinked first.

"Okay Errol, see you Friday at eight, be lucky." Satisfied with the setup, Eddie and Johnnie exited the Butchers Block and headed back to the Oasis.

Some recruiting needed to be done. Car theft a speciality on the C.V. would be appreciated. Word was circulated amongst known associates, Eddie waited for interested parties to apply.

Billy and Mel would be briefed on the protection scheme plus the car-lot nursing should be a doddle for them. The second meeting with Errol at The Oasis, dealt with all the financial stuff and was agreed on with a handshake with an unexpected bonus.

A Jag Mark 2 in ice blue, leather seats, complete with a wooden steering wheel would be on permanent loan to the guys doing the car-lot milk round collecting Errol's weekly takings. All kosher like, proper paper work, car tax and stuff. When the boys are not using it Eddie will, with Wossname at the wheel. He salivated at the mere thought of sitting in it, let alone driving it. Eddie made sure Billy and Mel were present so as to be introduced to Errol. He wanted Errol to see that he had men capable of handing out punishment in the good old East End smiling, friendly way.

Eddie was the psycho, his men, although rough and ready as anybody were to uphold the honour of the crew. Eddie would be the one to demand respect from anyone who crossed his path.

Any punishment metered out would come with a message. "Don't fuck with us," said with a smile of course. During the discussions, Errol handed a dossier over to Eddie, amongst other things it contained the addresses of the car-lots to be visited their managers names and average weekly takes, plus the location of the breakers yard over at Creekmouth. It was up to Eddie to sort out the arrangements for protection and money collecting.

He earmarked Billy and Mel to carry out the arrangements. They would need wheels and Errol had provided handsomely. From Errol's point of view the outlay and weekly outgoings to Eddie was well worth it. No more break ins no more skimming at the car-lots and designer cars coming in to be re-plated and sold on. Printing plates at Creekmouth safe once more. Nice bit of business to talk over with his dad when the time came.

Errol's dad Leroy-the-Second had popped over to Europe recently. He needed to contact certain people who could move up-market cars on to the middle East.

That part of the world had a voracious appetite for quality and were prepared to part with good money, no questions.

Cars destined for that part of the world would be packed and crated on site at Creekmouth, collected and delivered to the docks. Genuine looking paperwork to be stamped by customs, as long as there was a tenner or two accompanying, and off they would go to a destination in Europe. The next leg of the journey was of no interest to Leroy. As far as he was concerned, it was then no concern of his.

A Flourishing Business.

It was now a month or so on from Eddie's meet with Errol, money was coming in, not mountainous amounts just a steady stream. Enough for a reasonable type of income for Eddie and his crew. Lenny the Scrote was out of action. He experienced a bad kicking from the Stratford lads who set about him under orders from Eddie with no mercy given.

His two accomplices who helped the Scrote at the shop break-in were nowhere to be found. It was without doubt, as soon as Lenny was out of hospital he would do as he was told and offer up the missing pair for a brief chat with Eddie at the Oasis. Mrs Sharif and her two sons were more than happy regarding the arrangement. All was quiet on that front, she'd requested to see Eddie and talk things over when he was next in the area.

Mel and Billy dutifully visited Mrs Sharif on a weekly basis firstly to pick up the protection payment and secondly to be seen at the premises. It was assumed this was enough to put off anyone who thought they could do the place over. On a couple of occasions Mrs Sharif made the boys cups of tea upstairs. Outside, the ice blue Jag was parked up. It was akin to a dog pissing on a patch of grass, this is now my territory so, fuck off or get bitten.

When Eddie popped round to the mini market as requested, Mrs Sharif explained how happy she was with the arrangement and remarked on the boys.

"They are perfect gentlemen," she said. "Always please and thank you and my two sons look forward to them coming around. Your boys have time for my sons. Now that they have no father figure, well, I'm sure you understand."

"Only too well, Mrs Sharif, only too well." With a wave of assurance Eddie walked home to Plevna Street. A number of people caught his eye on the short walk home. To a man, they all greeted Eddie as Mr Coleman. "Hello Mr Coleman. Nice to see you Mr Coleman. Hope you are well Mr Coleman."

Friday meetings were set in place, downstairs at The Oasis. All needed to be present, flourishing businesses needed to have business meetings, even if it was protection rackets, car stealing, beatings and so on.

Careful planning is required to dodge the inquisitiveness of old Bill. Planning is also required to keep abreast of any intended start-ups poaching their business. At the Friday meetings, Eddie would lord it over the rest, he sat centre circle, Wossname to his left.

Johnny the Turk to his right, they were flanked by Billy and Mel. Bomber was a key member and would sit in as was his right to do so. According to Mel and Billy, protection of the Creekmouth Yard was successful.

They discovered the break-ins at Creekmouth Yard were conducted by a gang of lads going by the name of 'Cherry Boys'. The twosome from Stratford, explained at length about their visit to the Cherry Boys local, pulled the gang leader out to the back of the pub.

He was arrogance personified, so Billy and Mel had a stern chat with him. Within minutes all his gang mates piled out as Billy and Mel hoped.

All hell broke loose. The lads were no match, Billy was equipped with an iron bar and Mel with his persuader, the silver bike chain.

The Stratford two, smoothed down their double-breasted suits, then walked calmly back into the pub, had a brief and quiet word with the landlord instructing him some chaps out the back might be in need of an ambulance. They paid him handsomely to keep his trap shut or he would be next. Just as an aside, they mentioned the name Eddie Coleman simply as a bit of product marketing.

Next on the agenda was the car-lots not many problems there. Turning up in the Jag gave them plenty of Kudos. To begin with the managers of each car-lot were a bit bitchy and twitchy. However, the very presence of the Stratford two was met with fear by most. Mel came up with the idea of counting the cars on each lot plus the value per number plate. All scribed down and checked weekly. Skimming stopped overnight. It became obvious, the previous cash collector was definitely in on the scam. Mel was busy on Saturday nights knocking off some bird he'd met at the Butchers Block. So, it was left to Billy to call in to Errol's office, hand over the takings minus Eddie's cut. Once again, it filtered down to Eddie, the manners and courtesy shown to Errol by 'Stratford's finest twosome,' as he put it, was top notch.

Eddie was pleased to hear it. It made his decision to recruit them all the better. All good so far. It was now time to put the quality car nicking on the table for open discussion. The team currently being used could not be totally trusted and nothing had come back on the grapevine, no other takers for the job. Eddie waited for ideas round the table. As none were forthcoming, he suggested putting the black on anyone known to the crew assembled that might just be capable of nicking and driving away. Anyone with secrets to hide that the crew could lean on should there be resistance to getting them on the payroll. Blackmail would always produce. Meeting over everyone except Johnny disappeared.

"Tell you what Johnny, that guy you were sparring with, the one just out of clink. See if you can lean on him, he might just be the one dead right for the car nicking job. I mean, just out hungry for a side line perhaps, a nice little earner. Give him a bell and see if he might pop down to see us. Down here at The Oasis."

Precisely one week later, The Turk arrived at The Oasis with the guy he'd done the sparing come pitched battle with at the Gym over in Hackney. "Grab a drink from Bomber," he waved in Bombers direction indicating to put it on Eddie's slate. "Eddie and I will be waiting for you downstairs."

"He's knocking off some married bint over in Hainault, told me on the way here. Said if her old man got to hear of it, he might be in for a stabbing."

"Do we know the husband?" asked Eddie.

"Yea, its only fucking Reg Sullivan in it. He's well known for his use of blades. The rippers got nothing on im. Likes to slit faces with a razor up one side then down the other. Calls it facials he does. Got quite skilled at it."

"He's knocking on a bit now ain't he?" asked Eddie.

"Yea but this is wife number two. Gone right down the age range he has. Word is, Reg can't get it up no more and she can't get enough of the stallion upstairs."

"Well now, that's a right fucking pickle. We need to get our mate into the corner, you know on the ropes like and slug away. Make him toe the line and do our bidding. Make him an offer he daren't refuse like." Just then their visitor stepped down into the basement.

Eddie did the greetings and told him to sit. "Pal, we need a handle, what we gonna call you?"

"It's Dave, Eddie, Dave Conti."

"Okay Dave, relax, you're among friends, drink up, there's plenty more where that came from." Eddie dived straight in. He explained exactly what he expected of Dave Conti in fine detail leaving out that he was going to bin the guys handling it at the moment. Cars to be lifted from up West, driven and delivered to a yard over at Creekmouth.

Money would exchange hands and Dave would be under the protection of Eddie's crew from any unwanted interest from wronged husbands. Dave looked over at the Turk at the mention of wronged husbands, then dropped his angry stare.

He was in too deep now to back off. Besides, this looked like a lucky triple. Money coming in, freedom to get his leg over with a certain Mrs Shirley Sullivan, all this with a bit of protection thrown in, Bingo!

"Count me in Eddie, as it happens, when I was doing time one of my cell mates turned out to be a bit of a pro at car nicking, gave me some of the inside info. Like how to get in with the smallest of damage and that see. He managed seventeen before he got caught and only then got six months, out on four with good behaviour."

Eddie was keen to hear how this cell mate got caught. Dave explained, "He was a 'to order' car thief. One evening he spotted a car that somebody ordered. It was sat in Victoria Park down by the pond, on the hard standing under some trees. He waited about for a bit, went over and tried the rear door handle. The door was flung open. Instantly out jumped a bleedin' copper in uniform, trousers round his ankles, underpants at half-mast, all bollocks and no truncheon. Not a pretty sight you might say. The copper then slapped handcuffs on him uttering something entirely novel as in 'your nicked.' My cell mate was about to leg it, handcuffs and all when a female appeared from the back of the car too, very flustered buttoning up her white blouse and straightening her business-like black skirt.

"Looked like they might have worked together at the station perhaps. Knickers in one hand, car keys in the other, she deftly jumped into another car parked up nearby fired up the engine and roared off. He and the copper stood and looked at each other for a short while, one contemplating doing a runner, the other contemplating pulling up his pants and trousers. 'Look mate it'll go easy on you if there's no mention of what you've just seen.'

"The copper continued, 'Keep your trap shut about the woman and cough to anything else you've been up to.'"

"Gordon Bennet, bent coppers, don't you just love em?" added Dave.

"He coughed to the other car nicking's which helped old Bill's clear up record and kept schtum about the dame with her knickers in her hand. The copper who arrested him put in a good word, hence the short sentence."

"Right, Dave from now on your in my crew. I want you to continue with your boxing keep that going, keep fit and keep sharp. Good punchers who can duck and weave, knock guys down inside the ring and out for that matter are valuable commodities to me.

"As soon as I've had a word with Errol, Johnny here will be in touch with you then and only then, you can prize some tasty wheels away from their rich lazy bastard owners up West. If you get pinched by old Bill keep my name out of it. If you go down for a stretch, do your porridge, we will look after you inside and when you come out. Now fuck off and stay low for now."

Lies and More Lies.

Cigarette smoke hung heavily in the air from the many smokers in the room. Those that abstained from the filthy weed as they would call it, could only cough irritatingly or wave the smoke away to a different direction. The Murder Incident room set up within the gym behind East Ham Station was now fully functional and fully manned. Desks, telephones, filing cabinets, in trays, out trays, ash trays and typewriters had all appeared almost overnight. A large pin board at least six feet across by four feet down had been hastily screwed to the gym's wooden climbing frame that was attached to the wall. This would act as an information board upon which photos of potential suspects would be pinned.

On a long table near the back-wall opposite to the suspect board a hand-written sign hung marked 'Essential Police Equipment.' Somebodies attempt at humour.

On it sat a tea urn bubbling away surrounded by dozens of cups, teaspoons and an overly large basin of sugar. As if this wasn't enough to warm the cockles of the coldest of hearts an equally large basin, filled to the brim with Garibaldi biscuits occupied centre stage.

A general hum was about the place, it was 07.30hrs and briefing number one was to begin at 08.00hrs prompt. A number of the detectives started combing through their note books searching for snouts or snitches to lean on. Others were busy chatting to each other, wondering how quickly they might get this mess cleaned up and be able to return to their normal duties. A couple of bods decided to take a leak before the fun began and wandering off to the toilets, absently following paper signs pinned on door frames offering directions. They made it back with seconds to spare. Two high ranking Police officers swept in to the Murder Incident room at 0750 hrs together with D.I Mike Bright bringing up the rear. Ties were straightened, fags dogged out some even donned their jackets.

None of the detectives assembled actually stood to attention or saluted However, they were riveted to these high-ranking officers as a matter of course. The Chief Inspector motioned that all present were to relax and pay attention. "Any questions must be framed at the end," the Chief Inspector deliberately started at the beginning.

The first briefing was to deal with the basic facts. Clearing his throat, he started, "A murder occurred within Stratford Police Station on June the 17th at approximately 0800 hrs.

"The victim is known to be Sergeant Frank Bullymore who was on shift from 0200 hrs hours to 1000 hrs hours. He was attached to K Division and based at Stratford Station. Sadly, he never made it past 0810 hrs. In addition, a relief constable, one P.C. Halliwell who was also on duty at the time of Sergeant Frank Bullymore's murder has gone missing." A photograph of Halliwell was pinned up on the board as the Chief Inspector spoke. A murmur of mutterings emanated from the assembled detectives.

"And, as if this wasn't enough, two police vehicles were set on fire within the vehicle compound of Stratford Station, as far as we can ascertain, at precisely the same time that Frank Bullymore's dying body was discovered. He was discovered by D.I. Mike Bright. D.I. Bright is stationed at Stratford Station also in K division. We are awaiting SOCO results from site one, the murder scene, and site two that of the police vehicle fires. An ambulance was called to Sergeant Frank Bullymore. The ambulance crew declared the Sergeant 'life extinct'. This was duly followed up by the on-duty police Doctor. All correct procedures as in declaring the front desk and car compound at Stratford Station to be designated as crime scenes by D.I. Bright, who then admirably conducted the remaining duties to preserve both scenes. It is now the 19th of the month so, we are two days in from both the incidents.

"Until we get information from scene of crime officers, we will have to get things moving without their findings. Top priority is to locate Halliwell. He may well have all the right motives for doing his disappearing act or then again may not. Alongside this we need a team to concentrate on the murder. Get out and about, talk to locals, visit gambling dens, strip joints, pubs, clubs, you know the drill.

"Get amongst the thieves, pickpockets, pimps, safe-breakers, local hoods and bandits. Get as much out of them as you can. Somebody will know someone who is involved. Knock on doors, break them down if you have to let's get them all jittery. Even their lot can't be too enamoured with a cop killer, especially if you circulate in and around the Stratford area and push on into their seedy world. Shake trees until somebody squeals, squeeze snouts until you get to the pips. Cut through to the bone and beyond and don't stop until you reach marrowbone jelly." Astonished looks all round.

The Chief Inspector spun round to look at the photo of Halliwell pinned up on the information board. He seemed almost to be silently asking, where you are now you fucker and what did you see or do to make yourself scarce.

Turning back, he said, "I need a team on Halliwell. Use your information conduits. Who has he nicked lately? Who has gone down due to his coppering? Apply for an immediate warrant and get his home address searched. Take a SOCO team with you."

A voice from the back of the room completely ignoring the Chief's opening statement about questions to be framed later said,

"Sir, could it be a case of mistaken identity?"

"Explain," the Chief Inspector requested.

"Well sir, just suppose Halliwell was the intended victim, the murderer got his wires crossed, assuming it was a hired hit man, and killed Frank instead. Halliwell's done a bunk because he knew the knife or whatever was used as the murder weapon, was meant for him."

"Yes, that's plausible. Keep that in mind all of you, as you are going about your business. I am now going to hand you over to D.I. Bright who was as you now all know first on the scene." The two Inspectors had privately talked to Mike beforehand and therefore were well aware of what was coming next. Mike stood up outlined his carefully thought-out story missing out that he knew the killer. The same voice came from the back of the room. "As you were first on the scene guv, any idea who might have murdered Sergeant Frank?"

Mike lied through his teeth,

"No, I haven't. My focus was on saving his life, being on the floor down behind the front desk my view was restricted to any would be possible runners." This was of course true, but still he held back that vital and telling piece of information regarding the dying Frank, whispering the name of his killer. A phone rang. "It's for you sir, crime scene blokes have something for you." Mike inwardly panicked. It was going to be very unnerving to take this call following on from what he had just explained.

"Mike Bright," he snapped into the receiver. The room fell silent, all were straining to catch a word or two. It was rare for SOCO to interrupt a briefing.

All anyone heard from Mike was,

"Okay, I see, yes, yes, I understand. Right, okay. Thank you." Mike hoped the relief and his facial expression didn't seem too obvious. He returned to his spot by the information board.

"The crime scene officers dealing with the car fires have ruled out arson. Relief spread quickly all-round the gym.

"Following the brigade dealing with the blaze, no trace was found of any propellent or traces of any kind. The chief fire officer who was present complied. Having established this fact, the crime scene lads set about checking what was left of the electric cabling. A wiring fault was established as the cause of the fire. Exact details will be presented to us in due course." Same voice from the assembled detectives,

"Both cars had an identical fault sir?" Mike replied,

"No, not at all. Car number two was in close proximity to car number one. Car two caught fire from the blaze of car one, according to the log, car one had been used for a mobile patrol and was parked up in the compound at 0745 on the morning of the fire. Can one of you circulate this info including the make of both cars to all other stations in the Met. If there is a fault it will need to be notified as soon as we have finished here.

"So, this bit of welcome news, means that we can dismiss any thoughts of arson and fully concentrate on establishing who killed Frank Bullymore plus the whereabouts Halliwell. As I am sure you are all aware, the press is camped outside. They will be shadowing our every move. I needn't have to tell you, all and any information that is passed to them will be via controlled press releases only. And only then, when we deem it necessary. For us to succeed we need to have a near black out, other than the contrived releases. I look to you all to adhere to this request. Thank you, gentlemen, if there are no further questions, I suggest we get on with the two jobs in hand. Next briefing will be 0800 hrs tomorrow morning. Murder scene forensics, I am sure will have turned up something by then."

West End Wheels.

Wossname got the right hump. He was severely pissed off that he, the driver of drivers was not picked to do the car nicking. It's not that he was strapped for cash, not totally boracic lint like. It was more to do with pride. Didn't want to see himself selling rosettes up at Wembley for the rest of his life. So, he decided to front it out with Eddie at the first opportunity. What was in the way of a meet with Eddie was this, Eddie was fully pre-occupied with this guy Errol.

Thing is, Wossname couldn't see the bigger picture, Eddie was building a crew capable of jobs they could do standing on their heads, if necessary. The Stratford two, were more than capable of seeking out trouble makers and settling them down even if it was with an iron bar, hammer or bike chain. Not only that, they were raking in a fair bit of wedge from the car-lots which was boosting the takings for Eddie and Co.

West End toffs' motors were being nicked regularly and being delivered to Errol's plant, so that job was adding to the pot nicely. Eddie put all his crew on fixed incomes whether they earned it or not. When things are running smoothly why fuck it up. Wossname however, didn't think like that. "He's lording it up in the back of the Jag with my dad's gun tucked in his belt and me working as bloody chief wossname." Dave on the other hand, was on fire regarding car lifting up from up West. Unbeknown to Eddie, Dave had enlisted a couple of young scouts. One to spot target cars, the other to go doggo, remain motionless nearby to where Dave was busy getting to grips with a car worth nicking. Youth two was to remain unseen quiet, on watch as it were in case plod appeared on the scene. Both Eddie and Dave believed, due to the amount of prime automobile metal being lifted and never recovered, old Bill would be forced by the gentry of the West End to increase their patrols forthwith. For the moment though, Eddie said,

"Let's push our luck and perhaps be active at differing times of the night and spread the nicking about in different sections of the West End at random. The coppers can't be everywhere and at all times of the night." Wossname had not been party to the meets between Eddie and Dave and therefore was not aware of the contents, or discussions.

He felt that he was being passed down the food chain, becoming a tad unwanted. Maybe it was because he'd diss'ed Eddie that one time over at his house in West Ham. So, he decided to chew things over with his dad. "Look at this way son, you get to drive a Jag with a wooden steering wheel you get a regular income and you're mixing with a great bunch of blokes. If I were you, I'd stay shtum for the moment and watch how things develop."

To be fair, Wossname had not explained the whole story to his dad about Eddie and his ambitions. He'd spoken a bit about the car-lots being visited, about Errol's operation and about the two blood brothers Billy and Mel, always so smart looking and clearly a pair of gentlemen villains. So, on balance, he decided to agree with his dad's advice. Telling the whole story especially about Eddie holding on to his Dads gun might well provoke differing advice.

Diamonds Never Lie.

The plate glass window threw in the towel at the first hammer blow. Massive cracks appeared in all directions. Gave a crazy crazed patterned look about it. Instantly the store alarm bell started ringing. Tiny electrical tabs could be seen hanging loose, their circuits broken triggering the alarm. Very little jewellery was left on display in this window overnight to be grabbed following the smash. This was of no consequence to the two guys who by now were kicking in the cracked glass.

It yielded even further. The integral wire mesh was easily cut away leaving enough room for either of the two would be smash and grabbers to get a gloved hand in the opening, to swipe any stuff within reach. It was 2.00am as they grabbed the smallish amount of jewellery left in the display cabinet, sitting close to the smashed window.

It was all pinchbeck stuff, cheap jewellery not really worth a jot on the black market. Didn't matter though, this blag was being carried out as a diversion. Pretty soon old Bill would be responding here in numbers at the Gem Palace Jewellers, Mayfair. The distraction was designed to draw the cops on night-shift away from a much more daring raid elsewhere. The elsewhere raid was going to be the main attraction that night. The target being a very up-market Jewellers who were trading in Regents Street for many years. This second raid was definitely not a quick smash and grab job, no way. Plenty of planning had been undertaken. The outlet had been visited a number of times to assess what's kept location wise especially overnight. On occasions, observation visits took place late in the afternoon just prior to closing time in order to spot where the best trays of sparkler's might be stored.

More information was gathered at the rear of the premises by a couple of other guys wearing work coveralls. They climbed all over the scaffolding-clad building next door. Recent renovations had been carried out next door and whoever was responsible for erecting the scaffolding, had yet to return and de-erect. Wearing work coveralls and clambering all over the scaffolding and such like, did not arouse suspicion. They were able to take plenty of photos and look for entry points at the rear of the target jewellers next door without being sussed.

The two break-in teams now in action at Mayfair and Regents Street had been recruited by Eddie and Johnny the Turk. The first team were instructed to carry out a fast noisy smash and grab, leave a bloody great mess everywhere and scatter some of the jewellery on the pavement outside the shop. They were further instructed to leave no clues then scarper and make themselves scarce. Dump the hammer in rubbish bin about a mile or so away, then go and lie low keeping their traps shut.

The second team had by now, forced entry to the jewellers in Regent Street. Both of them had previous experience of jewellery raids and knew the drill. Their point of entry at the back of the building, happened to be a fire escape door which when forced, immediately triggered the obligatory alarm. If their timing was spot on, coppers would be attending the first robbery over in Mayfair.

They both took a look at their watches and signalled five fingers to each other, five minutes to do the place and be long gone. They knew there would be no time to open safe's but it wasn't cash they were after. Two more internal door locks were drilled out and forced. They found themselves in a small window less room surround by trays of high-quality jewellery and expensive watches. Beams from their mini torches set off a profusion of sparkling light, bouncing off the walls.

Canvas holdalls were un-pocketed quickly filled and zipped up. Another signal, two minutes both grinned at the silent two finger signal. Piece of cake one mouthed to the other. Hard rapping and much door banging was heard from the pavement at the front entrance. The alarm had attracted a beat bobby who was intent on getting noticed. The pair shot upstairs to the rear fire exit. Leaving it wide open, the pair ran across the flat roof ignoring the metal staircase leading down to the rear yard used for staff parking during business hours.

High locked wooden gates enclosed the yard which would have impeded their escape. Canvas bags thrown first, a short leap onto another flat roof of the building next door, grab the bags and throw them again, across that flat roof to yet another.

Then it was down the side of this building by means of a ladder left there conveniently by a window cleaner-paid handsomely-earlier in the evening, then away down an alley-way leading on into Beak Street. The two bundled into a waiting car parked up at pre-arrange spot.

The car having been acquired by Dave some thirty minutes or so before hand from an underground overnight car park, on the basis that the rightful owner would not report it missing possibly stolen until the following day. Dave drove the three of them to Creekmouth where they dumped the lifted car. All three piled into Eddie's Jag.

Wossname and Eddie waiting patiently for the trio, greeted them warmly and listened intently to how the blag went. It was a bit of a squeeze as they drove out of the Creekmouth breakers yard heading West towards The Oasis. It was now 3.00am. Most of the East End back streets were pitch black. Bomber had been briefed and was ready and waiting. The caff kept in darkness as Eddie and the others filed in, Bomber closed up behind them and followed the team downstairs. Grins all round. "Fuck me, that went well," remarked Eddie. "Piece of cake, sweet as you like. Can you Adam and Eve it two bloody break-ins in one night 'and' a nice motor nicked for Errol. That's what I call a good night's work." Contents of the two canvas bags were decanted onto the circular meeting table. Whistles and more grins all round.

"Anyone got ideas on value?" inquired Eddie.

"Well, that Rolex has got to be a monkey for starters," one of the blaggers said. "I recon there must the best part of ten grand there." More whistles!

"Okay, well done lads, jobs well and truly in the bag, or should I say bags. Shows you what a bit of pre-planning will do," said Eddie. "Let's keep stuck to the plan, you two guys go about your normal day to day stuff. Keep to normal routines and stay low for a bit. Bomber, business as usual at the caff."

"Wossname, get on home and get the Jag over to Billy and Mel in the morning. They'll be needing it for the car-lot milk round tomorrow. I'll kip down here for the night. The Turk knows a safe fence for the tom, but we will need to stall the fencing while it's still hot. The tom stays here up in Bombers flat." Eddie carefully put the jewellery back into the canvas bags. He looked closely at some of the diamond studded items admiring their beauty. He held one of them up to the light and almost gasped at the raw quality, whispering, "Don't you lie to me lovely little beauties of mine."

Bomber, let the others out the back entrance and made his way back down to speak with Eddie. He was busy digging out a blanket and pillow from a cupboard in the corner getting ready to bed down for a short kip. "Got a minute Eddie?"

Eddie looked up, "Of course mate, never too tired to chat what's on your mind?"

"Well, as it happens, I've been thinking. I've been thinking, for a long time actually about selling up. I ain't getting any younger you know. I know this place was supposed to be my pension and that's all very well except I don't want it to be like a working pension. What I really want, is to be able to put me feet up of a night. Maybe train it down to the coast now and then and smell the briny." Eddie dropped what he was doing opened a couple of brown ales flicking the bottle lids on the floor, offered one to Bomber and sat down.

Bomber took his cue and sat also. A silence descended for a few minutes while they both took a few swigs. "Tell you what Bomber, give me first refusal. There are ways and means of doin this, I'd be keen to get hold of the caff, bar and downstairs here. That leaves you the flat above. In other words, you ain't got to move. We can arrive at a cost. If I haven't got all the readies, we could have an arrangement of so much per month until the final amount is paid up. That way, I don't have to apply for a liquor licence as it will carry on under your name."

"I dunno, Eddie, before you came and helped me get rid of the rowdies, I wanted to shift the lot as one item."

"Okay, how about I buy the lot off you and you live in the flat for the next two years rent free."

"Why would I want to do that?" asked Bomber.

"Well, I will tell you. You ain't no mug Bomber.

"The way you waded into those mods proved that. Plus, you have always treated me with the utmost respect. I like that and I happen to like you. You can be a handy bloke to have around. Besides you could still be the holder of the liquor licence because you will be resident and on the premises."

"Any more sweeteners Eddie?" asked Bomber with a wide grin.

"Behave yourself, Bomber," laughed Eddie. "You're starting to take liberties."

"It's a good offer Eddie, tell you what, I'll get an agent round tomorrow to get the placed valued."

"That's fine Bomber, just make sure the tom that was grabbed earlier, is safely tucked away."

Guns in the Dungeon.

Eddie's law was starting to get noticed. He was seen as a bloke to gravitate towards, especially for those that had fallen into crime at an early age. Eddie was seen as a bit of a hero to young tearaways. He was seen as the man who could catch a pig by his tail, everything he did seemed to work and work out well. Plus, at 22 he was about their age, it was like he had a Midas touch. Following formal chats with Bomber, the Oasis, lock stock and barrel had been signed over to Eddie. Both Eddie and Bomber Brown were happy with the arrangements drawn up by a tame solicitor, Eddie now had a proper head-quarters.

It was to become his castle with Bomber in charge of the drawbridge. It was here that 'would be' crew members would hang out in the hope of becoming part of Eddie's gang. Bomber was given a part time job evening only, serving beers, Rosie was given the job of running the caff six days a week. She was well up for it having had plenty of experience working in caffs down on the docks. Plus, it meant better wages for her. Eddie and Johnny the Turk would preside in the basement where they could plan raids and much more importantly, count all the reddish that were pouring in. Happy days all round.

A small but heavy metal safe was installed downstairs. It was ancient and weighed a ton and a half, only one key would open it and that was held at all times by Johnny the Turk, Eddie's most trusted aide. It was in this safe that all the money was stashed. The Tom from the raid at the jewellers in Regent Street had been fenced for seven grand or so in the death, big money indeed. Probably worth four times that but the fence has got to earn a living too. All four baggers were paid off well and told to keep their heads down for a couple of weeks or so to await a signal for another job. Errol kept up his end of the bargain paying Dave Conti up front for the nicked cars and the same with Billy and Mel for dealing with the car-lot protection. Eddie thought it was high time to put his mum well in the picture. He was already handing over three times as much housekeeping and Val was asking questions.

She knew something was going on but decided discretion the best part of valour. Sometimes it is better to avoid a dangerous situation than to confront it! She needn't have worried. Eddie explained the basis of the extra income, acquiring the deal on the Oasis, and of course, the Jag.

He carefully left out the jewellery heists that took place up West, which still had the Met police scratching their collective heads. It was Friday, meeting day. Eddie decided to get everyone together in the dungeon as he now called it for a pow wow.

The delegate list included The Turk, Wossname, Errol, Billy, Mel, Dave Conti and Bomber. Outlining the agenda, Eddie explained Bomber and he had come to an arrangement. "As of today, I own this building." Johnny and of course Bomber were in the know. The others didn't seem to take it in immediately. Billy and Mel looked at each other with raised eyebrows but that was it. Wossname almost cried, left out in the bleeding wossname again, he thought.

Errol warmly congratulated Eddie, he was a man of substance himself courtesy of his Dad, instinctively knowing the benefits of property ownership, even if it was for wrongdoings. Eddie went on to explain that Rosie a friend of Errol's was to run the caff Mondays to Saturdays and Bomber would run the bar in the evenings.

He then said, "I would be grateful if you looked kindly on these two, as although they are not crew members, they are definitely in a very important support role. To the outside world I want The Oasis to seem to be a nice little caff by day and a quite bar for a beer or two in the evenings. Obviously, people in our trade so to speak will know different.

"It is up to all of us to let it be known, loose tongues will be cut out of mouths. We're doing well just now and I want The Oasis, our bloody castle, to be well off old Bill's radar. Next, I want us armed, we've enough cash to buy some proper working shooters. I don't want any of us to be cornered by rival gang members without a means of a way to talk our way out of it peacefully of course.

"If you open your jacket and the enemy sees a holstered luger or some such weapon, well, you know the rest. If you can help it, as and when you are forced to use a gun, just the legs, no killing just maiming.

"Word on the street has it that we have caught the eye of other minor gangs operating around us. Not the firm I might add, but small-time shit bags who fucking fancy themselves. A couple of leg shots should keep them out of our way, Errol can you do some digging and find us a dealer?"

"Yea, sure thing Eddie, I'll get on it first thing tomorrow morning."

"Errol, you're up again. We need another set of wheels; I want a Daimler. Let the blood brothers keep the one we've already got; I want a newer one for Wossname to cart me around in. I want it customised so that I can stash a sawn off in a secret side pocket. All clean paper work and reg proper like, in case we get pulled over." Errol looked at Dave Conti. Who grinned and said,

"It'll be with you later tonight Errol."

"Okay gents, that about wraps it up, bars open." Two weeks or so passed since that last meeting, without any problems arising. The tame solicitor who did legal stuff for Errol's dad recently hand delivered the deeds to The Oasis plus the floors above and below into Eddie's possession. Errol contacted a couple of guys in the Romford area, who were able to lay their hands on some shooters. They called in later that week to find out what was on Eddie's shopping list. Within hours, enough fire power to start a small war was delivered to The Oasis on the face of it, looking very much like a delivery from a wholesale grocer. Crates of this and that with the shooters hidden under the this and that.

Mostly it was hand guns along with three shot guns, one sawn off, plus plenty of ammo. The armoury was dished out to those that needed them. Wossname was given the peacemaker.

It was now obsolete and needed to be returned to the box in the under-stair's cupboard at his house. Eddie spent some time becoming more conversant with the building he now owned. Digging around here and poking his nose in there.

He made it a personal rule however, that unless invited Bombers flat was totally out of bounds. In point of fact, in all the time Eddie ruled at The Oasis, it never happened.

Esme Wren.

Summer was slowly turning into Autumn and soon the nights would be drawing in. The spend on the weaponry had put a large dent in the money pot, so some armed robberies need to be put together to fill up the pot again. The caff was doing very well. Rosie was a tad better looking than Bomber and therefore was attracting a great deal of new customers mainly young blokes up from the Docks.

She introduced take away this and take away that, all boosting the earnings nicely. "Ahem," Rosie cleared her throat. Rosie had popped down to the Dungeon with someone in tow in order to speak with the boss. "Eddie, can I introduce you to a friend?" Behind Rosie stood a right little charmer. Eddie glanced up from his paper, finding it difficult to mask his interested expression. He smiled and nodded in her direction. She was a stunner alright but in an old fashion way which appealed to Eddie. Youthful but with none of today's youthful young ladies' looks or demeanour. Eddie always felt a little nervous around women-folk and this was certainly no exception. Butterflies weren't in it.

Rosie didn't have to introduce the young lady she stepped forward herself, held out a hand all business like and said, "Hello Eddie, I'm Esme Wren and I'm very pleased to meet with you." Eddie responded and held his hand out too.

They shook but held on to each other for a bit longer than was normal. Esme had lovely green eyes and he remembered his mum Val telling him a while ago, people with green eyes have good reason to be happy about it.

She wore gold framed specs that had a thin frame holding in the circular lenses. Couple this with a lively smile which implied being full of life and energy. "Hello Esme, welcome to The Oasis, downstairs here doubles up as my office. Please have a seat." She moved to sit down, Eddie ever the gentleman, scraped a chair back for her then another for Rosie. He noticed that Esme was a little shorter than he. That's a bonus he said to himself. Rosie made her excuses and went back upstairs to the caffe, it was still trading time and she needed to be behind the counter serving customers. "So, Esme, how old are you and what brings you to The Oasis?"

"I need a job basically, Rosie and I are old mates all the way back from school, she's been telling me the caff upstairs is taking off and thought it might be a good idea to ask you if I could join the team and give her a hand. Oh, and I'm eighteen."

"Yea, course you are love. About the job why not." Eddie rushed in made an impulse decision without much thinking time. Didn't know why. For all he knew this girl could be a plant. A plant to see what's occurring at The Oasis. For all he knew she could be in league with another gang or worse still, in league with old Bill. "Tell you what Esme, you can do three days a week in the caff say, Tuesdays Wednesdays and Thursdays, from opening time to closing and on top of that two nights working with Bomber at the bar on Friday and Saturday nights. Pay is cash in hand, ten quid a week, keep all your tips. How's that sound to you?" Esme thanked Eddie, finished sipping her tea and left to see Rosie upstairs. As she made her way up stairs Eddie watched her go and promised himself that would he get to see lots more of this Esme Wren.

Eddie's employment plan for Esme worked a treat. The three days Esme was on up in the caff were Rosie's busiest and the two nights she worked in the bar were Bomber's busiest. Talk about the face that launched a thousand ships. Esme dragged even more customers in for both caff and bar. She seemed to be straight as a dye, so for now, Eddie's suspicions of her being a plant were slowly and surely forgotten.

It was six am. Eddie looked out of Esme's bedroom window at the grey misty slated roof tops and above the chimney stacks, to a grey and misty dawn over Stoke Newington. At least the rain had stopped hammering down. Esme's little flat was all of three floors up and may just as well have been in the loft.

From this vantage point despite the mist, the top third of the recently constructed Post Office Tower in Fitzrovia could be seen, a stone's throw away from Regents Park. The tower seemed to be poking its head up toward the heavens and lording it up over all its pathetically short neighbouring buildings.

It was a sight to see and he wondered if such lofty buildings were to become the norm in London. Eddie didn't care too much for heights promising himself that we would not venture up a tower, post office or otherwise.

Down in the street below Eddie's Daimler sat waiting patiently for its new owner to return. Wossname slumped and asleep at the wheel. He thought of the sawn-off shotgun nestling in a hidden compartment in the rear door where he sat and felt a warm glow.

It was an odd sight in this dank and dowdy part of London. Stoke Newington was not the most up market and exciting of areas. Row upon row of Victorian houses, for the most part converted into multiple flats. Not everybody living here owned a car.

The tube was nearby and plenty of buses ran towards the city and West End for people that lived here and worked there. Hence the Daimler possibly sticking out like a sore thumb. If this was going to be a regular haunt for Eddie, a chat with Dave Conti and Errol was on the cards to find a more suitable motor.

Eddie didn't want any questions asked of Esme from neighbours or otherwise. Her flat in Gladding Terrace, was a hop skip and a jump away from Stoke Newington Police Station. If they spotted a Daimler parked up on a regular basis, especially with bleedin' Wossname slumped over the wheel, there no telling what aggro it might cause. Best get a different motor on the hurry-up.

Esme coughed following her third fag within thirty minutes. Eddie turned his naked body to look at Esme and smiled. She too was naked lying on top of her bedspread, inhibitions flung to the four winds. "How did we end up here Esme? Don't get me wrong, I think you're lovely, but how did we end up here?"

Esme refrained from saying Wossname drove us over in your Daimler and you asked him to wait, but thought better of it. "Eddie, look it's a one off. Right from the moment we met, I don't mind saying I fancied you fiercely. All those weeks we were at The Oasis together, me up and you down, one thing and one thing only was burning inside me. I wanted to feel you in my body. Do you remember the little smiles when you walked past me on your way downstairs?"

"I certainly do Es, gave me a tingle made the hair on the back of my head stand up it did, amongst other things," he grinned.

"And do you remember those little winks of your eye you threw back at me? Made me tingle too." Eddie moved over to the bed where she was lying. He gently pulled the cigarette from her mouth stubbed it out and clicked off the bedside light, he laid down beside Esme. Her body warm and welcoming, Esme reached up and curled her arms around Eddie's neck and whispered, "My body is all yours." Then began Eddie's second warm glow of that early morning. Wossname sitting below saw the guttering of the room light thinking right, he was now determined to have it out with Eddie once and for all. When Eddie finally dragged himself away from Esme's embrace, he thought to himself these moments of bliss are all too brief and they still make me wait.

Sleeping with the Fishes.

Dramatic news halted the man hunt for Halliwell at the Gym in East Ham Station in its tracks, almost before it had begun. A body had been discovered on an isolated foreshore of the River Thames close to East Tilbury. A dog walker alerted the local police. It was spotted washed up on an expanse of muddy banks at low tide, at first the dog walker thought it was a dead seal! The location was some twenty-five miles or so East of Stratford as the crow flies. Early indications seemed unequivocally to prove that it was the body of Halliwell. The Police uniform which was still on the bloated and battered body, although torn, covered in slime mud and other detritus from the Thames still held Halliwell's ID number and indeed his warrant card was found with him.

Essex police had been called to the scene and discovered the identity of this grisly mess of a body. This happened to be quite a remote spot. Luckily a single lane led down to the scene from East Tilbury village, passing Coal House Fort then stopping short of the Thames.

The remaining part of the journey had to be tackled on foot. Not an easy task what with it being marshy here and there. "Who would want to walk a dog down here?" mentioned one of the first coppers on the scene.

"Well, he didn't hang about, so we can't question him. Just phoned it in from a coin box in the village. I expect we'll be able to track him down though." The local police radioed the findings back to their station who in turn via all the correct upline Police channels alerted Scotland Yard. The Yard in turn passed the information on to the incident room at East Ham. The man hunt was over. Resolved by the missing policeman helpfully turning up himself.

Two teams consisting of officers from crime scenes and four detectives shot off to the location. local police secured the area with some difficulty.

It had been raining hard visibility was limited. Having to go back time after time to their car which contained only basic equipment, not anything like remotely required for a job like this, their backwards and forwarding beat a bit of a path amongst the tall grasses and thorny bushes.

The call about the body in the Thames had come in to the police via a 999-call logged at 1000 hrs. It was now 1100 hrs.

The body of P.C. Halliwell lay on a mud bank foreshore, very close to where land meets water. His body on its side facing outwards to the River. There was a short step down to the mud bank from the grassy water's edge. It was not difficult to see how and why the body had washed up at this particular spot. The local police were first on the scene, just minutes before the fire brigade arrived followed by not one but two ambulances. It was judged, at high tide, one could still stand on the mud bank. It stretched out some twenty foot and about thirty foot to the left and right of the body. At high tide it might just be possible stand on the mud bank and still only be ankle deep. A few feet further out passed the twenty-foot mark, the bank shelved deeply.

Other jetsam lay on the mud bank, a couple of old tyres, bits of wooden pallets, even an old TV carcass. It was now a race against the tide, the River Thames had fierce tidal currents at this point. It flows from London down to the Estuary and returns some hours later. Information was requested from the local port authorities regarding tidal movement. They now, according to the information from the authorities, had the best part of four hours to remove the body from the raised mud bank.

Following much blood sweat, swearing and tears the body was safely lifted from the mud bank, just as the tide started to swirl inwards. A black Moriah was summoned for Halliwell's return journey to Stratford in East London, not a conveyance he would have wanted of course. The remains of his body now lay in the morgue waiting to tell the story of how its owner ended up in the Thames to the examining pathologist. Rumours ran riot, not only throughout Stratford nick but the Incident hub at East Ham in particular. Arson had been firmly ruled out by crime scene officers. Now that the missing copper who was actually on duty at the station at the precise time of Franks murder had turned up, all be it in a body bag, all that was left now was to establish who murdered Frank Bullymore plus exactly how Halliwell had actually met his fate. The following morning to when Halliwell's body was found and identified by his mother, it was laid out on the slab, ready and waiting anxiously for a full pathology examination. D.I. Bright called the a.m. briefing in order to bring all those present right up to date and requested results from the officers if any. The detectives who chased snouts for info had nothing. The detectives who had been shaking local trees had nothing. The detectives who ransacked Halliwell's home had nothing.

In fact, the incident room had very little to go on except, there was one suspect nobody was able to question whose photo was still pinned to the board, D.I. Bright was sceptical that Halliwell was involved. However, Halliwell did disappear and had it away on his toes and definitely should have some bearing on the case. The order of the day, was to drill down further into Halliwell's recent activities. "Widen the search," Mike ordered, just prior to closing the briefing. "Okay boss," came the collective answer sounding more of a resigned sigh.

"There has to be something that ties him in with the murder. I want you to break into teams. Team one, circulate round known fences, pimps and other low life put the fear of Christ up them. Team two, visit local gambling dens between Forest Gate and the West End ask to see lists of punters owing large sums of money. Has he frequented any of them, when and why? Team three, back to his abode, if you didn't first time, pull up floor boards, scour the loft space. A thorough search short of digging up the flowerbeds. Off you trot. Back here at 0800 hrs tomorrow."

Rocking and Rolling.

"Listen Eddie, straight up, guitars, drum kits and that is the newest black-market wossname in it? Mate of mine works in a music shop down in Southend right on Cobweb Corner."

"Cobweb Corner?" queried Eddie.

"Yea well, they call's it that, cause of all the overhead power lines and cable that were used for trams, should have taken them down years ago. They span outwards above the round-a-bout at the top of Southend High Street like a bloody great spider's web, where his shop stands.

"Anyways up he said his shop has had no end of break-ins recently just for guitars and amps and stuff." Wossname was quite excited to pass on this little tad bit as he thought it might elevate his standing within the crew. As far as he was concerned his standing was at an all-time low and it might as well have been actually sitting instead of standing. Eddie and he were at the bar in the Butchers Block pub in Stratford.

The publican noticed them as they entered and made a mental note to keep a well-trained eye on them what with Eddie in his smartly cut suit, crisp white shirt and dark coloured tie, along with someone looking every bit as his big ugly minder. The pub was as busy as ever, had a great reputation for live music and very lively evenings. "No wonder it's billed as the best pub in London." Wossname drew Eddies attention to a poster advertising Lucifer's Kitchen, a night club just round the back of the pub.

"That's a must," said Wossname. "But I don't think it would be a good idea to offload any guitars and stuff anywhere near this pub. The landlord would sniff us out soon enough, and we'd be history."

"Tell me more about the music business and what's the take, what's in it for us?" Just then the landlord who was busy helping out collecting empties, came over and introduced himself. Following a short exchange of pleasantries, he moved on satisfied that neither of these two presented any threat or trouble.

Wossname remarked,

"You would struggle to find a fairer bloke than him, he's run this place along with his brother Keith for a number of years and apart from the odd one or two major skirmishes, it's basically trouble free. If anyone proves to be a nuisance, it's out on their ear followed by a swift kick where it hurts. He's a tough one but fair with it. Its rumoured the top hard nuts drop in here from time to time, so that can't be bad see."

"Yea okay, I get the point, but apart from being a quality gaff, why are we here?"

"I've arranged for us to meet up with this mate from Southend, he works in the music shop I told you about earlier you know the one under Cobweb Corner. He's coming up tonight by train with another guy who can shift musical equipment bent or straight, by the cartload. Thing is Eddie, there are hundreds of bands starting up all over the country. Guitar and drum suppliers are getting on the band wagon so to speak and hiking up the prices. In some instances, putting band gear as it's known out of reach of many a new set up. So, let's plug the wossname and earn some readies…"

"I have to say, me old mate I think you might have something there. But why here?"

"For you to see the popularity of groups and bands that are doin' it live see! Just look at the place Eddie, its heaving. Bands, groups live music, got to be something in it for us, hooky guitars and stuff for starters. Besides the Butchers is close to the train station in it."

"Christ Wossname, you've got a Daimler to run us around in, you could have driven me to Southend and met up with these guys on their own turf, then maybe have some candy floss after." Wossname frowned, his plan to up his placement in the scheme of things was running aground again.

"Tell you what then as soon as they arrive, one drink then I'll drive us all over to the Oasis."

"Thing is mate, we don't know fuck all about guitars and the like and I'm bloody well not going start learning now." Wossname grinned,

"You don't have to the bloke coming up to town with this mate of mine is an expert. He can tell us the best places to hit. Most shops selling this stuff are weak as shit security wise, when they do wise up, we will have moved on to something else. Let's exploit it now while the goings good." Eddie leaned in to be heard above the music and general hubbub raised by a couple of hundred people out for a good time and said,

"Exploit? you swallowed a fucking dictionary or what?" He gave Wossname a broad grin and gripped his shoulder, "like it," he said. "Like it."

Shame was, the programme was not be tonight, at least. As the evening wore on it was becoming obvious that the two guys from Southend, Wossnames mate and guitar man, either didn't make the journey in the first place or had gotten lost on the way. So, the two of them settled in to a drinking session. Wossname was overjoyed at having Eddie all to himself for a change. He passed on a story his mate Roy from Southend had told him. Roy was working away in the shop one busy Saturday dealing with all the customers. Some came in for albums by their singing hero's. Others came in to squeeze in three at a time into listening booths, having asked to hear a particular artist currently in the top ten.

Roy selected the single, shoved it on to one of three turntables on a bench behind him, then direct the listeners to a numbered booth. In the booth they could hear the music without disturbing the rest of the shop. Also, in that day was a local band called the Rivals who were currently filling out a dance hall in Romford called the Willow Rooms and on occasions the Whickham Hall down in Kent. Members of the band would call in to the shop in from time to time to see Roy, check out any new sheet music and try out any new guitars on sale.

Things were running smoothly when in walked a giant of a guy, jet black hair swept backwards into a pony tail heavily brylcreemed down at the front with a kiss curl hanging down over his enlarged brow. He wore a teddy boy style red drape jacket, tight black jeans, luminous yellow socks and brothel creepers on his huge feet. It was a fascinating sight Roy explained to Wossname, who was clearly enjoying telling the tale. Getting up to the counter the big guy informed Roy, "I want a guitar!"

Roy swept his hand towards the thirty or so guitars hanging on the wall behind him and said,

"Any particular style sir?" Nothing was forthcoming. Roy asked another question. "What sound are you after sir, Hollies? Stones?" The big guy said,

"Dunno, all I know is I want a red one to match me drape mate." Silence fell. Most of the shop's customers were riveted to the scene playing out in front of them, except of course, those in the listening booths. The nearest red coloured guitar, an acoustic Fender was painstakingly and carefully lifted down from its display setting, handed to the big guy who said without even touching it, "Ain't cha gonna wrap it pal?" Paid his money, slung the guitar over his shoulder shovel-style, and marched out of the shop heading in the direction of Southend Pier.

After he disappeared out into the street, Roy said to the Rival's lead singer who was standing with his mouth open, "Got some competition with that one mate. Probably see him on opportunity knocks soon Hughie Green would love him, might even win it. I mean who's going to argue the toss with a guy that size. Christ did you see the sizes of his hands?" Meanwhile Wossname having spun the story out had loads of things to ask Eddie. Issues that were sitting right on the end of his tongue. Things like was this really serious stuff with that Esme? Was he going to remain Eddie's driver for ever?

Where does he fit in with team long term? The light ales were beginning to mellow him into a false sense of security. He didn't have the courage to front

Eddie out on these subjects, preferring just to be with what was now basically his boss and paymaster and with no one else around for the moment, to push him down the ladder by a couple of rungs or three. Eddie on the other hand had no intention of bettering Wossnames position in the scheme of things. Unlike the Stratford two Billy and Mel, Wossname was a non-starter, and definitely not street-wise.

Whereas the other guys had taken an apprenticeship in crime and came through it with distinction. Okay, he came up with the musical instruments angle, yea, give him that one he thought.

Not five star though. But whilst the meat was there to be stabbed and sold on, all good. Still, he would need to come up with more long-term money-making angles in the near future. Knocked off guitars, amps, drums and stuff, in the short term would provide cash but Eddie for one reason or another didn't think it was long term. No, until something told him different Wossname was the chauffeuring goffer. They were both made aware that time was being called.

The Butchers Block for all the correct reasons had an excellent record for chucking out on time. When Eddie and Wossname looked around them the majority of the customers had drifted out on to Stratford Broadway.

Some were chasing down eager black cabs that suddenly appeared from nowhere. Others hopping on the last of the buses operating and then there were those not able to stand fully making their way gingerly from shop doorway to shop doorway, grateful for something solid to grab hold onto thus preventing them from falling. Back inside the pub Eddie Coleman watched as the publican professionally but firmly prized the hardened few still left at the bar, away from the dregs in their glasses and steer them in the direction of the main exit. It was none of Eddie's business, but he got the impression this publican's night was just beginning, work-wise.

There was a huge number of half empty beer glasses spread around the place. Some on various shelves tables and some balanced-on bar stools waiting to be collected. Ash trays piled high with dogends to empty, floors to scrub, bars to polish, not to mention restocking bars and changing over barrels downstairs ready for tomorrows lunch time trade. There seemed to be a well-oiled army of helpers getting to grips with what was needed to be completed before final lights out. "Let's take these over to the bar," he said waving his glass at his companion. No longer had they done that they heard the publican make a point of thanking them, which to him was common business sense and of course common courtesy.

114

Somehow Eddie knew he had benefitted by being in the Butchers Block that evening. His subconscious was registering something which he could not yet put his finger on.

It did however, have a lot to do with mine host. Something stuck with Eddie Coleman. He made a mental note to visit the Butchers Block again, maybe over lunch on a weekday as he did so with Errol not too long ago. But this time he would take a closer look. Stepping outside, the fresh air hit them. They took a while to find where the Daimler was previously parked up. Behind the Butchers, there was a maze of back streets none of them well lit. It dawned on Wossname that he might have left the car unlocked and someone might be stupid enough to nick an already nicked car which now belonged to Eddie Coleman. Stupid twats he giggled to himself. If that was the case someone was in for a bleedin good hiding.

Before long though it was found and Eddie let himself into the back of the Daimler, Wossname at the wheel gently eased off from the kerb taking all the back roads to avoid getting a pull from old Bill. "Where to then, boss?"

"Esme's mate. Esme Wrens, drop me there and pick me up around nine in the morning. Meanwhile go on home and get yer head down."

Eddie fell asleep. One hand on his sawn-off shotgun the other in his pocket clasped around a bulging bank roll of at least five hundred one-pound notes, tightly bound by elastic bands.

Silence is Golden.

Just four weeks on from the failed meet with the Southenders, Eddie and the Turk did indeed get Wossname to drive them both to Southend. The Southenders requested to be met in Prittlewell just outside and North of Southend, being about halfway between the town centre and Southends football ground Roots Hall. Eddie and company had been directed by the Southenders to a quiet off the main road café. There they sat and waited. Eddie looked sideways at Wossname indicating irritation at the waiting time whilst Johnny, who had already donned his worn and scratched spectacles, was busy scanning the racing tips for tomorrows races.

The time of 2.00 o'clock was set for the get together. It would be dark around the four thirty to five mark. Not that it mattered to Eddie, Wossname would be at the wheel to drive them back up to the smoke. At ten past two the Southend pair turned up grabbed some coffees and seeing the three of them, made their way over to where Eddie and friends were already seated. Following introductions one of the Southenders produced a hand-written list.

On the list was information about high quality guitars, drum sets and amplifiers. Top brands of course as promised along with locations of selected stockists throughout Southern England. Thirty-seven to be exact all stocking the best of the best. This valuable document was handed over to Eddie. He quickly scanned it gave it to Johnny for his once over. Johnny handed it back with a shrug of his shoulders. First on the list were names of quality very saleable guitars noted down. This was way outside Eddie's knowledge.

To him a guitar was a guitar. He read them through without speaking. Fender Stratocaster, Fender Telecaster, Hofner Very Thin, Gibson Les Paul, Rickenbacker Gretsch and Epiphone. Then the Drum kits, Pearl, Ludwig, Premier Olympic, Finishing up with the amplifiers, Marshall., Vox, Fender and Selmar. *Christ,* he thought, *this a lot of gear to be shifting.*

Conversation between them was kept to an absolute minimum. Basically, if you were sitting anywhere nearby, all you will have overheard would be grunts and murmurs. All you would have witnessed body language wise would have been nods and head shaking. It was now Eddie's turn. He glanced at Johnny who produced a sheet of paper that had been drawn up days in advance. On it neatly typed by Esme, were Eddie's terms and conditions, including percentages payment dates and the like. All very professional and proper. The Southenders glanced through the notes together nodded their agreement then signed it. What was needed now from them and vital to the success of the venture, would be some helpful information concerning the location of a safe warehouse. Somewhere the stolen musical instruments and various associated items could be deposited, awaiting to be sold on. This had been left to Wossnames music mate. During the run up to today's meeting, he'd been scouting round for a suitable outlet.

The best he could come up with was a warehouse cum distribution centre not massive, but then again, not too small. It was located within a busy trading estate in Basildon Essex, just off the A127. Any comings and goings would be virtually unnoticed. Next door to the intended warehouse in question was a local van and car hire company. According to Wossnames mate, vehicles were in and out of it all day long. A small private security looked after the whole estate security wise.

They were based in Laindon just up the road a bit and did random checks by van, two up maybe three times a day. It was decided that a bung was needed to keep them sweet. A dummy company name would need to be erected to the building or gates if there were any, thus making it looked used and in business to the casual passers-by.

Johnny would see to that, along with acquiring keys to the premises. He would also arrange a short lease, say 6 months with the landlord who ever that might be to keep it more than kosher. All seemed to be in order. Eddie, bade his new 'musical' business partners goodbye, jumped into the Daimler with his team and roared off down Victoria Avenue towards the A127.

The short journey from the café in Prittlewell to the start of the A127, took them under the flight path to Southend Airport. Johnny the Turk looked skywards and noticed a queer looking shaped plane on its approach flight flying low, just above them. He never mentioned it at the time, preferring to seek information on such a weird looking plane at another time. Much later, he discovered it was a revolutionary car carrying aircraft called Carvair. Apparently, it was able to take some cars on board plus their owners, due to its unusually long and bulbous nose opening at the front and swinging to one side.

A ramp was lowered and one by one each car was lifted up by the hydraulic ramp and driven straight inside the aircraft. Passengers, for obvious reasons needed to be seated elsewhere in the plane. Eddie, who was deep in thought asked Wossname that he drive home via the trading estate in Basildon so as to get an eyeball on the premises. It didn't take long to find it. On the locked gates was a 'For Rent' sign, indicating 10.000 square feet was available, including racking. The agents name and telephone number, was hastily noted down by Johnny.

All three sat in the Daimler looking through the metaled mesh gates directly at the building. It was a single-story brick faced building. A small office area to the front with a flat roof above together with windows looking out to the gates.

Venetian blinds were closed making it impossible to see inside especially from where the three were sitting. The rest of the building looked to be nearly all warehouse space. Vehicle access was to the warehouse, according to the lorry signs would to be at the rear. "That's a bonus," breathed Johnny.

"That'll do," Eddie muttered. Then asked Johnny.

"Yep," he said, "looks fine." Wossname waited for Eddie to ask his opinion sadly it wasn't forthcoming. Bloody ell, here we go again he thought. Right down the pecking order once more.

"Fuck me," he muttered maybe just a little louder than a whisper.

"What's that?" asked Eddie.

"Just decided I need a piss boss."

"Yea well, tie a knot in it mate just get us back to The Oasis and don't spare the horses." Inwardly, Wossname was beside himself, he was beginning to hate ever getting mixed up with bloody Eddie Coleman. *Drive 'im ere, drive 'im there, no bleedin' thanks or please, sitting outside Esme's flat when he's avin an all-nighter, I should bloody coco.*

He became so distracted by his evil thoughts his attention to driving took second place. They ended up exiting the trading estate in the wrong direction and were now heading back to Southend instead of London. As pure luck would have it, within a mile they hit a round-a-bout, he deftly swung the car around, now facing the correct way home, hit the accelerator.

The Daimler responded and burst into life responding to the extra fuel supplied to the engine courtesy of the accelerator being pressed hard to the floor. Heads were jolted backwards as the Daimler flew away from the round-a-bout in London's direction. "What the fuck Wossname," Eddie needed to raise his voice above the screaming engine.

"Don't spare the 'orses you said boss."

"Yea well you don't need to sodding well scare them at the same time. If you get us pulled by old Bill for speeding, I'm gonna have to fuck you up some." Wossname bit his tongue until it bled.

He decided now was not the time to speak his mind, he eased off the gas and hit the national speed limit and stayed there. They journeyed on all quiet in their individual thoughts. Gallows Corner at Romford came and went as did Gants Hill, Ilford then on into Wanstead, still at steady speeds.

Now on more familiar ground Wossname gently threaded the Daimler and his two passengers like a needle through the East End of London to their required destination, The Oasis.

Porridge and Jags.

Dave Conti opened his eyes to a corn flower blue sky. It took him a while to work out where he was, indeed, how had he arrived at this beautiful spot and more importantly how long had he been snoozing? Laying by his side head on his chest was the young Mrs Sullivan. A shiver ran through him knowing of her husband's fearsome reputation for facial slicing but then remembered he was under the protection of Eddie Coleman. Slowing pulling himself up onto his elbows his companion murmured softly not awakening fully. Dave took in the surroundings. They were on a grassy slope, a couple of hundred yards behind them on a gravel path stood a gleaming bright red Jag, the keys of which lay beside him on the picnic blanket together with a near empty bottle of Blue Nun.

In the distance he could see the coast and guessed judging by their journey earlier in the day, they must be close to Brighton, or at least overlooking it out to the sea. Alarmed and worried he rose up to a standing position and looked around for some kind of land mark. The wine had made him woozy. Standing up sharply reminded him he was still a bit pissed, he nudged the young Mrs Sullivan with his foot asking, "Shirl, where the hell, are we?" She looked up at him and smiled,

"Devils Dyke init, don't you remember you said with a name like that you insisted we come here." He continued to look down.

"Oh yea, I don't remember seeing too much of it though," he giggled.

"Christ what would your old man say if he got wind of what we've been up to." She grimaced at the thought of Reg re-arranging Dave's face. For a moment or two, Shirl, and not for the first-time studied Dave.

Gave him her personal once over so to speak. She had always like tall men and Dave must be well above six foot. He had that lived in look for his age. At the age of twenty-seven his face though, told a different story. A story of a much older man. A slim frame with lovely hands nice and smooth. They felt wonderful especially when he was stroking her inner thighs. Not like Reg's hands, rough as sandpaper. Long jet-black hair swept back and held down with Brylcreem. During their love making sessions with Dave on top she adored it when the front of his hair hung down over his brow, to Shirl it looked extremely sexy made her gasp inwardly.

A typical East End bashed in nose gave him the look of a boxer which he was now and then of course, but had yet to tell Shirl that bit of info. His deep powder blue eyes looked down at her and he smiled that smile. Hmmmmm she purred my ideal lover. "Come on girl, time we, was gone." Shirl nodded, then jumped up and ran down the grassy slope kicking off her high heels, laughing and giggling like a teenager.

"Sorry Dave need a pee and don't you bloody well watch!" The further she ran, the steeper the downward slope sloped, thereby lending a hand to her ever-increasing running speed. Within seconds she was out of sight. Dave started to gather up things from where they had lain and began walking back to the Jag when he heard Shirl screaming blue murder. Dave threw himself over to the Jag grabbed his gun from the glove compartment and dashed back down towards where the screaming was coming from. Shirl ran past him followed by what looked like a bleeding great bull. It was only a matter of seconds before Dave and Bull met head on, he levelled the gun at the bull's eye and pulled the trigger, twice.

Dave hadn't fired this gun in anger yet, in fact, he'd not fired it at all. Luckily for him and the bull, it had one hell of a recoil. Consequently, both rounds flew harmlessly over the bulls charging brute force of one ton of muscle, and on into some bushes someway down the slope. The noise of the gun however, was not a noise the bull had previously heard.

It changed direction like a jet in the sky veering off, not much but enough for Dave to skid to a halt on the grassy slope, he conducted a rapid U-turn and legged it back to the car. By now Shirl was in the passenger seat shaking like a leaf having seen the whole thing. Dave gathered up the blanket, wine bottle and other miscellaneous pieces, shoved them into the boot and threw himself in the driver's seat. "I don't mind tellin' you Shirl, I nearly shit a brick out there. I've fought many a man, but that. That scared the livin' daylights outa me. Come on let's get out of here in case he changes his mind."

An hour or so later, they were crossing the Thames on Vauxhall Bridge when Shirl asked of Dave, "Why do need to carry a gun Dave? It's a simple question. You see, ever since my mates' brother was shot, I don't like guns. In fact, never have, noisy bloody things. You can kill people with guns Dave and if old Bill finds one on you, you can go away for a bleeding long time."

"Look Shirl. We're lovers, right? What I do outside of that is not of your concern. The business I'm in means that sometimes I come up against people that want to hurt me, so it's there to keep agro like that at bay." Just then, Dave's attention was forcibly re-focussed elsewhere. A couple of bloody coppers were walking alongside the traffic, now moving at a snail's pace, towards a set of traffic lights. The Jag was edging along at a walking pace towards the lights on the North side of the bridge.

The coppers were looking at car registrations and checking their note books. Dave swallowed hard and loudly. The cops were now along-side them nearest the passenger side. Should they have been informed of the stolen car's registration, indicated for the driver to pull up for a chat, Dave would have to ram his foot down and bash his way out of the jam. Another little snippet Dave had held back from Shirl, was she was sitting in a shiny red Jag that he nicked during the early hours of this morning. If these coppers had the reg then the balloon would go up.

All hell would be let loose as Dave rammed his way clear. Jail birds especially, don't usually go from porridge to shiny Jags. "Shirl do me a favour and get those coppers numbers please girl, just in case and all that."

Dutifully she rummaged in her handbag drew out a lipstick holder took the top off, twisted the base until the pointy bit protruded and scribbled the coppers numbers on a spare hanky. "Cheers girl." One of the coppers gave Shirl a cheeky wink as they cleared the lights and went from snails' pace back up to speed again. Shirly was about to give him the 'V' sign and mouth a fuck off, but thought better of it.

Dave felt both severely relived and happy at the same time. If the theft had been reported, the cars registration number had yet to reach those two coppers. As they cruised on, Dave let his left-hand rest on Shirl's knee and began slowly moving it upwards to her inner thigh then gently squeezed. His hand bridging the gap between stocking top and bare leg, the giggle factor he called it. Shirl let out a gasp but didn't resist she loved it too much. Besides in a short while Dave would soon be dropping her off, therefore, any time spent with Dave was precious, not knowing when they would meet again worried her.

That worry became much more important than the issue of Dave carrying a gun and the strange request for the copper's numbers, so she chose to block both issues out lodging them in the back of her mind somewhere, to be challenged at a later date. Before long Dave parked the car up in a side street close by to the usual tube station on the Central line. They embraced heavily kissing each other almost in a frenzy. Shirl reluctantly pulled away from Dave, she delved in her handbag brought out her powder compact and began the ritual of donning the war paint. Neither liked these goodbyes so within minutes she was out of the car, making her way to the station. Dave sat and watched. *Nice arse* he said to himself. Shirley Sullivan was not a petite dress size. If anything, she was a tiny bit plump, exactly how Dave liked his women.

Something to get hold of, ran through his mind. Wasted on her old man-can't get it up-Reg. Long blonde curly hair naturally blonde, he had since discovered, cheeky smile with a brain sharp as a pin. Good dresser too.

Must be all the dough from Reg's ill-gotten gains. Shirl turned the corner and was gone. Dave fired up the Jag and was away too in the direction of Creekmouth to drop of yet another nicked motor.

A Botched Word.

"Who the fucking hell are you?"

"No questions pal, just drive and keep yer trap shut." At the same corner where Shirley had just vanished, Dave stopped the car waiting for the busy London traffic to leave a gap for him to move out onto the main road. Three men piled in to the car. Two in the back seat and one to Dave's left in the passenger seat. This one was holding a cosh, Dave glanced in the rear-view mirror to get a look at the two heavies in the back. Cosh holder said,

"Reg wants *a word* with you, been a naughty boy pal ain't ya, dippin' yer wick like." Dave took a quick glance left at his passenger, he thought bloody ell, is this the best Reg Sullivan could muster. The two in the back both looked old enough to be his dad and cosh man looked abnormally thin almost emaciated. Made his black Crombie look well oversized, should these three have tried to take him other than inside the car they would definitely have come off worse. Dave could well handle himself.

He had once seen off two thugs on the platform at Fenchurch Street station. Both were hospitalised for many weeks. This minging lot in due course, would soon suffer the same fate. A grin appeared on Dave's face. He remembered; his gun was stuck in his waistband following the debacle with that bleedin' bull. Luckily it was out of sight of these three goons. They'd missed a trick, should have given him a shake down found the shooter and turned it on him. Bloody amateurs thought Dave. "Where the fuck you going?" asked cosh man. Mistake number two thought Dave, he was told to shut his mouth and drive, but they had failed to offer any directions, Dave was beginning to enjoy this.

One of the back seaters announced he needed a piss and soon. "You and your bleeding prostate," came from his companion sat next to him.

"Yea well, at least I don't get the shits like you when things go noisy." Cosh man intervened,

"Shut yer traps, you two." He then turned to Dave and told him to head for Hainault.

"Don't know where that is boss," Dave lied.

Dave grinned again, a bit more obvious this time and the grin was noticed by cosh man. "Don't know what you're grinning about pal, but I'll tell you this, Reg can't wait to leave his calling card on your boat race. You'll 'ave a permanent grin from earhole to earhole." Mistake number three, telling him his fate, Dave mused. They were still heading in the opposite direction for Hainault. It soon dawned on Dave they had not a notion of how to get to Hainault by car. They must have travelled to the snatch point by tube. Finally, Dave spoke, he couldn't resist the question.

"How did you know where to make the snatch?" Prostate, rather unfortunately for the other two spilled the beans. Apparently, they had been there on doggo, watching and waiting.

The trigger for any doggo, was this, Shirl mentioning to Reg she was going up West to do some shopping. So, under orders from her suspicious and jealous husband, Cosh man was to follow her. He watched her as she got off the tube from Hainault at Stratford Station, then walked a few hundred yards to where a car and driver were waiting. He witnessed a loving embrace before she and the driver zoomed off laughing and smiling like a young couple very much in love. When he heard this Reg was furious. The next time Shirl announced she was going up town Reg ordered his three best men to hang around the area that cosh man first spotted the waiting car, snatch the driver and escort him back to Hainault for a facial. So far so bad. Prostate was screaming for a piss and very near to wetting his pants.

His back-seat companion was hoping against hope that things did not go noisy and possibly kack himself in the process. Cosh man was becoming a great deal more agitated.

The road signs announced they were heading West. Dave was getting bored and now wanted to end this comedy.

The car they were in had been nicked earlier the same day, primarily for an outing with Shirl. By now the owner would have registered the missing car presumed stolen with the police.

Probably, most mobile units would have the registration on their list of stolen to watch out for. It would have been oh so easy to jump out at the next set of traffic lights on red and leave them to it. With a bit of luck, the confusion of an abandoned car in the middle of the road might well attract the attention of old Bill. These three would then have to explain why they were sitting in a stolen car without a driver.

Dave had no idea if any of the three could drive a normal car let alone an automatic Jag. He assumed not. He was not however, inclined to ask. There was a slight problem with this plan, Dave's dabs were everywhere to be found inside and outside the car. Although he was transient i.e., of no fixed abode, it wouldn't be that hard for the police once they identified it was Dave's dabs to track him down. There was also the possibility of bringing his bosses name into disrepute and that was a huge no-no.

Eddie told Dave to keep his name out of any frames. If old Bill tracked him down to The Oasis, that would be the end of his employment. As they cruised into White City with Wormwood Scrubs being close by, the car came to a stop. Dave knew the area well. He'd spent a bit of his youth in and around Shepherds Bush which was about five minutes' drive away. As a lad he often went to see the Hoops at Loftus Road and remembered a run-down trading estate not too far from the Queens Park Rangers stadium. "That'll do for me," he said out loud.

"Wasat?" shouted the now near maniacal cosh man.

"Sorry mate, just realised where we are, I'll be in the right direction for Hainault soon." Within minutes the car was entering the wasteland that was a trading estate at one time.

Derelict buildings to the left derelict factories to the right every window smashed by stones no doubt thrown by kids. Giant weedy type bushes creeping up all over the place. *Conti's last stand,* thought Dave.

"Here we go," Dave hollered. He raced the car towards a six-foot high, sixty or so feet wide brick wall, which stood between them and South Africa Road on the other side. With one hand, he spun the wheel to the right.

The car skidded sideways, banging into the wall trapping the nearside front and rear passengers. With his free hand he pulled his gun from his waist band. As soon as the car stopped moving, he was out like a hot knife through butter.

Dave slammed the driver's door shut flung open the rear door and grabbed hold of prostates companion by the scruff, dragged him to the ground and stuck a foot on his exposed throat. No noise emanated from the grounded man, only gurgles as he began to run out of breath via his very restricted airways.

"You, with the cosh ditch it, then get your fucking arse out here." Dave was now at screaming pitch. Cosh man crawled over to the driver's side shoved open the driver's door and made a valiant attempt at attacking Dave. The gun in Dave's hand descended, making heavy contact with cosh man's head.

He went down like a sack of spuds, blood running down his face from the guns whipping wound. Satisfied that these two had been rendered harmless, Dave now turned his attention to prostate. This poor little lamb had pissed himself and remained stuck in his seat in the back of the Jag.

His head had been bashed by the force of the car hitting the brick wall. Prostates head had swung violently against the side window. He was basically out of it he couldn't exit the car easily and looked to be half dead.

Dave, having taken his foot of the guy on the deck leaned into the car seemingly in an effort to gently help prostate out, instead he shouted, "look what you have done to the lovely leather seat, you've pissed all over it. Naughty little boy ain't cha," then proceeded to punch the fuck out of his face. Cosh man was the only one of the three who was now anything like compos mentis. He had some control of his mind, only some. Although still bleeding, down on his knees, he managed a threatening sneer. Dave told him he'd fucked up big time. If it happened again, he would seek out Reg sodding Sullivan himself and give him a taste of proper violent disorder. Also, if he got wind of Shirley having a bad time at Reg's hands or anyone else for that matter, he, Dave Conti would see to it personally that Reg would meet his maker following hours of torture.

His body, what was left of it to be dumped in the Thames. You make sure he gets the message. A final kick in the groin to cosh man, Dave slowly brushed himself down, turned on his heel and walked back to the main road then on into the Bush to find a pub for a pint or two.

Only then did he shout out over his shoulder, "Oh by the way, that Jags nicked." The three hard men looked at each other. Not wishing to get pulled for nicking and driving away, Regs men set about destroying the car for good.

First, they found the blanket in the boot, forced open the locked compartment which housed the petrol filler tore a thin strip off the blanket and with the aid of stick found nearby poked it down into the fuel tank. In minutes the petrol soaked upwards. Roughly twenty or so inches of petrol-soaked cloth hung down from the fillers spout almost to the ground, the other end embedded firmly in the petrol tank. Cosh man lit a fag drew heavily, then touched the cloth with the lit match. It flamed up immediately, all three had about thirty seconds to get clear. As they walked away, they heard first a thump as the reserve tank ignited instantly followed by a huge bang as the main tank blew. None looked back at their collective handiwork. The massive blaze and pall of dense black smoke would no doubt get noticed soon enough and they didn't want to be around, especially when the fire brigade arrived, followed no doubt by the Police. Their main objective now was to find a working telephone box, get on the blower to Reg and pray that he sends a car for them.

How they will be able to explain the three of them had lifted Shirls lover, let him escape and got beaten to a pulp into the bargain, was anyone's guess. They would need to concoct a story between them, and stick to it. God, talk about thieves and villains within thieves and villains.

Two Dead Coppers.

A post mortem report for Police Constable Halliwell was delivered by courier to Mike Bright who was at his desk as he opened the sealed envelope. Glancing through the several pages of pathologist findings, none of it made good reading. The pathologist discovered three deep stab wounds Halliwell's body to his upper middle back, this was a complete surprise. Cause of death therefore was uncertain. Yes, his lungs were full of Thames water and yet, the massive blood loss caused by the stab wounds rendered his death a convincing murder. The team of detectives within the incident room behind East ham Police Station had now two murders on the boil, that of Frank Bullymore and now constable Halliwell. A briefing would need to be called in order to bring everyone up to date. As of yet despite intensive investigative work, no clues had emerged that might lead to Franks killer.

Halliwell's murder was probably going to be just as tough, his body had been in the water for quite some time, bloated and mangled. Mangled no doubt brought about by the number of times it had been bashed against bridge cutwaters and other assorted fixed and stable Thames water furniture. The questions that would need to be answered is, where and when did Halliwell enter the Thames. Also, did he drown as a result of clinging to life as he hit the water. Thing is, he needed to have been half alive to be able swallow that much of the filthy water.

Upper most in Mike's mind was this. Did he jump or was he pushed? The report made no mention of impact damaged. If a limp, dead body was flung off of one of London's bridges, impact damaged would have occurred. The average height from bridge to water on London's Thames crossings, dependent upon tidal movements is eight to ten metres. A dead weight of say thirteen stone would gather speed during the drop increasing the likelihood of severe bruising and or possibly broken limbs. Mike searched the report once again for any tell-tale evidence of this nature but found none. He therefore concluded that the body might well have been slipped into the water at low tide, there being a number of areas along the edge of the Thames at low tide that afforded an area of muddy shingly foreshore which might just be useful enough to off-load a body onto, especially late at night. Halliwell would have simply floated away with the next high tide.

His next thoughts were, did who-ever murdered Halliwell, stab him the back three times at the point of offloading the body onto one of those tiny mud banks or before? Then deciding to dispose of Halliwell's body in the time-honoured way of London's criminal fraternity for centuries; flushed away by Father Thames. Either way, it pointed to someone a bit savvy regarding movements of the river and where to dump the body knowing that a high tide would take it away. It was a slim chance, but he would seek a meeting with an expert from the Port of London Authority. Someone familiar with the terrain, someone who might have charted all the low tide banks say from Tower Bridge to Battersea Bridge, both sides of the river. If they could identify areas of muddy shingle banks which revealed themselves at low tide, there was a slim chance that if searched by his team and anyone else he could rope in, even the tiniest bit of evidence might be waiting to be discovered thereby offering up a clue. He scanned the report once again. The pathologist had measured the depth and width of the stab wounds. The report indicated a serrated blade on one edge only the other edge being blunt and possibly thicker. Blade size was estimated at approximately one- and one-half inches wide by twelve to thirteen inches long.

No hilt marks were visible around the stab wound entry points which meant it was not a dagger. Christ thought Mike that sounds awfully like a bread knife. Sparked up, he thought he might get a detective or two to trawl through police records perhaps to see if someone had a modus operandum of killing or maiming with such a weapon. If that was the weapon of choice and someone's name popped up, then Mike wanted to know about it post haste. The briefing had been set for the following morning at 0700 hrs.

That same evening following receiving the report on the pathologist's findings, he found himself taking a stroll along the Thames embankment close to Cleopatras Needle.

He stopped a while looking down at the river just below him swirling around. It was almost high tide now with the river being, a fair way up. The evenings weather was cool. London's night lights were coming on whilst the office lights in the buildings across on the South bank were being switched off. Soon office workers will have all made their way home for a meal, a glass of Chablis, switch on the tele then fall asleep to Simon Templar in 'The Saint'.

Night life fun seekers and theatre goers would soon replace them, the younger set hoping to get lucky. Looking to his left, he could make out the iconic shape of the mighty Tower Bridge and Mike shuddered. Shuddered at the thought of being dumped unceremoniously into the waters below from its walkway. What a fucking waste.

Two coppers murdered and for what. One closing in on retirement the other by comparison, a lifetime of policing in front of him. People do die he thought, but not the way these two did. One with his carotid artery slashed open, allowing no way of halting the inevitable. The other stabbed or drowned, which ever came first.

Looking down again towards the waters below, he whispered to the Thames flowing through the middle of London then out to sea, "What secrets do you keep guarded and what secrets will you ever yield up?" Mike had all but banished the fact that the desk sergeant had whispered the killer's name. He pictured the killer in his mind's eye and shuddered. This was one secret he was going to have to take to his grave. When eventually he arrived home, it was to his office he sought sanctuary with a very large gin and tonic, and started to write up some notes ready for tomorrows briefing.

Whipped, Stripped and Beaten.

"Come on Billy for Christ's sake, this bloke's heavy, give us a hand." It was one o'clock in the morning. Billy had drawn the car up as close as he dare to the rear ground behind the hospital. The instant he stopped; Mel was out of the car. Running to the boot he flung it open, there lay bound hand and foot, Mr sticky fingers in the till, the car lot manager. This particular one had had, a big a dose of sticky fingers, up near the hundreds somewhere and needed to be dealt with.

Naked, apart from his tiny leopard skin style briefs, that didn't leave much room for imagination. Frightened eyes staring up at Mel, the poor sod was quivering and not because it was cold.

He was quivering with fear. Badly beaten with Mel's bike chain then pushed unceremoniously into the boot of the Jag. The chain whipping had left its mark all over his grotesquely large belly and lower chest. He rightly assumed that this was it, the end is nigh! From where he was lying, he could not see the hospital sitting in the gloom over to the left of Mel's shoulder. The hospital that was eventually to become his salvation. Just now however, fearing the worse he started for the first time in his miserable life to pray. Pray to the lord any lord, for mercy. He promised faithfully to God and anyone else who might be tuning in, he would not steal from Eddie or Errol, never ever again. The mumbled prayer didn't reach Mel's ears.

During Mel and Billy's weekly rounds of the car-lots, they discovered this chap was on the hey diddle-diddle, big time.

The discovery was discussed with Eddie at the most recent Friday Oasis meeting. Eddie reacted immediately. "The fucker," he shouted. The boys were instructed to lift the guy give him a severe beating then dump him in the grounds of Bethnal Green hospital.

"Billy, will you get your arse out here, I can't get this slag out on my own," Mel whispered hoarsely. Reluctantly Billy shut down the idling engine and joined Mel at the back of the car. Billy heard the prayer mumbling emanating from the boot. Fearing that it might increase in volume and attract attention, he picked up a tyre lever and smashed into the side of the man's head, at the same time as pressing his other hand over the victim's mouth.

Just as well, the wild screaming needed suitable action. There was plenty of cloud cover that night, no shiny moonlight to pick them out luckily for them. They were bathed in near pitch darkness. Mel rummaged around in the front of the car, after a few minutes he found what he was looking for, a reel of industrial tape.

Ripping a portion off he returned to the boot area and proceeded to gag the now ex-car lot manager's mouth. A home-made hood was pulled roughly over the hapless man's head and tied with a long bootlace tightly round his neck. He was now effectively blind to his surroundings and unable to call for help. The wounds on his lower chest and his large belly were still weeping blood, as was the new wound to the side of his head. The two Stratford boys literally dragged him out of his temporary home in the Jags boot onto the wet grass beside the parked car, this action added to the man's woes. His naked back didn't take too kindly to being dragged over the lip of the boot which cut into him opening up yet another wound. Had he been a tad lighter lifting him out would have been easier on his body. There he lay quivering, bleeding, waiting for the inevitable gun to the head the one he'd seen Billy wielding earlier followed by the bang, followed by oblivion. He sent a silent goodbye to his wife and daughter then clenched his eyes and waited for the gun muzzle to be shoved against his head, minutes passed. No gun to his head. No shot.

He was breathing so hard; he couldn't hear what was going on outside of his hood. "Now what?" Warm liquid on his chest wounds? He smelt the strong unmistakable aroma of urine. "Fuck me, the bastards are only pissing on me." As he strained to hear anything, anything at all, he thought he heard soft laughter from his captors. When the boys had finished pissing on their prisoner, Billy silently motioned to Mel to push the car away from their victim. "Don't want him to know we've gone."

Billy pressed up real close to Mel's ear and whispered his getaway plan. About fifty yards away in the direction the car was facing, there happened to be a slight incline. They could free wheel the car down this incline, fire up the engine out of earshot at the bottom, and be away. Unaware the Stratford two had scarpered the beleaguered hooded, beaten and pissed on car-lot man, lay still, as quiet as he possibly could. No sense in aggravating his assailants possibly bringing about further pain to his body. Shivering now from the cold as well as from fear he tried sitting up, wincing with pain as he did so. His mind went back to earlier in the day when Billy and Mel popped over to his particular car-lot. He thought it a bit odd as they normally visited on Fridays and here it is Monday, almost at going home time.

He was looking forward to locking up and getting home. Monday nights was Shepherd's Pie night and his misses cooked up a mean Pie-n-chips. Plus, he was starving into the bargain. The two guys entered the static caravan that doubled as his office, as usual looking quietly dangerous. They were smiling thank God, he thought. Then one of them said, "We need to go for a little drive pal." He couldn't remember which one uttered those very unwelcome words, In East End parlance, when spoken it almost always ended up in violence one way or another.

Sweat was gathering on his brow. They suggested he lock up and hand over the keys. "Oh, fuck," he inwardly panicked, "Don't like the smell of this at all." He remembered being driven to an old abandoned warehouse, not far from Limehouse, an area he was not too familiar with. Once inside, he was ushered into a room about 24 by 24 feet. Windowless but with no ceiling. He looked up and was able to see the old warehouse pitched corrugated roof. Two skylights afforded shafts of light down towards where they were standing. Thick metal beams ran across from one side of the factory to the other and were visible twenty foot or so above him, as was a chain hanging down. Attached to the chain at about three foot from the ground was a wicked looking meat hook. His blood ran cold. In an instant, he knew his fate.

Billy pulled his shooter from a shoulder holster aimed the muzzle two inches from the poor fuckers left eye and ordered his captive to strip or get shot in the eye. The choice was his. Slowly he took off his suit, then shoes, followed by socks and finally shirt and tie.

Mel bound his wrists together then pushed them roughly onto the hook. He moved over to the wall to where the other end of the chain was attached to a bracket. Mel grabbed it and pulled it downwards. The chain was looped over one of the metal ceiling beams. Mel's pulling action produced a loud clanking noise, reminiscing of a thick chain being let loose from its housing when a ship drops its anchor. The movement lifted the car-lot managers arms above his head and a little beyond until he needed to stand on his tippy toes for comfort. His whole body was now defenceless. He remembers Billy producing a sheet of paper the contents of which he read out like he was bloody judge and jury. Get on with it for fucks sake he thought, just get on with it.

Billy continued the diatribe, the words pointing out that neither Eddie Coleman or Errol will stand for being turned over. Not now, not ever. He read, 'You have been thieving from us and will be punished accordingly. Henceforth your services will no longer be required.' All too well the next action he remembered acutely; a metal chain whipped across his chest. The pain and burning sensation for him, was too much to bear. He heard himself scream in order to release the pain only to receive a second and third lash, a much louder scream echoed all around the bare torture chamber. He glimpsed large blood splatters on one of the walls. They had done this before? At this point, mercifully, he passed out. He didn't remember anything more only being dragged painfully out of the boot onto the wet grass where he now lay, then being pissed on.

The rest was a blur. His lower chest and belly felt like they were on fire. Hunger pangs had totally disappeared, so to it would seem had the Stratford two. It was six o'clock in the morning before he was discovered. He had been in and out of consciousness several times following the disappearance of Billy and Mel. His discoverer happened to be a maintenance man who originally thought he had come across a dead body. However, when the body started moaning, he jumped back more in surprise than anything else. It's not often he thought that a cadaver starts moaning and complaining about the weather! He raced in to the hospitals rear entrance just up ahead to summon help. It took another ten minutes or so to get enough people to lift him onto a stretcher, get him inside and begin remedial treatment. Naturally the police were called and naturally they would be told nothing. No one squeals to old Bill. Especially if one's life depended on keeping schtum.

Strike First and Strike Hard.

"You fucking did what?" Eddie roared, oozing badness. His words echoing throughout the entire Oasis building. Punters in the café upstairs looked at each other nervously. Some developing an immediate dose of twitchy bottom syndrome. The management in the basement as they were referred to usually conducted their business, like any other businessmen in the city or elsewhere. The screaming was totally out of character.

One or two of them perhaps a little more tuned in to Eddie Coleman's bad moods than some of the others in the cafe, decided it was time to depart whilst they were still in one piece. Bomber looked at Esme, Esme looked at Rosie, Rosie looked at Johnny. All four shrugged their respective shoulders, carried on as if nothing had happened, or was about to. Dave Conti was currently on the end of a severe tongue lashing from Eddie. And Eddie didn't quite know at this stage if he wanted to kill Dave then and there or simply pat him on the back.

"You fucking did what?" repeated Eddie, now finding a new upper level of volume. Dave had felt it necessary to tell all. Right from using a stolen Jag to whisk Shirley off to a patch of grass somewhere above Brighton, to the Jag being torched. Now he was beginning to regret telling the story. He was slowly losing his bottle "Look," wailed Eddie. "We know about you shagging Regs new bride. We also know your job is to lift cars from the wealthy up West which you are then supposed to drive straight to Errol's." The next bit found Eddie up to full volume again. "But you don't use the fucking nicked cars for your own ends. All it would take is to be stopped by old Bill.

"You'd get collared and then what? Not only do you go for a shag with the Jag, you half fucking murder three of Reg's men in the car. Christ give me strength.

"Then, the Jag gets bashed around, and torched! You couldn't fucking make it up!" Dave sat silently. He had had wind of what the Stratford boys did to the hapless car-lot chappie. He sat waiting for them to be tasked by Eddie with doing the same to him. Eddie, quieter now half smiled at Dave and said "Three of them eh? You stuck it to three of them. What were they, fucking old age pensioners? Look Dave, I can feel a mini war coming on because of your brainless actions.

It won't take long for Reg Sullivan and his not so merry men to work out where to find you.

As it happens, I offered you protection provided you did a good job on the car nicking front and I certainly can't complain in that direction."

"Thanks Eddie." The relief was dawning across Dave's face. "If, there is going to be a war even if its only revenge, I will keep to my word. What I now want to happen is this. You go and keep the flash cars coming, I'm going to ask Billy to shadow you and step in if any of Reg's boys jump on you again. Let Billy do the sorting out. You just concentrate on nicking decent motors. Meanwhile, Johnny the Turk will drop into Hainault and find Sullivan's drinking den. Okay?

On your way out, ask Johnny to come down, will you?" Dave nodded and disappeared hot foot upstairs. He motioned to Johnny with his thumb waving in the direction of the basement, indicating Eddie wanted to see him. Johnny almost fell down the stairs to the dungeon. Immediately wanting to know what the shouting and screaming was all about. Johnny had wrongly assumed that Eddie was in danger.

Eddie was busy taking in major gulps of air to slow his heart rate down a trick he had picked up from training in the gym. Having settled himself at the round table, Eddie explained all that Dave had told him, leaving nothing out. "Okay," said Johnny, "So, what's the plan. Where do we go from here?"

"Right, this is it. Get Wossname to drive you over to that slags back yard; Hainault."

"His turf, where he feels safe like. Don't front Sullivan out just yet. At the moment he won't have no idea who you are. I just need to know which boozer he frequents. Where he meets members of his gang and when. In the mean-time, we'll be needing some serious fucking shooters, two or three maybe with plenty of ammo. Those guys in Romford said they can lay their hands on them at a price. Sterling machine guns I think they called them. Real noisy and scary in confined places. Scare the shit out of 'em I should think. So, on your way back from Hainault get over to Romford and talk to them. Do a deal on the 'urry up, I want to hit Reg before he hits us, I want a solid fast attack. Get in. Get 'em, then stroll out, all casual like."

Johnny the Turk was nodding throughout. "You've got the key to the safe, so grab a ton. That should be plenty for the shooters, then, when the times right I want you Mel and Dave to do up Reg's fucking meeting place. Clear out any innocent drinkers first and be gentlemanly when requesting they leave. Don't let Reg or his men get out. Strike first and strike hard, put the fucking frighteners on 'em big time. No killings like, just wreck the place. If Sullivan is not there, tell anyone who's listening Eddie Coleman is not a happy bunny. Next time they pull a stunt like jumping on one of mine again they will face the consequences. Tell 'em we won't stand for it. You tell 'em Johnny, loud and fucking clear. Wossname will drive you three over to Hainault and wait outside whatever pub it is. When you've done shooting the place up torch it good and proper and for fuck sake don't run out like bleeding cats on an 'ot tin roof. I want you three to stand around for a while then walk slowly out. Tell Wossname not screech off, it's not a bank raid, nice and calm like. When you get to London tell Wossname to drive over Tower Bridge. When you get there, you lot dump the machine guns over the side in the drink. Then as soon as he's dropped you off get him to drive the Daimler over at Creekmouth."

0800hrs East Ham Station.

Mike Bright strode purposefully in the briefing room and took up a position at the head of the room, close to the information board. "Morning everybody, let's be having you, listen up, come on now we need to get focused. The Chief Super is breathing fire mostly down my neck. The press is like a bunch of baying hounds gathering like dog packs around any-one who so much as glances in their direction.

"Now, regarding the murder investigation of Halliwell. From the notes and information that has been trickling in, it is now clear that he has run up a substantial debt with a gambling den or spieler in Soho that goes by the name of Maddison's. Its rumoured to be controlled by Jake Speck. He, is a cold bloodied character who is well known for his brutal activities in his crime ridden world. This new information has surfaced via the officers tasked with going back over Halliwell's movements whilst being out of uniform as it were. The thinking or theory is now pointing to Halliwell being unable to pay a gambling debt, and possibly, just possibly being used a conduit of information from us to them. Each little snippet passed back to the gambling dens management would thereby reduce his outstanding debt." A question arose from the assembled team.

"What little snippets might be passed back sir?" Mike was about to ignore the question. He thought the enquiring detective might be taking the piss.

He looked over at him, waited for a full thirty seconds before answering in order to give his answer gravity and said, "Impending police raids on illegal gambling dens that Halliwell would have been in debt to for starters." Silence all round. Mike continued. "I have instructed the team dealing with this side of Halliwell's investigation to bring in further information that might support this theory. If Jake Speck is involved in anyway shape or form, we could well be opening a large can of worms which might lead us on into police corruption on a larger scale, or then again it might not. In this instance, the Chief Super has given me the go ahead only if we tread gently amongst the criminal fraternity. Officers from the police corruption arm will be joining us imminently. You are to share with them any and all information that may be relevant to their investigations; because, there may well be police officers involved. We do not want to scare anyone back down the holes that they live in." This information rocked the room.

Police corruption and illegal gambling dens had a reputation, albeit in the past was rife. Was this current situation going to bring it back to life once more? It was hard for the officers assembled at the briefing to contemplate such a bizarre situation. They were to a man, of the new breed of detectives and unable to think even remotely like criminals. Mike watched them as they glanced at each other in disbelief. They had assembled at the briefing to establish how the two murder investigations were progressing. Here then on top of that, the possibility of corruption and not just any old corruption, actual police corruption. "Okay, a little information for you here. Take one fictitious copper, let's call him copper **A**. Gets a bit behind with his bills and rent etc. His bank will lend him only so much, but usually, never enough to pull him out of the shit lake where he stands with the slurry up to his neck." Somebody murmured,

"Copper **A** would do well to avoid the devil shooting past in his speed-boat." Supressed laughter and giggles.

"May I remind you gentlemen," Mike cut in, "this is a double murder inquiry coupled with possible police corruption." Silence fell over the room once again. "As I was about to explain. Copper **A** decides he knows of a quick fix. Let's imagine there are at least two or three gambling dens on his beat.

"It's a given that any-one connected with the dens will have clocked him as he passed by on his beat. You just never know these days, what they would or could be thinking, one day he might actually come in wearing his civvies. Copper **A** doesn't want let them know he is a serving officer. Oh, but they would know, wouldn't they? But perhaps best not to let him know, that they know he's old Bill. So, in he goes, nobody so much as looks up. He creeps over to the bar for a beer and the gambling dens mechanism kicks into gear. A young lady escort already at the bar befriends him, which is phase one of the plans. Copper **A** tells the young lady he's a bit of a rookie at the roulette wheel. 'Come on' she says 'I'll give you a few tips.' Having bought some low value chips from the dens cashier, said young lady walks with him to the roulette table, discreetly winking at the croupier as they both approach the table. Phase two begins. Copper **A**. loses his first two or three bets-all part of the plan, then begins to win and win big. His new-found lover squeals in delight as he keeps winning. This is amazing thinks copper **A**. At the end of the evening, having come into the den with a tenner, he's trousered the best part of fifty quid almost but not quite enough to clear his rent and bill debts. Back he goes within a week. Phase three. Same bird, same croupier. Now he's starting to get greedy. This time the winnings fraudulently go up a notch. This is too good to be true; he thinks. Fifty quid last week. This week more nearer a hundred. So, instead of banking it he splashes it, saving just enough stake money for his next visit to the spieler.

Phase four. That's odd he thinks as he starts losing, and losing heavily. It's then that the management step in and allow his gambling debts to mount up. 'Of course, you can, your good for it son,' says the management, 'Good customer good for the loan.' In no time, he's back in debt up to his neck again. This time, due to who he owes the money to he's beginning to sweat like a race horse. Sooner or later, copper **A** is asked to step in the manager's office. They offer him a way out. No violence necessary my son. Copper **A** is told they know he's a copper and he is now firmly in their grip. His only way out of the gambling debt run up to the den is to pass police information back that might be of use to the gambling den he frequented and for others owned by the same firm."

Shocked and amazed at the devious criminal mind, the assembled team sat and listened for what was coming next. Only one of them spoke up and asked,

"So, if perhaps the information passed to the gambling den was either false or in fact it simply dried up, do you think sir, that this is the reason he was found dead by the side of the Thames? Couldn't or wouldn't pay up, mistakenly thinking, that being a copper he was in some way protected?"

"It's the line we should be working on, yes."

"As this is now highly sensitive stuff from us in this room at least, there has to be a total news black-out. The Chief Super will be solely responsible for any press releases, which will be as limited as possible. Right, let's get to work. Find out as much as possible about all the gambling dens and cheap spielers between here and the West End. Let's see who's who in these so-called clubs. Who owns what? I want a list and their management teams and who they report to. Who are the big boys behind the scenes pulling the strings? Because you can bet your bottom dollar it will be someone at the very top who will have put a contract out on Halliwell. Franks murder is right up there regarding investigations as to his murderer. That is all chaps. Next briefing two days from now at 0800 hrs. Let's get weaving."

Code of Omerta.

Long bursts of machine gun fire blazed, bringing true and unimaginable fear to those who happened to be on the wrong end of the three bullet blasting barrels. Eddie's men were blasting away, making a fine mess of the pub's interior. It was ruthless. No pity or compassion for any of Sullivan's men currently huddled on the floor in a corner of the pub. At best, all they could do was watch and wait for death. They had no fire power to retaliate with, no ability to defend themselves, caught like rabbits in a torch beam, they froze, not daring to go up against these characters. Not five minutes before the furore they were discussing retribution for Dave Conti. Not only is he knocking off Reg's new bride, he had the audacity to get the better of his boys, beating the fuck out of them mostly in the confines of a car. Apparently cosh man was doing a short stay in hospital. Prostate and his mate had simultaneously retired themselves from the gang.

The atmosphere in the pub suddenly turned toxic. In walked three heavies, all wearing long black Crombie style coats. Reg looked up and was the first of his group to move, he instinctively smelt danger. As he slipped out of the door that led to garden at the rear of the pub, he told his men to stand firm. Reg's men had little idea of who these three tough looking men in Crombie's were. What they did know however was that things were looking decidedly dodgy; they began to edge towards the same door that Reg just exited through. Mel moved to bar their way; he made his intentions meaningful by waving the machine gun in the direction of the now extremely worried group of Sullivan's henchmen. The pub door leading to the garden was bolted shut.

Mel turned around exposed the Sterling machine gun from its hiding place inside his Crombie, raised the machine gun barrel to knee level pointing it towards Sullivan's finest. He flipped off the safety and fingered the trigger. As far as these boys were concerned it could go off at any moment. Fearing imminent danger hands began to go above shoulder height. Tools of their trade started to clatter on the floor, Mel mimicked a kicking motion meaning for them to kick the hardware over to Mel that currently lay at their feet. Whilst this little play was playing out Johnny the Turk was busy ushering everybody else outside and told to stand well clear. "Might even be a good idea to wander off home and stay well out of the way." He was talking almost at a whisper. No panic in his voice, almost as if he was saying nice goodbyes to a bunch of happy party goers.

This included the Pubs manager and his staff. Once the decks were cleared of innocents all three simultaneously raised their machine-guns and opened fire. The noise was enough to wake Satan himself. Instantly Reg's boys hit the floor hands over ears in an attempt to block out the terrible destructive noise. In a closed environment such as they were in the eardrum-splitting noise was amplified ten-fold. A full magazine per each machine gun was sprayed around the pub. Huge damage was inflicted. When the firing finally stopped, silence descended at least for those that didn't have loud ringing in their ears.

All three shooters removed little plastic ear plugs and dumped them on the floor. It was now time for Johnny to bring to the attention of the rabble still laying on the floor, the reason for this visit. Slowly they picked themselves up off the floor banging their ears to rid themselves of the ringing. Some slumped into any remaining undamaged chairs in complete shock. Johnny spoke. "Our boss Eddie Coleman is not a happy bunny. Any further attempts to highjack any one of his team and I mean anyone, for any reason, will face serious consequences.

"We expect you to keep to the code and keep your mouths shut tight as a duck's arse, especially to the filth. You tell that to your boss; Reg Sullivan and tell him this, you don't come after us, we don't come after you.

"Now, clear the place, walk out don't run. We have people outside to make sure you leave in an orderly fashion. Now go, go on fuck off the lot of you." Dutifully the men walked out as if nothing happened, leaving the tools of their trade at Mel's feet. Next on the list was Eddie's final request to be carried out on his behalf. Dave Conti, obligingly found a bottle of Whiskey that had escaped the onslaught, he poured the contents all over the bar and set light to it. Whoosh, the flames from the ignited alcohol burned fiercely. Dave threw some table cloths onto the flames together with a batch of the Sunday papers that were there for the customers to read whilst enjoying a pint. Well, they fucking well wont now thought Dave.

138

The fire caught some soft furnishings and nearby net curtains alight. Flames beginning to take a hold reaching up the walls. Satisfied that the torching was well underway Johnny signalled to the others, it was time to leave. Machine guns were returned to their hiding places, inside the Crombie coats and the three of them strolled casually to the waiting Daimler. Wossname, knew the drill.

He made sure the guns were stowed in the boot, all his comrades seated comfortably then gently and quietly drove off. Nobody in the Daimler spoke. A mile or so down the road Wossname having spotted the plume in his rear-view mirror, reported seeing a pall of black smoke emanating from where they had just come from. Nobody made any attempts to speak.

The job was a good one once again proving that planning paid dividends. A few miles further on Johnny asked Wossname to drive up to the City, hang a left and drive slowly across Tower Bridge. By the time they got there night was on them. Traffic was light a couple of London busses passed in the opposite direction half empty lights blazing out of the windows. A single black cab was to their rear. Johnny told Wossname to stop the car halfway across.

The cabbie behind hooted in disgust driving very slowly round the stopped Daimler. As he passed, Mel and Dave casually walked to the back of the Daimler opened the boot grabbed the machine guns and threw them over the side of Bridge. The cabbie obliged by looking the other way, wife and kids to support, he rehearsed his speech to the police in the unlikely event of him being questioned. Me guv. No guv. Saw nothing guv. Guns guv? Pull the other one guv, it's got bells on it. Honest guv, I saw nothing.' Down they went, on into the waters below.

It was all over in a matter of seconds, back in the car Mel and Dave breathed a sigh of relief. It was one thing to be arrested for travelling in the back seat of a hookey Daimler.

Quite another thing to be nicked for carrying machine guns around. Especially those that had just been used in a major shoot out. Hainault to the City was only 12 miles or so, an immediate connection would be put together. All four of them would have had the Hainault raid pinned on them.

Without the machine guns however, it might be a bit harder for the old Bill to do so. Just then Johnny informed Wossname that he was to drop him, and the others off at The Oasis. "Drive the Daimler over to Creekmouth."

"No worries Johnny, what's the story there then."

"Think about it Wossname, a pub in Hainault shot up to fucking kingdom come, then torched.

"The people hanging around rubber necking the show probably couldn't get in touch with the old Bill quick enough, probably the papers too if they've got any sense.

"Three hoodlums strolling to a waiting Daimler, shoving machine guns in the boot, and driving off without so much as look backwards or a bye or leave. The reg of your beloved Daimler will be circulating quicker than a Black Mamba strikes its prey. It's got to be crushed at Errol's place. The guys at Creekmouth are expecting you so no dilly dallying. Errol will be there too. If you ask him nicely, he might drive you over to West Ham." Johnny then spoke to Dave.

"Lift a Bentley tonight mate, get it over to Creekmouth pronto, cause the boys are waiting around for you too. As soon as you deliver they will get to work on it and turn it around within 24 hours."

"Wossname, you pick it up when you get the nod from Errol. It will be all kosher proper paper work and all that shit. Drive straight over to The Oasis and pick Eddie up, he wants to have a butcher's hook at the pub 'that was' in Hainault."

Narrow Escape.

Johnny the Turk couldn't have been nearer the truth when he warned Wossname about the filth jumping on the pub shooting sharpish like, spot on he was in fact. Following the shootout then the torching of the pub, Hainault nick was besieged with 999 calls. On duty police at the station immediately alerted neighbouring stations. Twenty or so coppers from various stations screamed over to the pub now burning furiously. It was way out of control. The fire service collectively, and based on the information phoned in from the public saw fit to dispatch a number of pumps to the fire from a number of stations. They, having tried to keep the fire contained and couldn't, decided to let it burn out.

The fire officer in charge of all engines and pumps on site, due to the pub being a stand-alone building, with no neighbouring properties, plus fearing for his firemen's lives, took the decision to let it burn. The police of course were severely pissed off as most if not all evidence was now being bar-b-qued right in front of their eyes. All they would be able to do once the fire burnt itself out would be to sift through the ashes. They would not be allowed anywhere near the place until the chief fire officer was satisfied the fire was utterly and completely out with no danger to the police who would need to begin searching for evidence. This could and frequently happened on a regular basis and of course frustrated the police no end. Large numbers of onlookers, some with camping chairs to sit on gathered, albeit kept well out of harm's way. One chap who was a bit of a short arse brought along a pair of decorator's steps in order to get a better view.

They were all held back behind the red, 'Do Not Cross' tape running from tree to lamp post to tree again, then on to other helpful places to wind the tape around.

Following the instructions from an attending Sergeant, uniformed officers now present started to question individuals standing in the 'on lookers' audience hoping for information that might lead to an arrest or two. When the officers checked their gathered statements with others also taking statements established instead of a pattern emerging, they discovered wildly differing eye witness statements. One witness statement read there was eight of them, another said three. Another eye witness statement read the getaway car was definitely a Mercedes another said it was a Ford.

Yet another read thus, 'the gang used hand grenades which blew out the pub windows.' Another said shotguns were used over and over again. However, the police will at some stage, be in a strong position to dispel the grenade and shotgun theories.

Eventually, scene of the crime officers will discover the empty shell cases amongst all the ashes and will no doubt, firmly point proceedings towards machine guns being employed, thereby, ruling out once and for all hand grenades and shotguns. Loads of differing versions about what had occurred that afternoon trickled through.

One thing was common though, all eye witness statements had the car registration written down correctly. Some on the back of their hands, others on bits of paper, one on the back of a bus ticket! The registration number was very quickly circulated along with the possible make of car.

Meanwhile, Wossname having dropped off his companions at The Oasis was making his way over to Creekmouth in order to dump the Daimler. Purposefully, he avoided where possible any main roads preferring to slink around the back doubles well off old Bill's radar. A mile or so from Creekmouth a cop car flew by, he expected them to pull to their left thereby cutting off the road ahead. He'd already primed himself to do a runner, especially if they jumped out tooled up.

The cops on board the passing squad car were obviously on the hunt for a Mercedes or Ford first and registration second, although Wossname was not to know of this bit of information.

On they raced past him and on down the road, the smirking and giggling Wossname might have been a bit of a give-away but the cops as far as they were concerned, were not looking for a Daimler. Within seconds the squad car was long gone. Wossname by now was approaching the breakers yard gates. They swung open on his arrival, he and Daimler deftly disappeared behind the 12-foot-high wooden gates, safe and sound.

At a signal from one of Errol's boys Wossname jumped out and made his way to Errol's static caravan which doubled up as his yard office. In a matter of minutes, he heard the screaming uncomfortable sound of metal scraping against metal. He turned to see a giant fork lift truck with extended forks lifting the Daimler, wooden steering wheel and all, lifting it across the yard towards the waiting hungry crusher.

He closed his eyes tight; he simply could not witness such a lovely motors death roll in the crushing machine. Soon it would be an anonymous block of metal like so many other anonymous metal-blocks, scattered around Errol's yard cubed up, ready to be melted down.

With his back to the demise of the Daimler he whispered an epitaph to his dying friend 'So long Pal, hope you get to drive the big man round his Kingdom in the clouds.' News in the underworld spread like wild fire. It was none too often; one gang shoots up another then sets fire totally destroying a favoured haunt let alone used as target practice. Two reputations were hit fast one negative the other positive. Reg Sullivan's days were now numbered his decent from a position of power was a little short of spectacular, He'd suffered a humiliating defeat and what's more he'd scarpered leaving his men to face the music and subsequent machine guns. Shirley his cheating wife, was utterly disgusted at his cowardly exit leaving the men in his employ to stand tall and face off the shooters. She of course threatened to leave him but only if it should become a regular occurrence. Since the enormous and humiliating defeat in Hainault, most of Sullivan's men drifted away from his gang looking for other employers in the same line of business, telling their tales as to why they had departed from the craven fucking coward into the bargain. Some even knocked on Eddie's door. Things were not looking good for Reg. However, in Eddie's corner things improved no end. The raid at Hainault was going down in East End ganglands history. Eddie was becoming a notorious ruthless legend in his own lifetime.

More and more would-be gangsters from the East Ends criminal fraternity began to migrate in the direction of The Oasis. Eddie had the pick of blokes with varying GCE's in varying criminal skills. Of interest to Eddie, even more than skills offered, was respect and loyalty. If these two elements were in place then by all means let's talk. As the numbers grew, so did Eddie's area of criminal activities. The original idea of just working on the Isle-of-Dogs, his home patch was long gone. Greed and hunger for notoriety blinded Eddie to the possibility of ever being extinguished by other gangs.

Board Meeting at The Oasis.

Johnny, Mel, Billy, Dave and Wossname were consulted. A late-night get-together at The Oasis was convened. As usual, Bomber sat in. Esme and Rosie shared the duties of bringing the beers downstairs, Esme more often than Rosie, emptying the ashtrays as well as manning the busy bar. Eddie thanked all those present. He took a little time to look round the table and looked from face to face, these men were his most trusted. He would listen to all and any suggestions they came forward with, which were then to be fully debated. Eddie spoke.

"We don't want any fucking mob breathing down our necks, all agreed?" Nods all round. "Anyone here heard anything, even the tiniest little whisper about any of them getting edgy about us?" Heads shaking from side to side all round. "Anyone here got any ideas how we get to the next level without pissing off the really big boys. Wossname was the first to speak.

"Why Eddie, what's the matter with what we're doing, it's only the same as them, ain't it?"

"How's the Bentley Wossname?"

"Gotter admit Eddie, it's a fucking diamond. Knocks spots off the Daimler. To think, I was sorry to see it go."

"Pissing off the really top firms' mate might well see the Bentley pushed into the canal on fire with you locked in it and that's just for starters." Dave chipped in with,

"I had heard, mind you it was some time ago, Sullivan and his team were treading on a few East End toes. So, we might be might be okay just by basically putting Reg out to grass."

"Don't see it Dave still you could have a point, might be an idea to pick up on it. Bang a few drums, ask around see if what you're telling me, has some substance. Just don't strong it, Dave keep your fists in your pockets.

"Ask only people you know and trust. The boxing gym you go to might be a good place to start."

"Johnny what's your thoughts?" Johnny the Turk looked at Billy and Mel, true Stratford boys through and through.

"I think, if we want to grow the crew's activities, we may well want to look in the direction of Essex. By that I mean East of Romford. We've got the warehouse in Basildon filling up fast with guitars and stuff. It may be a bit of a trek but there's places like Southend with all the amusement arcades that might chip in for protection. Plenty of Seaside pubs that might do the same, got to be gambling dens we can get on the books too." Billy and Mel usually quite passive with unmoving eyes and unmoving facial features, visibly grimaced. The body language was not lost on Eddie. He spoke directly to the Stratford's usually, non-caring villains.

"You two are doin a blindin job with the car lots. Errol says profits are well up and that's each and every one of em, and so is ours profits as a consequence.

"That spanking you handed out definitely sent a message to all of Errol's car front managers. According to Errol no more skimming and no more shady deals on the side are happening. We need to find other car lot owners that can do with your type of help and consideration; for a bob or two of course. Get the word out and see if you can recruit any. A bonus for them might be that Errol can supply a regular dose of done up cut and shuts at very reasonable rates. If you get a sniff of the serious mobs at any time, give it a miss.

"Secondly go and see those Cherry Boys you banged about a bit recently. See if they are still operating find out what they are up to then just take it over. Tell them, they're under our protection. Offer them a small percentage you keep the rest put it in your sky rockets. Use iron bars to negotiate with if necessary." This was a major step up for Billy and Mel and well they knew it, he gambled it would bind them in to his crew even further. Bit like moving up from privates to sergeants.

"What you want me to do Eddie?" asked Wossname. Eddie turned to face him.

"First off, take over from Mel and Billy the protection of the shop on the Isle-of-Dogs. Go and see Mrs Sharif and explain to her you're taking over. Make sure each time you go; you take the Bentley and stick it right outside her shop. It'll act as a beacon and send out a message. Be nice to her two boys. Keep a shooter on you at all times.

"If you get a hint of trouble get Billy and Mel to deal with it, don't fuck it up cos it's a nice little earner. While your there have an ask around about Lenny the Scrotes known associates, we still need to sort out the two of them that were involved with the shop break in.

"When you find them go really fucking noisy on 'em. Knock 'em to the ground if necessary, then bring them here to me for a littler chat. When you've done that slip down to Basildon and do a bit of a stock take on what's coming in. We need to get that Southender out and about flogging to bands and stuff, is all that okay with you Wossname mate?" Wossnames eye widened. His chest expanded, he thought he might yell out with bottled up frustration mixed in with bubbly joy. One minute he's just a bleedin driver, next minute a full-time part of the wossname, with acceptable aggro thrown in. This indeed was a leg up for him.

"Yes boss." He almost saluted. That was Wossname sorted thought Eddie. He knew for some time he was pissed off and he knew he was taking a big chance getting him to carry out these duties, but time would tell.

He was assured however that Wossname could and would lean on the boys in the event of any major trouble. "Johnny, Wossname will drive you down to Southend. When you're there have a scout round to test the water, not literally. See how many of the amusement arcades can be gently forced into a protection scheme. Let's get some numbers together and add them up later.

"If it looks good then we'll get Dave here to go back down with you to put the frighteners on and start collecting the readies. Its seasonal, best get started right away. You okay with that Dave? I recon the two of you will make a right fucking menacing pair. As with Billy and Mel taking on the Cherry boy's activities, if you find someone else is in there and already at it, find them, do 'em and take over. If you need a small army, recruit from upstairs, go back and lay every one out. Any questions?" Silence all round.

"Esme," he shouted. "Beers all round, upstairs and down here." Eddie winked at Bomber who sat stony faced.

"Bomber, see Johnny, he will cover the costs."

"No worries Eddie, just didn't want a repeat of the scooter boys, you know all pissed up looking for aggro." Eddie smiled,

"Your right Bomber. To put your mind at rest listen to this, most of the bloke's upstairs are trying to get into our crew, you couldn't be better protected if you paid for it."

Just at that moment a cheer could be heard as Esme informed that all present was to get a beer on Eddie Coleman. "It's a down payment Bomber, a down payment for future free services."

Bomber returned back up to the bar amid cheers and whistles. The remainder of Eddie's inner circle drifted off. Their minds firmly fixed on their new duties. *Right,* thought Eddie. *That's the troops sorted.* He too drifted upstairs to the bar. Moving over to one of the occupied alcove seats, as he approached, it rather quickly became un-occupied.

Three young men dutifully picked up their half-drunk pints then made their way over to the bar. Eddie nodded his appreciation. Once sat down, Esme who was standing nearby said, "What's it to be then Mr Coleman?" He looked up sharply to see her cheeky grin, her eyes sparkling behind those thinly gold rimmed circular glasses.

"You avin a giraffe Miss Wren?" he replied.

"Certainly not, sir. Now what's it to be?" she whispered, "a glass of whiskey or my body?"

Eddie's mind raced back to when they were last between the sheets. He felt the sap rising and said, "I'll have both please and bring a drink over for yourself. I've got a feeling that you might like to join me."

"Certainly sir," she produced a little note book and wrote in it.

"So, that's one large whiskey for you, a Babycham for me, followed by a night of naked lust for us both." Eddie was taken aback. He was not then and never would be, comfortable with women being a bit previous. Keeping up the charade though, he said with a broad smile.

"Put it on my account miss." Esme disappeared back over to the bar, just before she left to get the drinks, she popped a folded note that she'd written on the table in front of Eddie. He picked it up, wondering what comes next, it read, *'Darling, please fuck me senseless tonight, all night. Your Esme.'*

Eddie took a long look at Esme who was by now leaning over the bar requesting the drinks from Bomber. He thought she was probably telling Bomber that she would be leaving soon. Eddie eyed her legs, then moved his eyes up to her pert little bottom and thought, *enough! This little minx is romancing me, seducing me, driving me to distraction. I will have to make this night, the last night…well, perhaps.*

The Chase.

Wossnames breathing came in gasps and rasps. There was no way he was going to keep ahead of the pack. A group of six young men calling themselves 'Razors' due to cut-throat razors being their preferred weapons, were almost upon him. Exposed wicked looking blades flashing intermittently as the chasing pack ran below each street light in pursuit of their quarry. Wossname heard one them shout, "Come 'ere you fucking turd." *On your bloody bike*, thought Wossname. As if he was going to respond to a polite request like that! A little earlier in the day as requested by Eddie he popped into see Mrs Sharif. He explained everything and she seemed pleased that the protection cover was to continue.

Mrs Sharif served tea and Peak Frean bickies, Wossnames favourites, introduced her two sons, then paid the weekly stipend for continuation of Eddie's protection service. All was well. Wossname said his goodbyes and wandered out to the waiting Bentley. To his horror, the car had been attacked. Paint stripper or something close to it was busy stripping paint off the bonnet and roof. Wing mirrors dangled from their original mountings. The car would have been drivable but for the two front tyres being slashed.

Eddie will not like this he thought. *Eddie will not like this one little bit. What did Eddie say? In case of any trouble, get hold of Mel and Billy. Fuck that, I've only just been promoted. No way am I going to run to them. I can deal with this, any-how Errol can put all this right. Or, Dave can nick a replacement. Nah, I can sort this.*

He looked around for any likely culprits. The mistake he made was underestimating the seriousness of the situation confronting him. He really should have twigged; this was no school boy prank.

That which also should have come to mind, if the damage was not inflicted by school boys, odds on it could well be young local hoodlums. And if it was young hoodlums, they would know that Wossname and the Bentley might have belonged to Eddie Coleman. Knowing this would they have been willing and prepared to stamp on Eddie Coleman's toes, the architect of the Hainault pub demolition, in such a fashion?

Indeed, metaphorically kick him right up the arse. It should have dawned on Wossname, this was a trap. He knew part of his new job spec; was to track down two of Lenny's mates. The two that along with Lenny done over the Sharif's. Lenny the Scrote was still in hospital thanks to the attentions of Mel and Billy. More importantly Lenny had kept his trap shut, therefore the Old Bill were no further forward with a potential arrest. Lenny's two accomplices on that fateful night, now thought they were untouchable and invincible. In a way, in their eyes the fact that Mr Sharif had died during the shop break-in, had elevated them to a pair of murderers. Better still, as of yet, unconvicted murderers.

Their tiny minds turned these thoughts over and over till it convinced them to start up their own gang. Word got around about the boys being murderers. This was too much for other hoodlums living nearby to hold back and not to join them with a view for an imminent dose of retribution regarding Lenny being done over by the Stratford two.

Between them a plan was set. They were all to a hoodlum, more than aware that Billy and Mel were responsible for Lenny's hospital vacation and knew also they visited Mrs Sharif's shop once a week in order to deter further break-ins or any other such aggravation.

One Razor gang member was ordered to hang loose close to Mrs Sharif's shop to time the Strafford Boy's visits. This was done for no particular reason, other than to see if the pattern changed. All of the Razor gang members which now numbered fifteen on and off depending on school hours feared the Stratford two and rightly so. Billy and Mel's reputation for sheer unadulterated violence was becoming very well known.

Today however, a different car arrived with only one bloke getting out. Making his way over the grass verge to the shop and whistling as he sauntered in to see Mrs. S. The lookout couldn't believe his eyes, if this guy was here instead of the Stratford two, it would even things up nicely. Although he was a big fucker bit dopey looking too, six or seven against one seemed fair enough.

He legged it back to the flat that was deputising as the Razors den and reported back to his superiors. A group of half a dozen hoodlums were mobilised. Most of them shitting themselves at the thought of aggro for real, instead of just sitting around pretending they were hard arses to each other all day and night.

Cut-throat razors were pocketed paint stripper, previously purchased from Mrs Sharif's was grabbed as they exited the flat on the 13th floor.

Below them over by Mrs Sharif's shop it looked to be mostly deserted. It was not its usual busy-self. Did the locals sense a problem was looming? Why were they staying away? Birds disappear from the sky when a storm is due.

Similarly, people in the East End did the same. Disappeared if trouble was smelt in the in the air. They had been there before, so it was, get back home proto and draw the curtains. If they saw nothing, they could legitimately say the same to old Bill. The gang of Razor hoodlums piled into the lift on the 13th floor and spilled out at the entrance lobby.

Casually, they made their way across the grass rectangle, to where the Bentley was parked up on the opposite side of the road.

A lookout was sent to keep an eye out by the doorway of the shop, with instructions to let the others know when the big guy who was spotted earlier, was on his way out. The gang quickly went to work on the Bentley, pouring the paint stripper on the long and wide bonnet then across the gleaming roof, slashing tyres and generally kicking the fuck out of it. A at signal from one of the two might have been murderers and they moved back to the entrance area in the block of flats across the way and hooded up. They could just see from their vantage point the Bentley and above its roof, the entrance to Mrs Sharif's shop. Twenty minutes passed and by now the paint stripper had done a superb stripping job.

Some of the lads were silently wishing they were somewhere else. Scared glances were exchange by some of the younger members.

It wouldn't do though to back out now and be branded a rank coward. Worse still branded a yellow scaredy-cat, banned from the Razor gang for life. At last, Wossname exited the shop, all casual like still whistling. Pleased how it had gone with Mrs. Sharif. The hoodlum's lookout sauntered along behind him, walking in the same direction about ten feet or so back. The trap as far as the waiting Razor gang were concerned, was now set. Wossname took a look at the Bentley. He yelped, "Shit a brick, what's happened here then!" He was alone. The Bentley was wrecked and as usual, he was unarmed.

'Bollocks, why do I always leave my fucking shooter at home'. Too late now. The gang member behind him overheard and smiled inwardly. This is gonna go well, he decided. Wossname sensed rather than saw people charging towards him across the grass from the block of flats, some waving nasty looking cut-throat razors. Spinning round to face them, Wossnames blood ran cold.

A group of hooded young thugs were heading his way, joined now by the lookout charging up from behind. This one yelled out to his mates, "No guns on him, get stuck in." They were closing fast; his options were about as good as none. No way was he going to nip back into Mrs Sharif's shop and bolt the door, and no way was he about to stand his ground, despite his size and girth. The only option left was to run, Wossname sadly, was no sprinter. For sure the shouts and yells behind him screaming, "Let's cut him," helped him on to an unaccustomed and hitherto unknown level of speed. But there was no way he was going to keep it up for very long. The other bit of poor planning; Wossname was in unfamiliar territory. He should have visited the area previously, done the knowledge so to speak in case just a situation as this one took place. The Razors however were on home ground and knew every twist and turn of the area. At a crossroad, three of them branched off and used the alleyways to circle round in order to trap their quarry. Wossname still running, was fast running out of steam. He saw up ahead what he thought was another three of them standing in his path, waiting menacingly, hoodies up, scarves covering their lower faces Razors held at arm's length towards him. Just at that moment the chasing pack was on him. He stopped breathless, hands on knees gasping for oxygen, head lowered down, reminiscent of a marathon runner who had completed the distance, just.

The shop was a good one hundred yards plus back, a length Wossname only ever ran once before; and that was during his school days. He looked around to see if any of the locals might helpfully intervene. Sadly, they had all gone to ground.

Front doors were slamming shut, followed by bolts being rammed into place. Houses on both sides of the street developed a serious bout of twitchy net curtains. Others had their main curtains rapidly fully drawn. He thought this a bit strange although it was twilight, it was only six o'clock in the evening.

A low brick wall at the end of someone's garden fronting on to the pavement, provided him with somewhere to sit down. A semi-circle of hooded hoodlums' scarves up to cover their faces, glared down at him. They all seemed reluctant to carry out their 'cut him' threats.

Nobody wanted to make the first move, Wossname took this opportunity to reason with them. "Listen, I work for Eddie Coleman, touch me and believe me he will fuck you up one by one."

"What happened to Scrote…" Searing pain. That's as far as he got, at the mention of Lenny the Scrote a cut-throat razor made deep slashing contact.

Wossname felt a stinging sensation to his leg several inches above his left knee, within seconds, another stinging sensation to the side of his head then another on his shoulder, then another and another. In all five deep razor wounds were inflicted, although he didn't know it, he was screaming like a piglet caught up in a rogue abattoir. The hooded hoodlums having finished the job, decided to scatter, have away on their toes. As far as they were concerned Lenny had got his revenge by their hands.

Wossname, now bleeding profusely from the number of deep wounds inflicted, managed to crawl on his hands and knees a little way back towards Mrs Sharif's shop, managing only some twenty yards or so before passing out, then finally collapsing face down, half over the kerb and half over the grass verge. If suitable help had been on hand to administer first aid, he might, just might have made it. However, help was not forthcoming, Wossname was no more. He bled to death in a matter of minutes down in the gutter. His life blood running through the metal grill of a convenient council installed drain.

Two of the gang hived off from the main bunch of runners. On reaching Millwall's Den it was decided they had run far and fast enough. So, they carried on at a semi fast walking pace, de-hooded and de-scarved. The taller of the two said, "We wade in slash the poor fucker, and what do we get from the boss, not so much as a bye your leave, kiss your arse, or even thanks."

"I know, I know, it's expected of us, but still, your right," the shorter one replied,

"What the fuck have we done? If that geezer we slashed really is part of Coleman's set up, we're dead, history, finished. Think I'll go and stay with my aunt in Chelmsford for a bit."

The taller one said, "Good idea, I'd do the same, but I haven't got any aunties, or uncles for that matter." Neither of the two realised what serious trouble they were in. Apart from the police doing local door to door enquiries then launching a gang hunt, they would all be also hunted down by Eddie's Crew and beaten with iron bars, tortured, maimed then possibly murdered. The shorter one asked,

"How did it make you feel slashing that big guy?"

The taller one replied, "It made me feel like ten men."

"Eh!" said his companion. "Yea, nine dead and one dying." Not what you would call a rosy hoodlums future. To their horror, they were informed by the morning headlines that were splashed across the papers *'Gangland Murder on the Island. Five Hooded Youths Sought'* Under the banner headline the story continued. *'This was a brazen and brutal murder in broad daylight, in a normally quiet housing estate, on the Isle-of-Dogs. According to a police statement released last night, exhaustive questioning on a house-to-house basis local to the murder scene, no persons had anything to say about the awful murderous activities taking place within yards of their homes. However, the police are convinced arrests are imminent.'*

No Comment.

Police activity in the East End of London was at an all-time high. Two policemen murdered, one at Stratford Nick, the other supposedly stabbed and dumped into the Thames. A possible gangland revenge murder of a young man found dead on the Isle-of-Dogs. A pub in Hainault shot to pieces with machine guns then burnt to the ground. Potential police corruption within known gambling dens. Police colleagues in West London dealing with a spate of quality cars being stolen, along with two major jewellery raids.

All this on top of normal day to day police activities such as house break-ins, road traffic accidents, school crossings, traffic duties and the occasional cat stuck up a tree. The press was having a field day, they had never known activity at this level for quite some time. It didn't help things for the police very much either as most, if not all the reported crimes had yet to culminate in arrests. One of the Red Tops had decided to rub the police noses in it, by printing a daily count.

As in *'Day **Seven**, Still No Nearer to Solving Hatful of Crimes.'* The Chief Inspector dealing with press releases was confined mainly to 'No comment. No Questions, we are working on a number of leads etc. etc.' This stirred the press up to point of frenzy. They were not looking for the 'No Comment' comments. Newspaper editors simply couldn't and wouldn't print 'No Comment' at the best of times. Even more so now, what with so many unsolved crimes hanging in the air. Dozens of detectives were drafted in from all around the home counties to help. This of course to begin with, was more of a hinderance.

Local detectives and officers together with other staff currently trying to solve all the various cases, now needed to stop what they were doing and go over the many and fine case details with the seconded officers from out of town. Most of the anti-corruption team were put on stake-outs, usually all-nighters, who sat in their cars freezing their bums off outside selected gambling dens, in and around the East End. It was a particularly tedious task, as they were there to note down who came and went. If anyone of particular interest as in one of their superior officers visit any of the sites under surveillance, they were to be put on individual twenty-four-hour watch. D.I. Mike Bright was subsequently taken off the murder investigations regarding Bullymore and that of Halliwell. Apart from the little or no progress in tracking down the murderers, he himself appeared to be complaining of feeling quite unwell. Inwardly, he was mightily happy at being relieved of his current duties.

Keeping up the pretence of pursuing an unknown murderer was proving to be very difficult for Mike. He knew who killed Sergeant Bullymore.

It was becoming almost too much for him to bear, every time he was called into the Chief Supers office he broke out in a cold sweat and had a bad case if the jibbers. He knew at the time it was wrong to hold key information back.

As days went by however, he actually convinced himself that it was the right and proper thing to do. He'd say to himself, "I must have been mistaken," thereby, essentially blocking out the awful consequences that would befall his career in the Met. A bit like memorising a car number plate then trying to recall the type of car it was attached to. But now it was far too late to confess, far too late indeed. Imagine the mess he would be in if he decided to fess up now! Instant suspension, followed quickly no doubt, by being asked to leave the force without a pension. Withholding vital information much needed to apprehend a killer is a crime in itself, *whoever* is withholding it. Following being dropped from the murder investigations Mike decided that he needed time off to recover his health. All folders and information on the cases so far were to be handed over to his replacement and dutifully they were. Mike was officially signed off for an indefinable period on sick leave.

Just for now, for a while he was at peace with himself. He decided he would spend more time with his family in an attempt to forget about Franks whisperings during his last dying moments. It would however, take much longer for the nightmares to fade away. For the time being Mike could pretend the whispering never happened. With a bit of mind over matter, he might even persuade himself it never actually happened.

His first week at home compared to the working pressure of the last two or so weeks was almost bliss. A day out here and a day out there did wonders for him. But he still endured the nightmares. In his troubling dreams, Mike found himself in the Whispering Gallery inside St Pauls Cathedral. In the dream, the whisperings were shrieked at him, echoing all-round the gallery and leaking out into the surrounding area. Climbing higher and higher in an effort to silence the screaming, he climbed even higher until he was at least thirty metres above the ground below.

The stairs on which he was climbing somehow to him resembled a rickety wooden ladder, the top rung of which had been half sawn through. Mike didn't spot this and missed his footing. He began falling towards the stone flooring way down below.

Looking up above him as he fell, he could see the beautiful carvings on the inside facades of the great dome. As he fell, he gathered speed. The vision of the dome above him whilst floating downward looking up, became blurred. A face appeared instead.

That of Sergeant Bullymore, fountains of blood spraying up either side of the weirdly contorted face looking at him with crimson bulging eyes and mouthing, "Tell them tell them." Mike was falling so fast now; he was preparing himself for the inevitable bone crushing flesh splitting impact below. It was always at this point he would sit bolt upright shaking and sweating all over.

His distraught wife arms round him, cradling him, protecting him, from some unseen horror. Smoothing his brow, gently bringing him back down to earth. "What is it Mike?" Sarah would enquire, he would simply shake his head, unable to unburden himself.

Sarah, for these last two to three weeks felt like she was sleeping next to a person who she didn't know anymore. Almost an interloper a stranger to their bedroom. She harboured thoughts that he might sit her down soon and tell her what he was dreaming of what it was that was so bad, so bad that it was making him shout and scream then suddenly wake in the middle of the night, sweating and shaking. Occasionally after a nightmare episode, Mike would get up get dressed leave the house and walk for miles. Returning only when daylight was filtering through the clouds above the streets of London. The crazy thing was, by day Mike was as he had always been, happy charming a loving husband and great dad for little Leo. Sarah had a chat one morning over a coffee with a close friend.

Hearing what Sarah had to say her friend suggested Mike might need some professional help. Someone capable of getting into Mikes brain and do some re-wiring. "Re-wiring?" enquired Sarah, her friend explained that sometimes the odd cassette in the brain gets a bit tangled up. It needs pulling out rewound the correct way then slotted back into its housing. "Oh, you mean a psychologist."

"That's the ticket love, it'll be a devil of a job to get him to agree. You will have to use a bit of blackmail. Something like, if you want our marriage to survive you have to go and find professional help. The trick is once you've sown the seed let him find a professional himself. He needs to go voluntarily actually wanting and needing for any course paid for, to work. If you press gang him into it, it's not going to work. He needs to think this is actually his idea." Sarah sat staring at her cold untouched coffee. She needed to let this advice from her close friend sink in, she asked, "Do you know of such a professional?"

"Of course, my lovely. Me and the husband had several sessions with a lady psychologist over at Seven Kings near Ilford. Very discreet she was.

Handled the old man's problems a treat."

"And what were they?" Sarah asked.

"Oh, come on now Sarah, I've told you too much already, so I'm definitely not going to tell you about his bed wetting.

"Oh bollocks, he will kill me if he knew you know." They both giggled like little girls in the playground. "Seriously though," said Sarah. "How does a psychologist sort something like that out by some re-wiring? Surely a doctor could have given him some pills or something."

"Well, listen to this," said Sarah's friend. "It all dated back to his childhood, as a young boy. Once she had established which cassette needed attention the childhood one, bingo pissing the bed stopped overnight."

"And when did this all happen," enquired Sarah.

"Couple of years ago."

"Fingers, legs and eyes crossed, never a reoccurrence. No more plastic sheets under the bed sheet no more nappies for the old man, bliss!"

"Well, that's it then, when you can let me have her details? I will have a chat with her, and will have to think of a way to put her name in Mikes frame so to speak."

"I suppose once the idea has sunk in with, him he might take the bait, I could get you to drop her name into the conversation next time you come over to pick Leo up."

"Will do my lovely, now let's get some more coffee these two are stony cold, my shout this time."

Missing.

Eddie Coleman sat sipping his morning cuppa down in the dungeon. Esme brought it down with a couple of the days papers for Eddie to read. "By the way Esme, have you seen Wossname today yet? I need a ride to Errol's over at Creekmouth, said he wants to see me about a new line of business. Frankly I think we've got plenty enough going on right now. Johnny can ride with me. On the way he can tell me how he got on down at the coast."

"Can't say I have seen him, last thing I heard, he was driving over to Mrs Sharif's shop to collect the weekly, then locate Lenny the Scrotes two absent mates and bring them back here for you to have a chat with them."

"Christ, I hope he hasn't fucked the job up."

"See what you can find out. I'll give Errol a bell and tell him I'll get over there this afternoon instead." Esme disappeared back upstairs; Eddie's attention was drawn to the Mirror's front-page headline *'Gangland Murder on The Island. Five Hooded Youths Sought.'*

"Bloody hell," he said to no one what's been happening in my backyard? The Island rarely had a story good enough to get into a national paper, sometimes the sports pages maybe specially if Millwall Lions had a good win at home and the fans had torn into the opposition. Eddie screwed his face up in deep thought; trying to piece things together. It would eventually come to him but only sometime later, he would realise that he made a grave mistake in under-estimating the situation regarding Scrote and his two absent shop breaking oppo's. His team of spies recruited from the bar above had not informed Eddie of any possible trouble on the Island especially potential gangland killings.

A murder on the island a missing Wossname, he simply couldn't bring the two facts together. He read on. The story didn't hold back any punches. The reporter reported the unknown victim was knifed to death. His killers, all five of them were still at large. A major manhunt was underway with arrests imminent. *Arrests imminent*, he thought who the fuck are they kidding. The Islanders are well known for the unusually high and wide wall of silence. After finishing the article, he put the paper to one side and slurped at his morning tea, Esme was back at his side again flitting round him, refilling his cup and stirring in two sugars. "Thanks Esme," he said for the second time that morning. "Have a look at this." He shoved the newspaper over towards where Esme was standing.

Esme needed to mask her horror at reading the story, she instantly put two and two together, instantly, instinctively knew who had been killed, not the killers though. "Bloody hell," she remarked. "That's a bit close for comfort. I wonder if Mrs Coleman can throw any light on it."

"Actually, Esme, as it happens, that's an excellent shout. Ring for a cab and I'll pop home and have a chat oh, and find out where the fuck is Wossname, can you."

"Righty ho Eddie, I'll get on it right away." Soon after Eddie left Bomber took a call from Wossnames old man. He was both livid and screaming with agony at the same time. "Who the fuck is this?"

Bomber shouted down the phone. Verbal abuse wasn't even in it. In between loud sobs there was effing and blinding more sobs, more swearing. Bomber was non-plused, he had neither seen the papers reporting the Isle-of-Dogs murder or absolutely no idea as to where Wossname was. Wossnames whereabouts was not his responsibility. Bomber had had enough, he roared down the phone like a beast in the jungle. The tirade coming from Wossnames dad ceased abruptly. After a few seconds of golden silence from both ends, Bomber said, "Calm down, tell me who you are and what you want?"

Wossname's dad explained who he was and that old Bill called on him just this morning and informed him that his son Vince Gander had been murdered. They wanted me to identify the body." More sobs. "I hoped they'd got it all wrong, but no, it was him alright. Next thing there bleeding well questioning me! How was our relationship? Did we have any arguments lately? Did I know who the killers might be? I said—"

"Hold on," Bomber interrupted. "Did you say killers?" Wossnames dad talked over Bomber.

"What the fuck has my son gotten into with your lot?"

Bomber didn't reply, his mind was racing ahead of this conversation, did this guy tell the police that Wossname worked for Eddie Coleman and did he tell the police about The Oasis? Up until now the Oasis was well below the police radar. If this address had been blabbed to the police, they would have field day probably solving several crimes, in one day.

Wossnames dad spoke again a bit calmer this time. "Look mate, I think I know what's running through your mind. I didn't think it would be a good idea to talk about Eddie Coleman nor about The Oasis. If that's why you've gone silent then you lot over there needn't worry."

"If old Bill do come and turn you over, I can assure you it won't have come from me. I think I knew my boy would 'get it' as soon as he told me he was mixed up with yous lot. Thing is, if I spilled to the cops, I wouldn't have your lot to go torture who evers done this thing to my boy."
He slammed the phone down, Bomber called Esme over.

"Wossnames dead!"

"I know," she said.

"Murdered on the Island,"

"I know," she said.

"More than one killer,"

"I know she said."

"Wait a minute," said Bomber. "How the fuck does you know?" narrowing his eyes.

"Are you on old Bill's team or something?" Esme cheeks reddened.

"No," she said softly. "I read it in one of Eddie's newspapers this morning. He showed the story to me. It didn't give the name of the deceased. I just put two and two together."

"Did you tell Eddie?" asked Bomber.

"Not bloody likely, I didn't want to be anywhere near him when finds out its Wossname that got done. You know exploding with rage and all that."

"Where's he disappeared to, then?"

"He's popped home to see if his mum can shed any light on it."

"Oh, so you know."

"Well, I sought of guessed," whispered Esme. "I know. Fucking Wossnames dad knows. And probably Eddie's mum knows."

"But Eddie doesn't! Fuck me, he gonna go stark raving mad, I think I'd better grab a black cab too and get over to his mum's before he does anything stupid. Oh, and don't tell him I said that."

"Good idea Bomber, I can look after the café."

"Okay Esme, make sure you don't let on to anyone else, that includes Billy, Mel, Dave and Johnny if fact no one. Ditch the newspapers from downstairs, don't leave 'em lying about."

Ed let himself in to his home. "Hi Ma, you home?" No answer. His mum kept a works time table pinned to a cork notice board in the kitchen. It would seem he'd narrowly missed her by just ten minutes. She would be half-way to the bus depot by now. No way of knowing which route, she took. He was just about to leave when he noticed a hand-written note tucked into the corner of the living room mirror. It had Eddie scribed on the folded front half. Inside, just a few notes that read as follows. Canteen gossip at the depot points to Scrotes gang. They call themselves Razors now. Talk is, they did for Wossname.

Right at that moment, Bomber appeared on the doorstep the front door was wide open, he could plainly see Eddie was about erupt. Bomber lunged forward and threw his massive bulk at Eddie, gripping him in a bear hug. He squeezed him for all he was worth, Bomber became a human straight jacket pinning Eddy to the spot.

They were now face to face, as close as any two alfa males would want to be. Bomber grimaced but he knew it was the only way to hold Eddie until he calmed down. Eddie let out a blood curdling long, extremely loud scream enough to wake the dead.

The scream was followed up very quickly by, "I'll kill them, I'll kill the fuckers, I'll strip the skin off their fucking faces, I'll kill them one by fucking one. They've got a nasty fucking shock coming their way." For more than a minute or two, Bomber thought Eddie would have a heart attack. *How would he explain that to his mum,* he thought? Instead, Eddie slumped to the floor, a big bag of snot, shit and tears. Bomber took the opportunity to pop into the little kitchen and stick the kettle on. It's what we do he thought in moments of crisis. Behind him, Eddie jumped up and followed him into the kitchen. Opening the cutlery draw he grabbed the biggest kitchen knife and was about to steam out to the road ready to cut the first person innocently passing by like a crazed lunatic on the run from a nut house. Once again, Bomber lunged forward and gripped him.

This time from behind, swearing, cursing and hoping Eddie doesn't use the knife on his hands or arms that were binding him. A major struggle ensued, Eddie was now doing the swearing and cursing. However, the more Eddie struggled the tighter Bombers grip became. Bombers mind was racing Eddie might just turn on him to satisfy his lust for revenge. Here he was almost squeezing the life out of his boss. Eddie had gone ballistic with some blokes for much less.

Sometimes just for them looking at him the wrong way. To Bombers relief, Eddie let the blade point downwards then he slumped to the floor for the second time. On this occasion he stayed where he slumped. Bomber, anxious that he might jump up again, let him lay there for a minute or two. This time no rage, no jumping up, just laying quite still. Bomber gingerly leant down over Eddie's prone, face down body, gently lifting him to a standing position and said in a commanding voice, "Eddie, hand me the blade." As he did so he held out a shovel like hand.

"Sit down and we can talk, but first, a cuppa." The commanding voice had the right effect, Eddie looked around him. He began to surface, to realise where he was.

It was familiar surroundings, his home in Plevna Street, his home and sanctuary. It was where Val his Mum always had a calming effect on him. His mum wasn't there just now but might as well have been. He imagined her scolding him asking him to promise her no violence to be brought to our doorstep. He meekly picked up the knife handing to Bomber, handle first.

At the thought of brutally killing Wossnames murderers, his eyes began to glaze over, as he hummed very quietly his favourite nursery rhyme, "*Half a pound of Tuppeny rice.*"

Island War is Declared.

"Pull everyone in Johnny, send some of the lads from the caffe to go and suss out the lie of the land. I made a mistake underestimating that bunch of slime that topped Wossname. What a bunch of cowards eh, teamed up five or six handed against one." It was a stark reminder of Eddie's school days only much worse. When he was jumped on after the school the worst that would happen, apart from the humiliation was a cut lip, a boot in the guts and possibly a black eye.

Bad enough but this, severely slashed to death by five or six tearaways, all armed with cut-throat razors. "How come Wossname wasn't tooled up?" Eddie asked.

"I specifically told each and every one to stick the guns I give 'em in their shoulder holster and point to it, if and when you think it might frighten idiots like those wankers away. If he was armed, none of this would have happened.

"Those bleedin' hoodies that did him would have shit themselves at the sight of a real weapon and fucked off."

"Get everyone down here in the dungeon, we need to get on a war footing." Johnny shot off to make contact with the necessary faces. Before leaving he deputised a number of the lads upstairs-he had no problems recruiting help. News of Wossnames demise was still very fresh in their minds. Any amount of them were more than willing to be a part of what was about to take place.

Many of them saw this as a golden opportunity to show their worth to Eddie, and in the long run get into the crew proper and on the lucrative payroll. As it happens, the lad's findings over the next few days on the Island would prove to invaluable to Eddie and his knights, as he liked to call them of the round table in the dungeon. Information filtered down like a coffee percolator, down to Eddie's ears. From the info gathered, Eddie now had most of the Razor Gangs names, descriptions and addresses. The lads upstairs have done good. For two solid days, he sat alone at the table staring ahead refusing any type of refreshment, be it beer, teas or comfort from Esme. Most of the money-making machine that was of Eddie's creation was slowly grinding to a halt. News of the brutal slaughter by the Razors was beginning to reach the ears of some of the more notorious gangs in the East End. There was even a hint of help and assistance from one such outfit. Eddie Coleman would need to refuse any helping hands very diplomatically.

This job needed to be sorted by his own hands and his alone, previous issues were capably carried out by Eddie's most trusted. This one however, was his to deal with alone. He'd misjudged the position with the Scrote mob, and he, had put Wossname in the firing line. No, Eddie Coleman was to sort this himself and alone. When Eddie eventually surfaced from his revere having picked over the various bits of info, brought to him via the lads upstairs, people were summoned to The Oasis for a meet. Eddie explained to roars of disapproval that he needed and wanted to avenge Wossnames demise all by himself. Not for status or notoriety simply for personal pleasure. Pleasure of dealing with the scum one by one, leaving the Scrote till last. He had two requests for help from his team.

One, was as much information as possible from the gang of lads recruited by the Turk, as to the daily whereabouts of the Razors and number two, "Best as you can, keep them all on the island.

"Use more of the lads upstairs to create an iron ring. Not to confront or stop anyone, don't want no one else razored. Just monitor to see who scarpers and identify them to me." Eddie requested to be alone again so as to mull over things and how best to make these razor bastards suffer. Very evil thoughts came to mind. Dare he see them through?

Reprisal.

The morning was chilly but bright, lovely early morning sunshine dappled on the still waters of Canary Docks. It was seven o'clock. Two massive ships stood anchored, motionless waiting for many hands to unload their fresh cargo of exotic fruits and bananas brought to England from the Canary Islands, a journey of some fifteen hundred nautical miles from point to point.

Warehouse workers, dock workers, crane drivers and assorted 'day-only' labourers poured into Canary Wharf with one thing on their minds. Get in, get the job done and get down the pub for a couple of jars. Today however was destined not to be a normal day.

161

Information had it that one of the Razor gang regularly turned up at the Canary Docks and applied for a day's work here and a day's work there. It was not always guaranteed that this lad would get work. Various foremen hiring labourers for the day would need perhaps five of six blokes from a crowd of twenty or so who turned up hoping.

The rest might be turned away, it really depended on how much work there was to be done at the dock-side. With two big fully loaded cargo ships there was plenty of work to be done. Today all that turned up for spot work, got it. One of them happened to be Eddie.

His usual fancy garb left at home, today he reverted back to jeans, T-shirt and his old bashed up leather jacket. He blended in well especially with his dads old peaked cloth cap on top of his head. Eddie knew it would be pot luck if he was to be picked today. His luck held out.

He was picked and more importantly so was Razor boy. Nobody at The Oasis knew the whereabouts of Eddie, he'd insisted on a whereabouts black out. They would in due course become all too aware when street talk mentioned a blatant brutal attack on a dock worker at the Canaries, suffering multiple cuts to his back face and hands, possibly with a boning knife.

The uniformed guardians at the Docks security gates had counted twenty 'day' labourers in first thing that morning, but only nineteen going through the security gates flush with readies, eight or so hours later. The Dock area security controlled was huge. Quay-side, warehouses, docked ships, recreation areas. All would have to be searched for the missing twentieth man. It wasn't Eddie's intention to murder this guy, his plan was to give him a taste of what he'd done to Wossname. During the day Eddie cornered Razor boy in a quite part of a warehouse, dock side. They were hidden from view by piles of old pallets, stacked twenty or thirty high. Razor boy needing a piss decided the location behind the pallets was ideal. It was midday break and the warehouse had emptied out. Eddie told Razor boy he was gonna do to him exactly what he'd done to Wossname. The cornered hoodlum raised his hands palms out to Eddie.

He protested, "It was all the others mate they all cut the big guy, not fucking me mate." He was quivering with fright and stammering his words. In a flash Eddie whipped out his boning knife and slashed it across both Razor's up turned palms.

"Firstly, I'm not your mate. I'm Eddie Coleman secondly, the bloke you and your mates cut up worked for me. Get it? So, when you see your mates who you say cut him, tell 'em they've got it coming to them an all." The boning knife swished again with surgical precision. Skin from Razor boys' cheeks fell to the ground, he was marked good and proper. It would take months to heal, if ever.

Eddie's eyes glazed over, he needed to be aware they both could be discovered by anyone else deciding to take a piss in the same spot. He shook his head vigorously in an effort to regain control of his mind. The boy, yelping with pain fell forward onto his blooded and split hands. Eddie stood on the back of his legs and with the boning knife played noughts and crosses on Razor boys' torso. It was a barbaric, crazy thing to do.

But Eddie was doing this for pleasure, he saw this as the right and perfect thing to do in return for what the Razors did to poor Wossname. At least this was one on one not six to one. "Fucking cowards," he whispered to the limp sobbing mess on the floor. "Don't you forget, tell the others to keep looking over their shoulders." It wasn't until midnight the body was found by security, the sight which greeted them, sickened them.

Thing is, if this body belonged to a 'day-only' labourer, security wouldn't have a name. Names were not needed for spot workers. Paid in cash, no paper work etc. Seemed to work up until now. However, from now on, issues like names and stuff, would need to be tightened up.

Police were called to the scene to begin yet another murder investigation. The following day Eddie was informed by the press that a body of a young man was discovered by the dock Security team at Canary Wharf.

The story didn't go into much detail other than to say, whoever the killer was, due to a kid's game of noughts and crosses carved on the victims back has to be a psychotic madman and needs to be apprehended quickly. Thence to be immediately sectioned. *Bit out of order that,* he thought. Papers always jump things up a bit. Bet old Bill are a bit pissed that this has actually been printed. It went on to say. What happens now?

If the killer strikes again before being caught, will it be 'Hangman' this time on the victims back? "Dead though, that wasn't in the plan, Eddie said quietly to himself."

"What do you think Johnny?" quietly sitting beside him.

"Well, he did have a hand in killing Wossname. I wouldn't tell his dad about it yet though. I know he wanted from what Bomber relayed on was an eye for an eye, and he is expecting us to do it. He's gonna have police blokes beating a path to his door again, and probably knockin' it down following this killing. It's likely going to run through their minds that he's put a contract out on the killers of his son. Keep him well out of the loop. If he gets on the blower to Bomber and all that, mixed messages could lead the filth back here."

"Right, you go and sort it with Bomber and the two girls to act daft if he does call. Meanwhile, I want more information on the next hit.

"One a week seems fair and I'll try not kill the next fucker." Johnny the Turk sighed inwardly. He was a practical man and could see the small but growing empire, centred around The Oasis crumbling without his boss at the helm while he was on a killing spree.

Eddie had been making wise decisions for the crews forward motion, it was as if he was destined for such a role. Blessed with the Midas touch, up until now they all enjoyed the activities and opportunities to earn good dough, ride around in quality motors, have the pick of the birds. All this and a growing sense of respect from people they came into contact with. Sorry as he was for Wossname, the daft bugger, why didn't he use the grey matter sitting right behind his massive forehead? He brought it on himself by being unarmed. A shooter, if only fired once in the air then levelled at his attackers would have produced a different ending.

An ending that would have kept Wossname alive and Eddie steering the ship. Johnny remembered a conversation he once had with a guy that worked in the city for some conglomerate or other. The managing director had turned a bit queer and was making bad mistakes. Share price falling and all that, Johnny enquired as to how things were resolved. he was told, his deputy, and with approval from the board of directors took hold of the company reins. The managing director was to temporarily step down, go away and sort his life out, while the deputy deputised. Worth a try Johnny thought. To even think of this course of action was utter madness, diplomacy and plenty of it was going to be needed.

If anyone was going to front Eddie out with an idea of temporarily taking over the day-to-day duties of running the team, it was Johnny the Turk.

Best not approach the idea like the board of directors did, Eddie would see it as everyone ganging up on him, in the end Johnny had a brainwave. Two days later Johnny cajoled Eddie to go on a trip to London Zoo, Eddie stared that stare at first, then grinned like a schoolboy having nicked his first Mars bar from the local sweet shop. "As it happens mate, I've never been there. My old man always promised to take me but never did, the old git." Eddie left instructions with Bomber and Esme and the pair exited The Oasis in search of a London cabbie.

"See that Eddie, that big fucker with the huge mane, he is in complete charge of the whole pride." It was feeding time at the lion's enclosure.

"The large in-charge male always got the best bits; the lions share I think they call it Eddie." Johnny went on. "In the wild, they don't get food chucked at them they have to go and hunt for it."

"Yea, okay, thanks for the lesson mate."

"What I'm getting at Eddie is this. Your main aim right now and for all the best reasons is to avenge Wossnames death by the Razor mob. It's going to take time."

"You said to all of us remember, you want to handle this alone on your tod, right?" Eddie nodded and smiled.

"Oh, I get it, while the cats away an all that. Well, why didn't you tell me before we came here? I recon you ought to sit in for me. Keep the wheels turning like."

Eddie looked back at the lions feeding their faces then to Johnny and back again at the lions. "You're a sly fucker you are, you had all this planned didn't you. Tell you what mate," Eddie said with a big grin. "You'd better do a good job or I might just slice you up." For a second Johnny got a bit worried, but it soon passed when Eddie suggested they go and see some of Johnny's relatives, in the monkey enclosures.

Val's Day Out.

Things were definitely looking up for Val Coleman. For the umpteenth time that morning she looked at the beautiful watch adorning her wrist. Eddie took his mum on a trip up West and bought two Omega watches, one for Val and one for him. He had the neck to make an appointment at the Regent Street Jewellers, the one he ordered the hit on not so long ago. They were back in business the following day after the robbery, massive insurance claims indented no doubt.

The Omegas together, cost two hundred sov's. The manager explained the watches are beautifully crafted jewellery items and not time pieces. "What does he mean by that," Val whispered to Eddie.

"Dunno Mum, but if they don't keep good time, he'll regret it." Next was a visit to the Ritz for afternoon tea, then a walk across Green Park towards the Queens residence. They stood outside Buck House for a few moments, no sign of Royal life so Eddie flagged a cabbie down, instructing the driver to drop them off at Trafalgar Square.

Val had passed by all these famous landmarks from time to time whilst working on the busses, seeing all the sights of London from the open platform at the rear of the bus, but it didn't compare one iota to doing in style though. On the tube journey back home, Eddie explained to his mum that he'd organised an account with a local private hire taxi firm, belled them out of the blue. No recommendations or anything like that. The chap at the other end of the telephone was told who it was calling.

He was only too aware of Coleman's reputation. He looked at his misses in despair, mouthing, "Oh fuck." This could only lead to one destination, big trouble. Their business had taken him and his wife years to build up to its current standing. They had ten cars, and a pool of drivers to call on. Being private hire, they were not licenced to pick up punters who waved them down in the street, although occasionally they did. Every fare needed to be booked in advance usually by telephone. The drivers didn't require any special licensing.

A standard full licence sufficed. Based in Leytonstone the taxi firm was busy with regulars plus did airport stints which always paid a good wedge. Their main income however, was a contract to taxi round the executives of Bearman's Department Store which was opposite the Picture Palace on the High Road in Leytonstone.

Eddie told his mum she could use the taxi firm whenever she wanted at no cost. The boss, on instructions from Eddie was to give Val priority even if they were stretched. They were under orders to miss bookings in preference to Mrs Colman's requests. In return Eddie offered muscle and protection at no cost. Val, of course had her pass for the odd bus ride or a couple of stations on the tube but when she was feeling she wanted something a bit special, she used the taxis. After a while, she got to know one or two of the regular drivers who came to pick her up.

One chap who was always very courteous towards her and cautious as a driver was to become her regular; if she had anything to do with it. He happily offered up his name when requested. "It's Jimmy, Mrs Coleman. Jimmy Toomey," he said with a gentle pleasing Irish lilt. "Over from the Emerald Isle so I am, been in London now for a couple of years, so I have."

"How does it compare to living in Ireland?" enquired Val from the back of the taxi.

"Well to start with," he said, "It's mostly green over dere and mostly grey over here. The Guinness tastes far better in Ireland too, told its brewed with water straight out of the Liffey in Dublin." Val's knowledge outside of London being virtually nil, asked,

"What's the Liffey when it's at home Jimmy?"

"It's the river dat flows through Dublin Mrs Coleman, you can cross over it from one side of Dublin to the other, by way of the Ha'penny bridge."

"Oh, sounds very charming it does, must try it someday." Jimmy always turned up looking smart. Clean crisp, open necked white half sleeved shirt. Tan slacks together with highly polished shoes. Would have doffed his cap if he had one.

His chiselled jaw, often sported a five o'clock stubbled. Jimmy's smiling sparkling blue eyes missed nothing either. Inside his head, he was having a thing with this lady. Wrongly, he thought she was wanting it too especially as it was forever him when she booked a taxi and, her bookings were on the increase.

Each time Jimmy picked up Val for a job, he would jump out open the rear passenger door for her all gentlemanly like, discretely looking away as she climbed in. When he pulled away it was, "Where to my lovely?" She began to use the taxi firm more and more, almost daily. Always asking for her favourite driver, Jimmy. Whenever she called for a taxi, she'd have a laugh and ask for 'Jimmy in the Liffey'. The radio operator at the taxi firm had no idea why she added the Liffey bit.

This was Mrs Val Colman on the line. No questions asked. Val's daily demands, gave the taxi firm a bit of a headache, what with having to switch drivers around to suit her and provide Jimmy in the Liffey. But they did and from then on it was Jimmy, whenever she called. More than once they needed to dig Jimmy out of bed, or drag him out of some pub or other. After all, we are talking Eddie Coleman's mum here. Eddie was offering free protection for the taxi firm, not paying any fares, no contest they thought. Besides, ferrying Mrs C. around might add a bit of prestige and publicity.

Why, Eddie himself had made use of their services on a number of occasions. Sadly however, the publicity gained, was about to backfire.

Eddie Coleman had gathered a fair few enemy in his steep climb up the psychotic criminal ladder what with all the violence and mayhem happening. He played his gangland games in the big boy's playground now. Some looked on with admiration and let him be, others looked on in complete envy and jealousy.

One such envious team, headed up by the Derkin cousins and associates was an ambitious mob of blokes on the South side of London wishing to emulate known gangster groups. Wishing to stamp their own brand of brutality on London.

Spies to Die.

"Esme," A friendly shout rang out from the basement. Esme, currently knocking up a couple of bacon rolls for two very hungry customers pretended not to hear the shout. "Essssmeee." This time even louder. She looked around for Rosie, hoping she might take over her duties and finish off the rolls. She knew that Johnny who was calling from the dungeon was more laid back than Eddie. He would understand, she couldn't drop everything and run-down stairs to him at a moment's notice. Looking across the caff she saw two young guys had cornered Rosie over by one of the booths.

At least that's what it looked like. On closer inspection, Esme might have seen that Rosie was encouraging the two lads giving them the old come on as it were. Esme couldn't quite see what was occurring, one of the lads had his back to Esme; the other was standing very close by his mate, screening movements from other nearby customers who might be looking on. She could see that Rosie was grasping the nearest lad to her, but couldn't see exactly where or what she was grasping. Fearing the worst, she called "Hey, Rosie, put the customers down would you please. I need a bit of hand over here." Esme called out in such a way, hopefully in a manner, not to stir up problems in the caff. It didn't take much for things to kick off, what with half the customers either being hardened criminals, the other half being lads who wanted to join Eddie's crew. Rosie managed to surface from the huddle, face burning red with embarrassment.

She was about to extract herself from them, when the two guys who were now on a mission, roughly pulled her back. One started clawing at her breasts leaning in tongue hanging out, going in for a snog.

The other started to put his hand up Rosie's shortened mini skirt; Rosie was none too impressed. She knew of a few 'fending off' moves for unwanted amorous advances, having had years of working in the docks, warding off advances from a small minority of dockers, swiftly heaving a knee in the groin of the nearest lad.

His reaction, considering whose roof he was under, was nothing short of astonishing. Instead of curling up in a ball dealing with serious pain in the men's department, he drew his arm fully back and behind him, then swung an almighty punch hitting Rosie square on the jaw. She fell, unconscious. Sprawled backwards across the oblong table, legs akimbo, mini skirt riding up, not leaving anything to the imagination.

Fearing the worst seeing Rosie stretched out defenceless and extremely concerned as to what these lads had in mind to do next, she sucked in a gob full of air and was about to let out a piercing scream, when 'bang!' a shot rang out. Everybody but everybody froze!

Johnny the Turk stood at the top of the stairs that led up from the dungeon, gun held at arm's length up towards the ceiling, barrel end smoking, now levelled deliberately towards the two lads. They sobered up rather quickly. Their combined thoughts had gone from ravishing to rushing; rushing out of the establishment.

It was if they were a pair of badgers caught in the headlights of lampers out for a night's kill. Minutes passed. Their pulse rates climbed way beyond normal.

An apology was out of the question they were caught red handed, Rosie laid out behind them was stirring, beginning to murmur now groaning and in pain.

From this point on it was if everything happened in slow motion. Johnny waved the gun slowly and purposely to his left, indicating that the two lads should make their way to the top of the stairs, once they had reached the spot the barrel was guiding them to, instructions were calmly uttered by The Turk.

"Yous two remain motionless. The slightest movement will result in your death. It's your call. Don't even want to hear you breathing." Johnny the Turk was old school, brought up proper like.

Brought up to respect women, shout and bawl a bit now and then, but knock 'em out? No fucking way. Esme used the frozen hiatus to go the aid of Rosie who was accordingly drowsy, stroking and rubbing at her jaw. "Come on Rosie love, let's sit you down. Would you like a cup of tea, or something a bit stronger?"

"Brandy would nice thanks Esme, me 'ead is spinning a bit, for all the wrong reasons. Yea, a Brandy in me tea would be lovely ta."

Esme still shaken by what might have happened, did the honours. She took the liberty of having a snifter herself to steady her own nerves. Something akin to normality descended on The Oasis. Frankly she needn't have worried, any amount of Eddie's young army would have steamed in. Thing is Eddie was not around so they were without a defined leader. Johnny was in charge of day to day running of the kingdom, so they stalled until the gunfire put a halt to the proceedings. Johnny still held his shooter and it was still in the direction of the two offenders. They remained at the top of the stairs leading to the dungeon, hardly daring to breathe. Hearing the shot from his flat above the caff Bomber appeared on the scene. Seeing customers waiting he dutifully finished off the bacon rolls for the two shaken, but patient customers. He offered the rolls and cups of tea at no charge, seeing as how late their meal was being served up. Both customers thanked Bomber warmly remarking to each other, what a gentleman he is, secretly glad most of the aggro was over.

Bombers instincts told him to fly at the two bastard lads and bundle them head first down the stairs followed by a bit of midriff kicking. He didn't though.

He could see Johnny the Turk had things under control, and could well imaging what Johnny had gotten in store for these two. If they had parents, then the parents would not be seeing either of their sons again 'ever.' He drifted over to Rosie. "You alright, girl?"

"Yea, I'll live," she replied. "My dad taught me how to roll with a punch It was banging me head on the table that knocked me clean out."

"I hadn't seen those two lads in here before," Bomber said, more of a question, rather than a statement.

"Neither have I, they were up from South of the Thames, Crayford I think they said."

"Oh, so maybe they didn't know who owns this place?"

"Spose not Bomber," said Rosie. "Anyways look, the Brandy's done the trick, so let's get the customers to feel comfortable again eh? Stick a record or two on the Jukebox, bit of Cliff or Elvis should do the trick." Bomber complied and a sort of peace descended on The Oasis.

Meanwhile, Johnny ushered his captives down-stairs, then straight out of the door that led to the back yard bundling them into the shed. Inside the large shed it was well cold, musty and almost pitch black.

Various odd bits of furniture were stacked to ceiling height filling at least half of the entire enclosed space. Some old rolled up carpets lay on the deck. These served as a place to park themselves, the pair of them sighed with relief.

For now, at least they were alive and able to tell the tale back in the Derkin's den, assuming they got there. The shed door didn't have a proper lock, so Johnny slipped a lump of wood through the staple part of the steel hasp and staple lock, which should hold them until Eddie's executioners were summoned.

"What you done with them?" Johnny padded up to the caff and was about to exit the building. Bomber, whilst trying not to be hostile, wanted to know the full story. It was not often in fact never; a shooter had been loosened off in The Oasis. Bomber stood in the doorway, blocking Johnny's way.

"Err, they are in the shed out in the back yard, sort of locked in."

"Why the gun mate?" Bomber enquired. "Look mate, I don't answer to you. As it happens, from what I saw young Rosie was about to be attacked. You know what I mean? Physically." Johnny was well pissed off, didn't need to be cross examined. Bomber was now just an employee. "Look at it this way Bomber. I did what I thought was necessary on the spur like, and it worked. Now let me pass, I need to link up with Billy and Mel." Bomber nodded totally forgetting to mention to Johnny, the two caged captives no doubt by now shivering in the shed, were from out of town.

A Soft Target.

Teams with many gang members were growing in numbers rapidly. Parts of London, South of the river included recruiting tough, rough young guys was definitely not a problem. Gangs in the sixties are very fashionable some, both idolised and feared by many out of work young men. They saw how ruthless violence paid well, in some cases being the only way to secure much needed cash on the hip. The Derkin's hailed from Crayford, South of the Thames. The cousins being part of a large family of Romany descent, decided the way forward would be to snuff out rival gangs, pick up the pieces take over any protection rackets, or deals, then move on to the next victims.

The Oasis would be a good base for them, close to the East and West of London, closer than the Pom Poms pub in Erith. Eddie's crew with his growing reputation looked at least to be a sitter. Grind them into the ground and take over the assets was their game plan.

The Derkin's narks had been keeping tabs on Eddie's movements. They Incorrectly assumed, with a bit of muscle, they could make a move on Eddie hit him and his crew even harder, take over his business interests before Eddie, even fell to the deck. For a few quid, narks passed back information regarding Eddie Coleman's movements directly to the Derkin's. Information the cousins had been waiting for now presented them with a golden opportunity. Apparently, according to the narks Eddie Coleman had gone to ground, vanished like Dr

Who. Someone who went by the moniker of Johnny the Turk was now minding the operation at The Oasis, it was too good an opportunity to miss.

The psycho was away on his holidays or whatever, so this might be the best time ever for a takeover raid. One thing this rival outfit knew for definite, there was a tie up with a taxi firm over in Leytonstone. Narks had spotted the cabs calling at The Oasis, picking blokes up, and dropping other blokes off. Word had it that Eddie's mum used the same taxi firm regularly. The taxi firm was therefore designated as the place to hit, it was a soft target. The big idea they had was to petrol bomb the taxi firms' premises. This they reckoned would lure Eddie's team out from the protective walls of The Oasis. The Derkin's, along with twenty or so of their blokes, could steam in when The Oasis was half empty of Coleman's thugs and stamp all over it. So, the plan was hatched to fire bomb the Taxi firms' office and adjacent garage where the most of the cars were housed in the dead of night. That should bring them running.

At 11.00 o'clock the following Monday night, in the pissing rain three men armed with Molotov cocktails and a heavy looking sledge hammer, purchased the day before pulled up in a van twenty-five yards or so, downwind of the Taxi firms' premises, which was in total darkness.

A quick look round to make sure nobody was about, one of the men smashed his way through the street door and on into the front office. With the use of the sledge hammer the door, bottom half wood, top half glass, printed with the Taxi Firms name, gave way after the third blow.

The other two followed him in, one holding two milk bottles filled with petrol, the other a single bottle.

Another door, this one through to the cars out back was smashed down too. The sledge hammer was flung to the ground, the door breaker handed a bottle as he ran through to the garage area. Several of the company's shiny cabs were parked up, sweat was pouring down his forehead stinging his eyes.

Don't fuck this up he thought, sparking up the crude cloth fuse he blindly slung the glass bottle filled with petrol which smashed against the driver's door of the nearest car, immediately bursting, igniting the petrol.

Flames engulfed the car. Running back to the front office eyebrows smoking from being singed, a nod to the other two who were waiting for his signal. They too lit their fuses, two more bottles full of petrol were thrown then smashed. One against the back wall the other at the two-way radio system. Access to the garage area was now blocked as flames leapt up threatening to leap into the office area.

No one was going to pass through that door now, even if they wanted to. Near-by girly mags got chucked onto the blaze, followed by company ledgers, account books, drivers' rosters, anything that would help the fire take hold. Satisfied with their handiwork all three exited by the same way they came in. On the way back out to the street, one of the three thought he heard a shout as they sprinted to the waiting van, but momentarily dismissed it. He stopped to listen again cocked his ear upwards. Amongst the crackling and roar of the flame's windows breaking, glass shattering, there was a definite human type hollering noise. He looked up to what looked like an occupied flat above the offices. Perhaps he thought, someone's up there, trapped, the other two fire bombers were beckoning for the third man to jump in the van.

All those two wanted to do was stick the van into gear and speed off. "Can't," said the third man.

"Don't wanna get done for murder, do we? just wait here a sec." Across the road there stood telephone kiosk and by good fortune it was lit, a single bulb illuminated the interior. This was definitely a bonus, most public telephone boxes were completely vandalised glass windows smashed, light bulbs either nicked or smashed. Dashing across the road, very nearly slipping over on the rain wet surface he prayed the telephone at least was in working order. Opening up the heavy door, he was greeted with an overwhelming stench of piss. It was up to gagging level, of course there would be piss in there.

Has to be piss in there, where else do right thinking drunken bastards take a piss on their way home, can't piss in the gutter, might get a pull from the law! Grabbing the receiver, he was grateful to hear the dialling tone. Quickly dialling 999, immediately a female operator's voice said, "Police fire or ambulance."

"Fire," he grunted trying hard not to breath in the aroma of stale piss. It lent a hand to mask his voice.

"Can you tell me the location and address please sir?" Panic set in.

"Where, the fucking hell are we?" he yelled to his companions. They were busy revving the van wishing to put many miles between them and the burning premises. they could make out where their accomplice was, but couldn't make out what it was he was shouting about. Neither had taken an exam in lipreading or body language. Was he telling them to fuck off or stay and wait or what? What the bloody 'ell was he doing over there anyway. They looked across the bench seat of the van at each other. One said,

"Let's go, get out of here, if he wants the police to nick him, that's his sodding lookout."

The other said, "No, let's give 'im two more minutes, then we will have to shift."

From the telephone box fire bomber number one, looked back across at the taxi office. It was now well alight black smoke pouring out of the front window, panic returned. He thought his mates might well just drive off and leave him. Looking around inside the box for divine intervention, it came. He saw right in the centre of the dial the telephone box number and location printed on the circular plastic insert, he read it out in quick fashion to the telephone operator. Old habits die hard, before bolting he pressed button 'B' just in case someone had inadvertently paid for a call, didn't get through and forgot to get their four pennies back. No luck.

Either somebody had taken a piss in here and got himself fourpence for doing so, or the last person to use the box got through to their call. Running back across the road to the waiting van leaving the receiver dangling, he flung himself in banging his head as he did so. Off they roared, within minutes they were almost out of the district. Had they stayed a few moments longer, they would have heard terrible agonising screams as opposed to the earlier shouting. Unbeknown to any of them one of the cab drivers having had a skin full that very night, decided to get his head down in his taxi rather than risk getting caught driving under the influence, possibly losing his driver's licence.

The taxi he was using for the night's bed was parked up in the garage area set behind the front office. His was the first car to be set ablaze, semi-conscious but realising the danger he was in the stricken driver made feeble attempts to escape via the driver's door. Pulling frantically on the door handle the door swung open but he was beaten back by the intense heat. He was trapped. The passenger door, courtesy of the car next to his being parked up far too close would only open a fraction. No way could he squeeze out of that small gap. He screamed and yelled, banged on the windscreen pounded on the roof for help, but no help came. Mercifully before the flames got him, thick black acrid smoke was inhaled. It caused him to at first vomit violently followed by choking, gagging then convulsions. Unable to breath, he finally passed out. It was a horrible death. The fire service attending eventually had the fire under control, finalised the damping down, and began searching the area for evidence in order to establish, exactly what started the blaze. Oddly enough, the office area remained reasonably intact.

Mostly scorch and smoke damage, nothing much to fuel the fire, the firemen when they arrived aimed two jet hoses directly through the broken windows that looked out on the street playing the high-pressure jets directly onto the fire, extinguishing it rapidly. The covered garage to the rear was the tricky bit. More hoses were needed. A second fire engine was summoned, eventually that fire too was brought under control but not before all the cars present were fire damaged in one way or another. A body found by two fire fighters was reported to the fire officer in charge, he in turn informed the senior police officer on site.

A radio message back to the station regarding that this was not just a fire but a suspicious fire, resulted in a D.I. being despatched the scene. It was a miracle that the flat above suffered mainly smoke damaged, but that was it. The fire crew had been up there and established it was unoccupied, its main usage being a paper storage area for the taxi firm below. The key holder was contacted by the police. It was the first thing they did on arrival at the site having found the information in an unlocked metal filing cabinet. Officers who were eventually given the all clear to enter the rear building were the first to see up close the gruesome sight of a very dead body lying in the burnt-out wreck of one of the taxis.

Its charred hands had melted onto a half-opened passenger side window in what looked like an attempt to pull it away and make an escape route from the inside of what appeared to be one of the taxis. So intense was the heat at the height of the inferno metal had warped and buckled making the car unrecognisable from its former self. It was the same with the body. Unrecognisable in terms of black or white, male or female. Its mouth frozen wide open, flesh burnt back revealing upper and lower teeth and jaw lines.

To the officers looking on, it gave the impression the corpse was emitting silent screams. Most likely though it was the body of an adult. But who's? By now the key holder had arrived, hands held over his head impersonating football fans, when their team missed a sitter.

The scene he was confronted with at 2.00am was one of controlled chaos. 'Do Not Cross' tape surrounded the entire building. Reels of hoses were being rolled up. Ambulance men were busy getting a stretcher ready for the body. A black Maria was just arriving and police were crawling all over the place. He stood for a while and surveyed what was left of his business. Silently wishing, he had not skimped so much on the business insurance.

"I'm the owner," he said to the first person he came into contact with.

"And who might you be, sir?"

"As I said officer, I am the owner." He said sternly.

"Yes, of course you are, sir, still need a name though." "Nick Godly, me and the wife own and run this business, what's left of it. Will you let me through please?"

"Sorry, can't do that sir, will you follow me please?"

"Hang on constable, I need to get in there to see if anything can be salvaged. What started the fire anyway? Dodgy electrics or something?"

"We don't think so, sir, we think it might have been deliberate."

"Now, would you step over this way sir, I need you to talk to this gentleman here, Detective Inspector Moon." Moon was on his haunches going through some ashen residue with a pen. He stood up. The lanky bugger, towered over Nick.

Before greeting him, Moon dropped something into a plastic evidence bag, took off his thin rubber gloves and held a hand out as if to shake hands. Nick refused. "Good Morning, sir." D.I. Moon proffered.

"What the bloody hells good about it?" Nick raved.

"Sorry sir, bad phraseology, please accept my apologies." "Right introductions over, can I now go and see what can be salvaged of my business. It happens to be mine and many others sole source of income." D.I. Moon answered,

"Sorry sir, at the moment no. It is designated as a crime scene. Until crime scene officers have been and gone, only myself and the Sergeant here are allowed in."

"We might well be here for quite some time. You said earlier, this business is the sole income for yourself and your wife Mrs Godly I assume, and many others? It will be of great help if you can tell one of my officers who they all are, how many, just names at the moment. We would also like to know if you, your wife or any of your drivers can remember upsetting any one recently."

"Oh, for Christ sake," replied Nick.

"We upset people on a daily basis. Sometimes we can't do wrong from right. If we are late picking a fare up, we get a bollocking, if we are too early picking up a fare, we get a bollocking. If we are busy and turn down a fare, we get a bollocking."

"It's clear you don't know much about taxi work. Anyway, why do you ask."

"Well, we think this is deliberate sir, we have found large fragments of broken milk bottles here and there. The favoured container used for Molotov cocktails."

"Fuckin hell," Nick shouted, "You think this was the result of us being fire bombed? Then why are you standing here wasting your sodding time cross examining me?" D.I. Moon was about to say, you know precious little about policing do you sir, but refrained from doing so.

"There's more sir, a body has been found. As we speak it is being removed by the ambulance chappies over there who will pop it along to the coroner's vehicle just over there. He pointed to both locations with each hand simultaneously. A full examination via a post mortem to establish the cause of death will be carried out in due course. Now, I urge you to talk to one of my officers. Please inform him with as much information as you possibly can, especially as to the names and possible whereabouts of your staff and drivers. Please include anyone that you may have dismissed for whatever reason going back for at least twenty-four months."

"Just before you pop off to do that sir, have you any idea who might have been in the building at the time of the fire. Are any of your drivers in the habit of staying behind after you've locked up? You know kipping down in one of the cars perhaps."

"Why on earth would you want to know that?"

"Well, sir, the deceased was in one the burnt-out cars. Now if you will excuse me sir, I need to get on with the investigation." D.I. Moon turned on his heel and walked over to the fire chief for a chat.

Nick was in a daze. His business fire bombed; a corpse found in the locked-up premises. He needed to know more. "Inspector, I need to know more." He followed the inspector to where he was now standing. "What makes you think it's a driver, can you describe him?" Moon dragged himself away from the fire chief and turned to Nick.

"All we can tell you sir at this point is, that it's an adult. We cannot tell if its male or female, black or white, or very much else."

"Why?" asked Nick.

"Well sir, due to the intensity of the fire, we cannot establish any facts other than it is the body of an adult." Nick was taken aback. He turned ashen and thought he might throw up,

"My God. Look I will give you as much help as I can, meanwhile I need to get home and tell my wife what the hell is going on. Get your officer to come around to my house whenever you think it's appropriate, I will more than fill up his notebook. As it happens, we keep records at home of who's who and who's where etc. Sorry for being belligerent."

"That's okay sir. Very understandable in the circumstances. Now if you will forgive me, I really must get on." He spoke to his Sergeant suggesting at an appropriate time this morning house to house, flat to flat, basement to basement might yield up some leads. "Get some bodies on it Sarge let's try to wrap this up sharpish like. We also need to question the key holder, a Mr Godly."

"You met him earlier, send a couple of constables over to his home. Better send a WPC and all. Mrs Godly will probably be in a bit of a state. Apparently, they can do a short cut for us, finding out who's who. He's holding a staff and drivers list at his house. I'm going to attend the post mortem. Who the bloody hell would want to fire bomb a taxi firm, I mean there quite useful most of the time; whoever did it used at least two Molotov cocktails? Someone must have a right old grudge. See you back at the station."

East Ham Station.

Mike Bright's replacement, Detective Inspector Jackson, addressed the assemble officers and detectives. "Do we have a prime suspect?"

"No." he said. Speaking for them.

"Do we have 'any' suspects?"

"No." he said again.

"Right, in which case we are going to start again from scratch." Gasps and moans filled the gymnasium. "I see we have a joker or two amongst us." Jackson was referring to the sign on the twin gym doors that had been altered from incident room to indecent room. "Whoever it is please be aware if it's not dealt with correctly by our next briefing, any overtime logged will be paid at normal time rates. I want the teams dealing with sections of the investigations to swap them around. Fresh eyes and fresh questioning may throw up new leads and new lines of enquiries.

"Reporters are hounding our press people and there is only so many times we can trot out hackneyed phrases. As I am sure you are all aware one of the red tops is rather cheekily taking the piss with a daily headline, announcing *'Still no Arrests at Day Sixteen'*." He held up the offending paper before scrunching it up and disposing of it in a handy swing-bin. "The deputy police chief is rumoured soon to be dropping the newspaper an official letter. What will be in it, only he, God and probably his wife will know." He paused for a moment to take a swig of water. "If they print it, or even part of it, more shit from them and a bigger fan.

"So, get swapping your individual sections with the exception of the anti-corruption squad. You lot, keep up the surveillance duties. Anything suspicious bring it with me immediately." He paused again, hands held behind his back to let all that information, sink in. "Now, due to financial constraints the officers drafted in to help us will need to return to their own stations at the end of the month. That's just two weeks away so make good use of them.

"One last thing and I've saved the best till last." Voice lowered leaning forward, to lend the announcement gravity. "We have an officer working under-cover at the very heart of a den of thieves. An under-cover officer who is able to hear and see things that we don't see or hear.

"Up until yesterday we've had zero information back from this officer. This is not unusual for someone on the force and working covertly." The gym fell silent. If a pin was dropped it would have sounded like a cannon going off.

"Do we know who and where, sir?"

"No and we are not going to. That's the meaning of deep-cover. This officer, the D.I. being guarded regarding gender, has been trained by professionals for this type of job. It is highly dangerous, working under-cover means just that.

"This officer cannot be closer to the hub of a particular gang and would be in in danger of death if discovered. Therefore, I need not remind you this information is not to be spoken about outside this room.

"Thing is, what's come back from our under-cover officer earlier this very morning is this. It is very likely that most if not all of the recent unsolvable crimes in the East End, point to one or two individuals. Someone somewhere, possibly two persons at most, are pulling all the strings."

"So are we talking about a gang, sir."

"Make of it what you will son, but yea, that's about the size of it. Concentrate on groups, gangs, mobs, firms, and stuff like that. We need to take any and all suspicion away from our under-cover officer. Bring people in for questioning. Charge them for loitering, petty larceny, poor parking, anything that will enable you to keep them for twenty-four hours.

"Whilst anyone you do bring in for questioning do make sure they understand, that during their short stay at the station here, their homes will be searched. Let's build a thick enough portfolio to put people away. You know what Crown Prosecution Services are like. Evidence, evidence, evidence. We need to be on the front foot from now on. No more chasing shadows." A wag asked quietly of his partner,

"Where is Hank Marvin anyway?"

"Start closing in on the criminal elements. Now then, let's get on to secondary target's witnesses. Somebody somewhere will have seen something that will have clues for us. They always do. Question people close to the vicinity of the crimes we are investigating.

"If they come up with the usual old chestnut, 'I've told all this to the other officer,' tell them that you need to hear it again first hand, some witnesses crack the second or third time around. Tell them that it's very easy to forget something and that you will not be charging them for withholding vital evidence.

"You'd be surprised how much will come tumbling out once you have put them at ease, so to speak. Next on the list, anyone know of clearing houses for crime?

"If yes, get in get the top boys and bring 'em in here. I do not want us to be plagued with instability any more. What I do want is the interview rooms bursting at the seams. Right, if there are no further questions, get to work. Next up-date tomorrow at 08.00hrs." D.I. Jackson, twenty years' serviceman with the Met, an old boy to most of the coppers in the Gym, moreover he was an old hand, very good at sparking coppers up. They watched closely as he marched military style out of the incident room. Back ram rod straight.

You either liked him, or loathed him, Nothing in between. Luckily for him the majority of the officers and detectives present were on the 'like him team'.

The buzz in the gym soon turned to nattering about the under-cover officer. As with all police gatherings, rumours, gossip, tittle-tattle and general hearsay entered the conversations. Some had Mike Bright as the under-cover cop, others had others in the role.

It hit home though to all present, that D.I. Jackson had asked everyone to focus on, gangs, mobs, firms and the like. The inference being just like ten pin bowling, one ball to strike the king pin with a bit of luck the other nine pins fall too. The strategy put across by D.I. Jackson looked tangible and workable. The teams now had fresh directions to follow, fresh questions to ask, fresh evidence to unearth. No longer fiddling and farting about with low life, snitches and nobodies. Much better to be working from the top down.

For sure, they were all now fired up ready to go. Suddenly it looked like a great idea to start from scratch. Not as the way they had originally thought, but with solid substantial, well-defined parameters. The pep-talk convincingly woke them right up.

Nest of Vipers at the Pom Poms Pub.

"Well, that was a waste of bloody time wasn't it?" Jesus wept. Voices kept low to barely a whisper as they discussed the debacle regarding torching the Taxi Firm. As of yet, the Derkin cousins were unaware that a body had been discovered on the taxi firms' premises. The police had yet to release any information of that nature to the press or otherwise, until next of kin had been located informed and the body identified. The only thing the Derkin's had seen or heard about it so far, was a short story reporting the fire on the inside pages of the popular Evening News. That's all they had to go on. Tom and Neil Derkin were sitting in the Poms private bar in Erith, drinks on the table for two only.

Having called in the three responsible for the firebombing they wanted to know when, the three were told otherwise, why the hit took place at eleven pm. and not at the set time. Pom Poms, a nick-name for the pub they now all sat in was a natural. Manufacturing of the QF two-pounder gun took place at the Vickers Armstrong's factories nearby in Crayford. The gun was christened Pom--Pom due to the sound it made when being fired. The private bar at the Poms, doubled as the Derkin's den.

"We had a team waiting outside The Oasis from nine o'clock, nobody came running out for us to jump on, because you didn't light the place up as you were told to do so, spot on at ten," said Tom Derkin.

One of the three responsible for the torching, became the spokesman. They were all shit scared of the Derkin's, the spokesman just a little less so. "Had trouble nickin' a van, didn't we?" He turned to the other two, who nodded vigorously in unison. "First one broke down on the way to Leytonstone.

"Second one we nicked had a bloody great dog tied up in the back. Vicious great black bastard it was, Yappin' and snarling at us it was, kicked up a right commotion."

Again, he looked at the other two for support, again, they nodded in unison. "Third van thank fuck was fine, we were on our way over to Leytonstone when

181

we realised, we'd left the can of petrol in the first van. So, we had to go back and find it. Still, we did a good job of the taxi outfit didn't we? By the time we left it was well on fire." Tom and Neil exchanged glances then both stared at the three sitting on the opposite side of the table. All one could hear, was silence. Eventually the elder of the cousins Tom, spoke,

"As far as we're concerned you fucked right up. We had it planned to do that place called The Oasis and timing was bloody important. If this gets out and about, we could be laughed at. And we can't have that, can we?" All three shook their heads in unison. "We don't want another fuck up, do we?" All three shook their heads again. "Right, Neil and me decided before you got here on our next move. You three are gonna take the Turk or what-ever he's called and stash him in one of our warehouses in Dartford.

"Keep him hostage tie him up. Do a twenty-four-hour watch between you. We will get a meet arranged with this Eddie Coleman when he surfaces and front him out. Do some people bargaining. Do you think you can manage that?" All three nodded. They sat for a moment or two until Tom Derkin looked across the table and sneered, "You lot still here?" Standing now outside the Poms in the evening drizzle nobody spoke. Kidnapping was above their paygrade.

Besides, the one who heard the cries for help was convinced someone in the building had come to grief. It was now time to spill to the other two. "Why are you telling us this now?" one said.

"Yea why now?" the other one joined in.

"I dunno, I just can't get it out of my head."

"The shouting for help you know, kidnapping and holding a hostage is one thing, but say someone did get hurt or even killed over at Leytonstone, that's life or a ten stretch at best. Fuck this for a game of soldiers, there's got to be other ways of getting the readies in." From that moment on, the three desperados never set eyes on each other again. The Derkin's were three men down. Something they would discover sometime later.

In With the Boss.

"Come in!" Jackson marched in, back ram-rod straight as usual into the Detective Chief Inspector's temporary office, at East Ham Police Station. "Take a seat, what's happening any news?" DCI Ellis asked.

Jackson cleared his throat wishing now that he hadn't had that last smoke before coming in here. "Yes, sir somethings come up on the radar, which I think you should know about."

"Okay, let's hear it but make it brief, I need to have a report written up soonest. Since you're stirring up of the troops at the last briefing, I need to re-set our strategy and operational policies, regarding our situation here. Got to get it off to the Chief Super today some time."

"Well sir, I think you might want to hold off your report until you have heard what I am about to tell you."

"Okay go on."

"The tactics employed at the briefing have paid off sir. Anti-corruption officers have discovered, that Halliwell had indeed run up a massive debt with a gambling den known as Maddison's which is located on his beat."

"Interesting, what is the value of the debt?"

"Around the £500-mark, sir."

"Christ, as much as that, serious money then."

"Serious enough to kill for I would think, especially if Halliwell was not doing as he was told, sir."

"What do you mean by that?" asked Ellis.

"Well, as we thought earlier in our investigations which has been confirmed, our line of enquiry was that he needed to pay off the debt by becoming a conduit for information from us to the gambling den owners."

"Do we know who the owners are?"

"Working on it now, sir. Earlier indications pointed to Jake Speck."

"Earlier, have things changed then?"

"Possibly, sir, mixed messages are coming in we need to evaluate the merits of each one before acting upon it."

"If we do track down the correct owner, will that alone lead us to the killer?"

Ellis enquired, "And what sort of information would Halliwell pass on to them that might be of any use to them, other than who's who?"

"These gambling dens sir by-and-large are illegal. If we decided to arrange a raid, catching them at it has always been a problem. They break down the kit stuff it into large suitcases and nip out the back, or sometimes disappear via a network of old unused cellars and tunnels.

"It would be even more impossible to catch them in the act, if Halliwell is as we suspect informing them of a potential raid, in advance of us carrying it out."

"So, let me get this straight, Halliwell runs up a debt with an illegal and unlicensed gambling den known as Maddison, which the people there encourage."

"When he cannot pay with actual cash, they get him to turn on us and be a gambling den snitch."

"That's about the size of it, sir."

"Well, I'll be damned," said the DCI breathing out heavily as he spoke.

"Thing is sir, it's going to be awfully difficult to prove that he was a conduit, snitch or snake in the grass. He is unquestionably dead. What we do know, he definitely ran up the huge debt, was murdered, then unceremoniously dumped somewhere in the Thames." Detective Inspector Jackson liked to throw in the odd long word at this level of discussion.

He thought it lent him a smidgen of kudos.

"Please, you do not have to state the bloody obvious."

"No sir, sorry sir. I didn't mean to be obsequious."

"So, what's your plan, how are you going to piece this together?"

"We need to pull in Jake Speck and if it's definitely not him."

"Well do it then," the DCI cut in.

"Easier said than done, sir." Ignoring the glib comment, Ellis ventured.

"Hmmmm, I seem to remember reading in one of Mikes reports before he went on leave, that the stab wounds to Halliwell's back were inflicted possibly with a bread knife."

"Furthermore, Mike put a constable or two on it to search records held here and at other local stations for any bread knife related stabbings and or murders. Might be a good idea to follow that up today. See if the two constables have found anything."

"Yes sir, that will now be my next move."

"You do that and you might find that it was one of Speck's associates that did for Halliwell."

"While I'm here sir I might add, we are now getting slow but regular snippets of information from our under-cover officer. Nothing substantial enough to make any arrests yet, but it seems we are nudging ever nearer to that end."

"Great, keep me well in the know. It will be an excellent day when we are able to shut up the newspaper drivel, especially the one with that 'date-nothing done-yet' story. I know the Chief Super will be delighted." Jackson, seeing the meeting was over, stood up to leave.

"Before you go Jackson off the record, what do you make of this business with D.I. Bright?" Jackson sat down again unaware of what was coming next. As far as he was concerned Mike had gone off on sick leave and he, D.I. Jacko was parachuted in to replace him, temporary or otherwise.

"Off the record sir, how do you mean?"

"I wish I could put my finger on it. Recently made up to D.I. First class coppers record and all that, this double murder enquiry that's caught the attention of the public in a big way, to some, it would be seen as a gift.

"To be involved at his level with the possibility of promotion prospects if successful. I mean how many times would a D.I. get the opportunity of leading a major enquiry with the sort of help in officer numbers as he did then sign himself off sick?"

D.I. Jackson, looked down, kind of deep in thought. Ellis took it that Jackson was concealing something. "Come on Jackson if you know anything, you have better bloody tell me." Jackson squirmed in his seat on the opposite side of the DCI's desk, who was now leaning back with his hands behind his head. Somewhere in the past for one reason or another, Jackson read a book entitled 'Body Language at Work'. Surprisingly little importance was attached to the art of reading peoples body speak in the sixties. Jackson had delved into it, in an effort to get ahead in meetings just as this one. It was why he marched around with a back like a ram-rod. He knew it silently conveyed the message, 'you *will*, look up to me!' He watched DCI. Ellis as he clasped his hands behind his head, lean back in his chair almost to tipping point and recalled that according to the body bible, it is a classic signal 'I know that I am better than you, see!' The DCI repeated his request. "Come on, you must have some idea why Mike dipped out?"

D.I. Jackson hesitated once more. If he told Ellis what he had 'on the grapevine' heard, what hell would follow. No way was he going to instigate an investigation or a disciplinary action against D.I. Bright. On the other hand, would it be tantamount to withholding information that might possibly lead to an arrest, which would put Jacko firmly in the shit.

Saturday Night at the Pom Poms.

"How much longer Dave," muttered the Turk, "I'm getting cramp in here?" Johnny, Billy and Mel were sat in the back of the Bentley, tooled up and ready for the coming battle. Eddie sat in the front alongside Dave.

"About another twenty minutes," said Dave, glancing in the rear-view mirror. "Were just coming into Woolwich so that's about halfway." Eddie had his eyes closed. In his mind's eye, he was visualising the coming massacre, rehearsing his moves, practising his public performance. The Derkin's sealed their fate, torching the taxi firm in Leytonstone had seen to that. Pikey lineage or not they were about to be snuffed out. Travelling behind the Bentley a small army in two more motors, recruited from The Oasis bar. There was no shortage of volunteers, only too eager to come along and get stuck in. Eddie was severely pissed off about the taxi firm. The two lads who had tried it on with Rosie, confessed all to Billy and Mel just prior to losing their young lives. They told all, who the Derkin's were, what their plans were, where they hung out on Saturday nights, everything.

Even confessed to checking out The Oasis for the Derkin's. Checking out entrances, likely exits, all kinds of stuff in order for a successful raid. It still wasn't known yet, who got stiffed that night in the blaze at the taxi firm.

Eddies' mum Val, prayed that it wasn't Jimmy from the Liffey. Before long the Nordenfelt pub in Erith, loomed into view. "Is this the one the local's call the Pom Poms?" Eddie asked of Dave. "You were the one who came down here last week to suss it out?"

"It is," replied Dave. "The Derkin's got a private room at the back."

"Right, everyone these Derkin's apparently get in here on Saturday nights. Dave, go back and tell the others to park up and give us lot about fifteen minutes, then steam in."

"They need to cause havoc, smash the place up a bit. Cause a rumpus and take people's attention away from us and what we're doing." This night's work by Eddie's crew ably assisted by a small army of lads in balaclavas, armed with pick axe handles, was about to shoot Eddie Coleman's hard man reputation into the stratosphere.

Due to the utter seriousness of the event at the Pom Poms, coupled with poor intelligence from the under-cover police officer it was muted by police top brass whether or not it was worth risking the under-cover officer's life any further. Gangland warfare spawning cold bloodied murders was not to be tolerated. Not to mention putting innocent Saturday night drinkers in the firing line. Moves must be made they said to smash these gangs, lock them up and fling the keys into a foreign ocean.

Sunday Morning Stepping Mount Hotel.

"Wake up Es, get us a cuppa."

Esme groaned, "Just a sec Eddie, bloody hangover's hurting my head. Hold on," she said looking around, "we're in a private suite, aren't we? This Hotels opposite Hyde Park from what I clocked last night!"

"Yea I know," Eddie grinned, "I was only pulling your leg. I'll call room service. You put a fair bit of champers away last night, glugging it like little miss Faunt-Le-Roy you were, no wonder you've got a bad head."

"That's not the only reason Eddie, when you were banging me, I was banging me head on this wooden headboard. Can you have a word in case we stay here again, get them to put a softer one in here instead?"

Esme had a sudden urge to relieve herself, all the drinking at the hotels bar the previous night, meant that Esme didn't get to see much of the suite.

Making her way to the huge bathroom she stopped to glance out of one of the full-length windows. Enormous drapes hung to the floor either side of both windows, drawn back, held with curtain stays halfway up.

Long frilly net curtains obscured the view to an extent, in and out. Putting her need to wee aside Esme pulled back the net curtain of the nearest window to the bed. The view was little short of spectacular, both windows looked down on to the busy Bayswater Road and over to Hyde Park. A bright and sunny Sunday morning greeted her gaze as she moved a little closer to the huge widow.

"Bloody ell Esme, put something on, standing there for all to see stark naked, you'll have a pile up on the road down there." Esme dropped the net curtain, turning to Eddie, with a wicked smile, opened her arms and legs wide, like a star fish. She spoke, "Only you can now." It was a come-on Eddie couldn't resist, throwing back the covers he made a dive for Esme. She was too quick for him though scuttling, mock squealing, skipping to their overly large 'his and hers bathroom', locking the door and calling out, "too slow." Eddie ran to the bathroom door pretending the fall from the dive, hurt him in some way. Fearing he was in trouble; Esme unlocked the door turning the gold-coloured lock until it clunked, opened the door an inch or two and peered out. No Eddie to be seen, she opened the heavy door a little further and stopped to listen. A low groaning sounded like it was coming from the other side of the extra-large, extra king-sized bed. Slowly she crept towards the groaning expecting to see Eddie curled up on the floor in agony. Eddie however was now behind her creeping softly.

187

Esme got to the other side of the bed and then realised what was happening. Too late, he was on her turned her around and flung her backwards onto the bed. "Who's too fucking slow now girl?"

The stay at the Stepping Mount Hotel was all part of Eddie's plan. Bomb over to the Pom Poms at Erith, kill the Derkin's, get back to The Oasis, grab Esme book in, and enjoy a bit or R&R, blot out the killings so to speak. Esme, got up again and made her way to the bathroom, this time wrapping a bed sheet around her nakedness as she moved across the huge room. Eddie laid back, remembering the events of last night. "To the victor go the spoils," he said quietly to himself.

Leaning over to the rather grand regency bedside table he lifted the phone.

"Reception, how can we help?"

"Room service, please," requested Eddie.

"We can deal with that for you sir."

"Tea for two please, in about an hour from now."

"Yes sir, certainly sir, tea for two at ten o'clock." Click and she was gone.

"Esme, get your arse out here, I've got something to show you." Subtle as a brick as usual he was.

Later that morning the pair of them took a stroll along the Bayswater Road on Hyde Park side. Dotted along the wide pavement were dozens and dozens of stalls displaying very much for sale, artists work. Most were hung onto the park's railings, paintings and artwork of all descriptions, ranging from absolute shite, to the untrained eye to the 'how come that's not hanging in the Tate over at Millbank?' Nothing hit them hard enough to make a purchase. Besides, many items were not priced, Eddie wasn't keen to ask, he thought as soon as you did, the seller would look you up and down, then decide on a price dependent upon how well you were dressed.

There was he, a double-breasted suit, crisp white shirt, sober tie, finished off with shiny black brogues. On his wrist an expensive Omega. Nah, I think I'll come back next week as a rag-n-bone man. Knock fifty percent off straight away wont they. On they strolled in the lovely morning sunshine. Yesterday's murderous events shut away. "I like it up here Esme, stinks of money. In between all the black cabs, every other motor looked to be a Jag or Roller or Bentley. Bugger Southend that's small fry, seems to me, this is where it's at."

"Whatever you say Eddie, just so long as we can lord and lady it up occasionally, like last night."

188

"Yea right, was good fun, weren't it?"

Feeling peckish, they dived into a Chinese restaurant conveniently placed just across the Bayswater Road to where they'd been strolling. It was busy for the time of day, almost full. Finding a table near the front window, before they could get seated a smart Chinese waiter with a stitched-on smile handed them menus. In the centre of the restaurant was a small island surrounded by a wide circular worktop. On it, cooked meals awaiting a waiter to take them to their destined table. In the middle of the island a young lady of Chinese descent worked slavishly over a large circular hot plate. Food cooking on the hot plate sizzled and hissed as she continually turned the food being careful not to overcook it. Eddie being unused to such things asked the waiter who she was and what was she cooking.

The waiter replied in excellent English, "that is my wife Sui (pronounced Sue) Sui Lin. You can make up your own dish from the ingredients on the menu and Sui Lin will cook it especially for you. Many customers call her 'Chuck it in Sui Lin.' Very famous she will be someday!"

Eddie and Esme looked at each other across their tiny table smiled and shrugged. "Okay, we'll do it." The waiter grinned and said,

"good, then you will be able to tell all your friends that you have been Sui Lin'd." An hour or so later, much satisfied with Sui Lin's style of cooking they exited the restaurant heading in the direction of Notting Hill Gate Underground station in order to make their way back to the East End. As they reached the entrance to the station Eddie mentioned to Esme that whilst they were in the restaurant, he noticed a car parked across the road with two blokes sitting in it, as if they were keeping tabs on him. When they came out of the Chinese, he looked for it but it was gone. Just before stepping into the underground station, he thought he saw the same car with the same men in it, but had only just caught a glimpse as it passed by not full-on like.

"Any ideas Esme? You got a bleeding minder or something." Esme laughed hysterically, perhaps putting it on a bit more than was absolutely necessary.

"Apart from all the other things you are to me my lover, you're my minder Eddie, the best a girl could have, a beast of one at that!" Ed smiled. *A beast eh,* he thought, *like the sound of that.*

"Listen Esme, when I'm with you I feel that I can take on all-comers. I need to show London how powerful I can be. I can take whatever I want, just like a bleeding king." The last bit was drowned out by a tube train arriving at the platform.

The DCI's Office.

"Okay, Jackson, 'Jacko,' if there is even the tiniest bit of information you may be withholding, or even something of the nature of a rumour going about, I am not asking you to explain I am ordering you to tell me. God, this is like pulling teeth!" Ellis growled.

Jackson thought, *I've no choice now. Cursed if I do, cursed if I don't.* Still, he held back. Looking at his direct boss, he could swear he saw steam coming out of his ears. "Right sir, this is only a rumour.

"Tittle-tattle that sort of thing, nothing substantial." Ellis stood up, walked round to Jackson's side of the desk, parked his bum on the edge and repeated what he had said earlier, "This is off the record." Jacko stuttered aware of the trap he might fall into, he stood also. They were now face to face, too close for Jackson to read the DCI's body language. *well here goes my pension! He thought.*

"Thing is sir, and I repeat its very much on the grapevine some of the detectives are convinced that…" he paused just a mite too long.

"That Mike Bright could well be aware of Frank Bullymore's killer. Apparently, he was seen leaning over Sergeant Bullymore face whilst he was barely alive. Frank, so the story goes was whispering something to Bright sir. Whispering the identity of who stabbed him, maybe?"

The sentence tumbled out of Jacko at about a hundred miles an hour. There it was done, rabbit out of the bag. "Sir you did say completely off the record, sir?" DCI. Ellis returned to his seat and flopped down.

"Is this true?"

"Which bit, sir?"

"What do you mean which bit?" The DCI addressed Jackson by his full title. "Detective Inspector Jackson, the bit I am referring to is this. Is it true that D.I. Bright knows the killer of Sergeant Bullymore?"

"Cannot say for sure sir, it's just a rumour going around."

"Well, it's the first time that it's been brought to my attention and I thank you for that. Bring him in for questioning, let's hear what he knows first-hand and not second or third hand or even fourth. Good grief, may God rest the Sergeant's soul, he gives up his killer's identity with his last breath and Bright sits on it. My giddy aunt. No wonder he's signed himself off sick, if this rumour turns out to be true, well, let's just say, it will have far reaching career implications. Bring him in," repeated the DCI.

"Yes sir, consider it done, I will inform you the moment he steps into the station."

D.I. Jackson stepped outside the office, feeling a great deal the worse for the wear. The words 'career implications' now spinning wildly round and round inside his head. Implications for who, Bright, or himself? Or perhaps both of us. He consoled himself, that one, it was just a rumour and two, he had acted upon it, positively. He knew though from situations of the same type in the past, shit sticks but at least he didn't have to deal with it silently and alone. Jackson, convened a brief meeting with two of the visiting detectives.

They were requested simply to locate Bright and escort him to the station. They were also instructed to tell Bright, there had been a development in the ongoing murder cases and his corroboration of new facts that have emerged would be required. "And if he refuses?" one of the detectives asked.

"Well, then you will have to arrest him, won't you?"

"On what charge?"

"Withholding evidence, but it won't come to that," Jackson answered.

"On no account are you to enter his premises. We do not want to have an entry to his home without a warrant.

"We are unlikely to get a magistrate to issue one for that sort of charge. If he slams the door in your face call it in and we will have to think again. You might have to sit and wait for him to leave his house. When he does, nab him. Finally, there must be no mention of this action to any of your fellow officers. It's all a bit hush, hush. In the scheme of things, it is vital that you report directly to me and me only please gentlemen. If you have to call it in, ask for me first and foremost. Got it?" Heads nodded. "Good, sort yourselves out with an area car and get on with it. First port of call, his home address." He handed them a piece of paper with Mikes address written on it by hand.

Creekmouth Yard.

"How did you get over here, Eddie?" Errol enquired.

"Only you haven't got a driver since what happened to Wossname." Eddie snapped back, "I cabbed it." Errol didn't like Eddie's attitude, just lately at the mention of Wossname, Eddie stiffened up somewhat, Errol wasn't aware of the

Derkin's demise and not at all sure what was going on with Wossnames killers over on The-Isle-of-Dogs. Eddie liked it this way, better that Errol stayed on the edge of things, Errol was not party to the previous few meetings up at the Oasis. Had he have been present; the talk of murders here and there might have spooked him, frightened him off.

As it was, cars were coming in from Dave's efforts up West and making good dough too. The car-lot scheme was also going well, Mel and Billy had recruited quite a few more to protect, which was also pulling in good wedge. No, Eddie didn't want Errol to bottle it. "Anyway, Eddie since you are here let's have a drink and you can tell me what's on your mind. I've got a drop of malt whiskey in a draw somewhere but it'll have to be out of mugs. This okay with you?"

"Sure thing, that's kind of you." Errol located the whiskey and poured a good measure for both, Eddie spoke first. "The Bentley's got well and truly trashed outside Mrs Sharif's shop, it's probably still there, bit like a war trophy for those that did for Wossname."

"Do you want me to send a team of my lads over and bring it back here then?"

"That's exactly what I want you to do. Get it out of sight of Mrs. S. Bring it back here and crush it."

"That's no problem Eddie it will be gone by this afternoon."

"Fair do's mate, I cannot ask for better than that. I've asked Mel to cover the weekly visits to Mrs. Sharif's for the moment."

"Do you want a replacement motor Eddie?"

"Yea, that was going to be my next question, a Jag this time, the Bentley was a bit over the top like."

"Look, I might be mistaken, but I think I am being tailed. Could you ask one of your lads to leave the yard maybe go and get some fags or something. I need to know if there is a car parked somewhere outside with two shifty looking blokes in it."

"Off course, Eddie no probleemo, just wait here a tick and I'll get Little Allen to run me an errand and keep his eyes peeled."

"While he's doing that Errol, I was thinking of asking Dave to drive me around as well as supplying you with motors. It will mean a slowdown for a short while, until I can find someone trustworthy enough to do the chauffeuring."

"Sounds fine, but why are you asking me?"

Eddie took a swing of the malt letting it burn gently down his throat. He turned his back on Errol and gazed down through the grubby window that looked out on the breakers yard below. Watched for a moment or two, as yet another end-of-life car was dumped into the crusher, the hydraulic pistons making short work of reshaping the car into a metal cube.

"Out of courtesy mate. You see, you get to see a lot more of him than I do and only then when he drops into the Oasis on a Friday night with the weekly reddies." Just then Little Allen popped into the office.

"Well?" Errol asked.

"Yep," Little Allen replied enthusiastically. "Two geezers across the road in a dark blue Ford Zephyr. Two hub cabs missing, reg number 308 DCL. Starter motors fucked an all, I know that cause as soon as they clocked me clocking them, they had trouble getting the car to start. I could hear the starter motor whinging and whining before the engine caught. When they shot off tons of blue smoke came out from the exhaust. I would say that motor isn't long for this world." Eddie looked a surprised look towards Errol.

"That's great Allen, very observant of you." Errol nodded to the door for Little Allen to get back to work in the yard. "He's well into cars is our Allen, great mechanic too." Eddie turned back to face Errol.

"That's not the filth outside then? Can't see them running around in a dodgy banger." Errol looked over at Eddie.

"Then if it's not the filth as you put it, who then?"

"Dunno mate, but whoever it is, they won't be long for this world either. Anyway, let's not worry about them, I've got enough blokes that would be only too willing to have a chat with them and chop them up a bit. Listen, how long has Little Allen worked for you?"

"A couple of years off the top of my head. Do you want me to get his employment record for you?"

"No, just tell me, do you trust him?"

"Yes, I do Eddie."

"So, you don't think he made all that stuff up about the car outside just to impress us."

"Not for a second, cars have been his life. Worked at Ford over in Dagenham before he came here."

"Why did he leave Fords then?" Eddie asked.

"Nicking parts; hang on I think I see where this is leading."

"Sharp as a pin you are Errol, ask him if he wants an 'in' with the crew, mainly as my driver. I promise you he will not get into any fights and that, just got to drive me around and possibly me mum."

"What do you think Errol? Have a word with him today like. Right, I need to be somewhere else, can you ring us a cab. Oh, and before I go, why little?"

"We've got two Allen's working here. His proper name is Allen Little, so to unconfuse us we turned it round to Little Allen. Bit like John Little in Robin Hood."

"Yea, whatever Errol. I'll go and wait outside for the cab, see if I can spot that Zephyr and suss out the blokes in it."

Equus Ferus.

"Come on you bleeding nag, I've got a tenner on you," Dave Conti, shouted up at the radio commentary coming from track side at Alexandra Park in North London. The flat season was well underway and Dave as usual was in his favourite bookies on Mare Street shouting a bit too loud. His protestations drew the interest of a couple of blokes also in that day but for very different reasons.

The mildly interested pair were accustomed to punters shouting up at the speaker's commentary, it happened all the time. What drew there attention acutely was the mention of a tenner. Most punters would bet a bob or two each way, maybe up to a pound or two if they were acting on an overheard stable boys cert. Just Dave's luck though his horse, appropriately named 'You Lose' trotted in past the post some way back of the other runners. Dave tore up his ticket then made a move to leave the bookies premises. For a few seconds he was held up by the door, one of the two interested party tried to exit at the same time. Expert hands without Dave even realising, told the owner of the hands that Dave was armed. The owner of the hands nodded to his mate to exit the bookies with him, in an orderly fashion. No need to arouse this armed and flash with money bloke. There may be more to add. And there was, they watched as Dave climbed into a gleaming jet-black Mark 2 XK6 Jaguar, fired it up and roared off South in the direction of Stepney.

When Dave disappeared, literally, the two men walked back into the bookies and told one of the tellers to fetch the manager. The manager appeared in a matter of seconds. "Good afternoon gentlemen, I have your weekly payment right here in this envelope."

"Cheers," said one of the two. "All okay, no bovver or anything this week then?"

"Oh no," replied the manager, "you are doing a wonderful job. Haven't had a break-in or any bother since you offered us your protection."

"Good, that's how we like it." His partner in crime asked, "A few minutes ago, you had a customer in here chucking tenner's around, has he been in before?"

"Oh yes, sometimes he might spend up to twenty or thirty quid at a time."

"Funny, we've' never seen him before."

"Well, he drops in different times on different days."

"Oh yea, that's interesting, seems he might not want to lay down a regular visiting pattern then." The manager nodded, and started to get nervous. These guys were collecting the weekly for a serious outfit. This conversation he thought might be leading to some sort of violence of some kind.

"The other thing is," Mr manager offered up, "nine times out of ten he turns up in a different motor. I've put him down as a car dealer perhaps, based somewhere not too far away." Neither noticed Billy over in the corner, listening carefully. The pair of money collectors left the premises.

"Look," said Alf as they walked up the road to their next payment victim. "As long as he's behaving himself, he can come and go as he pleases. I mean, the more he tops up their takings, the more we collect."

"Hmmmm," said his mate, "He was armed though, a luger by the feel of it."

Alf said, "You always was good with your fingers, must have come from all that dippin' you did at the races."

"Best let the boss know, you know what he's like, if he got this from someone else, he'd 'ave out guts for garters."

"Tell you what, let's sit on it for a couple of weeks, see what happens like."

"Ere, who's that big fucker behind us, he looks well mean." Billy was closing on them fast. Two strides and he was alongside them.

"What's your fucking game them?" Billy demanded.

"No idea what you mean pal but if you want trouble, you've come to the right place."

"Well, here's a friendly warning," Billy shouted. He crashed a huge fist directly in the centre of Alf's face.

It sent him straight to the ground. He sat up, blood pouring from a broken nose, grabbing hold of his mate with a vice like grip, Billy opened his leather jacket to reveal a holstered gun and said quietly, "Trouble has come to you."

Mistakenly they thought Billy was after the envelope whereas the truth was, he was simply carrying out Eddie's order to mind Dave Conti. For a while now Billy had been shadowing Dave, for just such a situation. Up until now, he was kind of redundant. Alf got to his feet and held out the envelope. "Here take it. Just want you to know, you've gotten yourself in at the deep end." Billy hit him again, this time it was a full body blow. Alf went down again totally winded.

"Keep your sodding money. I'm here to see that no harm comes to the punter you just met at the bookies. He's more than capable of taking you two on, I am however, more than capable of killing you." Billy glared at them, wagged a finger turned and walked away. Alf slowly got to his feet, some kindly motorists stopped to offer help, they were waved on angrily the last thing they wanted was a sodding audience.

"We've still got the money."

"Yea," mumbled Alf, "thank God. Not a word of this okay?"

"Yea. Spose so," said his companion, none too sure if he was doing the right thing.

Get Lucky.

"Left here Allen." Three weeks ago, Errol let Little Allen leave his employment to join Eddie Coleman's crew. Officially as his driver. Just as well, Eddie had never learned to drive, and unofficially as his gofer Allen didn't mind one little bit. The hours were certainly longer, but oh the glamour. Driving the top man around in a gloss black Jag Mark 2 XK6, exactly the same one that Dave rolled in with a week or two ago. Exactly the same one he changed the plates on and Errol had dummied up the official paper work for. Little did Little Allen know at the time he would have the Jag mostly to himself. Eddie had him drive him to meets and stuff two or three times a week and his Mum about the same. The best of it was though Errol said, if it didn't work out, he could have his old job back. "Every one's a winner." He told his girlfriend Monica.

"Drop me here son, this is Esme's place. Pick us up at ten in the morning."

"Sure thing, Eddie. Is it okay if I give the Jag a polish up, top up the water and oil and stuff?"

"Of course. Take what's her name out."

"Monica, Eddie."

"Yea, that's it, take Monica for a spin, never know you might get lucky." Little Allen smiled, not exactly sure how to respond. He waited till Eddie was out of the car and into the street door of Esme's place, then sped off.

Rolled Down Wellies.

"Eddie, someone to see you." Eddie was deep in conversation with the Turk. He didn't look up; it was as if he hadn't heard Rosie. She was standing halfway down the stairs leading to the basement. She was alone in the café and wanted to keep an eye on things upstairs, Eddie looked up, all he could see was a pair of legs.

"Did you hear something Johnny?"

"Yea boss, Rosie called out there is someone to see you."

"Look, we need to plan how we're gonna fuck the rest of the Razor Gang up. Tell who ever it is to piss off, tell them we're double busy." Johnny did as he was asked and followed the legs upstairs. A smart looking bloke in casual gear was chatting to a couple of customers like they were old mates.

"That's him over there at the bar," said Rosie, "apparently he knows Eddie's mum quite well." Johnny beckoned him over. "Okay pal, what's with you and what do you want with Eddie Coleman?"

"Me name's Jimmy, Jimmy Toomey sir and you might be?"

"That's not important, just tell me what you want."

"Well, the thing is sir, I ferried Mrs. C. around a bit in a taxi, but the firm got closed down. So, I'm out of a job see now and Mrs. C. once told me that her son employed people, so here I am!"

"Hold on," said Johnny, "was this firm over in Leytonstone, the one that got burnt down?"

"The very same, sir."

"Wait here, Jimmy." The Turk, dropped down into the basement. "Eddie, it's a guy from the taxi firm that got torched."

A driver he said, "drove your mum around a bit, I think he wants a job or something."

"I've already got a driver, ain't I, Little Allen."

"Well, considering your mum knows him it might be the right thing to do, to have a chat with him, at least."

"Okay, Johnny, inform him I'll be up in a mo, grab some coffee and sit with him in one of the booths." Ten minutes passed before Eddie appeared. They were on their second cup by then, Eddie sat down opposite Jimmy and studied him as he talked, after a while he said,

"Your Irish ain't ya?"

"Spot on, Eddie, over from the Emerald Isle for these past two year or so."

"What else do you do apart from driving?"

"Well, sir, I'm very good with a pencil and paper, I trained as an accountant, so I'm good with figures, tax avoiding a speciality." Eddie raised his eyebrows monetarily. "We don't pay tax here, it's all cash in hand. We have money coming in from many different sources, all sorts."

"Well then Eddie, I'm your man, lead me to the books and I'll sort them out for you good and proper, on me life I will."

"Books," said Eddie, "we don't have books. We've got a safe downstairs stuffed with cash. When we need some dough. we ask Johnny here and he doles it out."

"He holds the one and only key."

"That's fair enough though so it is Mr Coleman, but here's another thing. Say you was to buy into a legit club or casino or something, they will have books.

"If they were to try it on with little porky pies about their worth, I could tell you in a flash if they were telling you the truth, or porky pie's just by looking at their books, see. Then there's wages and out goings that you might need to keep an eye on." Eddie glanced at Johnny, who was sitting alongside Jimmy. A wry grin, told Eddie all he wanted to know.

"How much we got in the safe Johnny?"

"Exactly or roughly?"

"Roughly will do."

"Nineteen thousand one hundred and eleven pounds."

"And exactly?" Johnny grinned again saying,

"Plus, eleven pence." Jimmy chipped in,

"More than enough to buy your way into club possibly in the West End, I would say." Eddie looked at Johnny again, This, was new territory for him. To date, he been acting like a king just took what he wanted without batting an eyelid. Johnny was nodding slowly, giving Eddie the green light as far as he was concerned. Eddie leaned back in his chair and visualised him and Johnny, surrounded by his most trusted, sitting a in a pucker club watching all the punters spending their weeks wages, and at least half of it going into their safe downstairs. New territory indeed. What was it he said to Esme that Sunday morning? "I love it up West, it stinks of money."

"Okay Jimmy, you're in, actually you'll have two jobs with us. We will supply you with a classy motor and you can use it to ferry my mum around whenever she wants. Deal?"

"I'll be glad to do so sir, a proper lady is your Mum."

"I'll let her know so that it doesn't come as a surprise. By the way what happened to the taxi firm owners?"

"Living it up in Spain to be sure. The insurance on the property saw to that."

"Happy, then are they?" Eddie asked.

"As sand boys, no regrets, it's what they were driving towards anyway."

"Who was the stiff then, that got torched?" Eddie enquired. "It was a relief driver chapiee from Tiszaujvaros in Hungary by the name of Tibor, all very sad so it was.

"No next of kin and a pauper's burial, paid for by Leytonstone Council, may God rest his soul. When would you like me to begin at all?"

"Give me a couple of days to get a motor for you and brief me mum and all that."

"Thank you, sir, thank you, I was not looking forward to digging up roads again. I was a navvy in me younger life, back in Ireland. You could spot me a mile away on the beach at Inch near Annuscaul over in Kerry." Eddie looked at Irish with blank eyes, his geographical knowledge outside of London, being about as bad as his mum's. "We used to trek over there for a week in the summer. Some of us navvies would roll our wellies down when at work, so I was left with a red ring round both me legs from the wellie turn downs rubbing the skin, it marked me out as a labourer, so it did!"

"Well, thanks for that bit of information."

"Before I go sir, may I ask a little tiny favour?"

"What's that then?" Eddie said irritatingly.

"May I have a little advance on me wages please, I have no money as what I was due from the taxi firm was not forthcoming and I'm living hand to mouth just now you see."

Eddie turned to The Turk. "Johnny, bung him a score will you and put an I.O.U. in the safe." Turning to Irish, he said, "Call back in here Irish Jimmy sometime next week and we'll set things in motion." Jimmy left the Oasis whistling an Irish sea shanty as he stepped outside on the pavement.

It might have been raining in fact it was drumming it down but to Jimmy, it was a beautiful day. "Well, what do you think then, Johnny?"

"Do it on appro, Eddie, suck it and see, he seems innocent enough and it will be a lovely surprise for Mrs Coleman."

"Yea, it will an all, I'd best get over to the house and have a chat, can you get hold of Little Allen and he can run me over."

"Hang on a second Eddie, before Irish arrived, we were discussing your next move against the Razors."

"I know, while you were waiting for me to join you up here, I decided to let the Stratford two, Billy and Mel sort them out, specially that head case Lenny. I want him done proper. Perhaps they can have a bit of help from Dave if he wants to. Keep all three of 'em sharp like. I'll have a word with them, sound them out like."

Mirth and Mischief.

Val was well pleased and relieved to hear Jimmy from the Liffey was alive and well. Even more pleased he was on the team and under Eddie's wing. She didn't like to ask too many questions about Eddie's work, but she thought it was worth pressing on a bit more about Jimmy.

Eddie explained Jimmy's dual role. "He's gonna be our accountant as well as ferrying you around, as and when you want him."

"Accountant," Val looked shocked but laughed because of the good news regarding Jimmy cos he was safe and well. "What do you need an accountant for?"

"All sorts Ma, mainly though, if I was to decide to buy into a club, he can scan their books make sure there's no jiggery pokery, you know dishonest and deceitful entries. On my life Ma, you can't be too careful, there's lots of bad people around these days, all more than ready to turn you over." Eddie smiled innocently. Val looked at him sideways and smiled too, then laughed again. Her son was growing up fast, becoming a shrewd operator, here come the beach huts maybe!

"And, what about this ferrying me around business?"

"I'm getting him a nice motor to drive you to – wherever, use him as much as you like. He'll be based at the Oasis so all you need to do, is to bell Rosie or

Esme and he will, like the genie, appear. By the way Ma, I've got a new driver for me, Little Allen's his name. If for any reason Jimmy can't make it, Allen will do the honours for you. While I've got you, what's the story with you and the buses? You know you can jack it in if you want."

"Not right now, thanks Son, wouldn't know what to do with myself, it gets me out of the house and I can by my little personal things without having to tap you up. Its improved at the depot a fair bit and I'm making some nice friends. Ask me again in a while or so."

"Okay Ma, as you wish, but keep it in mind anytime you want to quit, I will look after you."

"Thanks Son, I will." Then Eddie was gone. Val peeked out of the window just in time to see her son take his suit jacket off fold it neatly, and climb into the back of a well posh car. With a nod of his head the driver pulled slowly away. She waited for Eddie to turn and wave which would have been nice, but he didn't. *Well,* she thought, *let the neighbours get an eyeful of that!*

On the way back to the Oasis, Eddie explained to Little Allen regarding the new employee. Jimmy was to be heading up the ferrying around of Eddie's Mum, therefore he, Little Allen was to be exclusive to the boss unless directed otherwise.

News was on the car radio, it was carrying breaking news story regards an explosion in a property in East Ham Lane, East London today at twelve noon. The news carried the story further. The end terraced dwelling was all but demolished, adjoining properties needed to be evacuated, due to being rendered unsafe.

The main road taped off, but was now open again although areas alongside the damaged property was down to a single lane, controlled by temporary traffic lights. Police and the Fire brigade had been in attendance for some time. Early indications pointed towards a gas explosion. The Police have sealed the building off as it is deemed too dangerous to enter, therefore, they are unaware at this point as to anyone who might be trapped in the rubble.

Contractors are due to assess damage to the adjoining properties to establish if they can be made safe. Sniffer dogs will then be able to search for any survivors. 'Now on to other news' the radio said.

"Turn it off son and take a detour I want to see this for myself." Eddie didn't want to see the site of the explosion out of some macabre curiosity. There was something about the address that made him want to do a drive by.

A Door that Doesn't Fit.

Two Detective Inspectors were issued with orders to bring D.I. Mike Bright in to the Station. Either nice and calm like, or an arrest and caution coupled with good old-fashioned hand-cuffs. One of the D.I.s had his hands on the wheel of the area car, the other had his hands on the piece of paper with Mikes address. They definitely had the right road; it was on the same road as the police station they'd driven from. The driver was counting down the house numbers. "Must be almost there," he muttered, in the distance they saw a convenient place to park up. The spot was beyond Mikes house, meaning the car was out of his eyeline. Walking back, the two were preparing what to say if D.I. Bright opened the door. Should one of them jab his foot in the door, so that it could not be closed or simply allow him to shut the door in their faces and play the waiting game as requested by Jackson? They needn't have bothered; their decision was made for them.

They were just fifty yards or so from the door when an almighty bang and flashes of flame blew the front door of Mike Bright's house down the five steps, and out on to the wide pavement straight into the road. At the same time, both front windows and curtains followed. Glass and curtain material flung wildly in all directions by the force of the explosion. The two detectives staggered backwards feeling the intense heat of the blast. Passing traffic was littered with shards of glass and bits of wooden window frames. Some stopped dead in shock, others drove on as fast as they could. The detectives gathered themselves and decided to attempt an entry as there might be people that need rescuing. As they neared the site the end wall collapsed exposing upstairs bedrooms. The collapsed walls main job in life was to hold up part of the roof.

Seeing as the end wall had now retired proper, a substantial part of the roof decided to join the wall on the ground. The noise was horrendous, roof timbers splitting and cracking, tiles tumbling, bedroom contents sliding into view for all to see. Abruptly, the noise stopped, the house avalanche for now, was over. Brick dust was everywhere making it difficult to see clearly.

Windows either side of the once busy road but now halted were either cracked or blown in. One if the D.I.s ran back to the area car and called the station. The desk sergeant answered. "What the fuck was that, we heard it from here?" The D.I. explained who he was and relayed on what he had just witnessed, adding, "bomb disposal, as well as fire and ambulance needed, plus a ton of bobbies for traffic duties and to secure the area."

"What's the address?" asked the Sergeant. The D.I. read out the address from the bit of paper held in his now very shaky hand. "Are you okay, sir? Any injury to yourself?"

"Just a couple of minor scratches from flying glass. We were just outside the main blast area and luckily no pedestrians were hurt."

"Sir, did I hear you say we?"

"You did. Look just put D.I. Jackson on the line please."

East Ham Station.

"Morning everyone." Once again, fags were dogged out, plastic coffee cups set on desks, chair scraping as attending officers moved to form a semi-circle around 'Jacko' Jackson. D.I.

Numbers attending were down the visiting officers and detectives seconded to 'K' division, already returned to their respective stations in the various home county divisions. "Right, we will begin with the extremely sad news, which I am sure you all know by now, detective Mike Bright's body was found in the rubble of his near totally demolished home. At the moment foul play has been, unless evidence to the contrary comes forward, ruled out. A date has yet to be set for his funeral and I am sure many of you will very much wish to attend.

"Mike Bright's wife and son were out at the of time of the explosion. They are now in a safe police house with a specialist team put at their disposal. According to information received the extent of the damage to the adjoining buildings is minimal. The owners have been notified and will be returning to their homes as early as next week. Various bods including the gas supplier, the fire service etc., are investigated the cause of the blast. It seems an underground gas feeder pipe below the kitchen floor ruptured.

"Therefore, a large amount of gas collected in the kitchen, all it would require, would have been to switch on the lights to set off an explosion. In all a very unfortunate set of circumstances leading to Mike Bright's demise. Any questions? No, okay on to the next subject. The specialist corruption team have been stood down, three weeks of observations at various gambling dens have not produced anything worth following up other than Halliwell's massive debt at a Club known as Maddison's. That leaves us with tracking down the killers of Frank Bullymore and Halliwell. So, carry on." D.I. Jackson marched out of the incident room and was gone. The remaining officers and detectives currently sat in a semi-circle looked astounded at each other. Where was the direction, where was the usually determined and hard-bitten Jacko? It took quite a few moments and lots of chatter about what just occurred. Someone said, "I think he's taken the death of Mike in bad way."

"Could be that he will go off sick too, just like Mike did," said another. Yet a further voice popped up!

"So, will this mean another Inspector taking over the murder enquiries?"

"Who knows," said another voice, "perhaps we will all be asked to stand down next. What a bloody shamble eh?"

Growing Pains.

Reg Sullivan's operation in Hainault effectively got shut down. A number of his team joined Eddie's ranks bringing with them some lucrative protection jobs out Walthamstow way. The Derkin's from Crayford who hoped to snuff out Eddie's crew had the tables turned on them and were snuffed out themselves. Gone for good. Razor Gang on the Isle-of-Dogs were on the run, in hiding or actually leaving the Island to hide elsewhere. The fearsome twosome from Stratford were responsible for that, just the one stayed on, mostly because he was short of brain cells.

That would be Lenny the Scrote. Eddie asked Billy and Mel to bring him, almost dead please or barely alive to the Oasis for a little chat. On the business front, all was going strong. Musical instruments which Eddie like to call 'contraband stuff', car-lots, protection rackets, in-come from the Oasis café and bar all bringing in good wedge. Then there were the payments from Errol for the quality motors that Dave was nicking up West. The only fly on the ointment as far as Eddie could see, is that Dave had gone rouge again. Billy mentioned in passing to Eddie about the loud mouthing in the bookies and flashing tenner's about.

'Thing is' thought Eddie, Dave is very good at what he does. Rapping his knuckles over this might have the wrong reaction, Eddie asked Billy to find out who the two collectors he threatened, worked for and where they could be found to be spoken to. Until he found out, things could bloody well stay as they are. No need to upset the apple cart or even the orange cart, halfway into the race.

Irish Jimmy however did sow some seeds in Eddie's mind. Up until now, he hadn't giving a 'buy in' any genuine thought. Eddie popped up stairs to the café area. Looking out through one of the windows he could see the bright lovely

London sunshine outside. In all, considering it was East London, it looked like a nice day. He called Little Allen in from outside who was busy buffing up the Jag.

"Look son, I'm taking stroll over to me mum's house."

"Walking did you say, boss?"

"Yea, it's a lovely day and I fancy a bit of current bun on me boat race."

"Oh, okay then."

"I want you to drive slowly about a hundred yards behind me, when I get home park up outside and wait." Off they set. Little Allen feeling a bit strange about Eddie wanted to walk, Eddie, strolled along suit jacket slung over his shoulder not a care in the world.

They hadn't got very far when a uniformed copper out on his beat began to approach Eddie, his truncheon already drawn. He was well big this copper and he looked like he meant business. It was then and then only Eddie realised what was happening, like a fool he had his gun and shoulder holster on full view.

The copper was striding towards him now and about to blow his police whistle to summon help. Eddie stood his ground and unbelievably drew his gun from the holster pointing it directly at the copper. "Come any closer you fucker and I will shoot you," shouted Eddie. The policeman now running towards Eddie was closing fast truncheon raised above his head. Eddie clicked back the hammer with his thumb ready to fire, twenty yards away now Eddie held his nerve. He knew he would shoot fuck the consequences, ten yards away and Eddie was aiming directly at the copper's heart. He started to squeeze the trigger; five yards away, here goes nothing thought Eddie.

Just then something large and black loomed into Eddie's view. It was the Jag with Little Allen at the wheel, it half mounted the pavement and struck the policeman at a good forty miles per hour. The poor copper didn't stand a chance. Up and over the bonnet he went. The Jag's bonnet mounted emblem 'The Leaper,' tore into the copper's flesh as his body was dragged over it by its own momentum. He bounced on the roof ending up in a heap in the middle of the road. Eddie looked around, his main activity now was to put some distance between himself and the copper who was lying very still. The Jag quickly reversed back to where Eddie was standing, the passenger door swung open. "Jump in boss." Eddie holstered his gun. They drove off not bothering to look back.

"Thanks Allen. I had it covered didn't want to shoot though, unless I had too."

"Yea boss, does this make me a cop killer now?"

"All depends son, the street was quiet, no other cars around from what I could see, as it happens though, I was concentrating on a heart shot, did you see any motors about?"

"Not a one Eddie."

"Well then, chances are it'll be put down as a hit and run wont it?"

"Better get this motor over to Creekmouth, get it tidied up again and maybe a bit of a respray here and there. Drop me off at me mum's, then shoot over there and sort it out. Just remember this son.

"You're in *my* crew now not Errol's. I demand total respect from all those around me and that means you too. If Errol wants to know what happened tell him you've hit a dog or cow or something, not a bleeding copper okay?" Eddie's calmness helped young Allen to calm himself down a bit. Although it was his decision to ram the copper, he had taken the action to stop Eddie actually shooting an officer of the law. Now he was wondering if it was the right decision. Even worse he was to lie to his ex-boss. What the hell would Monica think?

Sharps.

A street tinker sitting in a doorway of a derelict prefab sharpening knives for a living, observed the entire episode. Seen the gun raised, seen the truncheon raised, seen the copper raised-twenty foot or so in the air. He knew he should go to the copper's aid, knew he should raise the alarm, knew he should at least do something. He decided. With all haste, he put the knives and sharpening stones in his sack and disappeared. He would return the kitchen knives to their rightful owner sometime later, after the dead policeman got carted off to hospital that is.

"Alright, Ma."

"Hello Eddie, to what do I owe the pleasure of your esteemed presence," Val smirked.

"Leave it out, Ma, I've come over for some advice."

"Well, that's a first, I'm very flattered but I don't think I can help you. You seem to be doing very nicely without me."

"Tell you what Ma, stick the kettle on and let's have a cuppa."

"So, what's it all about then Son?" Val enquired.

"Well, I've not come here to sip tea and dunk biscuits, have I?"

"Go on." Val nodded, all agog.

"I'm thinking of going legit, buying a pucka business like." Eddie sat back in order to study his mum's face.

"What the 'ell do you mean legit and what do think I would know about it, you know, running a legit business and that."

"No Ma, I might want to buy a casino or club or something, and have you as the manager, not run it."

"Me? Forget it son, I couldn't manage a pedalo, let a casino. Besides, what's the difference, manage it or run it? Anyway, what's put this idea into your head?"

"The difference," Eddie sighed, "is I own it, you do the day to day running of it."

"Irish Jimmy put the idea forward."

"It's still a no Son." His jacket was half opened and she saw the monogramed logo on his shirt and for the first time, the lethal looking gun in his holster. Upon seeing the weapon, she physically jumped spilling tea on her lap. Horrified Val shrieked involuntary. "Eddie, get out of the house and don't you ever come in here again with a gun."

"Do what Ma?"

"You heard, get out and get out now." She screamed. This was serious, Eddie thought nothing of the cop who was mercilessly run down just over thirty minutes or so ago. But this, he fell over himself to apologies.

Telling his mum that he idolised her and promised that he, her little boy had been extremely naughty and would never ever bring a weapon into the home never ever again. Tears ran down his face, Val was his rock, 119 Plevna was his sanctuary and here was he despoiling it for want of a shooter. Val stood back totally amazed and deeply shocked, it was as if Eddie had dropped down to the age range to about ten! She walked towards the distraught little boy, held him in her arms. Smoothed his brow, and hummed a lullaby whilst gently rocking him. The sobbing subsided, his breathing calmed down, he looked up at his mum and calmness enveloped him, he swore inwardly that this would be the first and last time he entered his and Ma Val's home tooled up.

Very gently Val lifted the gun from his holster and put it in a drawer in the sideboard. She laid Eddie down on the settee and continued to hum the lullaby. Eddie slept for seven straight hours; he awoke to find the house in darkness apart from the hallway light. Val, already gone to work on the late shift, he stood yawned, stretched and noticed a note in the corner of the mirror over the little fireplace. It read. 'Dear Eddie, it's in the sideboard take it and go. Don't bring it here again like you promised. Love, Mum. Kiss, kiss.' Now he knew where he stood, there was work and there was home. Never again would he mix the two.

Thinking about how to get back to the Oasis he absently looked out of the window that looked out onto Plevna Street. There waiting patiently was Allen in the tidied-up Jag. Allen saw the curtain twitch, he waved to signal all was clear for Eddie to leave. Gun retrieved, out of the front door and into the Jag took Eddie just under a minute. "Where to Boss?"

"Find a restaurant Allen, I'm famished, how long you been sitting outside?"

"Not long Eddie. Mrs. C. came out of the house not long ago, so I ran her to the bus depot.

"She said you were fast asleep and not to wake you, so I hope that was okay?" Eddie smiled,

"You did well kid, you did well, now let's eat,"

"I fancy somewhere up West."

"Okay Eddie, were on the way."

"Let's hope Dave doesn't lift this car when we're eating." Eddie laughed.

"Didn't think of that one boss, I'll leave a note on the dashboard so he knows it on the firm."

"Good idea, now put your foot down. Toe nails in the radiator is the new term for speeding, ain't it?"

Confession.

D.I. Jackson, had good reason to leave the briefing in an abrupt fashion. All who were present without any new clues or fresh ideas, simply plodded on in the same direction as yesterday and day before and the day before that. Jacko's early exit from the a.m. briefing was more important than the briefing itself. The under-cover officer had requested to meet with him at a pre-arranged location at 10.00hrs sharp. The officer must have something really special to pass on, to break cover and meet in a public place. Jacko entered the appropriately named 'Downstairs at Micks' on the Silvertown Road. Making his way downstairs he was glad to be out of the bright London sunlight and entering into the gloom of the coffee bar below street level. He had a thumping headache and was cursing himself for not grabbing some aspirin tablets on his way out from the first aid box back at the station. Not too many people in at that time of day, thankfully.

A youngish couple at one table sipping from a single 'Seven Up' with two straws in the bottle neck. Another couple, two young ladies chattering something about last night's antics with their respective boyfriends, he was glad nobody had put any music on the Jukebox. A few minutes passed allowing his eyes adjust to the dimly lit interior. Jacko sauntered over to the counter and ordered a coffee, as he did so he heard the clacking of high heeled shoes making their way down the wooden staircase. He turned, recognised who owned the shoes and held up a 'T' then a 'C' indicating tea or coffee, a 'T' was returned. The owner of the high heeled shoes sat at the nearest table, removed her coat and made herself comfortable, Jackson, brought the drinks over, sat opposite and smiled a greeting. "Thanks for coming," the officer said. "Sorry about the short notice, but this cannot wait."

"I'm all ears," D.I. Jackson replied. They both leaned forward so that they could not be overhead.

Disruptive Diners.

Little Allen parked up. They were just off the Dilly, in Wardour Street. Allen found a nice little spot for the Jag on the corner of Peter Street. "Should be safe here Boss." Eddie smiled to himself, *proper little petrol-head this one, loves motors as about as much as I love money.*

"Don't forget to leave a note in case Dave tries to lift it." Soho was at its busiest.

They were in theatre land. All around one could fall over the many gambling clubs, strip joints, dirty book shops, Chinese restaurants, casinos, whore houses, coffee bars, drinking dens, pushers, users, queers, tarts the offing pot. Bit like liquorish all sorts, all cheek by Jowl. Couple of ladies of the night beckoned to them the moment they got out of the Jag. "Give it miss girls." They looked Eddie over and thought there was a bit of danger about him and so decided to ply their trade a little further down the road. "Didn't think much of your one," said the peroxide blond, "Probably a woolly woofter by the looks of him."

They linked arms giggling, hitched up their tiny mini-skirts a little further and disappeared down towards Piccadilly Circus, looking for some real men. Eddie and Allen dived into a Steak bar just up the road from the Jag and settled down to a well-earned steak and chips. Busy as hell, they were lucky to get seated, two beers arrived. "On the house," the waiter said.

"This is the bloody life, eh Allen?" He had to agree, this was the first time Allen had been in this part of London. *A far cry from Dagenham*, he thought.

"Let's live it up while we can, mate. I was thinking of buying into a club or something up this way, maybe this place will do. Watch this."

Bold as brass, Eddie instructed the waiter to send the manager over.

"Is there a problem, sir?" he enquired politely.

"Look pal, just fucking get 'im and do it now."

One or two of the customers who were sitting at nearby tables were beginning to take an interest. A party of lads who had been making a bit of a racket looked across the tables at them. Eddie beckoned one of them over and politely asked what the fuck was he looking at, before he could answer, Eddie upped him knocking him to the floor. His mates stood up and began rolling their sleeves up, grabbing steak knives from their table. Other diners sensing violence threw cash on tables and departed as fast as they could. Little Allen almost pissed himself. *Five against two. Bad odds*, he thought. However, he had reckoned without Eddie's resolve in such situations.

As the angry lads made their way across to Eddie's table, they upturned some of the now empty ones and empty chairs. China plates, with half eaten steaks fell to the floor of the restaurant, a chair was picked up and flung at Eddie. It flew over his head; he was smiling like a shark.

Little Allen was now close to shitting himself, the five were almost at their table, arms raised to shoulder height, hands bunched into fists, about to fly in all directions, others with steak knives at the ready. Even the one that was originally upped, now off the floor was going for it. Eddie whispered to Allen, "Now the real fun begins." He drew his gun and fired three times only slightly above their heads, close enough to make them dive to the floor, the bullets smashing into the optics on the far wall. Massive panic ensued, the remaining diners plunged under their respective tables, women and kids screaming.

Others including the waiting staff made a bolt for the comparative safety of the kitchen, the bovver boys were halted in their tracks. Guns, especially ones that went bang 'three times' were not something to be trifled with. Eddie, lowered his aim directly at them and quietly asked them to leave. When the dust settled and they had gone, Eddie finished off his beer. The staff and customers hiding in the kitchen slowly, cautiously filed out. The diners grabbed their belongings and coats then melted into the fabric of Soho. No doubt they would all be regaling the story to friends and family for some time to come. The waiting staff dutifully tidied the up-turned tables and chairs, being careful to clean all of the food strewn hither and thither on the floor. Eddie and Little Allen were now the only two customers. In due course a chap came over and said, "I believe you wanted to see me?"

"If you're the manager, then yea, that's correct," Eddie replied. "Please, take a seat."

The manger sat. He was a thick set man with a thick set Scottish accent. His eyebrows met in the middle; Eddie was sure he had heard something about that in the past but couldn't recall it just now.

"How much do I owe you for the lost business and the bit of damage over by the bar?"

"Well, I don't quite know, sir," the manager replied.

"How does a couple of ton sound?" asked Eddie.

"Och, well. I'm not sure what that means but it sounds more than enough thank you." Eddie pulled out a roll of bank notes and peeled off two hundred quid.

"There you go pal, now do me a favour get rid of the staff for the night and put the closed sign in the door." The manager did what he was asked, praying that nobody was thinking about getting in touch with the police regarding the shooting.

His main concern was not this armed thug and his gun, it was the deplorable state of affairs in the kitchen. For many a month now, he had ignored the kitchen staff constantly moaning about the poor state out back. If anyone from any authority stuck his nose out there the restaurant would face automatic closure and no doubt a heavy fine to boot. The owner would be none too happy about that.

"So, you're just the manager then, are you? Who's the owner then?"

"Mr Papadopoulos, Adonis for short." Eddie studied the manager.

"Do you have any one to protect you, you know, make sure animals like me don't shoot you up and that?"

"No, we don't. Adonis won't be intimidated."

"Oh really, well he fucking will now, you tell him this place is on our books for protection as of now. Its £100.00 per month, first month in advance. Oh, look you've got 200 nicker in your hands. Hand over 100 and you're covered with our brand of protection for at least a month."

"Tell Mr P. about that," Eddie said menacingly.

"Bit difficult," said the manager, eyebrows knitting even further. "He's gone home for a family funeral."

"Gone home?" Eddie questioned, "Where's home?"

"Athens," said the Steak Bar manager. Eddie looked confused.

"Greece, Athens. It's the capitol, bit like London is for England. Fuck off with the geography lesson mate can you get him on the dog and bone, or what?"

"What, now?"

"Yes now."

"Well, I suppose that will be okay, its roughly the same time over there as it is here, so he may be contactable." Eddie was getting uncomfortable, he wanted to speak with the organ grinder, not the bleedin monkey.

"Well bell him then," Eddie bellowed. The manager walked over to where the optics took the worst of the fusillade, swept broken glass off the phone and began the process of obtaining an overseas number, eventually the operator said your number is ringing.

Athens.

A deep voice answered after ten rings, "Kalispera." Mac the managers grasp of Greek lingo was zero, he thought and spoke only in a broad Scottish dialect.

"Hello, can I have a wee minute with Adonis please?"

"Anamoni." (Please wait).

"Yes, this is Adonis, who is calling?"

"Hello Adonis it's me, Mac from Soho."

"Yes, what do you want?"

Mac handed the phone to Eddie. Twenty minutes later Eddie and Adonis had begun a partnership, together they had cracked a deal on the phone. The basis of which was this, Irish Jimmy would be allowed to view the books. On Jimmy's say so and his only, Eddie would hand over £2000.00 in cash for sixty percent ownership and sixty percent of the takings.

They said their farewells and promised to meet at the restaurant when Adonis was back from Greece. Eddie turned to Mac. "I'm your boss now pal, it's in the deal struck with Mr P. We won't need to charge for the protection, so the £100 you've got, is for breakages and stuff that I caused earlier.

"Make sure you spend it wisely and keep any receipts. Little Allen here will be back tomorrow with our accountant for a glance at your books, be sure to have them ready." He looked at Allen, who nodded.

On the way back to the Oasis, Little Allen was deep in thought. *What the fuck have I done? In the space of one day, I've mown down a copper who's more than likely brown bread. Been an accomplice to a West End shoot up, and a witness to an aggressive buy in, to what looks like a successful legit business.*

Not only that, I'm due back tomorrow to sit with Irish Jimmy while he gives the books the once over. What on earth am I going to say to Monica?

"Nothing." Eddie called out from the back of the Jag making Allen jump out of his skin.

"Bloody hell Eddie!"

"Yea well, I was reading your mind as it happens, I could hear your thoughts from here."

"Thing is Allen, you are going to be working very close to me. You will see and hear all kinds of things that the others around me will not. Not as they will see things, anyway. For instance, Johnny and the others will be told about the 'in' with the Steak bar, but not about the shooting bit got it?"

"Mind you, they know I'm fucking mentally disturbed bordering on insane, so they would probably put two and five together and figure it out for themselves.

"But as I say, I don't want you repeating things and that goes for Monica too. That would be well out of order, got it?"

"Absolutely, boss." One thing Eddie kept back, Mr P. mentioned two other steak restaurants in the West End plus another in Dollis Hill on the Edge of Gladstone Park, all under his wing that he might be willing to have Eddie buy in too. What with all the stuff that had been going on, he felt suddenly extremely tired.

He invariably did where spending money was concerned. As he drifted off, he had a yen to change the name of the steak bar in Wardour Street to 'Steak-Away.' A dosshouse it was not, quite up market actually. *Yea like that,* he thought, as sleep descended.

Leaving the West End to West Enders, the Jag moved effortlessly from West to East, Eddie happily asleep in the back, Little Allen anxious and worried to hell up-front. It was all very well keeping his mouth shout but for how long? He began to wish he hadn't taken up the post with Eddie Coleman and stayed put at the Yard at Creekmouth. Time was getting on a bit; traffic was lighter at this time. They arrived at the Oasis well within the hour. Eddie woke up as soon as the engine was switched off and the Jag stopped its purring. Eddie gave Allen tomorrows rota. "Get back here about ten, pick up Irish Jimmy and get him over to Wardour Street. Stay with him, when he's done run 'im back here, rest of the day is yours." Eddie peeled off a tenner. "Tank up the Jag, keep the change. Get over here the following day and see what's what." Little Allen fired up the Jag. *Fuck it*, he thought, *I'm going over to Ripple Road, if it's still open, drop into the Ship and Shovel.* The ship was almost on top of Errol's yard. Occasionally, his workmates from the yard spent some late evenings having a drink and a game or two of darts in there. Little Allen had it in mind to be with them for a while and bring a bit of sanity back to his mind before fronting out Monica.

East Ham Incident Room.

"Morning gentlemen, apologies for my early departure yesterday." D.I. Jackson was once again at the helm. Standing by the information board which was now plastered with names, dates, connections, locations and many, many photos. Each photo had a name written underneath together with the date it was introduced to the board. It was now the Seventeenth of September, approximately two months since the murders of Sergeant Bullymore and Constable Halliwell. The weather forecast was for a hot and sticky day, an Indian summer they called it, short sleeved shirts were the order of the day. The gym currently being used as their incident hub was not a particularly cool place to work, during the last two or three days the indoor temperature had climbed to sixty-five degrees Fahrenheit, uncomfortable to say the least. Tea urns replaced by several glass jugs of lemonade, those attending turned their attention to focus on the Detective Inspector.

Jacko, pointed to a photo in the middle of the information board directly at the Madison. "This will be priority number one, it is thought that whoever owns it may have strong links to our murderer. Up until now information has it, the owner may well have paid someone one to silence Halliwell. Therefore, we need to bring in the owner for questioning.

"My feeling is, if we establish who killed Halliwell it won't be long before we unravel the mystery surrounding Sergeant Bullymore's murder. Due to conflicting information Jake Speck may not now be the owner. If we can establish that fact, we can one, eliminate him from our enquiries and two, press hard to establish who does own the Madison as of right now.

"Priority number two. Can we hear from the two officers who were requested by D.I. Bright, to trawl through police records both here and neighbouring stations for stabbings or murders involving a bread knife?"

"They were from the extra bodies brought in to swell the ranks sir," a voice stated.

"Right, well a couple of you, find and go through the paperwork handed over from the extra's before they left us and find the appropriate reports, if any. Third priority. Three uniform bodies over to Limehouse please to assist with the door to door. The P.C. involved in the hit and run incident has died of his injuries. 'H' division is dealing with the investigation and is asking for some help. Normally, with all that we have on our hands I would only respond to such a request reluctantly. However, information I have received from the undercover officer indicates the hit and run merchant may have a bearing on our two murders here at 'K' Division. That's all gentlemen. Next briefing, tomorrow at 14.00hrs."

Ropemakers. E14.

"Eddie, bleedin coppers are crawling all over the place about a mile away, down near Ropemakers. Any thoughts or ideas?" asked Bomber, who continued without waiting for an answer. "Rosie came up that way this morning and saw them knocking on doors, talking to people walking around and that, made her feel right queasy she said." Eddie as per usual, was sitting at his round table in the basement, Esme by his side stirring sugar into his second cup of tea. Johnny the Turk, nearby, putting the paper money that had just come in from Dave Conti into bundles of, fives, tens and twenties. Eddie looked up from the morning papers.

"Morning Bomber mate. My guess is, it's probably got something to do with that hit and run I would think. Say's in the paper here the copper died of his injuries. Don't let it get to you mate but thanks for letting me know. Send a couple of the boys out and about from upstairs, you know trusted ones. Perhaps they could take an innocent stroll over there and ask about a bit, you know do our own fucking investigation. Not immediately though let the law move on to other things, best not to arouse suspicions. Tell them to go over the same ground as the door knockers when old Bill has had enough of hitting brick walls. Probably get a hundred times more information from the locals than the filth ever will. Who's going to talk to them wankers anyway. They must get well pissed off with, sorry guv, no guv, not me guv, saw nothing guv. Wankers, all of them." As it turned out, Eddie couldn't have been more wrong. He winked at Esme.

"Okay," replied Bomber, "I'll get two or three lads to pop over there and ask about a bit." Waiting for Bomber to disappear, Esme whispered,

"Didn't you say you knew something about the hit and run Eddie?" He nodded.

"Look Esme, this is my manor, I've got lads out and about that keep me up to date, yea sure I know something. Want I want to know now, is what the police fucking well know. I'm sure they wouldn't do a door knocking job, unless they thought they were on to something and I want to know what they know, see. So, pour me another cuppa and stop your fretting. It's all under control." Esme wasn't so sure though, she secretly long harboured negative thoughts about Rosie. What was it, Bomber said earlier? 'Rosie came up that way this morning?' Wasn't her normal route to work passing by the Ropemakers Park area. What was she doing over that way with all the coppers in the world mooching around, stopping people and asking questions? Eddie snapped his fingers in front of her eyes. "Penny for your thoughts Esme."

"Sorry, bad night last night nearly dozed off then," she lied. The police door to dooring programme stretched wide of the Ropemakers area. Prefabs, houses, tents, businesses, shops, factories all knocked up and knocked up again. The three officers on secondment from East Ham Station, were about to climb back into the area car and head back to East Ham for lunch, when the driver said,

"Look, I know it's a wild duck chase, and I know you're going think I'm going mad, but I spotted a tinker earlier, knife sharpener perhaps or something.

"He was ducking and diving in and out of the alleyways he was, looked like he was trying to dodge anyone in uniform, bet you a pound to a ha'penny, he knows something." The two coppers with him, looked at each other, shrugged their shoulders and said,

"We take the bet. Let's drive around some, see if we can find him."

By now it was past midday, it was hot in the area car, even with the windows open.

"Look, over there," the officer sitting in the back almost shouted. Sure enough, a tinker type was sitting on the kerb outside someone's front door. In his grubby hands he held a pair of garden shears and was busy working on one of the blades buy putting it through the grating of a drain then bending the blade until it was relatively straight again.

At the same time, bellowing out something indecipherable with every other breath or so. The bellowing seemed to bring people to their front doors with various bits and pieces to be mended or sharpened. "Don't want to frighten him off, best be just the one of us drops in on him for a friendly chat. Whoever it is, helmet off, tie off, look a bit casual like." The driver was elected to interview the tinker. So, helmet off, tie off, jacket off, he sauntered over to where the tinker was working.

Sitting down on the kerb beside him he said, "That's a brilliant way to mend garden shears mate, I've learnt something from you today."

"Cost you a bob," the tinker growled holding out a knarled and blackened hand.

The driver coughed up the coinage. The driver started to talk about the weather; It fell on deaf ears. "You're the police aren't ya? Spose you wanna hear about the dead garda then?"

"You mean the policeman in the hit and run," the driver asked, hardly able to contain his excitement.

"Thasum boy, the dead garda."

"What do you know about it then?"

"Cost you a couple of bob an all." The driver dug out the correct amount. "Big n shiny black car it was."

"Did you see the number plate?"

"Aye."

"Did you remember it?"

"Cost you a tanner." A sixpenny piece changed hands. "Can't read or write."

"So that's a no then?"

"Ginger pulled a gun he did."

"Ginger, what do you mean?"

"Cost you a bob."

"Sorry pal, you've had more than enough, what do you mean by ginger?" The tinker got up to go.

"Okay, okay, here's half a crown, but before I hand it over you've got to tell me all you know." The tinker's eyes twinkled and his nose twitched. He loved the smell of silver coins, what with the money he had already gained the half a crown would see him a proper bed in the Sally Army hall next door to Limehouse nick for the next few nights at least?

"Him with a gun, ginger topped, like a bird's nest an all. All clean n smart he was. Pointed it right at the garda, but the big n shiny motor got in first, it 'im up in the air. S'all I saw. S'all I knows. God's me witness." The driver paid the travelling tinker and made his way back to the car. His two companions watched the whole thing from their vantage point. As the driver reached for the car door, he looked round just in time to see the tinker grinning wildly whilst sticking two fingers up at all three of them.

"Well?" the other two asked.

"Bingo," said the driver, as he climbed in to the driving seat. "Got a description. Looks like there was two of them, one with a shooter, the other driving a black car. The shooter bloke has ginger hair, armed and very dangerous by the sound of things. Apparently, he was about to kill our colleague for one reason or another but was beaten to it by the driver of the black car. Sounds like murder with intent to me. Let's get back to the station and report this to Jacko. He can decide if he wants to pass it on to the local force."

"I'm not too sure he will, you know," stated one of the watching officers. "Besides, that old boy will probably be of no fixed abode probably doesn't even have a surname. Some of these tinkers move around the country a lot, could be in Birmingham by this time tomorrow."

"Yea your right, fair do's," said the driver, "I'll have a wander back and see if I can get a name plus a fixed location where we can get a written witness statement." All three looked over to where the tinker had been plying his trade, there was no sign of him, gone in the blink of an eye. "Okay, let's split up and search for him," requested the driver. Thirty minutes later all three met up by the car, all three hot and bothered the tinker had vanished into thin air. As they drove away a net curtain twitched. The tinker took refuge in the house where he had been working outside on the doorstep. He asked the old lady who gave him the pair of shears to mend, if he could use her toilet, in return there would be no charge for the repair.

Mr tinker was still in the house supping tea and eating biscuit's when the three coppers drove away. Once again, this time from behind a net curtain, he grinned and stuck his grimy fingers up. As he made his way out of the house belonging to the charming and obliging lady of later years, he mumbled something to himself as he rifled through the handbag sitting on the polished sideboard. Gently closing the front door behind him he heading for pastures new.

It was then he transferred the cash from the purse to his trouser pocket, the empty purse tossed callously into a nearby garden hedge. Down the road a bit the street tinker passed a bunch of kids, two of which were holding either end of a long skipping rope. Three were skipping in the middle, in unison. Those that held on to the rope ends, sang a ditty as they swung the rope rhythmically.

'Say what you will.
School dinners make you ill.
And the Shepherd's Pie
Makes Davey Crocket Cry.
All School din dins.
Come from Pig bins.
And that's no lie.
That's no lie.'

A Spitfire Comes to Town.

The low loader slowly trundled into the Creekmouth breakers yard on Ripple Road, laden with what looked like a whale, covered in tarpaulin sheeting and securely roped down. The lads on site quickly got the ropes and sheeting off. They all stood back totally amazed, they were gazing minus it wings, which were due in later that day, on a W.W.2 Supermarine Spitfire in all its glory. Errol's was smiling, looking down at the great bird from his office. Smiling at the surprise of the chaps in the yard. Just lately they had all kinds coming in for breaking, but this. This for sure is a thing of beauty. It was minus part of its tail plane, shot off which no doubt caused it to crash land at Biggin Hill. It was there it had been mothballed until now. Errol took the call, arranged for the transport and was paid handsomely for taking ownership. They would of course break it down, but for the moment, Errol wanted to hoist it up on some steel girders so that it could be seen by the outside world. There was no end of yards like Errol's along the Ripple Road and the sight of such a bird might mean more spot business and further expansion. He could even stick a union jack up above the cockpit. The wings, when they arrive will be crushed as soon as. But the Spit up on girders, what a statement that would make. Good for business. Errol opened the widow and called down. "What do you think lads?" Thumbs up all round, it wasn't long before the local press got involved. Soon after it was hoisted onto girders and could be seen from miles away, it attracted a host of interest. Some good and some not so good. Pictures appeared in local rags, front page news. The Evening Herald featured it in a centre page spread. A picture of Errol appeared smiling, standing outside the yard pointing up to the aircraft. The reaction was a little short of spectacular. Vehicles were turning up from all over to be scrapped. The yard, crusher and smelter, lava bucket and all working now at full tilt. The recycling company responsible for purchasing and collecting the metal cubes and smelted base materials, were overjoyed at the increase in business volumes from Errol.

They too were thinking of re-investing and up-grading. Errol was preening himself, congratulating himself on his entrepreneurship. Not to mention the enormous influx of extra income.

All of this of course was very good news for Errol, no doubt his father would be delighted with the headway and strides up the income ladder implemented by his son. On the other hand, someone else would no doubt have the opposite view.

The Bridge House Canning Town.

Eddie listened intently; his gaze fixed keenly on Dave Conti. Dave briefly outlined what was happening over at Creekmouth yard. Eddie held a hand up to halt Dave in mid flow, the barman, saw the gesture and assumed, Eddie wanted another round. Within minutes two light ales were brought to Eddie's table, they both looked up at the barman quizzically. Nodded their thanks, then resumed their conversation. Dave went on to explain more fully. The Bridge House was relatively quiet at three in the afternoon, the barman whispered to his hired help, "Somehow it always goes quiet when Eddie Coleman appears, especially when accompanied by one of his minders."

"Got a bit of a reputation then has he?"

"Christ, I'll say so, stops at nothing to get his way, rumour has it he organised the demolition of a pub in Hainault. Raised to the bloody ground it was. Shot up first then torched." The hired help, gawped over at Eddie in awe.

"For fucks sake, don't stare at him!" stuttered the barman, "'e's got eyes everywhere." However, because of what Dave was telling Eddie, he was completely unaware of the conversation going on behind the bar. Just as well, as from what was being explained by Dave, Eddie was slowly going insane.

"Publicity," he spluttered.

"We've got nicked motors going in there at all times night and day, what the fucks he thinking of. If he's not careful, he's gonna get sussed and big time, he's handing us to the filth on a golden fucking platter. How long's this been going on?"

"Can't be exactly sure boss. I usually turn up at night. So, anyone that's keen to take a look's long gone. Spose about two or three weeks."

"Well, he's kept this under his belt. Were supposed to be business partners and he hasn't had the grace to fill me in about it. Something told me not to trust him as far as I could throw him." Dave could see the table between him and Eddie being upended any time soon, beers, beer mats and ash tray spilling onto the floor. He was well known for his dark moods, problem was, nobody knew what the triggers were. One minute he's slapping you on the back the next you're on the deck with his Cuban heeled boot rammed on your windpipe. On this occasion thankfully, he was comparatively calm. It was only hours ago; he and Adonis had agreed on a deal to 'buy in' the other two Steak Bars in Soho. He was not too keen on the Dollis Hill outlet as the location it sits in is predominantly a Jewish area. Eddie was none too sure if the Steaks that Adonis buys, cooks and sells are Kosher. So, he gave that one a miss. All that was necessary was for Irish Jimmy to check the books on the Soho pair, Eddie to pay the 'in' fee and that was that.

"Right Dave, sup up were going over to Creekmouth right now. Little Allen's due back here in ten minutes or so. He can run us over there. Just don't let him know why we're going."

Back at the Ranch.

Three constables were sitting in the station's canteen, nursing three cups of tea, when D.I. Jackson walked in. "Christ, you lot look a bit hot, you wanted to see me? I have got an office here you know."

"Yes sir, it's just that we were a bit thirsty."

"Well, what have you got that couldn't wait for a written report?" The driver of the three was elected by the other two to be the spokesman. He cleared his throat and took a final gulp of his tea. "Well sir, it's sort of good news and bad news."

"What!" asked Jackson sighing deeply, "let's have the bad bit first." The driver swallowed hard.

"We lost him sir." Jackson frowned.

"Sorry, I'm not here to play silly games, perhaps I should hear the good bit then and I can decide if it's good or not." A member of the canteen staff brought Jackson a cup of tea and placed it in front of him.

"The good news is sir; we questioned a witness regarding the possible hit and run on the constable."

"How solid is this err witness, then?" asked Jackson.

"Not the best sir, turns out he's a travelling tinker. I or rather we, saw him whilst helping out at the door-to-door initiative over at Ropemakers, he looked like he was trying to dodge anyone in uniform."

"Well, he would, wouldn't he?" Jackson remarked. "Probably wanted for all kinds of misdemeanours."

"Yes, you are probably quite right, sir. However, I, or rather we, deduced he might possibly have some information regarding the hit and run sir."

"Oh, did you now? And what prompted that thought between all three of you?"

"Just a three-way hunch, sir, and it turned out to be a right hunch."

"Right hunch! what sort of metaphor is that supposed to be?"

"It turns out, sir after a bit of silver coinage changing hands in order to prize anything out of him. Oh, and I would be obliged if you can organise for the money that I gave him to be reimbursed to me, sir."

"Get on with the story constable."

"Well as I was saying it turns out sir, this tinker bloke reckons he saw the whole thing." Jackson waited for the punch line, he truly hoped it would be today some time and not tomorrow.

"Are you referring to the hit and run on the constable?" "Oh yes, sir, most definitely sir." Jackson remained silent. He leant forward, arms now resting on the table. "Apparently, there were two men involved sir, well at least according to the tinker chap. The first one pointed a gun at the constable and it seemed he was about to pull the trigger when a black shiny car mounted the pavement, hit the constable throwing him right up in the air sir. The car reversed back to the man with the gun who jumped into the passenger seat and they roared off, leaving the constable in the middle of the road."

"Type of the car?"

"He doesn't know, sir, just black and shiny."

"Registration number?"

"He can't read or write, sir, or so he tells us."

"Description of the driver?"

"He didn't see him sir."

"What about the shooter?"

"Ah well, sir, that's where it gets interesting."

"Go on."

"Ginger hair and very dapper looking."

"Dapper, that's an old fashion saying. Is that it then?" "Yes, sir."

"Who interviewed this tinker?"

"I did, sir, well it was more of a chat." Jackson looked at the other two.

"And where were you two when this chat was taking place?"

"In the area car, sir."

"So, you didn't hear any of the conversation with the tinker?"

"No sir."

"So, you cannot corroborate any of what I have just heard?"

"No sir."

"So, it could all be hearsay?"

"I suppose so sir." The driver looked crest-fallen. D.I. Jackson sat back and looked at each constable in turn, then asked,

"Did you report this to anyone over at the Ropemakers door-to-door shindig?"

"No sir, we came straight back here because we wanted you to hear it first-hand."

"Right, I will talk to my opposite number over at Limehouse who requested extra bodies." Jackson leaned forward and almost whispered, "The description the tinker gave you regarding the shooter might just match a person of interest.

"Although we cannot use any of what you have just told me in a court of law, I can however, now tell you that a piece of jigsaw has fallen, 'hopefully' into place. Go and put you heads together and make out an appropriate report. I want it on my desk by tomorrow morning please. Your 'right hunch' might turn out to be a good right hunch. By the way, anything you can tell me about the tinker?"

"Yes sir, he called the constable who was hit by the car, garda."

"Garda! That's Irish for police, did he sound Irish at all?" Jackson refrained from adding 'at all, at all, at all.'

"Well, he did have an odd accent sir, part Irish part East End, I thought."

Jackson asked, "And as to his whereabouts?" All three shrugged their shoulders and looked down studiously at their empty tea mugs.

Ripple Road.

"Looks good Errol never thought I'd see an airplane stuck up the air like that no wings an all. Caused a right stir ain't it?" Eddie was standing outside by the tall wooden gates of Creekmouth Yard. Errol standing next to him looking up at the spit proudly.

"Did it not occur to you, all the interest shown might be a problem to our business arrangement."

"Sorry Eddie, don't see the connection."

"Take the fucker down now," he demanded. "We've got high end cars coming in here almost daily, thanks to Dave here. The old Bill up West are scratching their bloody heads not sure which way to turn. And you invite the worlds fucking press to see our operation for themselves. How long do you think it will take the filth to show an interest too? They ain't totally thick Errol. All it would take is a local copper who is looking for a quick promotion through the ranks to come to have a chat with you about your high-flying bird. In comes Dave with a Roller hot of the press like, then what. The balloon goes up, that's what. You must be creaming it what with all the motors going abroad, keeping your bloody head down at this end is essential." Errol took offence and went on the defence.

"This is my yard and I'll do as I please."

"Right, grab hold of him Dave, let's take him inside for a little chat." At the utterance of that East End threat of a sentence, Errol's legs turned to Jelly. Dave twisted his arm behind his back and frog marched him across the yard towards the steps leading up to his office. This was new territory for Errol, he was a self-appointed elegant sophisticated businessman.

Rough stuff was not on his agenda. When they reached the stairs Errol's workforce felt compelled to come to the aid of their boss, their paymaster and to some their friend. Little Allen, who walked behind the trio of Eddie Errol and Dave, turned to his ex-workmates, raised a hand saying not now, not now just back off. They obliged, grudgingly. Upstairs in the office, things were beginning to get sinister.

Up until Errol chucked his rattle out of his pram saying 'this is my yard and I'll do as I please' Eddie would have been happy to leave it as a warning. Now though it had reached the proportions of disrespect, this was a sure-fire way to get Eddie's goat up as high as the spit. The yard blokes were not used to hearing screams coming from Errol's office, Little Allen walked into the office to find Errol tied to his office chair with Eddie slapping him about a bit, shouting, "Look 'ere sunshine, your little tin pot operation ain't going to bring the Oasis crew down." Little Allen nodded to Eddie to look out the window at the advancing workers. He told Dave to go stand at the top of the stairs and undo his leather jacket so that the nice chap's downstairs could see he was armed and dangerous.

Eddie continued to berate Errol, he put his face inches away from his and produced a chiv. Errol's eye bulged, Eddie stuffed a cloth in Errol's mouth. "To reduce the sound of you screaming."

Eddie pointed out. "You see pal, sometimes violence and pain is the best currency we can lay our hands on. What's more its free, which incidentally is my favourite word." Eddie laughed insanely. A pool of urine appeared under the chair occupied by Errol.

"You need tribal marks mate," Eddie held the chiv to Errol's face. "Whose tribe do want to be in eh? Yours or fucking mine?" Errol swung his head from side to side trying to spit out the cloth stuffed in his mouth. "Oh, you want to talk now, do you son." Errol nodded furiously.

"Okay mate, if I let you talk, be very careful and chose your words wisely." Slowly Eddie removed the cloth. Errol offered up a show stopping command performance of a grovelling apology. Eddie called out through the window. "Right, you lot, your boss wants the spitfire taken down now. Well go on, jump to it."

They hesitated needing confirmation from their boss who was otherwise engaged. Eddie turned to Little Allen, instructed him to go down to the yard orchestrate the dismantling and crushing of the wingless aircraft. He turned back to Errol and said, "Very wise pal very wise, cut him loose Dave." Errol stood up rather shakily, moved over to the window to have a grandstand view of the great bird being brought down to earth for the second and last time in its long life.

East Ham Station.

D.I. Jackson having been in deep conversation with Detective Chief Inspector Ellis the man responsible for heading up the murder investigation at East Ham nick, called the briefing to order. Three of the attending uniformed constables, those who had spoken to the tinker over at Ropemakers had indeed delivered a full account of the incident on paper as Jackson had requested. Jackson was about to give them some praise, which was why they had been invited. He explained to the assembled officers about the request for bodies to be sent over to Limehouse for the door knocking initiative at Ropemakers Field and the subsequent sussing out a witness by the three constables present. A witness regarding the hit and run incident had been uncovered. A tiny ripple of applause from the assembled detectives. The uniformed three were asked to leave the meeting and get back to their beat duties forthwith. After they'd gone, Jackson remarked, "This together, with other sources of excellent intelligence has brought to our attention a group of undesirables or gang likely to be involved in a major crime spree. We have established their base and the names of some of the major gang members. We are aware they hang out at an establishment known as the Oasis, the address of which is, corner of Mill Place and Basin Approach Limehouse." Jackson drew everyone's attention to a large street map pinned up on the board. He marked on the map the exact spot where the Oasis is located, he then drew another large spot. "This one here is precisely where the constable was run down. The distance from this spot to the Oasis, via Narrow Street, is just 0.9 miles. A seven-minute walk at most. Of course, we cannot run away with the idea that the gang concerned or anyone else that haunts the Oasis has anything whatsoever to do with running down the constable. The proximity however between the two dots, is something that we just cannot ignore."

D.C.I. Ellis interjected, "I have briefed the D.C.I. at Limehouse station of our findings and will be having a meeting over there later on this afternoon.

"My hope is that we can have a joint effort between our two stations which may help to resolve our murder enquiries down the road at Stratford Nick. This of course is still very much our priority. You are all aware that we have an under-cover officer working out in the field. I cannot reveal who it is, or where this officer is currently working. Security reasons and all that, you understand. So please do not ask, I repeat to you all, nobody outside this room is to hear of this, especially the press. We are closing in on a number of suspects. If this information is revealed, many weeks of tireless and sometimes dangerous police work will be lost." Ellis excused himself, left the incident room on his way over to Limehouse for his meeting. Jackson took up the reins, he pointed to the two detectives who had been trawling through police records looking for any information, however small, regarding previous incidents, murder or otherwise concerning the use of a breadknife. "Nothing as of yet, sir, we are about half way through the records kept here and at Stratford nick and we have requested records from other nearby stations and are waiting delivery."

"Anything else new?"

"Yes sir. We have had an anonymous call put through to the incident room. The call lasted about a minute. Most of it was silent, just breathing and soft sobbing."

"When you say most of it, what else other than silence and sobbing?" asked Jackson.

"And who took the call?"

"I did sir. There was a fair bit of mumbling, so I had to draw my own conclusions, but I think somebody was looking for somebody to grass up somebody else."

"Three somebodies eh! When did this call come in?" "15.00hrs today, sir."

"Well, could it be a crank a hoax or something?" Jackson asked. "We do get these from time to time, usually following a newspaper plea for information."

"That's right, sir, but this one makes me think it's for real. Could be solid information, information that we have all been striving for."

"Okay, keep me posted on that one. Anything else to get our teeth into?" No answer was the stern reply, "Nothing? Bloody hell, a crank call and that's it. Get digging everyone. Especially for ginger haired gun toting gangsters who get driven around in black shiny cars. If these chaps are locals, it might be worth checking with your local snouts. Can I suggest a few more of you assist in trawling through the records on the lookout for bread knife murders? Next Briefing in 48 hours." On his way out of the Station, DCI Ellis suddenly remembered something he wanted to set up as soon as possible. Much to the desk Sergeants surprise Ellis spun round right in front of him. He told the Sergeant, "Get my driver to wait another ten minutes or so." Then he flew back into the meeting room. He caught Jackson's eye, just as he was closing the meeting. They met in the middle of the room. All eyes were on the pair, as Ellis drew Jackson aside. Jackson looked around the room encouraging the officers to get on with whatever they should be getting on with and to cease the earwigging. "We need to set up surveillance on this Oasis place Jacko. Twenty-four-hour stuff, no cars they would stick out like the proverbial sore thumb in that neck of the woods. Probably best to commandeer an upstairs room across the road discreetly, of course."

"Of course, sir, discretion is my middle name," replied Jackson. Ellis frowned.

"Well get on with it as soon as. Oh, and do we have a beat covering that area?"

"Yes sir, it's the beat belonging to the constable who was run down."

"Yes, yes, of course." Ellis stumbled over his last sentence. He continued, "What with all that's going on I think I getting a mind like a sieve. Just get a surveillance team set up by end of play tomorrow. Three men I would think, one to watch, one to take notes as they are called out from the watcher, and one to go out for sandwiches. Discreet change overs and all that. Okay?"

"Definitely sir, consider it done." Ellis made his escape for the second time that day. He reached the car, climbed into his customary back seat, behind and to the left of the driver and mopped his sweating brow. *Must be coming down with something* he thought. He barked out an order to his driver. Off they went in the direction of Limehouse nick, for the planned meeting. "That'll put a hammer in the works!" The driver looked in the rear-view mirror at the DCI and politely pointed out,

"I think you mean spanner, sir."

"Yes, well, whatever. We will watch them; we will arrest them and we will prosecute them out of their skins." A thought went through the driver's mind, *who's he thinks he is? Bloody Winston, what's is name. Can't be, he's left out the bit about on the beaches.*

The Oasis.

"What's on the agenda Eddie," asked Johnny. Eddie Coleman wanted to have a round table meeting on the coming Friday night. The first for quite some time. Truth is he felt he was losing his grip on things and needed tighten up again.

"Thing is Johnny, I've had to give Errol a big slap, don't really trust him anymore you know. Might need to dump 'im."

"Plenty more breakers yards down Barking way, Eddie."

"Yea I know, but not with the kit Errol's got, you know transferring car documents from straight, to not so straight, then selling the motors on." Johnny put an idea forward.

"Why don't we wrench the kit from him and install it in another breakers yard?"

"Tell you what Johnny, that's a good shout as it 'appens, get in touch with the Cherry Boys who roam around a bit down that way, get 'em to break in Errol's yard. Trash the place, grab the kit and bring it here. Let Billy and Mel know so they can turn a blind eye, let the Cherry Boys have free rein on the place for a week or so. Once the kits been lifted, we can get another yard to carry on with changing the genuine official paperwork over to not so official. Set it up Johnny, stands to reason, we'll have to put a stop on Dave's activities up West for a while, no more nicking cars and that, find 'im something else to do."

"What about putting him the trail of those two who fronted him outside the bookies, before Billy stepped in?"

"As it happens, that's a good shout too," Eddie nodded. "Let's find out who their working for."

Johnny asked, "And what about the two in the car that followed you over to the Creekmouth Yard?"

"Yea, I forgot about those two fuckers. Let's get Dave on that one as well. He can probably pick up some info at that gym he goes to. As soon as he's got any of them sussed, he can turn them over to Billy and Mel. They put the squeeze on them, get them to cough who they work for. Then we deal with it accordingly, okay?"

"Yep, good enough for me boss."

"Meanwhile, I'll get Irish Jimmy to do a round of the Steak Bars over in Soho, I'll clear the way with Adonis." "What's the story there then Eddie?"

"I want Irish to grab the books from all three and cook up a programme that proves Adonis is havin' us over on the takings. Then you and I will take him behind one of the restaurants one night and teach him a fucking lesson he won't forget. Nobody puts one over on us see," Eddie grinned well pleased with his plan. "He either sells us his 40 percent for a knock down amount, or we slice him up. Bingo, three steak bars belong to us 100 percent."

"Nice one, Eddie."

"Doesn't end there, Johnny, we need to find out if there is any accommodation above the steak houses."

"What for boss?"

"Feather out the rooms for birds on the game of course. Rent the rooms out to a couple of tarts. Chuck in a few two-way mirrors, any one of any note visits for a bit of the other, MPs, Clergy, or high high-ranking old Bill, we can put the black on them."

"I'll get the word out for a meet this Friday, do you want Errol there?"

"Yea, why not."

"What If he goes wonky on the deal to shaft him?" asked Johnny.

"Then he goes home in a box."

"What if wants the Jags back?"

"Same thing Johnny, we hold all the aces mate."

"What about Errol's car-lots?" enquired Johnny.

"Carry on as normal. If Errol fails to pay for the protection, the car-lots get wrecked."

"Seems fair enough."

"Yea well, it's about time I stopped being Mr, fucking nice guy. Oh, and run down the music business in Basildon. It's going stale."

Ed winked at Johnny and went upstairs to the bar, beckoning Allen over, as he did so. "Listen Allen get the Jag over to Errol's and get it resprayed. Any colour but black. And do it before this Friday."

"Sure, sure thing, boss. I'll get over there now, should be ready by tomorrow." As Little Allen was leaving, Eddie called out,

"Not green Allen, not green, that's well unlucky." Little Allen nodded and was gone. Eddie heard the sweet purring of the Jag as it pulled away, he felt he had covered most corners, but for one.

That Friday meeting went well. Billy and Mel were happy to put the squeeze on anyone that Dave Conti put their way. They were well up for a bit of banging heads together, looking forward to flexing their torture muscles again. Also, happy but only on Eddie's say so, to wreck Errol's car-lots until money for their protection started flowing again. Dave was convinced he could come up with some names and faces regarding the followers. The Black Jag was now an understated sedate slate grey. A far cry from the shiny 'look at me' black lacquered look. Irish Jimmy was fired up by Eddie to do the Steak Bar rounds, chauffeured of course, in the sedate grey Jag by Little Allen. The saddest person to leave the Oasis that night was Errol, no more cars coming in from Dave, temporary or otherwise. Evil and cold looks from Eddie all evening. Spitfire crushed, ego crushed and cornered into continuing payments for the car-lots protection or face them being crushed too. As he left the Oasis the watcher across the road clocked him through his binoculars and whispered to the scriber, "Eh up Snowy, get this down on your clip board. 22.15hrs black guy leaving. Now climbing into a Humber Super Snipe registration RUK 554. Better phone that reg through to the station, get that chaps' details, right flasks out, sarnies out, let's have a nosh."

Due to Errol's fractious state of mind, he drove off completely in the wrong direction, realising his mistake he executed a three-point turn and headed back up the incline towards the Oasis. "Old on," said Snowy. "Who's that bird standing in the doorway?"

"Fuck me, ain't that WPC Wren, what the bleedin' hell is she doing in there?" The scriber, grabbing the bins, focused them to his personal level of sight, and took a gander.

"Bloody well is an all, Christ, what gives here then?" Just then another body appeared. Tall, male, broad and swarthy. Esme Wren linked arms with him. The couple disappeared into the night heading towards Limehouse Basin. The scriber put down the bins, picked up his clip board and wrote 22.20hrs WPC Wren exited the Oasis along with white gent noting down a brief description of the male. "That should make interesting reading for the guvnor."

"Now, where's those sarnies? Hope there's cheese and pickle in there."

"Bollocks!" The watcher almost shouted. "Camera quick." On the pavement outside the Oasis stood Billy and Mel. "I know those two fuckers. That's Maggs and Cooper. Wanted by the cops up West they are. This is getting better and better."

The watcher aimed the Nikon in the direction of the Stratford two. Unfortunately, due to his excitement of a possible promotion the watcher forgot to turn the off the flash. The surveillance team could well have been compromised immediately if anyone below caught the flash. Their collective bacons were saved by the main beam from Errol's Humber momentarily blinding Mel and Billy. For the moment it would seem the surveillance team would be safe from discovery. Neither of the Stratford pair, courtesy of Errol's full headlights saw nothing of the Nikon flash. "Christ, that was a stroke of luck imaging having to explain that one to the governor." This from the sandwich supplier. The watcher answered,

"Yep, that was clumsy of me, been on so many stake outs of late you'd think I should be able to do something as simple as that wouldn't you? Anyway, seems that neither of them caught the flash, thank fuck." His mates started to sing in harmony, "Sing something simple, as years go by."

"Oh, very funny, very bloody funny."

Stepping Mount Hotel.

"Fancy Spain for bit, Esme?" asked Eddie. Both lay naked, she smoking, he sipping fine whiskey from a cut-glass tumbler.

"I do!" Esme replied secretly thrilled of a week or two in the sun. She sat up, looked around her. Bed clothes on the floor, mixed up with Eddie's shirt and suit, her blouse and skirt, all scattered in a frenzy to get at each other. They were back in the Stepping Mount Hotel. Same suite as last time, but this time with a soft velour bed-head to lean against. "I see you've had a word with the management." She glanced sideways at her lover.

"See girl, I listened. Your wish is my command and all that, give us a drag."

"No Eddie, you don't smoke now, and I'm not about to get you started."

"Okay, well get me started elsewhere then."

"God, your insatiable." he smiled. "Before that though, what about this Spain thing then?"

"Yes of course, I would love to have a week or two on the beaches out there."

"Esme, I'm talking about six months, maybe a year, I dunno, maybe for ever." She stubbed her cigarette out and turned to him. As she did so, the sheet dropped away exposing her curvaceous breasts. "They can come too if they behave themselves." Eddie had fits of loud raucous laughter then flung the entire bed sheet on the floor. "This lot too," he said pointing downwards, still laughing his head off. He serioused up. "Thing is Es. My life is revolving around the Oasis, Plevna Street, a few other places and not much else. I've got some real good guys on the team, plenty of good blokes joining all the time. Christ at the last count, we must be thirty strong. It's like a bloody army. Johnny's more than capable of running things. Besides, I need to duck the law, I can feel it in my piss, they're gonna suss me sooner or later. Can't keep going around killing and maiming people and playing noughts and crosses in their backs without getting my collar felt once or twice. However, there is one thing I absolutely have to do first, I promised me mum." Esme's head was reeling. He continued, "The blokes that have been killed or maimed fucking well deserved it, but the filth won't and don't think like that. They're bloody idiots. Can't they see that I'm ridding parts of the East End of low life vermin. I should get a bleedin' medal for that! I need to be one or two steps ahead of them though. Like I said, I can feel their presence. Bit like a shadow hanging over me. Fucking grim reapers, I call it. If there is even the slightest threat of them coming for me, I've got to take that threat seriously. That copper that got run over was down to us. If nothing else old Bill would make that one stick." Esme's mind was still reeling. On the one hand she had admiration for Eddie's foresight, on the other, it would be impossible for her to be away for more than a fortnight. Then it came to her, a compromise.

"Tell you what Eddie, we'll go. I'll come out with you for two weeks or so, get us settled in then pop back home and get things squared away at this end, then come out to join you for as long as you want."

"Nice one Es, let's do it, I'll get the ball rolling with Johnny and me ma."

She asked, "By the way, what's the one last thing you've got do."

Eddie whispered, almost in a state of secrecy, "I need to blow someone's candle out."

"Anyone I know?"

"Well, you've heard of him. Lenny the Scrote. I promised me mum didn't I."

"Sorry to be thick, Eddie what does blow his candle out mean?"

"He did for Wossname, didn't he, so I'm going to put him in the ground, in little pieces. Word has it that he sometimes hides in the walk tunnel that runs from the Dogs under the Thames to Greenwich on the on the South Bank. The plan is, to get my lads to block off both entrances while I do 'im in the tunnel. Now then, Esme my lovely, get your kit off girl, you've pulled. Oh, hang on I see you already have, come 'ere you little tart."

"God Eddie, I love it when you talk dirty."

East Ham Station.

DCI Ellis, was in conference with DI Jackson. Following the gas explosion at the Bright's residence and subsequent death of Mike B, investigating officers had combed through the rubble searching for anything that might possibly lead them to their investigations going forward in the right direction. Ellis initially cast doubt on the search, reluctantly signalling his agreement. "You did the right thing sir, something turned up."

"Really," said Ellis, "I thought it might." Smart arse thought Jackson, only last week you were pissing all over the idea. "Well, what's turned up then." Ellis couldn't contain himself, "Go on, go on."

"Well, sir," Jackson stalled, dragging it out as far as he dared. "In what was left of Mikes home was a two-draw metal filing cabinet, still intact. Most of the contents being the sort of things most households keep. Bills and things, just general stuff. But the big find for us, is this. In the top drawer of the cabinet, they found his police notebook. And what's more, there was a single entry in the note book with just one name and the entry date corresponds with the date of the two murders at Stratford Station."

"Bloody hell, Jackson, bloody hell! Go on. What was the name?"

"Well, I assume it's a name, sir. The word say's Rizla."

"Rizla, Rizla, who the fuck's Rizla, and what kind of name is that?"

"Possibly it's a sort of nick name, sir, lots of the underworld adopt nick names rather than use their own, adds a bit of colour I assume. You know like Micky the Mouth, Dangerous Dave, Slasher Haines.

My initial thoughts were, Mike knew this person, so I did a bit of digging, and I think I have discovered his true identity." The telephone rang, irritated by the interruption, Ellis grabbed the phone and barked,

"Yes. Oh, good afternoon, sir how may I help you?" He put his hand over the receiver and mouthed, 'Commander Crawley' – better known behind his back as 'Creepy.' Jackson stood up and motioned to Ellis, that he would go grab two coffees, whilst his boss, talked with his boss. *And bloody good luck with that* he thought. "What did the commander want, sir?" Jackson now back in the office with two coffees, Ellis ignored the question.

"Sit down, sit down Jacko, you're making the place look untidy." Jackson reluctantly did as he was bidden. "You said you did some digging regarding this, this, what was his handle?"

"Rizla, sir."

"That's the chappie, yes."

"Well sir, Rizla, luckily has form, grievous bodily harm in the main, he's on police records under the name of Jack O'Leary."

"Sounds a bit Irish to me."

"Got it in a nutshell, sir, where's more though, he is on remand presently at Pentonville prison." Ellis looked up,

"What for?"

"Brawling in The Eastern public house on East India Dock Road, sir, whilst brandishing a flick knife."

"By the cringe, this is beginning to add up at last," said Ellis. "Sergeant Bullymore suffered a fatal knife wound to his neck, who's to say it wasn't the same knife! Who was the arresting officer, we'll need to talk to him pronto?"

"PC Williams, sir, based at Limehouse Station."

"Right, we need to interview Williams first, then get over to Pentonville and interview O'Leary. Set it up will you, Jacko. I will talk to the people over at Limehouse Station and clear the way for you. Brief your team as soon as. Let them know what's happening."

"Will do Sir." Jackson left the room. Two full cups of coffee remained intact, untouched on Ellis's desk.

Tunnel of Evil.

Yelling loudly in a tunnel, echoes and amplifies, depending on its shape and length. The walk tunnel under the Thames from the Isle of Dogs to Greenwich is all of 1200 feet from end to end. Late one Saturday night into Sunday morning Lenny the Scrote was busy meeting his maker, somewhere about in the middle. Either end was blocked off to all but Eddie's crew. Those closest to the action needed to cover their ears, the amplified, echoing wailing and screaming was not nice to hear. Eddie had decided to fulfil his promise, mainly to himself, to gain revenge for Scrote arranging Wossnames demise. He walked the Scrote to halfway before throwing him to the ground, Scrote landed face down. Instantly, Eddie pulled out a boning knife and without much ado began carving a crude noughts and crosses symbol on Scrotes back. The screaming intensified. When Eddie was satisfied with his artistry, out came the revolver. By now, Lenny in an effort to stop the blade work, spun over to lay on his back. Delighted by the move, Eddie smiled and murmured "That's good of you scum now you can watch me kill you." The tunnel guards at either end could have sworn they heard gentle singing, Eddie on this occasion looked directly into Scrotes eyes.

"You're the fucking pig devil you are you bastard, go on then, fucking well kill me." Eddie smiled and whispered.

"As you wish." He pulled the trigger, Scrotes whole body lifted momentarily off the ground. His killer dug two very rusty three-inch nails from his jacket pocket. Scrote lay face up with a hole where his brow had been, Eddie knelt down beside him and proceeded to pull his eyelids down then push a nail into each of Scrotes dead eyes. He whispered, "Where you're going mate, best not to be able to see." As Eddie calmly walked past the guys standing guard at the Isle of Dogs end, he ordered, "Tidy up in there please lads, leave the body but don't leave no clues though, or no evidence, got it?" Little Allen was waiting patiently in the purring Jag, they both heard the guys whistle a signal to their mates blocking the Greenwich end. The two teams went into the walk tunnel to do as Eddie had asked, prompting a second team to guard both entrances.

"Christ, that Eddie's a maniac," remarked one of the clean-up men. "What a mess and what's with the bleeding nails? Fuck me that takes some believing."

"Can't say I've heard of that one before," said another. "He's not a geezer to cross. When this gets out it'll be a very brave fucker who tries." All four agreed.

"Yea well, for my money he's gone well past the post." All four agreed once more.

Arresting Officer.

The interview with O'Leary's arresting officer was conducted at Limehouse Police Station. Ellis looked on as P.C. Williams read from his note book the notes he jotted down at the time of the arrest and then the charge sheet subsequently written up back at the station whilst O'Leary aka Rizla, was sitting safely in one of the stations holding cells. "What happened to the flick knife," asked Jackson.

"Sir, when I arrested O'Leary for brawling sir, he was about to use it on me. I managed to disarm him and knife fell to the floor and what with so many people in the bar area, it got kicked under a bench seat by the front bay window. O'Leary was struggling so much I failed to get him handcuffed. It took two of us to wrestle him into the back of the police van, sir."

"And the knife, Williams?"

"I went back into the bar area sir, the mood and lighting in there was extremely dark. I instructed two customers who were sitting on the bench seat in question to move out of my way. A quick search proved fruitless, I then instructed the landlord to search for the knife at closing time, which would have been about the time I'd be back on my beat." Ellis sighed deeply. The constable would not have known the significance, evidence wise that the knife would hold.

"Have you been back to the Eastern, Williams," asked Jackson.

"No sir."

"Okay, might I ask that you return there today and conduct a full search, rip the furniture up if you have to. Suffice to say, we want that knife. Would you wait a moment outside please?" Williams left the interview room and did as he was asked. "Go with him Jacko, go with him."

The two left Limehouse Station enroute to the Eastern public house. A feeling of anxiety and dismay had befallen P.C. Williams, whatever was about to happen Williams needed desperately to locate that knife. They walked on in silence which added to the consternation raging in the head of young Williams. D.I. Jackson broke the silence. "Where did you do your training, Williams?"

"Peel House, sir over in Pimlico."

"Not Hendon then?"

"No sir, just visited Hendon once to do the swimming test you know swim down in the pool with my pyjamas on to retrieve a brick."

"How'd you get on?"

"Quite well, sir, I spent my youth living by the coast near Bournemouth, so swimming comes easy to me."

"So how come your stationed in the East End then?"

"Not by choice, sir, I was told Limehouse was to be my posting."

"You okay with that, Williams?"

"Love it, sir, the East Enders especially the cockneys are on the whole great people, well, so far that is." Rounding a corner, they were now but a few steps away from the Eastern Pub. As soon as they stepped into the bar, the publican beamed a toothy grin with two missing upper fronts which somehow made him speak with a whistle. He whistled loudly,

"I've got some good news for you, constable." He whistled.

"Thank you, sir, and what might that be?"

"The publican held up a paper bag, our charlady found that knife you mentioned. It was wedged right at the back of that two-seater bench. So that's a bit of luck ain't it?" Williams nearly fainted with relief, but tried hard not to let anyone know.

"Okay sir, hand it over, I need to inspect it." Williams peered into the bag. He recognised it instantly nodding his agreement to Jackson.

"Are you sure, Williams, it's important that we get the right one."

"Oh yes sir, you don't forget even the tiniest of little details regarding a knife when it's waved menacingly in front of your face several times."

"Okay," Jackson said, "no need for all the amateur dramatics, just doubly confirm it's the right one." Williams peered into the brown paper bag once more.

"Yes sir, I guarantee it."

"In which case, let's get it back to Limehouse for further examination, you never know, there just might be a fingerprint or two on it."

"Yes sir, I was thinking that myself. If the knife was undisturbed whilst under the seating arrangement, the only two prints should belong to the charlady and O'Leary's."

"Exactly Williams, not forgetting Mr Whistler of course. Fingers crossed eh?" On examination by the forensic team there was indeed three sets of prints. Two indecipherable but one, clearly matching that of Jack O'Leary. Following the forensic examination, the knife was bagged up and sent over to the original pathologist who dealt with Frank Bullymore's post mortem examination. The blade of the flick knife matched perfectly to the incision made to Franks throat. Breakthrough. The police now had a major suspect for Franks murder, at long, long last. Jacksons team were brought up to date, and made aware of this turning point. Some were tasked with establishing O'Leary's recent movements up to his arrest, others tasked with developing O'Leary's known associates. Ellis appointed himself along with Jackson, to interview O'Leary soonest over at Pentonville Goal in the Borough of Islington.

"I think we need to thin down your team Jacko, there are other cases to be sorted. How many bods have you got?"

"Since we lost the services of the detectives from the provinces, we're down to ten, sir."

"Halve it then, Jacko, keep hold of a hardcore of experienced let the rest get on with other duties."

"As you wish, sir." Jackson wasn't too sure himself; he thought his boss was jumping the gun a bit, his decision though and time will tell.

Sun Sangria and Shite.

"Take up the reins Johnny, me and Esme are pissing off to Spain." Eddie and Johnny the Turk were in the back of the Jag on their way to a meet with Adonis.

"Spain! What's brought this on?"

"A beano mate, only a bit further than Margate." Little Allen butted in with,

"We're here boss." The Jag came to an almost silent stop outside the Steak House in Wardour Street. Eddie gave instructions.

"Look son, Johnny and me got a bit of business with my partner here, park up as near as possible to the back of the steak bar as you can and keep the motor running. If you see any old Bill nosing about pop the bonnet and fuck about with the engine, rev it a bit so as we can hear it okay?" Little Allen nodded. Johnny grabbed the accounts books, the together they marched into the Steak Bar. Adonis was expecting them, he smiled a warm greeting type smile, opened his arms wide in a form of welcome. Unfortunately, the warm greetings were not reciprocated.

The blank expressions from both Eddie and Johnny exuded a warning of evil intent. "Out the back you," Eddie spat. Before Adonis could move Johnny spun him around, faced him towards the kitchen and frogged marched him straight through and out into the tiny back street yard. It was here he threw Adonis down amongst the tall metal dustbins. The Greek fell badly amongst the waste food and general rubbish, Johnny put a boot on his gut pinning him to the ground, Eddie could hear the Jag nearby engine purring gently, not revving, sending him an audible signal to move things up a level. He pulled his gun. Stabbing it in the

Greeks heart, he growled, "You've been havin us over old son." Adonis added to the mess in the gutter he was sat in.

"I don't understand," he stuttered, Johnny shoved the trumped-up piss poor figures, trumped up by Irish Jimmy, under his nose. At first glance they looked genuine. Adonis was not going to get a second look, Johnny whipped them away. At the same time Eddies' gun was whipped across the face of Adonis. No cries came from the Greek, just trickles of blood from the corner of his mouth, some from his nose, whilst an eye started swell. A number of the kitchen staff appeared at the door. Johnny produced his gun and waved them back inside. "Listen mate, I know that would have stung a bit, but that nothing to what comes next. Nobody has it over on me and my crew. We've just proved you have been, so now it's down to you what happens next. Here's your choices. A severe beating, then a bullet in your head, or sell us your forty percent of the three steak bars in Soho, for a grand each, and we'll back off, as a bonus you can keep Dollis Hill." 'Ever the business man Eddie' said inwardly to himself, always give 'em an option. There was however, no option for the Greek, he wanted desperately to see his family again. No way was he about to be shot whilst on his arse sat amid his own shit and other similar stinking rotten food waste. Eddie slung a roll of notes totalling two thousand, held tightly by elastic bands on to the ground next to Adonis. "Deal?" demanded Eddie. Adonis nodded. Eddie spat in his hand and indicated the Greek to do the same and they shook. Whilst hands were clasped, Eddie pulled Adonis upright, looked him in the eye and waited for him to say deal. "That went well Johnny." Eddie spoke for the first time since leaving Soho. Little Allen was at the wheel steering the Jag back to the Oasis. "We'll get Irish Jimmy to shoot over there pronto and get it all signed over. He can rope in that bent solicitor to go with 'im."

"Do you trust the Greek," Johnny asked.

"Do I fuck mate. All I know is these Greek guys usually stick to their word. I'm sure he said, 'deal' before we left." All three laughed as they sped back to the East End. Job done.

"Right, so what's all this about Spain then Eddie?"

"All in good time Johnny all in good time. For the minute, I just need to know you will stand in for me?"

"Goes without question Eddie, count on me."

Watchers.

"That's three piling out of a grey Jag, MK2 registration 98 MLP. Bet that's a dummy reg," the watcher called out. He continued with further information. "Timed at 22.00hrs all three entering the Oasis. All white, all male, too dark for detailed description." The scribe jotted down notes as the watcher was speaking. The sandwich and tea fetcher wanted to know why the street lamp close to the Oasis entrance was not working. Still looking through the binoculars the watcher murmured, "Kids with catapults done for it yesterday. The stations been on to the councils lighting department, apparently, they've got a backlog of jobs and loads of people on holidays."

"Great planning then," the fetcher remarked mockingly.

"Can't we get priority?"

"Yea, of course," chipped in the scriber, "Let's all pop down to the council offices and tell them were doing a secret surveillance and need the lighting back on, as soon as, so we can identify brutal cop murderers. Might as well sing it from the roof tops." The fetcher fell silent.

Shut Eye's Murder.

Various headlines in various newspapers made grisly reading. There were differing stories, however one theme connected them all. 'Noughts and Crosses murderer still at large' said one. 'Noughts and Crosses murderer at it again' printed another. A third cheekily asked,

"Do the Police have a clue-no, they do not. Scrotes body was discovered and reported to the police by an early morning jogger. For a second time within twenty-four hours, the walk-through tunnel was closed. This time by the police. Scenes of Crime officers needed three to four hours at least to carry out their task halfway between the two entrances."

Funny, Eddie thought as he was scanning the papers, no news on the rusty nails. "Well, that was a waste of two monkeys' tails," he said to nobody. If he had scanned down a little further into the various reports, he would have seen, nailing Scrotes eye's shut, did indeed warrant a few lines, as in 'gruesome escalation of mutilation.' Eddie's clear up men, made sure the body was naked, leaving the police with 'nothing to go on' regarding clothing. Naked bodies didn't leave wallets, watches, driving licences rings or anything else that might help the police I.D. the victim. For the moment according to the press, the body was reported as unknown. The other dilemma for the police was, the body was found exactly halfway between the Isle-of-Dogs and Greenwich, so which Police division would be tasked with forming up a murder team and incident room. It was as if Scrotes body lay purposely right across, middle for diddle the imaginary half way line. Feet and legs to the North, shoulders, and head to the South. In the end after some painstaking measuring, it was decided the Greenwich division would take it on, there was a proviso however. Due to the first noughts and crosses murder happened on the island side of the tunnel, the Greenwich team would need access to any information relating to it, therefore an agreement was consented, paving the way for a double up of activities from both divisions, answering to a single DCI as of yet to be appointed. Following the re-opening of the walk-through tunnel and due mainly to the media coverage, deeply morbid interested people flocked to the walk-through tunnel to have their photo taken, close to the spot where the unknown victim was toyed with, then brutally murdered. The locals looked on calling them ghouls and blood thirsty weirdos. For a month or so though, the Isle-of-Dogs was firmly on the map. Someone wanted to launch a nought's and crosse's tour. One of the local brewers even thought about launching a new brand of beer to be called 'Evil Ale' but thought better of it. Death is always a money spinner, much enhanced on these occasions by the murders chilling carvings.

Out to Lunch.

"Come on Ma, you know you've always fancied Spain."

"I know, I did once son but that was years ago, I'm a bit set in my ways now." Eddie and Val were sitting in one of Eddie's steak bars in Soho. Val for once was out of her uniform. To be her son's companion for the day she needed to dress up a little. Today she wore a bright lemon blouse and paisley skirt. Eddie as per usual a dark brown double-breasted suit, white monogrammed shirt with sober tie. The table being the most prized table in the steak bar, was constantly reserved for Eddie. Mac, the manager hovered at about three feet away, making sure his new boss was well catered for. "Lovely steak son, best I've tasted for a while." Eddie moved the conversation back to Spain.

"Thing is Ma, I can't look after you, with me over there and you over here."

"Leave it out, this is my home. I've got a nice job on the buses, good friends and lovely neighbours, anyways, how long was you thinking of going?"

"I dunno Ma, a fortnight, a year or maybe longer." Val was shocked.

"What's brought this on then, son?"

"I don't want to be the richest man in jail Ma. I've talked it over with Esme, she's happy to stay out there with me as soon as she's squared things away back here." A police car drew up and parked right outside the window in plain sight of Eddie and his mum. Two uniformed officers emerged leaving a third in the car at the wheel. Eddie unconsciously looked away; he buried his head in the menu. "What's up son, you in some kind of trouble?"

"No Ma, they just make me nervous."

The two police officers walked across Wardour Street and disappeared into a strip joint. "What's all that about then?" asked Val.

"Just wait a couple of minutes then you'll find out." Four minutes later, the they appeared again, one of which was holding a white A4 envelope. "Hush money Ma. They're on the bleedin' take. Christ, how am I supposed to make an honest living by offering protection? No wonder takings are down if the filth is in on it as well." The officers got back in the car and right there, under the gaze of Val and Eddie, they divvyed up the contents of the envelope.

"Christ, must be a pony each,"

"Minimum Ma. Thing is, they get free clothing; free car, free petrol and they get wages on top. Talk about bleedin' greedy!"

"Look son," Val intervened, to get back to the topic of Spain, "If you want to get away for a bit, then you don't have to worry about me. I will be fine. What about the Oasis and stuff?"

"Johnny's running the show till I get back, he's already had meets with the boys, all is well all system in place. By the way, you can tell your mates at the depot, Lenny the Scrote will not trouble anyone anymore." Val eyed Eddie, but thought better of digging deeper. "Ive instructed Johnny to get fifty quid over to you weekly and Little Allen will be at your beck and call with the Jag. I'll be taking Irish Jimmy with me." Val looked aghast. Eddie smiled, "Just for a couple of weeks, so don't panic, to sort out any paperwork needed to purchase a villa."

"A villa eh?"

"Well, I'm not going to bleedin' rent, am I? So, if and when you get some time off you can use it whenever you fancy. Just give me a bit of notice and when you do, I can come back home and catch up with things." Just then, Mac asked if sweet was required, Eddie waved him away. "Right Ma, I've got some people to see, Little Allen will drive you back to the island, it was lovely to catch up."

On the journey back, Val told Little Allen to make a detour to the Oasis, a place she had not yet stepped into.

"Okay Mrs Coleman, not a problem."

Watchers.

"Heads up you lot, the grey Jags back, displaying a different reg this time, it reads WHF 636." The watcher lowered his binoculars.

"Did we get a name and address on the first set of plates, or were they false?" The scribe rustled through his papers for the report.

"Registered to an Israeli somewhere indecipherable in Israel all kosher apparently," he announced.

"Yea sure as eggs is eggs, that'll be false plates again this time."

"One female alighting, yellow top, patterned skirt entering the Oasis at 15.30hrs, car running but stationary," called out the watcher. The fetcher, who was armed with the long-range lens on his Nikon, informed both his colleagues that he got some great shots. Watcher said, "Another one for the action board back at the station." A moment or two passed then the same lady emerged together with a lone man. Quite tall, casually dressed in white short sleeved shirt and tan slacks. If the watcher didn't know better, the chap with the lady seemed a bit unsteady on his plates. "Bit early to be pissed," he muttered. The scribe noted all the comments down whilst the fetcher got more good shots, this time their faces.

"I'd put her around fiftyish, the bloke she's come out with, we've clocked him a number of times previously and he's not been a person of interest, until now. Looks about mid-forties." The Jag whisked the pair away.

"A toy boy?" fetcher asked.

"Maybe, although I doubt it, but I did like the way he held the car door open for her though, very gentlemanly. Might be a minder perhaps? The strangest thing was however, he then walked around to the driver's door, opened it and almost sat on whoever was driving before he realised that someone was already there! It was almost as if he was collecting a fare, like a taxi driver." The scribe suggested this new information had better find its way back to the station and proto. Both turned to the fetcher. The watcher said,

"Off you go then and make it snappy, be sure to bring back some fresh sarnies."

An Irish Affair.

"Drop us here Allen, see you tomorrow perhaps." Val mentioned coffee to Jimmy making sure that Allen had overheard her before pulling away. She led Jimmy down the path to 119 Plevna Street. A great deal more was on her mind than mere coffee. Once inside, she pulled Jimmy to her crushing his lips with hers. He responded; this was unrequited love being requited. He flung his arms around Val, squeezing her as much as he dared. As far as he was concerned the sap was rising and fast, it had been some time since he had embraced a woman and nothing or no one was going to stop his flood gates from opening fully. Still crushing each other's lips, he managed to mumble bedroom. Val pointed an arm upwards. She began exploring his mouth with her tongue. They succeeded in climbing the stairs without releasing each other from their embrace, completely ignoring the creaking of steps two and seven. Moving like kissing crabs they entered Val's bedroom, falling onto her bed the kissing and embracing continued until neither party could stay clothed for a second longer. Many hours later, two exhausted sated and happy lovers began to come back down to earth. They talked some small talk then Val asked the question that was burning away in her mind. "Jimmy, you don't think bad of me because of this, do you?" Jimmy was a bit flummoxed by the question. To him it was what he had wanted from the moment he clapped eyes on her.

She took the two minutes silence the wrong way. "So, you think I'm just a tart then, do you? Picking you up at the club and dragging you back here?" Jimmy was heartbroken, to even think the love of his life would even think that way.

"Val, my lovely, I hold you in the highest esteem, to think you would think that, of all the thoughts you could have.

"Tonight, has been the highlight of my miserable existence on this earth. I have worshipped you from day one so I have."

"Thank you, Jimmy, I wanted to hear you say something nice to me, you did and I feel better now. So, how about that late-night coffee now my darling man?"

"As its 3.00 o'clock in the morning my lovely I think I'd prefer a cup of tea please." Dressed and back downstairs they sat opposite each other in the fireside chairs and chatted away for some time. Daylight from outside, started to creep into the room heralding that morning was about to be upon them. "I understand you might be going to Spain," Val said. "News to me," he answered, she bit her lip, perhaps he wasn't aware of Eddie's plans.

"Look Jimmy, I might have said something I shouldn't have."

"What's that exactly then, Val?" She explained all. The Spanish villa, Eddie going away, possibly taking Jimmy with him, hopefully just for a short time mind. Jimmy laughed,

"Wild horses wouldn't keep me from you now, for sure. Tell you what, when Eddie's living over in Spain, can I move into his room at all?" Val laughed.

"No, you bloody well can't Jimmy." He looked crestfallen. "You can move in with me full time and share my bed!" They both laughed and hugged again. Val pulled away. "What on earth am I going to tell Eddie. He'll go crazy if he knew that I've told you of his plans."

"Don't you worry your sweet little nose about a thing, I will say nothing and look surprised when he tells me. It won't turn into a 'paddies market' I can promise you that, so I can."

Pentonville.

DCI Ellis together with DI Jackson, offered up their warrant cards to the prison security officers. As with all prison visitors, they were both required to hand in any photographic equipment, along with anything else currently banned by security to visitors. Once they signed in a prison officer was assigned to accompany the two policemen through a number of locked heavy iron barred doors to, not the visitors hall, but to a lone interview room. It was approximately twelve feet by fourteen, half tiled with shiny white tiling from floor up to around five foot. The walls above and ceiling, emulsion coated in drab grey. One single barred window. A fluorescent strip offered some light to the room and emitted an annoying hum. The interview desk sat in the middle of the room. On it a single ashtray. Two chairs had been placed on one side for Ellis and Jacko and one on the opposite side. This then was the scene that would confront Jack O'Leary. Ten minutes passed before O'Leary appeared at the open doorway. With a sneer and a few mumbles, he shuffled in agreeing to sit in the single chair. The heavy door slammed behind him, for a few seconds Ellis and O'Leary stared each other out, Ellis looked away and opened up a folder. The Prison officer who brought O'Leary to them stood behind the prisoner pretending not to be there. O'Leary spoke, "What's all this about then, a bit of fighting in the boozer?"

"You pulled a knife on the arresting officer," DI Jackson cut in.

"Didn't slash him though did I, you bastards got nothing on me."

"You have used the knife before, haven't you O'Leary, on a different officer." Ellis, was not in the mood for fucking and farting about. He went into full detail regarding Sergeant Bullymore's murder at Stratford Police Station. Giving times dates and the fact that the knife in question, matched the wound causing the Sergeants death.

"So bloody what, it wasn't me. I nicked the knife from another bloke; it must have been him."

"Sorry pal," Jackson said. "Your prints are on the knife, the same knife that killed an officer at Stratford nick. We've got you, you bastard and you're going down for it."

"You can't do that!"

"We can and we will, get yourself a brief, see you in court." they signalled to the prison officer, to take him away. "Just before you disappear O'Leary, we will be having a word with the prison governor before we leave. We will recommend, in view of what we will be charging you with, you ought to be transferred to solitary."

"Charging me?"

"Yes, charging you. Charging you with murder and a copper at that. Your about to get your just desserts.

"We'll be back to go through the preliminaries in exactly a weeks' time from now. So, as I said, organise yourself some legal cover." As they made their way through security, signed themselves out then walked back to the car, Ellis remarked, "That'll give him something to think about, anyway it's started to piss down so let's get to the car double quick." Jackson took the wheel. They travelled in silence for a couple of miles, the rain was beating down now, windscreen wipers on full speed and still not coping. Jackson broke the silence.

"Maybe we could fit 'im up with Halliwell's murder as well sir, two deaths with one con as it were."

"Do you know Jacko; I was just thinking much the same. When we get back to the station get your team to dig around for as much incriminating evidence as possible. Do a search of O'Leary's abode, see if you can locate a nasty looking breadknife, one and a half inches wide and twelve to thirteen inches long. You know, the sort you can buy in a shop somewhere. I don't want this one to slip through the CPS net, you know what they are like." Jackson whistled at the DCIs inference.

"All too well, sir, all too well." Jacksons mind turned cartwheels, he wished that he had not opened his mouth and let those words tumble out. Fitting O'Leary up with two murders, put them both alongside the thieves, gangsters and low life. *No better than them,* he thought. *No bloody better than them. Have to hope it sticks.*

The Watchers.

"This is it then," the watcher almost shouted. "Get on the blower to the station. The operation is on, use Stingray, it's the code word for go." Two area cars tasked with periodic drive bys had already called in using the code word. It was the third call in, this time from the watchers. It fired up the initiation sequence leading to a raid on the Oasis. According to the watchers, all persons of interest were resident at the venue. It was time to put operation stingray in to action.

Diamond Heaven.

Johnny and Eddie were driven up West for a steak, then on to England's diamond trading centre at its very best, Hatton Garden. Here, on just one single street stood a concentrated collection of jewellers, watchmakers' diamond dealers and offices housing safety deposit boxes for the rich and richer. Eddie thought it might be a good idea to suss the place out, see what's what. Little Allen, having dropped the pair off parked up the Jag on nearby Leather Lane, close enough to the bustling street market. "Stinks of money up 'ere it does Johnny. A far cry from the Isle-of-Dogs matey Eh?" Johnny shot him a knowing glance. Jewellers, watchmakers and diamond dealers, all crammed together. Most with metal grilled windows. All but a few had locked entrance doors, with a sign quoting 'By Appointment Only.' "What we need Johnny, is just one of them to have a weak point, I guess most will be alarmed and even then, linked to the local nick." Johnny brought along a Kodak Instamatic. Eddie stood outside various outlets on either side of Hatton Garden, posing for the camera, as many a visitor would on such a famous street. They made their choice. A tiny almost insignificant Jewellers cum diamond trader, bordered on either side by much larger and more imposing diamond outlets. "That's the feller Johnny bet they've got more than the others next door, put together."

The weak point, as far as Eddie was concerned, was this one had a flat above, up for rent and therefore unoccupied. More photographs taken especially of the target and the flat until Johnny's film ran out. "Those two blokes we used for the jewellery heist in Regents Street, should be well up of this one, get them over to the Oasis for a meet."

"Will do boss, some meticulous planning for this job eh?"

"Yea, let's get back to the car and make a start." Little Allen saw them returning in the rear-view mirror. Just as well they were on their way back, he was parked in a 'No Waiting' area and a mountain of a copper was approaching him. Little Allen was not sure what to do next. It was probably out of order to ram yet another copper with the Jag, too many witnesses about. On the other hand, he had no wish to get done for parking where he shouldn't. *No contest he,* thought.

Not wishing to cause an incident he grinned weakly at the police mountain now on top of him rolled his window down and said, "Im just off officer." The officer bent down to take a brief look inside the Jag, but there was nothing untoward so he waved him on. Little Allen started the engine and gently pulled away. Johnny rather than Eddie, spotted what was happening, he whispered "Don't make for the car Eddie, look, Allen's talking to the filth. Let's cross over, don't fancy that copper getting hold of the camera. If the filth got hold of it, the job would be off."

"Right, flag a cab down," Eddie suggested, "and tell him to get us back to the Oasis. I'll sort Little Allen out as soon as he gets back. just have to hope he wasn't squealing to that copper."

"What do you mean squealing?"

"Look mate, walk in my shoes for a bit. In my position you have to keep your eyes open. Grasses to old Bill, ain't nothing new. Anyone of our crew could be a plant, you know under-cover and all that shit." Johnny thought, *fuck me, this guy is cracking up, losing it all over the place. Here we are in Hatton Garden, casing a joint, and he's worried about a grass! Hope he doesn't suspect me. Don't fancy him nailing my eye shut.* Eddie called out to the cab driver, "Hurry up mate and take your time, we've a meeting soon."

"What's the deal with the sparklers then?" Johnny asked.

"Down payment on a villa, ain't it." This at barely a whisper. He continued, "I need to have plenty of readies to spend over there. A bag of sparklers sewn into the lining of me suitcase is easier to take with me than bundles of readies."

Eddie slid the glass panel between them and the cabbie shut tight, but continued at a whisper.

"Don't want to leave you boracic lint, you need money to run the crew and it's not right for me to grab dough from the safe and scarper off for a while."

"So, what happens if the diamond job goes tits up then?"

"Do me a fucking favour Mr Turk," Eddie replied with a grin. "What's gone tits up so far then eh? Nothing, that's fucking what.

"Agreed a bit more planning on this one, have faith Johnny, have faith. The best of it is we order the blag get others more suitable to do that type of work. If it goes west our hands are clean. The two pros' that do the place for us will be paid well to keep their traps shut in the event of; if you see what I mean. Plus, if it goes well, which it will I'll fence the gear in Spain. Untraceable see! Cushty mate."

"Nice one Eddie." Meanwhile, back in Holborn EC1, Little Allen was going spare. He missed seeing Eddie and Johnny hopping into a black cab. He thought if he circled round anymore and that bleeding copper reappeared, he might be forced to run him down. Fuck it, nothing else to do but head back to The Oasis and face a bollocking.

East Ham Incident Room.

Ten uniformed officers listened keenly to DCI Ellis. "Right every one, pay attention, we are about to raid a club in Limehouse known as The Oasis." Ellis turned to the board pointing to a large red spot on the map. "We will be joined by ten officers from Canning Town Station and five from Limehouse Station. It is to be a co-ordinated raid, as we speak here now, identical information is being announced to the officers that will eventually join up with you from the other two aforesaid stations. In all, our numbers will be twenty-five, along with three police vans for carting off the arrested. There will also be two area cars to assist with ferrying the arrested to the various stations. I and DI Jackson will remain here at command central. The building which houses the Oasis, is spread over three floors. Limehouse will take the top floor. Although it is a flat of some kind, there may be people up there we want to interview. Canning Town Station, will take the ground floor. This is where drinks are served and will be the busiest by far. You gentlemen will take the basement, wide stairs, wide enough for three abreast to descend, lead down to the basement from the bar area. No matter how difficult it becomes as far as the officers from Canning Town are concerned, your objective, is to go straight past them and on into the basement where hopefully the richest pickings will be hiding." Ellis requested DI Jackson to take over. Jackson went on to explain whom to seek out, their general descriptions as being the most important to collar.

"The big fish must not be allowed to escape our net which is now closing in on them."

He continued. "The raid is timed at 21.00hrs. It is now 19.00hrs. This will allow time for all three teams to assemble in allocated waiting streets. At exactly 21.00hrs the co-ordinated operation known as 'Stingray' will commence." The uniformed officers were asked to show they all were in possession of their appointments. These being, truncheons, police whistles, and handcuffs. "One last thing gentleman, we have a spy in the Oasis camp, been there for a while now, feeding back all kinds of useful information." DI Jackson stood silently for a minute or two letting the news set in. "This person will need to be arrested along with the others, so as not to arouse suspicion. This person has, within the last twenty-four hours been issued with a code word. Assuming this person is at the Oasis when the raid takes place, they will be swept up with everybody else, and banged up in cells awaiting questioning like everybody else. This person, could well end up being held at one of the other stations therefore, right now, all other officers are getting this news at exactly the same time as you are now. If things turn nasty this person will tell the nearest officer the code word. If it is you that is spoken to and you hear the correct code word, then bundle this person out of the building and into one of two the waiting area cars, which by then will be as close to the entrance as possible. Do make sure to anybody watching, it looks like a genuine arrest. With all the uproar going on it should be easy to get this person out of the building relatively unnoticed. Pay attention now, listen up. The code word is Scarlet. Now, repeat the code word." As one, the assembled constables rang out with 'Scarlet.'

Party Time.

To coincide with the planned diamond robbery at Hatton Garden, Eddie Coleman threw a big party at the Oasis. He was to be on view to everybody there, all of the time. Nobody except the Turk knew that the job was going down at H.G. on the same night. Eddie's reckoning was, old Bill couldn't touch him for the break-in, even if they wanted to. Too many witnesses to swear that Eddie Coleman was at the Oasis, all night. The chaps brought in for the audacious heist at Hatton Garden were told to drop the nicked sparklers off at a bent jeweller over in Romford. The specialist there was to separate the ice from their gold housings, which he would keep melt down and sell on the world market. The diamonds would be collected within a few days by Eddie himself. Everyone's a winner.

So, word was circulated far and wide, Eddie would be throwing a party at The Oasis. Although licenced for wines and spirits, there was never anything other than beer on sale.

"Well," Eddie remarked, "You can't have a party without a bottle or two of Whiskey." So, prior to the party, plenty of whiskey was whisked in, along with bottles of rum, vodka and gin. Several bottles of Cinzano were made available as there might be a few ladies in on the night too. Heavies stood at the entrance; these would politely turn away undesirables. The watchers across the road were having kittens. They had not seen so many known crims under the same roof at the same time and still they kept coming. A steady stream of information was passing back to command central. Ellis and Jackson however were waiting, hoping and wishing the big fish was going to show. The raid was minutes away when the watchers announced his arrival, they breathed a sigh of relief. A grey Jag pulled up right outside the Oasis entrance. A figure emerged, stopped for a quick chat with the bouncers then disappeared inside. Although the watchers were ensconced in a building across the road, the cheer that went up from inside the Oasis, was unmistakable. The watcher said, "That's the boss man in then. Did anyone get a good look at him. I wish the council had fixed that fucking street lamp."

Scribe commented, "Well, he did have ginger hair and was dressed smartish, besides, that cheer nearly blew the roof off."

"Got to be him." This from the fetcher, "Stands to reason. I'll call it in, the raids almost about to go." Ellis looked at Jackson and smiled.

"We've got the ginger fucker Jacko."

"Not just yet, sir, not just yet."

The Canary Sings.

"So, what am I here for?" Eddie snarled at Ellis. "Well to begin with, Mr Coleman, we apologies for breaking up your party, but we needed to have a chat with you, about the following." Eddie sneered and folded his arms.

"I'm all ears coppa." He spat.

"We have two statements that point to you killing a metropolitan officer, whilst going about his business." Ellis went on to explain when and where plus the details of the hit and run tragedy. "There is also the matter regarding a killing of a young man in the walk-through tunnel."

"No way, I've got 'undreds of witnesses that will swear on the bible, that I was not there for either of those." Ellis didn't look up. From a folder on his desk, he pulled a further charge sheet saying,

"We know now it was you that ordered the shoot out over in Hainault, and we know now, that you were actively involved in the murder of the Derkin cousins over in Crayford." Again, Ellis explained the times and places.

"Word is Mr Coleman; we understand you might be popping off for a short holiday abroad soon. So, we were hoping that you might be able to cast some light on these events before you go."

"I've got witnesses to prove I was not there." DI Jackson had had enough. He launched himself at Eddie, it was only due to the intervention of the uniformed officer standing behind him, by grabbing Jackson, avoided any blows being swapped.

Eddie didn't flinch didn't move a muscle; such was his arrogance. Jackson, cooled himself down, and said, "This is wearing a little thin Mr Coleman, witnesses here, witnesses there, witnesses bloody well everywhere." A constable knocked twice, opened the door to the interview room, just enough to get his head around and said,

"Are you ready, sir?" he asked Ellis.

"Only I've got Scarlet here."

"Yes, yes, bring him in." The man known only by his code name; Scarlet entered the room.

"Do you recognise this gentleman Mr Coleman?" Ellis enquired. Eddie looked up at the chap now standing in front of him smiling a sickly grin. He half recognised the man but couldn't exactly place him. The face was vaguely familiar, but that was about it. Jackson spoke. "This gentleman worked as a bus driver a few years back, ring any bells now Mr Coleman?" Eddie's mind was racing, but nothing was surfacing.

"Look coppa, I need a brief. I've heard how you fit blokes up, pin stuff on 'em when it suits."

"All in good time, Mr Coleman, all in good time." Ellis, was in no mood to acquiesce to Eddie's request. At the moment he had the upper hand and was enjoying every second. "Let's see if we can nudge this thing on a little further." Eddie's mood was darkening. For the last five years or so he had total command of his mind and total command of his crew. He, did all the planning. He, masterminded the pub raids and murders on his gangland enemies. He, was top fucking dog.

He, was responsible for the welfare of his mum. '*Old on a mo, bam*' the penny dropped, Ellis had mentioned the buses, was there some connection. Buses, Mum, Mum busses, what was it they were driving at? What was he missing? "Get 'im out of my face coppa," he screamed. "If he's hurt or upset my mum, he's now top of my fucking kill list."

"Kill list, is it eh Mr Coleman?" Ellis enquired smiling. "Now, why would you have one of those?"

"Shut it coppa, you ain't getting nothing out of me."

"Oh, on the contrary Mr Coleman, we will, I can assure you, we will." Jackson motioned for the constable to take Scarlet out and to wait in the interview room just next door. *I don't know that geezer. What is he, some sort of grass or something?"* There was something well creepy about the bloke they called scarlet, thought Eddie. *What was his first name anyway, Will?* The thought made him smile. *Hang on a minute, Will Scarlet is one of Robin Hoods trusted. So, what the fucks this got to do with me, he's not one of my bloody trusted, no way.* Ellis broke into Eddie's thoughts.

"The chap who just left, might as well be called Canary because he's been singing like one. You sure you don't recognise him? He's been on your team for a least a four of years, since getting the sack from his job on the busses." Eddie was about to blow a number of fuses, one of his own it seemed had turned on him. What made it worse he'd stood in front of Eddie grinning like a bleedin' Cheshire cat. He must be thick as shit, and so must these coppers, parading him in front of me. Sensing a trap, one that would snare him for a lifetime in prison at the very least, he hurled himself at the nearest body, which happened to be DI Jackson. Big mistake. Jackson was well up for this. He grabbed Eddie's head in an arm lock and punched and pummelled his face. The officer who was supposed to be guarding Eddie managed to wrestle him to the ground then sat on him. Eddie's arms were swiftly pulled behind him handcuffs then applied. He was pulled roughly up-right. Blood streaming from a broken nose, both eyes were beginning to blacken.

Ellis shouted, "Take him away and lock him up, find an empty cell keep him separate from his cronies." Eddie was bundled out of the office. As they passed the adjoining interview room, the door of which was slightly ajar, Eddie saw the Canary sitting with a DI who was busily writing down every word that dropped out of his mouth. Eddie rammed his head backwards into the officer's face behind him, who released his grip. Instantly Eddie was in the room kicking over the desk in an attempt to get at Scarlet. Scarlet shat himself in fright and fell to the floor, Eddie fell on top of him. His only weapons now were his feet and his mouth. Scarlet screamed in agony as Eddie's teeth sank into Scarlets nose. It was bitten and ripped off whole in a matter of seconds. The constable whose face was messed up from Eddie's reverse head butting, managed to haul Eddie off of Scarlet, whacking Eddie's back with his truncheon in the process. Eddie wasn't finished, his feet now free, free to repeatedly kick and stamp on the grassing bastard.

The final, well aimed stamp, brought down with evil intention, crushed Scarlet's two oval shaped glands responsible for producing sperm. He spat out the remains of Scarlet's nose then let out a blood curdling roar, eclipsing Scarlets high pitched scream.

Oasis Raid Wash Up.

DCI Ellis and DI Jackson sat opposite each other. The den as Ellis called it, was his temporary office at West Ham Station. Decor and surroundings were drab compared to the beaming smile on the face of Ellis. "That went well then Jacko, three for the price of one. Maggs and Cooper will probably cough for the job in Kensington, just to get looked at favourably. Three years a piece I would think. Let the station over in West Ken know we've got them locked up. Let them come and take the bastards away."

"Witness protection, new name and address for Scarlet then, sir, when he gets back from hospital?" Jackson asked.

"Of course," replied Ellis. "Of course. We can leave that to the team in control of that sort of stuff, pity the surgeons couldn't stitch his snitch back on though. Coleman must have chewed it up a bit before spitting it out the uncaring ginger turd."

"Looks that way, sir, don't think Scarlet or whatever he's going to be called, will be pulling too many birds from now on."

"Quite Jacko. Our job now is to start the gathering of prime information in order to back up the statements. Evidence on paper alone, will not stand up. Get your team to take statements from all those being held. Go through the due process charge those that need charging then bail them, let off the rest with a harsh warning. This is going to go well Jacko; I can feel it in my water. Coleman didn't go down quietly, did he?"

"No sir, not at all, he's now in solitary as requested, the on-call station doctor has seen him and bunged a few sticking plasters on him here and there. I guess you want us to interview him ourselves and not one of my team?"

"That's is correct Jacko and that will include W.P.C. Wren, but first, I need to talk to my boss and fill him in on the details."

"Actually sir, I'm glad you mentioned her, she was not at the Oasis at the time of the raid. We've had no contact with her since. A constable has been round to her address, his report said the place had not been lived in for quite some considerable time. The constable door knocked a few doors nearby, but none of the neighbours had seen hide nor hair of her."

"Okay Jacko, put a couple of bods on her case and keep me informed. Meanwhile, we've a lot to get through if we are to come up with stuff that sticks within the next twenty-four hours, so let's get at them."

Remand Wing Wandsworth Prison.

"How is it, Son, are they treating you alright? Your face is a bit busted up."

"Yea Ma, busted but not beaten. Most if not all the inmates on this wing know of me so they leave me be." Val looked around the visiting hall. Looked at the inmates and their visitors. Up until now, all eyes were on Val and Eddie. As she scanned the room, all enquiring eyes suddenly looked down. "It's alright Ma. With my reputation, none of these small-time offenders expected me to be visited by me mum."

"Yea, but what about the screws?"

"Christ Ma, half of them is bleeding well bent, do anything for the promise of some readies, the other half are shit scared of me."

"Old Bill won't tell me what they fitted you up with. I've asked around, but everyone's tight lipped."

"Attempted murder, is the best they could come up with Ma. As they've got no actual eye witnesses as it were all they've got is what this tosser grass is telling them. Oh, and GBH. Apparently, I bit some blokes nose off at the station but he's yet to press charges, on account he's being stitched up in hospital, shooting in the dark they are, with blanks."

"Since you mention shooting, what about that gun?"

"Yea, forgot that, they're doing me for illegally possessing a fire-arm an all."

"Christ son, you do let yourself fall into their hands sometimes."

Val leaned forward lowering her voice to almost a whisper. "Esme's been in touch. Right old story there, I can tell you." Eddie's mood brightened at the sound of her name. "Esme, Esme, my little Esme. I don't think she got caught up in the fracas at the Oasis. Said something about a sick relative or other."

"That was a white lie Eddie. She didn't get caught up in the fracas as you call it, because she was the one who called the cops in!"

"Don't understand Ma. Why would she want to do that?"

"Cos she is a cop too, a plant, an undercover cop." Eddie stared at his mum in disbelief. Didn't believe what his ears was telling him, his brain had become a ghost town soon to be filled with raging demons. So, there was two of 'em.

His mind flew back to the day Esme first appeared in front of him, asking for a job. he remembered making a snap judgement, taking her on without a second thought. Then more came back to him, at the time, he remembered saying to himself, be cautious Eddie, be cautious. She might be a plant from old Bill or worse still, a plant from a rival gang. There was no-body to blame but himself. It was getting close to the end of visiting time. Eddie wanted to know more, much more. Ma Val explained that Esme had called on her at 119 Plevna Street. She was distraught, torn between her police career and her love for Eddie.

She explained to Val, she was about to resign from the Met, because she wanted to spend the rest of her life with Eddie no matter what the outcome at any forthcoming trial; if there was to be one. She was going to declare her statement null and void, withdraw it, or whatever she needed to do to ensure nothing she had put forward would be usable against you.

Eddie went, "I wondered where the second statement came from. If she pulls that, all they will have is what they've got from that snivelling no nosed bastard grass Scarlet the bleeding Canary." Eddie's cool down process was actioned.

The bell rang, announcing the end of the session. "Get back here soon Ma, as soon as you can. I need someone on the outside that I can trust and do a few errands for me. Do you think you can arrange this for me Ma?"

"I will try son, I will try. Meanwhile, promise me this, put plenty of paper down first. You never know what you might catch from the bogs in this place." They both laughed loudly, far too loudly for the likes of the nearby screws.

"Fuck them," whispered Eddie, "fuck them." Eddie was now on a mission to turn the tables on the filth.

The Forgotten Woman.

Esme Wren, went into hiding, hiding from the very people who employed her, The Met.

Following her visit to Eddie's mum, she shacked up with Rosie from the Oasis. "Christ Rosie, thanks for letting me kip here. It can't be for long. I don't want you to be dragged through the courts."

"Hang on Esme, what have I done? I only worked at the place and look where that's got me, it's all boarded up, while the bloody plod, go over every inch looking for clues and that."

"Yea your right, but you could still be done for hiding me I suppose."

"Look Esme, after what you've done to Eddie and his crew, not to mention Bomber and me I should really do us all a favour and kill you." Esme, visibly shaken by the statement asked,

"You don't really mean that do you?" Rosie raised her eyebrows and nodded furiously. "Look Rosie, I intend to withdraw my statements thereby keeping any charges against Eddie to a minimum. Besides, as I understand it one of the blokes under Eddie's wing has turned Queens evidence. His information will be almost useless without proper witnesses." "Yea well, they will find fuck all at the Oasis. Bomber and me slipped back in later that night. The plod guarding the place, for a bung conveniently looked the other way. We were able to clear out anything we thought they could use against Eddie."

"Good God Rosie, that was bloody brave."

"We did it for Johnny too you know. He was the one who saved me getting attacked by those two losers from the Derkin's mob." Esme looked puzzled.

"The Derkin's mob?" Rosie went,

"Best you don't know about that."

"I remember that Rosie, they were all over you like a cheap suit, knocked you out cold if I remember, hands everywhere."

"Like I said Esme, best you don't know. So, what's your plan?"

"I know how this thing works. If they cannot find me by the date of a trial, it will put off for a later date.

"I will then officially be a wanted person and could well be arrested on sight. I tell you Rosie, I'm not going back on this. The Met can fuck off and leave me alone. All I want to do is spend the rest of my life with Eddie. We've planned to go to Spain indefinitely." Rosie almost fell over in shock.

"That's a new one to me." She sat down on the nearest chair to think this one over. Esme continued.

"I plan to send in my resignation by post, just days before any trial date. Then continue with getting over to Spain and carry on with locating a villa for Eddie and me to live in.

"The Met will then have a major problem on their hands, because if I'm in Spain for a while, it will be all that much harder to track me down."

"Seems like you got it all in hand then Esme. Just don't reckon without the old Bill. Someone high up in their ranks has their teeth into Eddie, and not about to let go. Going to Spain alone are you, and what about the money side of things?"

"Not alone Rosie, Jimmy Toomey didn't get pulled the other night because he wasn't there. As far as the money is concerned, I've got some savings, plus Jimmy will collect the takings from the three Steak Bars up West for a couple of weeks, it won't amount to much, but it should be enough for a deposit."

"Does Eddie's mum know about this?" Rosie asked.

"She does Rosie the plan has her blessing. She will be keeping in touch with Eddie about it. What I've got to do now, is keep my head down. Best thing I can do before going to Spain is to keep on the move."

Remand Wing.

"So, that's about the size of things Eddie, Esme's got most of it sorted. What's happening this end."

"Well, I've officially been charged. Magistrates court and that, then referred to Crown Court, might be the Old Bailey. Could be six months from now."

"Ain't they going to bail you?"

"Nope, bin too naughty."

"Well, you're just have to sit it out for now. Anyway, regards your request, Dave Conti's been let off with a severe bollocking."

"Has he now, that's interesting. Have you spoken to him then?"

"Yes, Rosie did the match making and I talked with. He is more than willing to run errands as you call it. He's clean and not being watched."

"Cushty Mum cushty. I shouldn't think he will be allowed to visit me, so here what I want him to do. He's to go over to a jeweller in Romford, he knows which one and pick up a package. Go with him Ma, make sure it's not opened."

"What is it, son?" Val enquired. He whispered,

"sparklers. Should be loads of them. Take them up to Hatton Garden. Tell Dave to act as your minder and rent a safety deposit box in your name. Every other building will have plenty. Get the sparklers locked away. Keep the number of the deposit box and which company you use up there." Eddie tapped his head. "That'll do for starters. Just one more thing Ma, I miss all the violence and stuff, its food to me and I'm now starving, So, I'm gonna have a game of noughts and cross's tonight with one of the screws. When I get out its new and violent horizons for me."

"Bye Ma."

"Bye Eddie."